What readers wrote about Rob Neto's debut novel, *Beyond the Grate*

I often felt the panic and intensity of the situation and had to stop reading to get my bearings and remind myself that it was only a book. – Anthony M. Harrington, author of Lamb of God

Beyond the Grate by Rob Neto is a fast-paced thriller that will keep you on the edge of your seat from beginning to end. – Joel Silverstein, author of several mixed gas diving manuals and producer Shark Night, Piranha 3D, and Lake Mead

It doesn't matter if you are a diver, fascinated by it like me, or just like a good "coming of age" story of sorts with a mystery wrapped around it, you'll enjoy this one. – Steve Grobschmidt – author of the Gamma Trita Trilogy

The story thread is skillfully woven, creating a web of suspense and intrigue. What captivated me even more was the fact that the actual incident that inspired the story remains unresolved. This intriguing void allowed the author's creativity to express itself freely, giving birth to a series of captivating events that unfold in a fluid manner. – Laurent Miroult, World-renowned cave diving photographer.

The dead body floating on the other side is more than enough to dissuade his progress, and his awkward fight to the surface with his oxygen tanks nearly depleted is claustrophobic and anxiety ridden. It is scenes like this where Rob Neto really shines. An expert diver himself, Neto really knows how to take his readers to the murky yet wondrous depths. – Darin Miller, author of The Dwayne Morrow Mystery Series

ALSO BY ROB NETO

Beyond the Grate

Sidemount Diving The Almost *Comprehensive Guide 2*nd *edition*
Available in English, Dutch, German, and Spanish

INTO THE DARKNESS BEYOND

ROB NETO

Published by Chipola Publishing, LLC
Greenwood, Florida 32443, U.S.A.
www.chipolapublishing.com

Cover photography by Laurent Miroult; Artwork & design by Rob Neto

Author photography by Jen Neto

Printed in the United States of America

PUBLISHER'S NOTE

This is a work of fiction. Names, characters, places, and incidents are either the product of the author's imagination or are used fictitiously, and any resemblance to actual persons, living or dead, business establishments, events, or locales is entirely coincidental. While the names of certain locales, such as Blue Spring Recreational Area, Jackson Blue Spring, and Morrison Spring, are used to add depth and reality to the story, they are in no way meant to disparage such locales or past or present ownership of such establishments.

ISBN: 9781961612044

DEDICATION

This book is dedicated to all the divers who place themselves at risk to attempt rescues of divers in distress and to recover the bodies of divers that have perished during a dive so that their families can have closure.

In Memory of Doron Nof, Ph.D.
May 1, 1944 – August 1, 2022

"Survival depends on being able to suppress anxiety and replace it with calm, clear, quick and correct reasoning..." – Sheck Exley

ACKNOWLEDGMENTS

I'd like to thank the readers of my first novel, *Beyond the Grate,* especially those who took the time to leave reviews. I read each and every review and use what I can to improve my writing. I incorporated many of the suggestions into this story based on the reviews I received on my award-winning debut novel. There are more underwater scenes and there are varying perspectives incorporated into the story. Because of those readers, *Into the Darkness Beyond* is a much better book than it could have been otherwise. So thank you to all the readers who took the time to leave a review.

I'd like to thank Forrest Wilson for his ageless stories and lessons. I enjoyed hearing them during our 8-hour drive to Missouri for a cave diving conference and then another 8 hours back. Also, thank you for designing the line arrows we all currently use.

I would like to thank my cave diving instructors and mentors that provided me with the invaluable information about the various cave diving incidents. Each and every one of them helped me to become a safer cave diver. Many of those stories are retold in this book. Any mistakes or omissions can only be attributed to my imperfect memory.

I would like to acknowledge Debra Reeves for the unwitting sacrifice she made to make cave diving safer. She lost her life but was able to leave behind an important lesson which resulted in much safer conditions in the popular underwater caves.

I would like to thank Doron Nof for his dedication to cave diving and trying to solve the mysteries of underwater cave collapses. I enjoyed talking with Doron over the years and enjoyed the few cave dives we did together. You are missed, my friend.

I would also like to thank my wife for supporting me throughout the completion of this second novel so soon after finishing and publishing *Beyond the Grate*. She had to endure countless hours of me talking excitedly about the story and how it was developing, all without any specifics because I wanted to get her true reaction to the story after the first time she read it. Not only did she endure my excessive rambling about it, but she also provided me with invaluable feedback once I presented her with the second draft to read, and then again, the second to final draft. The final version of this story is improved compared to the earlier editions because of her advice and recommendations.

FOREWORD
DO NOT SKIP THIS PART!

While writing *Beyond the Grate*, I came up with the idea for the story of *Into the Darkness Beyond*. Shortly after the true event that inspired *Beyond the Grate*, a cave diver located in Marianna, Florida happened to be at a local cave diving site while other cave divers found themselves in a situation in which they needed assistance. Had that assistance not been rendered those divers might have perished in the cave.

Another event occurred not long after in which a diver found himself stuck in a small passage in the same cave. He managed to get himself out of the small passage and get almost to the cave opening. As he was ascending to a shallower depth the same diver that had rendered assistance to the other divers assisted this one.

Much like with *Beyond the Grate*, I asked myself what if the stories were different. What if the reports that were being circulated about the rescues weren't exactly true? What if there was more to the story than was being revealed? Lots of what ifs, but that's what my books are about. With those questions, the idea for *Into the Darkness Beyond* was born.

* * *

While some of the underwater incidents described in this book did occur, such as the first incident involving Joey Simmons, and the incident involving cave divers Gary and Jim, only the ideas of the incidents were used. The details of the incidents written in this book are products of the author's imagination. The incidents were incorporated as foundations, but imagination dictated the rest of the scenes, including the ending results. The divers involved in the incidents did survive the dives and hopefully learned from any mistakes they may have made.

In no way is this story or any of the scenes included in it intended to disparage the reputation of any living or dead person. The story is fictional from beginning to end with only snippets of real events inserted to add a sense of reality. The actual divers involved in the incidents are not a part of this story and nothing in this story is meant to be applied to them or how they handled their own situations.

The diver responsible for the rescues in Marianna, Florida and other locations was recognized by various organizations for his efforts. The incidents that were used in this story simply provided the inspiration for the story. That is the only resemblance to any truth in the book. Jack Johnson is a fictional character. He is not intended to resemble anyone in real life. There must be an antagonist and Jack is that guy.

* * *

The stories included about Forrest Wilson and Debra Reeves are true, at least to the best of my knowledge. If I got any part of it wrong, blame that on my memory and not on Forrest. I heard these stories more than 15 years ago, so my memory is likely to be as cloudy as the water in the first scene of the book.

The story about the collapse in Indian Springs and the death of Parker Turner is also true. I have pieced together as many details about the incident as I could remember. I've also included simple details that do not affect the story and may or may not have happened simply to make the account more interesting. Any omission or inaccurate information can be blamed on my memory as well.

The monofin diver is a real person. He lives in the Florida panhandle and could be regularly seen diving at Vortex Spring just as he is described later in the book. When you get to that part, you won't believe it!

* * *

The rescue of a diver from Bat Guano Cave located in Marianna, Florida did occur. As with other true events that I have incorporated into this story, I have included as much detail as I could remember into this particular account. Some details may not be accurate, but the event itself did occur. It was a miraculous event.

* * *

I have included a section at the end of the book titled Author's Note. This section contains information that would spoil certain parts of the story, including the ending. It is meant to clarify some information about true events that were used in the story. Unlike the information about Forrest, Debra, and Parker above, those details couldn't be discussed here in the foreword. I encourage you to read those couple of pages as you might find them interesting.

* * *

This book is a work of fiction. The characters, incidents, and dialogue are drawn from the author's imagination and are not to be construed as real. Any resemblance to actual events or persons, living or dead, is entirely coincidental. While the idea for the story did come from the rescues referenced above, that is the only similarity. This story is simply one in which the author creates a tale based on his imagination of what could have happened. There are some snippets of fact embedded in the story, such as some of the information about Jackson Blue, Merritt's Mill Pond, and local landmarks. These things are included simply to give the story more depth and reality. They are by no means implicated in any wrongdoing by anyone.

There is no Joey Simmons. There is no Lindsey Carter. There is no Jack Johnson. And while one of the events that occurs at the end of the book did really occur (not divulged here to keep from spoiling the ending), there were no witnesses to it. These characters, as well as the other characters in the book, are all imaginative creations. This work of fiction simply takes a set

of circumstances that occurred and creates a different version of
fictional events to tell a story.

PART 1

1

Joey

Joey Simmons tried to back out, but something was keeping him from being able to move. He pushed forward again but only felt his scuba tanks squeeze him like a vise even more. The silt had gotten so thick in the tunnel he could no longer see the walls which were mere inches from his face.

He wiggled his hips, trying to get himself unwedged. That only seemed to make things worse. He noticed his breathing rate was getting faster. Rather than the nice, even, rhythmic respirations he had trained himself to do, the bubbles were escaping the regulator in his mouth almost continuously. He needed to regain control of his breathing. He had a limited supply of air and he was a long way from the cave opening where he could ascend to the surface.

Joey closed his eyes and concentrated on his breathing, something he had learned early on in his scuba diving experiences. Something he had learned during his first unofficial cave dive.

Unofficial. Yes, he had been diving in a cave, but he had not had the proper training to be there. He had barely completed his open water scuba training. The type of scuba diving where you could always ascend directly to the surface of the water if something went wrong. That wasn't the case with cave diving. When cave diving, you had to deal with issues wherever you were. Because before you could ascend to the surface, you had to get out of the cave and get under the surface. And at the moment, that surface was more than 2000 feet away!

Breathe in. Hold his breath for a second. Slowly release, letting the air escape his lungs steadily. Hold for another second. Resist the impulse to immediately take another breath. Then repeat. Breathe in….

Joey could feel a sense of calm enveloping him. He would figure a way out of this predicament he had gotten himself into. He had three tanks on him, the two sidemount tanks plus a stage tank he had brought along because they were diving so far back in the cave using diver propulsion vehicles, more commonly referred to as DPVs, or just plain old scooters. The additional air in the stage tank was necessary in case they had a DPV failure and had to swim out. Swimming out could take three times as long as scootering out. And their breathing rates were higher swimming than they were when being pulled along by the DPVs.

They… What about Mike? Was he behind Joey? Blocking Joey's exit from this narrow tunnel? Or did he manage to back out and wait outside the growing silt cloud for Joey to do the same? It did no good to wonder about Mike. Joey couldn't help Mike unless he got himself unstuck and out of the narrow tunnel he was in.

Joey's breathing rate had finally slowed down and resumed its normal calm rhythm. He tried to back out again. He moved a fraction of an inch before something jammed him in place. He could feel the tank on his right side pushing against his armpit. He must be A-framed, meaning the bottom of the tank that was sticking out was caught against a protrusion from the wall.

Joey felt around in front of him to try to feel if the tunnel got any bigger. He had his DPV in front of him and moved his hand around the outside of the round propeller shroud. The tunnel was somewhat oval-shaped, wider than it was tall. There was only enough room above and below the shroud for his hand to barely fit. There was a little more room to the sides of the shroud but not enough to pass through the tunnel without unclipping both sidemount tanks and pushing them ahead of him. And that wasn't going to happen at this point.

He was going to have to back out somehow. But to do that he needed to pull the bottom of the tank away from the wall and toward his leg. The problem with that plan was his arms were stretched out in front of him much like Superman flying. There wasn't enough room to pull them back alongside his body so he could maneuver the tanks and get himself free. It's a good thing Joey wasn't claustrophobic!

Eyes closed.

Breathe…

Stay calm.

Joey wiggled his hips again and tried to get the tank to pop up above his hip so it could get loose from its entrapment and allow him to back out. It wasn't working, though. The stage tank he had brought was riding on top of his sidemount tank and it wasn't allowing him to move up at all. He reached down to the D-ring on his chest where the top of the stage tank was clipped and found the bolt snap at the end of the bungee cord connecting it to the tank valve. He fumbled with the bolt snap for a few seconds trying to get the gate open and the bolt snap off the D-ring. The bungee cord was stretched too tight. He could get the gate open, but the bolt snap wasn't moving at all. He had to be able to pull it at least a quarter inch to get it off the D-ring.

He tried a couple more times without success. *Well,* he thought, *I'm going to have to cut the bungee cord.* He couldn't remember how much air he had left in the stage tank but cutting the bungee also meant leaving it behind. There was no way he would be able to hold onto the stage tank, light up the dark cave in front of him, and control the DPV throughout the 2100-foot exit from his current location.

Joey reached across with his right hand to his left wrist where his cutting tool was attached to the strap of his dive computer. He felt the hard plastic handle of the tool and pulled it out of its sheath. He brought his hand down to his chest and located the chest D-ring holding his stage tank in place. Tracing his finger along the outside of the D-ring to its edge, he found the bolt snap that was pulling on it. He then traced the bolt snap to the bungee cord.

The cutting tool was a double-edged blade secured inside the holder. It had a catch on each side meant to both protect the user from getting accidentally cut by the blade and also to use to pull in whatever material was being cut and hold it against the blade. The tool was shaped somewhat like an M with the blade being the V in the middle and the catches being the legs of the M.

He positioned the cutting tool next to the bungee and slowly swiped it down, trying to catch it in one of the legs of the M. He felt the end of the cutting tool slip over the top of the bungee cord. *Let's try that again,* he thought.

Positioning the tool above the bungee again, this time he pressed down against his chest harder. He really hoped the sharp blade wouldn't cut through his drysuit. The suit had seals around the wrists and neck designed to keep water out and the person wearing it warm. Cutting it would allow water to flood in and make for a miserable, wet, cold exit. Never mind the decompression obligation that was building up the longer he was stuck in that restriction.

Joey pressed down harder and slowly pulled the cutting tool across his chest. He felt some resistance, held his breath hoping he hadn't caught a fold of the drysuit in the cutting tool, and pulled harder. A second later he could feel the tension the bungee cord had been creating on his armpit subside. He felt the stage tank shift slightly above him. This was it! He was going to be able to get loose from this vise. And the best part was he didn't feel cold water rushing into his drysuit.

Joey tried backing out again. He couldn't move even a quarter of an inch. The sidemount tank was still wedged against something. He wiggled his hips again to try to get it to move out of the way. *Nothing.*

He stopped for a moment and concentrated on his breathing. Suddenly it felt harder to pull each breath in. It was too silty for him to see his pressure gauges, but it had been a while since he switched regulators. He moved his hand to his neck and found the other regulator hanging from a necklace made from bungee cord. He grabbed the regulator with one hand and pushed the other regulator that was in his mouth out with his tongue, letting it drop below his head. He placed the regulator he was holding into his mouth and took a big breath in.

Cough! Cough! Cough!

He had just gotten a mouthful of silt. *Dammit!* He forgot to purge the regulator of the water and silt that had built up in it. He reached up and hit the purge button, careful to block the mouthpiece with his tongue so the silt would be directed out of the exhaust ports and not into his mouth and lungs. He then cautiously took another breath, and this time got a mouthful, and lungful, of air. Now that he had air to breathe, he could get back to getting himself unstuck.

The stage tank was still above him, hanging on by the bungee cord securing the body of the tank to his waist belt. He wiggled his shoulders to try to get it to fall off, but it barely moved. He tried to move forward again. This time he was able to move a couple of inches before meeting resistance. At least he moved though.

He wiggled more from this new position, but it did nothing. He tried to back up again. He was able to back up the couple of inches he had moved forward before the A-framing stopped him. It felt like the stage tank had repositioned itself though. He wiggled his shoulders. He had more room, but it still wasn't enough to make a difference.

Moving forward again Joey regained that couple of inches plus maybe an additional inch. He pushed back, feeling the stage tank shift position again. He reached back with his hand to push the valve of the stage tank away. Maybe that would help free him. He couldn't reach the valve though. The tank had already shifted too far down on his back for that.

He moved forward and backward, forward and backward. Each time he could feel the stage tank shifting position a little more. Each time he could feel himself gaining a little more room than the time before.

This went on for what seemed like forever to Joey. His air supply must have been getting low by this time. He had already breathed one tank empty.

He thought he was about 80 feet deep. At least that's what he remembered. He couldn't read the display on his dive computer through the silt to confirm this detail. Being 80 feet deep meant he was breathing three and a half times the amount of air he would breathe on the surface due to the pressure of the water. And despite his efforts at controlling his breathing rate he still found himself breathing a little faster than usual and having to calm himself to slow down the breathing. He had to get out of the hole he was in soon.

Forward.

Backward.

Forward.

Backward.

Thunk!

That was it! The stage tank had shifted enough that it finally rolled off his back! Joey wiggled both his hips and his shoulders, moving them more and more violently as his exasperation with his current situation grew. The more he wiggled, the more room he felt he had. He felt himself moving back a little farther in the passage than he had during previous attempts. His sidemount tank had finally pulled itself from the protrusion it had been wedged against. He stopped for a moment and focused on his breathing. He didn't know how much air was left in the tank he was breathing from, but it couldn't be much. He wasn't sure it would be enough to get back to the surface.

Joey pushed that thought out of his head and concentrated on slowing his breathing. Once back under control, he began to push himself back slowly, trying to not get A-framed again.

Wiggle. Tug. Wiggle. Tug.

Gaining a little bit of ground each time.

Wiggle. Tug.

No movement this time. Something was tugging back at him and preventing him from moving. Joey could feel something pulling at his waist belt. He pushed again and felt the waist belt tighten.

The stage tank! It was still attached to him. He had released the valve of the tank from his harness, but the body of the tank was still attached to a D-ring on his waist belt with a long bungee cord and bolt snap. Joey reached down and this time managed to squeeze his arm between the rocky, limestone floor of the passage and his torso. He was glad he had managed to lose that extra weight he had been carrying around otherwise he might be in a bigger predicament. Joey laughed at the pun.

He traced the shoulder strap down to the waist strap and found the D-ring. It was being held against his belly by the tension on the bungee cord coming from the stage tank. Joey felt around the bolt snap until he found the gate and opened it. He tried pulling the bolt snap over the D-ring. But just like with the chest D-ring, there was too much tension on the bungee. He pulled his arm back in front so he could retrieve the cutting tool. He was thankful he had remembered to place it back into its sheath after using it to cut the other bungee cord. He pulled the cutting tool out and squeezed his hand back between the floor and his torso to the bungee stretched across his belly.

This was going to be more difficult than cutting the other bungee cord. He had been working on losing weight, but he was still about 5 lbs heavier than he wanted to be, most of it in his gut. He pushed the cutting tool against his belly. He had to be careful because the tow cord from his DPV, the cord that pulled him behind it, was clipped onto a D-ring located on his crotch strap. If he cut that accidently he would have a really difficult time getting out of the cave.

Joey held the tow cord to the side with his pinky while trying to catch the bungee cord in the cutting tool. When he pushed in it pushed both his belly and the bungee cord in. He changed the angle on the cutting tool and tried to catch it again, still being careful to hold the DPV tow cord out of the way. He felt something catching onto the cutting tool. Hoping it was the bungee and not his drysuit or the tow cord, he pulled the cutter up toward his chest. *Snap!* He felt the tension of the bungee cord release from his belly. The stage tank was free.

He pushed the DPV forward away from him until the tow cord arrested its movement. *That was good,* he thought. At least that cord was still intact. And he didn't feel cold water seeping onto his belly so the drysuit must also be intact. Everything seemed to be going his way. Well, other than getting stuck in this godforsaken rathole.

Wiggling around more to make sure the stage tank was out of

the way, Joey felt it shift position. He slowly started to push himself backwards out of the crevice he had managed to scooter into at full speed, close to 200 feet per minute. He was finally moving backwards and felt the passage walls angling away from him. He also started to see the illumination from his powerful LED dive light again. The silt was clearing out. Or at least he was getting out of the thickness of the silt cloud he had created.

Joey felt around for his cut away stage tank as he backed out. All he felt was hard, sharp limestone under a layer of silt about an inch thick. He kept pushing himself backwards. The light got brighter with every inch of movement. The cave line denoting the exit from the cave finally came into view below him. *Wait! That wasn't gold line. That was white cave line!*

2

Somehow Joey had scootered off the gold line that denotes the main passage in the cave and gone into an offshoot tunnel. Joey was suddenly very thankful to Debra Eaves for her sacrifice back in 1988 that resulted in gold line even becoming a thing in cave diving. Joey's girlfriend, Lindsey, who was a cave diver when they first met and the reason Joey decided to become one as well, had told him that story shortly after he had finished his cave diver training. They had been discussing dives in which they would swim the passage alongside the main gold-colored line and explore tunnels off the side of the main passage that had thinner, white line in them.

* * *

Lindsey explained, "The passages in caves are initially lined with a #24 braided nylon cord by the first cave divers in the cave. They do this to stake their claim to finding virgin passage, passage that's never been explored before."

"Do you think there's any more virgin passage in the caves around here?" Joey asked.

"I'm sure there is sweetie. I've heard talk about some exploration that's still happening. They usually keep it quiet though because they don't want anyone else to get in there and push the passage beyond the end of the line they've laid. Sadly, there are cave divers who will try to scoop a find and claim it for themselves."

"Why do people do that? Isn't there any way for the original explorers to claim their find and keep others out?"

"There is, but it's an honor system. The first cave divers in a passage have the privilege of laying the line and leaving markers identifying themselves as the ones who found that passage. You know how we all carry line arrows with our initials on them? Most of us use them to mark the lines when we do jumps off the main line. Well, explorers typically carry arrows to leave behind on lines they've laid in virgin passage. The problem is not everyone honors that, and they'll pull those line arrows off the line and replace them with their own."

Line arrow belonging to Lindsey Carter

"Why would anyone do that??" Joey asked incredulously. "If they didn't lay the line to begin with, what good does it do to claim it?"

"It's just the way some people are, sweetie. Ego gets the best of them and there's no respect." Lindsey answered then continued with her explanation. "The lines serve a few purposes for explorers. They mark the new passage, provide them with a continuous line out to the opening of the cave, and they also give the explorers a means of surveying the passage so they can create maps of the caves."

"Most cave passages remain lined with the standard line we have on our primary reels and safety and jump spools. Until 1989 that's all that was used in cave passages," Lindsey continued.

"What happened in 1989?"

"In 1988, this cave diver, her name was Debra Eaves, had been diving with her boyfriend in Orange Grove cave over at Wes Skiles Peacock Springs State Park. Only back then it was just Peacock Springs State Park. During the dive Debra had a primary light failure. Remember that dive light you first got with your used equipment a couple years ago?"

"Yeah, that hardly lit anything up! I can't believe I ever thought it was worth using."

"Well, back in the 80s the lights weren't much better. Some cave divers made their own dive lights using car headlights and motorcycle batteries, but they were big and bulky and not everyone had the know how to build one of those and make sure they were watertight. So cave divers used what they could," Lindsey explained. "Debra's light probably wasn't any better than that light you had."

"And she was cave diving with that???"

"That's all she had available to her." Lindsey paused. "So, her light failed and while she was deploying her backup light from a pocket she *ascended to the ceiling of the cave. Her boyfriend noticed there was no longer light behind him and turned around to see what was going on. He noticed Debra was dealing with a non-functional primary light and swam back to help her."*

"How do you know all this?"

"I heard the story from Forrest Wilson. You know that cave diver with the long white beard? Such a nice guy. He's been cave diving for decades. In fact, he was involved with the training agencies back when this happened. Did you know he also designed the line arrow we all now use? Before Forrest's invention cave divers used Dorf markers — duct tape folded over the line in the shape of an arrow — to mark the lines. Those were named after Lewis Holzendorf, the cave diver that came up with the idea."

"Seriously??"

"That's what I've been told. Although, I haven't actually seen any in the caves here in Florida. I have heard there are some caves in Mexico that still have line in them from back when Dorf markers were being used."

"So back to Debra," Lindsey continued. "Once her backup light was deployed, she signaled her boyfriend that the dive was done, and they should exit the cave."

"Makes sense since they had a failure."

"They descended to the line below them and began swimming, with Debra leading the way out since she had the weaker dive light at this point. Now imagine trying to exit a cave using a light even weaker than the dive light you first used."

"I don't think she would be able to see very much."

"Not at all. Debra's boyfriend was still using his primary light, though, and noticed the tunnel looked different than he remembered. He signaled to Debra and told her he thought they were going the wrong way. He then signaled her to turn around, but apparently Debra didn't agree with him.

After a few moments arguing underwater, Debra turned and continued to swim the direction she thought was out."

"What did her boyfriend do?"

"Her boyfriend followed her for a minute and tried to convince Debra to turn around, but she refused. He watched his gas reserves and finally decided to turn and head back the way they had come. I think he was hoping he could get out in time to get help and save Debra."

"A couple of minutes later he came to the end of the cave line he had been following. He looked across the tunnel and saw another line along the wall going left and right. That was where Debra had her primary light failure. Her boyfriend surmised that when they had descended from the ceiling, they must have drifted over to a different line. That line was in an offshoot tunnel that did not lead out of the cave."

"Debra's boyfriend swam across the gap to the other line and continued his swim out to the opening. He rushed out of the water and called for help, but it was too late for Debra. Her body was recovered from the cave later that day, farther into the same tunnel where she and her boyfriend had their disagreement."

"Wow!" Joey exclaimed. "All because she didn't realize she was on the wrong line."

"Exactly. So a few weeks later, several instructors and board members from the various cave diving training agencies, Forrest included, met to try to figure out how that fatality could have been avoided. Back then cave diving fatalities were actually discussed and analyzed to see if there was anything to be learned about the incidents. Not like today in which no one talks about them."

"But I've read that people don't think there's anything new to be learned from the fatalities that happen now. The people that die in caves are dying

because of the same mistakes that have been made over and over again." Joey offered.

"That's true, sweetie, but we still have new cave divers getting trained all the time and many of them have never read and heard of the fatalities that happened in the past. And not many cave diving instructors bother to talk to their students about cave diving fatalities because they don't want to scare them off. I feel that if it scares someone off, then that person shouldn't be cave diving anyway."

"So, after several meetings, it was decided that having a thicker, different color line used in the primary cave passages would make them easy to distinguish from secondary passages both tactilely and visually. If that had already been the case when Debra was diving, there would have been no question in her mind as to whether she was in the correct tunnel or not. She would have noticed that the line they were swimming along was standard cave line and not gold line." Lindsey continued the lesson.

"The head honchos made a bunch of calls around to price out line and see how much of a budget they would need to reline the main passages in the popular caves. A distributor with an overstock supply of gold colored line was found and was willing to sell it at cost. Within a week the primary passages in the Peacock and Orange Grove caves had the white cave line replaced with gold line. Eventually, most of the popular caves in Florida had gold line in them."

* * *

Joey was very thankful to Debra Eaves. If not for her mistake and the lesson learned from it, he wouldn't know he wasn't in the main passage other than because of the size of it. The hole he was in was barely bigger than his DPV shroud! Joey couldn't think of any tunnel he had been in before that was this small.

As he was feeling around the tunnel to try to figure out how he was going to get himself out of the tight spot he was in, Joey found himself wondering where it led. He quickly pushed that thought back. He would have to check it out another time. Now he just needed to keep backing up and hopefully find the gold line of the main passage.

Joey had known it was a bad idea. For some reason he had let Mike talk him into doing this dive. Joey had been back this far in the cave only once. That was a few months earlier when the water current in the cave had been minimal.

Jackson Blue was one of 33 first magnitude springs in Florida. This not only meant a lot of water poured out of the cave, but it also meant the flow of that water was strong. The area had experienced a drought during the first half of the year and the current had reduced to almost nothing. The reduced current allowed Joey and Lindsey to be able to swim far back into the cave using a couple of stage tanks. It was one of the best dives he had with Lindsey so far.

The area they swam to was called the Trash Room. There was an old sink hole decades earlier that people apparently used as a dumping site. There was old trash scattered throughout about 200 feet of the cave passage – glass bottles, shoes, cans, and other assorted items. There was even an old traffic signal propped up on a rock in the middle of a large room where there was an intersection of gold lines. Most of these items appeared to be from the 1950s or 60s. Lindsey and Joey swam to the Trash Room and spent about 15 minutes checking out all the old trash before having to begin their swim out to the cave opening.

Joey had told Mike, one of his regular cave diving buddies, about the Trash Room and Mike really wanted to see it. The problem was that part of Florida had gotten a bunch of rain since Joey and Lindsey did their dive and the flow was back up to normal, meaning it was a significantly strong current, and swimming against it required a lot of effort. Joey and Mike tried to swim to the Trash Room the weekend before, but they only got about two-thirds of the way before being forced to turn back otherwise they wouldn't have enough air in their tanks to safely exit the cave.

So Mike talked Joey into taking their DPVs. Joey knew it was a bad idea. They had only purchased their DPVs a couple months earlier and had just completed their cave DPV class three weeks before this dive. They were still learning and trying to become proficient with them. The farthest they had taken them into the cave was about 1100 feet. That wasn't even as far as they had swum the prior weekend. And only about half the distance to the Trash Room.

"It'll be okay, dude! You and Lindsey have already been there so you're familiar with the cave," Mike told Joey.

One of the general rules taught during cave DPV training was to swim a passage before scootering it. The reason for this was to become familiar with the passage at a slower swimming pace before trying to maneuver it traveling three to four times faster while being pulled by a DPV. Mike was convincing though, and Joey really wanted to see the Trash Room again.

Lindsey, the more experienced cave diver of the three, was working that weekend otherwise she would have been there to talk sense into Joey. But she wasn't. And they went to see the Trash Room. And on the way out, at some point, while Joey was scootering out and looking around the passage, he lost sight of the gold line and followed the wall into the tight tunnel where he got himself stuck. And Mike had been right behind him. He hoped anyway.

Joey looked around but the silt hanging in the water was still too thick to see much of anything. However, he was finally in passage large enough for him to turn around rather than having to back out. He placed his right hand on the wall next to him and slowly rotated toward it until it was to his left. He didn't want to push off the wall into the silty water and get even more lost.

He followed the wall that was now to his left. The silt was beginning to clear even more, and he was starting to feel the flow of the current moving through the cave. Up ahead he saw the outline of the old traffic light propped up on the rock. He looked down at his pressure gauges. 200 psi remaining in his left tank. He looked at the other one, even though he knew what he would see there. *A big fat 0 – empty…*

Twenty-one hundred feet from the opening, only 200 psi left in his tank. And his stage tank was lost somewhere in the small, silted tunnel behind him. This wasn't good at all!

3

Joey darted toward the traffic light. Well, as much as he could dart considering he was swimming against a strong current. He knew the gold line wrapped around the rock holding the light so he could at least start making his way out from there.

Mike! Where was he?

Joey covered his light beam as he had been taught during training and looked for the glow of Mike's light around the cavernous room. Nothing. He removed his hand from the light and swept the beam around the perimeter looking for bubbles, or silt, or any sign that Mike was nearby. The only silt he saw was behind him where he had just been. *How long had I been stuck in that tunnel? Joey wondered.*

Glancing at his dive computer he saw he had been on the dive for 78 minutes. They had turned the dive as planned at 30 minutes to start making their way out of the cave. Maybe five minutes had gone by from the time they turned the dive to when Joey got stuck. *About 43 minutes had passed!* He had been stuck in that tunnel for almost an hour! His hope of running into Mike and breathing from one of his tanks quickly faded. Even if he did find Mike it wasn't likely Mike would have enough air for both of them to exit. Mike probably wouldn't even have enough air to get himself out. Joey dreaded the thought of finding Mike's lifeless body still in the cave.

As Joey neared the traffic light, he noticed something dark on the floor below it. *Was that a scuba tank?* Joey suddenly remembered there were a couple of local divers doing exploration more than a mile back in the cave and they had mentioned having some safety tanks staged along the main passage of the cave. These tanks were there as a precaution in case anything happened that required them to need more air than they could carry with them.

This must be one of those tanks. Joey quickened his pace and swam as fast as he could toward it. He grabbed the valve and turned the knob. He could hear the air in the tank pressurizing the regulator and hoses. He looked at the pressure gauge – *3100 psi!*

Joey unclipped the bolt snap around the valve from the gold line and clipped it onto his chest D-ring. *Hopefully the guys this belongs to aren't in the cave at the moment and won't end up needing this,* Joey thought. But it was either taking the full tank they had left as a safety tank or drowning. He would have to ask for forgiveness later.

He fumbled with the lower attachment bungee cord, but he couldn't get it clipped on. He was too nervous and worked up and his fingers weren't working like they were supposed to. He decided to just let the tank hang below him from the chest D-ring and deal with it later. The important thing was to start breathing from it and get out of the cave to the surface where he had an unlimited supply of air. And just as he had that thought his next breath was cut off after only a half an inhalation.

He fumbled for the regulator on the safety tank he had just clipped onto himself. He grasped it, purged it to make sure there was no silt built up inside, and put it in his mouth. The mouthpiece felt a little slimy, probably because it had been in the water for several days. But at least there was air passing through it. Taking in a deep breath, Joey started to relax again. He remained there for a moment enjoying the air from the tank.

After a few breaths, Joey removed the mouthpiece and rubbed off as much of the slime from it as he could. Satisfied he had gotten most of it, he placed the mouthpiece back in his mouth and took another breath. The mouthpiece definitely felt better than it had.

I've got to get out of here, he suddenly thought. Joey reached back for his DPV, which had been pushed behind him by the water current and swung it around in front of him. He turned in the direction of the arrows on the gold line and pressed the throttle switch. He heard the motor spool up and suddenly felt the tug on his harness from the tow cord attached to the DPV. This time he was careful to keep an eye on the gold line below him.

He steered the DPV along the white colored, windy path that led out of the area he was in. The gold line disappeared above him momentarily, causing Joey to have a slight increase in anxiety and breathing rate. Of course, this was also in a spot where the tunnel and the line took a sharp turn to the left. He had already gone the wrong way once. Fortunately, the white path was still below him and easily identifiable.

Joey was able to calm himself and focus on the white path, hoping there was no other white path in the cave, or if there was, that he was on the correct one that ran under the gold line. He was beginning to realize why it was smart to swim a passage and learn it before attempting to use a DPV in it.

Joey made the sharp left turn and saw the gold line slope down from the ceiling to the floor in front of him. He felt a wave of relief wash over him. He had lost his stage tank, breathed his sidemount tanks empty, and was on a borrowed safety tank. He knew there were no other tanks between his current location and the decompression tank resting back at the beginning of the gold line 100 feet inside the cave entrance. He didn't have much room for anything else to go wrong.

Joey concentrated on controlling his breathing rate so he could stretch out the amount of time he had on the safety tank. The traffic light was 2100 feet inside the cave. The water current was pretty strong and heading in the same direction as Joey. It had taken him about 15 minutes to get there going against the flow. He should be able to get back to his decompression tank in about 10-12 minutes. There was plenty of air in the safety tank to accomplish that.

Joey maneuvered the DPV through the winding tunnels, careful to keep an eye on the gold line. Fortunately, there was only one other place where the gold line touched the ceiling and that was at a duck under (so named because you had to duck under the ceiling drop to continue). At this location, the passage transitioned from a large room named the Hall of the Mountain King and the ceiling dropped down to a low, somewhat narrow tunnel, where it would be difficult to get lost again... *Joey hoped.*

He got through the Hall of the Mountain King, past the duck under, and into the lower section. About 100 feet later there was a breakdown area — a part of the cave where the ceiling had collapsed onto the floor. This had happened long before anyone had been cave diving and Joey hadn't heard of any recent collapses in any of the caves. Hopefully one wasn't due. He followed the line over the large boulders on the floor of the cave, around to the right and back down to the floor where the breakdown area ended.

That's also where the second gold line T was located. This cave had 4 gold line Ts in it. Ts are areas where the tunnel splits in two and both sides have line in them. Usually gold line is only in one main passage but both tunnels between the first and second Ts and the third and fourth Ts were about the same distance whether you went to the left or to the right so someone had decided both sides merited gold line.

At the second T, Joey could have gone left or right on the gold line since the distance was about the same. The difference was the size and topography of the passages. The left had less clearance from floor to ceiling but that also meant the current was a little faster and there was less silt on the floor. The right had a lot more clearance but there was a smaller restriction shortly after the T. The larger tunnel also meant the current wasn't as strong. That and the restriction would likely mean it took a little longer to travel that route.

This all went through Joey's mind in a matter of seconds as he was moving over the breakdown approaching the T. Joey decided to go to the left. He was more familiar with that side anyway. He followed the line along the passage and about 200 feet later encountered the first gold line T of the cave system. He was only 900 feet from the opening. He glanced at the pressure gauge on the safety tank he had borrowed – 2400 psi left.

Joey was most familiar with this part of the cave. He had

done plenty of dives swimming around this section before he bought his DPV. Traveling through this last part would be quick and easy. He didn't even have to watch the gold line anymore because he was so familiar with the passage. But he decided he would keep a close eye on it anyway because seeing it gave him comfort.

Shortly after the first T Joey saw another breakdown. This was commonly referred to as the second breakdown. It was actually the third breakdown, but no one counted the breakdown in the first couple hundred feet of the cave for some reason. The second breakdown was a section of ceiling about 50 feet long that had collapsed onto the floor. Joey didn't even ease off the throttle to go over it. He zoomed up over the breakdown, making sure to exhale as he did so, and back down on the other side quickly.

700 feet to go.

The first breakdown, as it was named, was a little different. There was no definitive end to it on the side farthest from the cave opening, or the side closest to where Joey was coming from. You only knew you were there when you saw Chicken Head Rock, a rock formation that had fallen from a fissure in the ceiling and come to rest on the floor on the side of the tunnel. When viewed from certain angles it resembled the head of a chicken, comb, beak, and all. That was located between the 500- and 600-foot line markers.

Popular Florida caves had line markers placed on the gold line every 100 feet with the number denoting how far from the opening they were. This way divers would know how far in they had gone. This seemed to be a common thing to discuss among cave divers. More importantly for Joey at this time, though, was how much farther he had to travel to get out.

Joey saw Chicken Head Rock ahead and shined his light on it as he scootered through the passage. Even with everything that had just happened and breathing from his last scuba tank, a borrowed one at that, Joey was able to admire the formations found in the caves located all over north Florida. He kept his light focused on Chicken Head Rock and admired it as he scootered by.

He left the chicken head behind and prepared to go through the restriction that denoted the beginning of the first breakdown when traveling into the cave. He maneuvered to the right of the line to take advantage of the larger opening on that side. Joey didn't understand why the gold line wasn't routed through that larger opening. Even swimming, most divers went through there and not directly over the gold line.

400 feet left.

Joey was now in a very large room; the biggest one he had been in during his short time cave diving. He always marveled at the size of this room. You could park two 18-wheelers in it and still have plenty of space to swim around and above them. There was no way anyone could be claustrophobic there.

He quickly made it to the far end where the gold line took a sharp turn up, ascending from 85 feet on the floor to 40 feet of depth at the top. This was commonly referred to as the chimney, but it was more of a fissure crack than a chimney.

300 feet.

Eddy Spring, where Joey had his first cave diving experience, even before he was trained as a cave diver, had a true chimney that was oval shaped and had walls all around it. The chimney in Jackson Blue was a crack in the ceiling or floor, depending on where you were looking at it from. There was only one light colored limestone wall to one side. The other side was open to a sloping, dark, silty bottom.

Releasing the throttle of the DPV, Joey slowed to a swimming pace just as he reached the point where the gold line began its upward slope. He glanced at his pressure gauge – 1900 psi. And less than 300 feet from the opening. *He had this!*

Joey slowly ascended up the chimney, or fissure, or whatever it was. He went slowly so not to off gas too quickly and risk getting bent. He had learned in his decompression procedures class that a slow ascent was critical in reducing the risk of off gassing the nitrogen bubbles that accumulated in the blood stream when you were scuba diving. The deeper you were and the longer you were at depth, the more nitrogen bubbles you accumulated. The ascent must be slow, and you must also stop at certain depths to allow the off gassing of the bubbles to catch up. If you ascend too fast, the bubbles grow in size too quickly and get stuck, causing decompression illness, also known as the bends.

The decompression tank filled with 100% oxygen that he had left at the beginning of the gold line helped accelerate the off gassing. Because the air scuba divers breathe is usually the same as the air breathed on the surface, there is nitrogen in it. The nitrogen is absorbed into the blood faster at higher pressures under water. Even when doing decompression stops, any nitrogen in the scuba tank will continue to be absorbed, although at a slower rate at shallower depths.

Breathing 100% oxygen speeds up the decompression, lessening the amount of time required to stay at depth, because there is no nitrogen in it to continue to be absorbed into the body. So divers will often take smaller tanks filled with oxygen on dives that will be deep enough and long enough to require decompression stops. This typically reduces the decompression obligation by about half. In Joey's case, on this dive, it not only would reduce his decompression obligation, it would also give him another tank of something to breathe.

Joey took about one and a half minutes to ascend the 45 feet in the chimney fissure. As he was clearing the breakdown at the top of the fissure, he saw a bright light ahead of him. That was strange, he thought, he shouldn't be seeing the light from the opening just yet, and definitely not that bright.

4

The light was coming from another diver scootering into the cave. Joey hadn't re-engaged his DPV yet since he was still ascending up the fissure, so he moved to his right to give the diver room to go by. The diver's light focused on Joey and the diver steered his DPV directly at him. Joey moved farther to the right, but the diver kept coming toward him.

Alright, what's going on here, thought Joey. *Why isn't he just passing through?*

Suddenly Joey heard the soft hum of the other diver's DPV motor cut off. The momentum the diver had built up while scootering kept him drifting toward Joey. Then Joey noticed the diver was holding one of his second stage scuba regulators out in front of him, offering it to Joey. Joey gave the diver an okay sign by forming a circle with his thumb and index finger. He then waved the diver off, but the diver persisted.

The diver swam into position next to Joey and grasped the back of Joey's upper arm. He started to lead Joey out toward the opening. Joey didn't know what was going on. What he did know was that even though he had plenty of air left in the safety tank he had borrowed, he didn't have the patience or energy to argue with this guy. He just wanted to get to his decompression tank and ascend to 20 feet of depth so he could begin his long decompression obligation. At least the diver was pulling him in the right direction.

Joey wanted to scooter to his decompression tank, but the unknown diver was holding onto his arm and wouldn't let go. Maybe this guy was in trouble and needed Joey to stabilize him. Whatever it was, Joey remained focused on doing what he needed to do to get himself to the surface safely. He would deal with this other diver once he was above water.

They reached the beginning of the gold line and the diver held out his hand toward Joey, palm down and fingers clenched into a fist, the scuba signal for hold your position. He let go of Joey's arm and descended to the oxygen tank that was resting five feet below them, unclipped it from the gold line, and carried it back to Joey. Joey tried to take it from him, but he wouldn't release it.

At this point, the daylight streaming into the cave was bright enough for Joey to make out the formations of the breakdown on the floor all around them. They were about 35 feet deep. Joey needed to get into the first room, appropriately named the Deco Room because that's where most of the decompression stops occurred, and where Joey wanted to be so he could get to 20 feet of depth and start breathing the oxygen from his decompression tank. Hopefully the diver would give him his oxygen tank once there.

They swam through the darkness toward the bright opening. There was a bottle neck restriction between the room they were in and the Deco Room. The restriction wasn't that small, but it was significantly smaller than where they were. The opening was about 15 feet in diameter and the room they were in, known as the Rock Garden because of all the rocks that had fallen to the floor from the ceiling, was about 60 feet wide and 25 feet tall. That meant the water flow increased in force as it transitioned from the much larger room through the smaller opening. The opening also took them from 30 feet to 20 feet of depth pretty quickly. If divers weren't careful going through it, they could get spit out of the cave and to the surface without stopping to do their decompression stops. Joey had seen that happen once before.

Joey tried to drop to the floor to get out of the flow but the diver holding his arm tightened his grip, not letting Joey move away. Joey was starting to panic at this point. He knew he needed to stop at 20 feet of depth. If he didn't, he risked getting decompression illness. This guy seemed intent on holding onto Joey though. Joey began to worry that this diver might try to pull him along all the way to the surface without stopping to do his decompression obligation.

As they glided through the opening, pushed by the current, the diver pulled Joey to the left, behind a wall and out of the water flow. Joey felt a wave of relief wash over him as the realization that he wasn't being forced to go directly to the surface came upon him. They moved to a corner where another oxygen tank was waiting. The floor there was 21 feet deep. They settled in and Joey made sure the depth readout on his dive computer display was 20 feet.

Joey watched the other diver open the valve on his decompression tank. He pulled the second stage regulator hose free from the retainers that kept it tucked alongside the body of the tank and pushed it toward Joey. Joey gladly took it, spit out the safety tank regulator he had been breathing from, and placed the decompression tank regulator in his mouth. He purged the water out of the new regulator before taking a breath from it. He then switched the gas selection on his wrist-mounted dive computers from the bottom gas setting (the gas he was breathing from his sidemount tanks) to the oxygen setting. This would allow the dive computers to calculate the time Joey was required to stay at 20 feet before he could safely ascend to the surface without getting bent.

Dive computers are essentially large watches that have many functions. They allow divers to program the mixtures of air they plan to breathe during a dive. They monitor the depth and time and calculate the decompression obligation throughout the dive. If a diver brings multiple gas mixtures on a dive, those can be switched in the computer as the diver switches regulators to breathe a different mixture. This allows for a much more accurate calculation of decompression obligation during dives.

Joey had planned his dive and knew how much decompression obligation he would have. But that was only if all had gone according to plan. He also had a couple of backup plans in case he was delayed by 5 or 10 minutes. He hadn't planned for a 45-minute delay, though. In the old days, before dive computers, divers had to bring stacks of dive tables with them and were forced to manually calculate decompression underwater if something went awry.

Joey was very thankful for the technology that allowed him to simply look at a display to see how long he had to stay at 20 feet breathing oxygen. Granted, things could go wrong. The computer could fail. That's why he had a second dive computer on his other wrist. And he also had his brain to determine if the time displayed on the dive computer seemed reasonable. If all else failed, Joey could simply remain at 20 feet breathing oxygen until the decompression tank was empty.

That thought made Joey shudder as it brought back memories of the times he had to remain on a safety stop breathing the last of the air in his scuba tank a couple of years prior. As he shuddered, the diver next to him immediately asked him if he was okay by holding out his thumb and forefinger in a circle. Joey responded with the same signal. *What's up with this guy?*

Now that Joey had settled in breathing from his decompression tank, he could relax a bit. He looked at his dive computer and noted the time he had to stay at 20 feet of depth to decompress and be able to surface from the cave – 33 minutes. While that wasn't as long as Joey had expected, it still seemed reasonable. He glanced at the dive computer on his other wrist and saw they were in agreement with each other.

The decompression tank was full, so Joey had plenty of oxygen to allow him to not only stay the 33 minutes but to stay a few extra minutes to pad the decompression stop and make sure he didn't get bent. He hadn't noticed any markings on the safety tank he had taken from the Traffic Light and didn't know what percentage of oxygen he had been breathing from it. It could be 32% enriched Nitrox which he normally breathed on these dives. Or it could be standard air with only 21% oxygen. He usually padded his decompression stop on his dives anyway. He definitely wanted to pad it this time after such a stressful dive.

Joey looked at the diver he had encountered a couple

hundred feet back. The diver was busy securing the oxygen tank that had been lying on the floor in front of them to his harness. Joey hadn't recognized him at first. The darkness in the cave, along with the scuba mask and hood, made it difficult to recognize other divers. And most of the dive suits and equipment made for cave diving only came in black so there was no way to distinguish one diver from another diver. But now that they were only 30 feet from the opening where there was ambient light, Joey was able to see the eyes of the diver through the mask. He also recognized the classic and uniquely shaped Poseidon regulator he was breathing from. It was Jack Johnson.

Jack was well known by most cave divers. He had moved to the area a few years earlier to be near the caves. He came from money and didn't have to work so spent a lot of time diving. In fact, he could be seen out on Merritt's Mill Pond almost every day preparing to do a cave dive or tearing down his equipment after a dive.

He had also built himself a reputation as a hero. There had been an incident earlier in the year where a couple of student cave divers had gotten separated from their instructor and Jack happened to be getting ready for a dive when the instructor surfaced and called for help. Jack was able to get in the water quickly and zoom into the cave on his DPV. He found the lost divers several hundred feet in, lost and confused, in a silt out, practically in tears, and led them out of the cave to safety. It was the first rescue of its kind in cave diving history. There was not only a lot of discussion on the social media sites about the rescue, but it also made it into the local news. Jack had become a local hero instantly.

Over the next several months after that rescue, Jack happened to be at the right place at the right time and rescued a couple more divers from the grip of death. Joey knew Jack spent a lot of time cave diving, but so did other cave divers. Yet, Jack was the only one that had done rescues rather than recoveries.

Mike, Joey's dive buddy, must have made it out of the cave and saw Jack preparing for a dive. Mike must have been the one who told him they had scootered off the main line and Joey was still stuck in the cave.

Mike!

Joey had forgotten about Mike after he found the safety tank and started making his way out. He turned to Jack and signaled "buddy" to him by pointing both index fingers up and bringing the fingers together and apart several times. He followed that by bending his right index finger into a curve to form the signal for a question mark. Jack just stared back at him, apparently not understanding what Joey was asking.

Joey reached into his thigh pocket and pulled out a set of wetnotes, a small notepad made of a special thick paper that can withstand the environment underwater and retains the graphite from a pencil even when wet. He pulled out the pencil attached to the wetnotes by a length of bungee cord and wrote "Buddy?" on one of the pages. He turned the page toward Jack and illuminated the word with his dive light. Jack read the question, and once he realized what Joey was asking, he gave Joey the signal for okay and pointed back out toward the opening of the cave.

Great, Joey thought, *at least Mike had made it out okay.* Jack remained hovering in front of Joey, apparently waiting for him to finish his decompression stop. Joey pointed to himself followed by the okay signal to let him know he was fine. He then pointed to Jack, pointed to the opening, and followed up with the okay signal again to let Jack know he could leave. Jack didn't move.

Oh no, Joey thought, *Jack thinks he's rescuing me.* This wasn't good. Joey liked to keep to himself. He had always been that way. But he had withdrawn more after the incident at Eddy Spring a couple of years back. He didn't even share much with his parents. The only person he was completely open with, and also completely vulnerable to, was his girlfriend, Lindsey.

Joey didn't want a bunch of attention focused on him, especially by people who thought he had screwed up on a cave dive and needed Jack to save him. And after the response he saw to Jack's previous rescues, Joey just knew another rescue so soon after would create more attention. Attention on Joey.

The cave diving community could be relentless when it came to Monday morning quarterbacking incidents. If it got out that Joey had an issue while cave diving, one that required a rescue, the rumors would be unbearable. Only it wasn't really if it got out, but when it got out now that Jack was involved. Because news of this would fly through the cave diving community quickly.

The stories that flew around the cave diving community after Jack rescued those student divers were pretty wild. It wasn't much different than the stories that got out after Joey had found the dead diver beyond the grate at Eddy Spring. The stories this time were so bad, the cave instructor never taught again. Joey wasn't even sure if the instructor had been diving since that incident.

Joey wasn't sure what became of the students. He didn't know if they quit diving after that or not. Joey hadn't come across anyone that he thought might be them and he was cave diving almost every weekend.

Joey didn't want to become known as one of Jack's rescues and become the focus of any fill station stories. Talk around scuba tank fill stations was worse than water-cooler gossip. And Joey didn't want to become Jack's first rescue of a trained cave diver. It was probably too late for that though.

* * *

After the 33 minutes had passed, plus another five minutes for good measure, Joey prepared to swim the last 30 feet to the opening where he could ascend to the surface. He reached back to grab his DPV, but it wasn't there. He looked around and noticed Jack had it clipped to a D-ring behind him. "Great!" Joey could kick himself for not paying attention. He was so used to relaxing, almost falling asleep, during his decompression stops that he hadn't noticed Jack unclipping the DPV from his D-ring and clipping it to himself. Joey thought about trying to get it back from Jack but that would only delay his exit to the surface, and after almost three hours in the water, the longest Joey had ever spent on a dive, he was ready to get out. He was hungry, thirsty, and tired.

With no DPV to push in front of him, Joey began swimming as Jack reached out and grasped his upper arm again. There was no use fighting it. Joey didn't know why Jack was being so persistent about holding onto him, but he just let Jack lead him out. They did a couple of fin kicks to get them back to the center of the Deco Room until the water current grabbed them and slowly pushed them toward the opening. As they exited the overhead enclosure of the cave, Jack pushed Joey to the right to get out of the water flow. They swam up the gentle sandy white slope located at the edge of the opening and ascended the last 10 feet until their heads broke the surface.

Just as Joey's head came completely of the water, he heard a bunch of applause. *What was going on???* Joey looked around the circular spring basin past the concrete dive board platform located just above the opening to the cave. He noticed several people standing on the concrete platform as well as on shore above the cinder block retaining wall to the left of the dive platform. Some of them were wearing uniforms. Uniforms with badges.

Then Joey noticed the ambulance parked about 50 feet behind the crowd next to the large pavilion closest to the edge of the water. After the ambulance, the worst part of this scene came into Joey's view – a long-bearded man holding a camera with a long lens on it that was pointing toward Joey and Jack. The guy was furiously snapping away taking dozens of photos. Joey looked past the camera and saw a laminated badge clipped onto the man's chest. It had the word "PRESS" on it in large, bold, capital letters.

5

The press had somehow learned about Joey getting stuck in the cave. How could that have happened? How could they have gotten to the spring so fast? That was all Joey needed. If this made the news and his parents saw it, that might be the end of his cave diving. No, not might. It would be the end of it. Joey's parents had been against him scuba diving from the very beginning. This would only turn them more against it.

His parents had been encouraging Joey to be more active. They told him he needed to do more than sit around the house playing video games. Then Joey came across what seemed like a good deal on a scuba diving class and thought that would be perfect. It was something he thought he would enjoy, and his parents would get off his back about being more physically active.

Except…when they found out he signed up for a scuba diving class they flipped out.

"Scuba diving is dangerous, Joseph! It's not safe at all," his mother lectured. "People get hurt and die all the time scuba diving, especially when they're diving in those caves around here."

In the Florida panhandle, where there were dozens, if not

hundreds, of freshwater springs, cave diving was popular. Every now and then, someone would die while cave diving. And somehow Joey's parents always heard about it.

Joey had learned to dive at Eddy Spring, one of the more popular freshwater springs in the Florida panhandle that also happened to be less than an hour's drive from where he lived. And it also happened to be the location where a diver had been last seen before his disappearance. This occurred about two years earlier, just one and a half months after Joey had become a certified scuba diver. That had caused quite a stir in his mother, and she didn't talk to him for days after that.

The thing is Joey wasn't a cave diver at the time, and he hadn't had any aspirations to cave dive. But his mother didn't like the thought of him diving in the Florida springs where the caves were located. Joey didn't know if she thought he would get sucked into the cave or if she thought he would venture in on his own. It didn't help that the body of the diver that had disappeared had never been found, even after two years.

Little had his mother known that Joey had found the missing diver just beyond the grate 300 feet in from the cave opening at Eddy Spring. Not only that, but Joey also pulled the body out of the cave in the middle of the night. And he was forced to help the manager of the dive park get rid of it.

At the time he had even told his mother *"Mom, I'm not a cave diver. I'm just an open water diver. That means I can always go straight up to the surface."*

And this was true. What he didn't admit was that he had gone into the cave, more than once, and that he was planning on taking a cavern diver course, which would train him to enter the first part of the caves that still had enough ambient light to allow divers to see their surroundings.

Eventually Joey completed that cavern diver course and earned his certification. What got Joey hooked on cave diving happened during the last dive of the cavern diver course.

Joey, his two classmates, and his instructor descended below the surface right above the cave entrance. The plan was to follow the line of their primary reel that they had placed in the cavern during their previous dive and left there for this one. They arrived at the primary tie off of the line and followed it into the cave and through the cavern until they reached the reel, which was tied off to a rock at the edge of the ambient lighted cavern zone. Joey's instructor grabbed the reel and unwrapped the tie off. He then proceeded beyond the daylight part of the cavern into the darkness beyond.

Joey hesitated. Over the past two days, his instructor had drilled it into him and his classmates that they were never to go beyond the daylight zone. Could this be a trick, he thought, a test to see if he would follow the rules? His instructor had told him this was the one time they would be allowed to go beyond the cavern zone. They were doing this so they would be able to get a taste of the next level of cave diving and be better prepared to decide if they wanted to pursue that. In other words, he was dangling a carrot in front of them. Was that true or was it a test?

What also made Joey hesitate was the fact that the last time he went beyond the cavern zone, he found a dead body. He still had nightmares about that. He was pretty sure that wouldn't happen this time. Besides, it wasn't just him. His instructor and two other cavern diving students were there with him.

When his instructor didn't stop and turn around, Joey decided to follow. As they transitioned into the cave zone from the cavern zone, Joey saw two cave divers with much brighter lights than he had ever seen come zooming out of the darkness right toward them. They were moving a lot faster than Joey thought it was possible to swim, even with the fast water flow of the first magnitude spring they were in. That's because they were using DPVs. Joey had seen divers at Eddy Spring riding behind smaller scooters. Those looked like toys compared to the scooters the two cave divers were using.

That was all it took to convince Joey he wanted to continue with the training and see what lies beyond and around the next corner. Joey wanted to go where those divers had come from.

It took Joey a little more than a year to save for the proper equipment and pay for the courses required to continue his training as a cave diver. He couldn't ask his parents for another loan, not after what he went through after borrowing money to help pay for his initial scuba certification. Once he had the money saved, Joey scheduled all the courses and completed his training within the following year.

It helped that he stayed on at the restaurant he had been working at even after getting a job at a local veterinary office as a vet tech. The vet tech pay was double what he had been making as a busboy at the restaurant and about 50% more than he made once he got promoted to wait staff. The only reason Joey stayed on at the restaurant to work a shift once a week was to save up for the expensive equipment and training required to cave dive.

Joey even managed to have enough money left over to buy a used DPV, one similar to the DPVs he had seen during that last cavern dive. And he found it for a steal. Truthfully, he should have waited another year or two before scootering in the caves. He still had a lot of cave passage to see within swimming distance of the openings. But the deal was too good to pass up.

Joey's parents noticed how hard he was working and stopped pestering him about diving for a while. Joey figured they must have assumed, incorrectly, that he wasn't diving as much, if at all, because he was working so much. And it never occurred to them to ask what he was doing with all the money he was making.

What also helped his case with his parents and being a scuba diver was Lindsey. His parents knew Lindsey was a cave diver and that helped ease some of the pressure off Joey. For some reason his mother didn't think of it as such a dangerous activity once she learned Lindsey was trained and actively cave diving. So she turned a blind eye to Joey and his scuba diving activities. Regardless, Joey decided it was best to keep the information about his cave diving training from his parents.

They found out about it anyway.

The cavern certification card had been mailed by the certifying agency, which was a cave diving agency, and this was reflected in its name on the return address. It arrived while Joey was at work and his mother had seen the envelope first. Suddenly, it didn't matter that Lindsey was a cave diver.

That was a day to remember. Joey spent three hours that evening defending himself to his parents. When Joey's mom saw that he had become a certified cavern diver she lost all sense of reason.

Joey walked into the house through the kitchen door. His mother was standing there waiting for him. She didn't look happy.

"Joseph, have a seat. Your father and I need to discuss something with

you."

Joey didn't know what she was upset about, but he knew it couldn't be good. It never was when she pulled his father into it. Joey sat at the kitchen table and saw the certification card lying on top of the open envelope. His heart sank.

"What is that, Joseph?" his mother asked once his father had taken his seat at the opposite end of the table from Joey.

"U-U-U-Ummmm."

"You told us you had no intention of ever diving those dangerous caves, Joseph!" his mother interrupted before he could say anything. "You know, I never liked the fact that you were doing this scuba thing to begin with. And we discussed this cave diving thing extensively at that time. You assured me you had no aspirations to do it. I don't want to get a knock on the door one day with some stranger telling me you died in a cave, Joseph."

"Mom! We've had this discussion before. It's really rare that anyone dies in a cave. The last time was two years ago at Eddy Spring and the body was never found so they can't even prove that's what happened." Crap! I shouldn't have reminded her of that! Joey thought too late.

"Caves kill people, Joseph," his mother repeated. "There are stories about all the people dying in caves all the time."

"Mom, caves don't kill people. Every single death that's happened in a cave, with the exception of one, has been because the diver violated one of the rules of cave diving. The training I received taught me those rules and I'll never violate any of them. Besides, I mostly dive with Lindsey, and you were okay with her being a cave diver."

His mother stood there with an incredulous look on her face, mouth hanging open, stunned and silenced by Joey's last words. She didn't like her own words being thrown back in her face and that was exactly what Joey had done. She let out a "Hmphhhhh!!!", turned on her heel, and stormed out of the kitchen. Joey looked at his father who just sat there with a sad look on his face. Joey knew his poor dad was going to be taking the brunt of this later.

When his mother stormed out of the kitchen, Joey got up and followed her. Usually, he would let her stew in her own misery, but cave diving was too important to him to let it go. He had already invested a lot of time and money and he really enjoyed it. He caught up to her in the hallway leading to his parents' bedroom.

"Mom, in training we're taught how to dive in the overhead safely. We have rules that we always have to follow."

His mother turned back to face him.

"I don't care, Joseph. Rules don't guarantee you won't become the next person to die in a cave."

"But these rules do! As long as they are followed. The people you hear about dying in the caves didn't follow the rules. The main one being not having the proper training. I have the proper training."

"I still don't like it, Joseph. It's a dangerous activity."

"But Lindsey has been cave diving for almost two years and she's still alive. She follows the rules and is very safe."

"It's different, Joseph."

"How, mom?"

"It just is!"

They returned to the kitchen where Joey kept trying to explain to his mother how safe cave diving had become and she continued to refuse to give in. And she never did reveal why it was different when it came to Lindsey cave diving.

Joey came to regret chasing after her. The three-hour interrogation finally ended with Joey storming off this time. He got up, walked out of the house, and left for a few hours. Nothing he said to his mother was going to change *her mind. She was convinced he was going to die in a cave.*

There was no point arguing with her. He had already wasted three hours doing that and it got him nowhere. The following week was very tense between the two of them. Joey's mother didn't say a word to him all week.

Eventually his mother cooled off and things started to get back to normal. Although, they never did get back to being exactly the same as they had been before that day.

* * *

Joey was more careful about where his certification cards were mailed. He began having the cards sent to Lindsey's address so his mother wouldn't see them. He thought that might be one of the reasons his mother was loosening up. She must have assumed since he wasn't getting any more mail from cave diving training agencies that Joey had given up that particular type of scuba diving. That and all the hours he was working probably made her think he simply didn't have time to dive.

The opposite was true. Joey spent every day off he had at the springs building up his experience. He continued with his cave diving training. In addition to completing the next level of training – introductory cave diving – he also took decompression diving courses and eventually completed his cave diver training – ten days of additional coursework over the previous year.

His parents learned all about it not long after he finished his training in the use of a DPV in a cave. Joey had chosen a different instructor than the one he had completed his prior cave diving training with. His usual instructor wasn't available to teach during Joey's days off for a few months and Joey was anxious to get his new to him DPV into the water. His impatience did him in.

Joey forgot to ask the new instructor to use Lindsey's address instead of his home address, the one he used on the training application paperwork. The cave DPV certification card was mailed to his house and his mother saw the envelope with the same cave diving training agency as the sender. Her reaction was nothing like it had been when she discovered the cavern diver certification card. Joey wasn't sure whether it was better or worse.

When Joey's mother opened the envelope and saw the cave DPV certification card, she was confused at first. She didn't know what the certification meant. So she googled it.

It wasn't so much the course description that set her off but rather the prerequisites listed for the course. All training agencies require the diver to have completed the full cave diver course and to have experience at that level prior to enrolling in a cave DPV diver course. The general requirement was between 25 and 50 cave dives depending on the training agency. So not only did his mother know he was a certified cave diver, but she knew he had been cave diving regularly for some time.

When he arrived home that evening it was a replay of the day the cavern diver certification card had arrived. The certification card was lying on the open envelope on the kitchen table. Joey's heart sank immediately upon seeing it. He quickly snatched it up and shoved it in his pocket. What should have been a joyous occasion quickly soured. He walked through the house looking for his mother. Usually at this time of day she would be in the kitchen preparing dinner. There was no sign that there was going to be a dinner that night.

Joey walked down the hall and saw her bedroom door closed. He considered knocking on it then thought better of it. Avoidance was probably the best option at the moment. He grabbed a package of pop tarts and quickly left the house to head to the dive shop where Lindsey was working. At least the replay didn't include the three-hour lecture. Two weeks later his mother still hadn't spoken a word to him.

6

When Joey told his mother that every single death that happened in a cave, with the exception of one, had been because the diver violated one of the rules of cave diving, he was telling the truth. There was only one documented case of a diver dying in a cave that was not a result of an error on his part. That was the Parker Turner incident in the Indian Springs Cave System.

Indian Springs is located on the grounds of a boy scout camp just south of Tallahassee, Florida. The entrance to Indian Springs cave begins about 10-15 feet below the surface, depending on the water level. It's fairly close to the coast so the tide affects the water level in the spring basin.

Parker Turner, one of the early Florida underwater cave explorers, and his dive buddy, Bill Gavin, the inventor of one of the first modern DPVs used in caves, were diving in Indian Spring exploring it looking for new passages.

Turner and Gavin dropped below the surface and immediately got into a horizontal position and assessed their equipment. All seemed in order. They turned toward the opening to the cave and squeezed the triggers on their DPVs as they descended to 20 feet of depth, just below the ceiling of the cavern. They passed from the safety of the surface above into the dark confines of the overhead environment. About 20 feet in, the coarse sand floor quickly dropped away down a sharp slope that ended about 90 feet deep. From there the floor kept getting deeper but not at as steep of a slope.

They reached the bottom, went through a quick mental checklist of their equipment and the dive plan, and continued to scooter deeper into the cave. The plan was to check out leads in the Wakulla Room, a large room at 300 feet of depth that they had found on previous dives.

After spending about 25 minutes in the Wakulla Room and finding nothing, Turner and Gavin began to make their way toward the exit. When they were about 1500 feet from the opening, Turner signaled to Gavin that his DPV was getting sluggish. Turner clipped his tow line to Gavin and Gavin increased the speed on his DPV continuing their exit. About 10 minutes later they arrived at a point in the line where another line tied into it, forming a T. They turned left to continue heading toward the exit.

Immediately after turning left, the visibility began to deteriorate. There were silt clouds hovering over the floor. The farther they went, the bigger the silt clouds got and the worse the visibility, until they couldn't see more than a foot in front of them. Gavin released the trigger and he and Turner made contact with the line to swim the short distance remaining.

Except soon after, they discovered the line they were following in the near zero visibility conditions was buried under the coarse sand. They began pulling the line up, trying to get it out from under the sand, until they reached a point where it was too deep to pull up. At that location, the sand also rose all the way to the ceiling. They were trapped.

For the next 45 minutes Turner and Gavin frantically searched for a way out of the cave as their limited breathing gas supply dwindled away. At one point, Gavin deployed a safety spool, secured the cave line on it to an unburied portion of the main line and began spoking out to look for an alternate exit. When he returned several minutes later Turner was gone.

Gavin continued to search, breathing the last of his stage tanks empty.

He went back to breathing from his backmounted double tanks with only 300 psi of breathing gas remaining. Gavin made one last effort at finding an exit when he came across another line T, one which he didn't remember being there before. He followed the new line not knowing where he was heading but having no other option.

Eventually, Gavin found himself in a larger area, looked up, and saw the permanent line above him. With only a few breaths remaining in his tanks, he picked up his pace to try to get to his staged decompression tank, which was waiting for him at 100 feet of depth. If the tank had been any farther, he might not have made it out of the cave alive.

Bill Gavin then had to endure four long hours of decompression stops knowing his teammate and good friend, Parker Turner, had not made it out of the cave.

There were other divers on the surface providing surface support for Turner and Gavin. They reported seeing the water in the basin drop by about a foot and the water current rushing into the cave. They didn't know if this caused the avalanche or if the avalanche caused it. Regardless, the exit was blocked.

It appears Turner had found a small tunnel through the sand and removed his backmounted double tanks to push them through in front of him. His efforts had resulted in this small opening becoming large enough for Gavin to be able to fit without removing his tanks.

Unfortunately, Turner ran out of breathing gas before he could make it to his decompression tank just 30 feet away from where his body was found stuck to the ceiling, his empty double tanks hanging from the main line below him. However, it was most likely because of his actions that Bill Gavin was able to get out alive and there wasn't a double fatality that day.

To this day, Parker Turner holds the dubious distinction of being the only cave diver fatality that is not attributed to a violation of one of the cave diving rules.

7

When Joey saw the photographer with the press badge, he immediately turned the other way and kept his face turned away from the camera. He also tried to keep his mask and hood on so he would be difficult to recognize if the photographer did happen to get a shot of his face. Jack wasn't being helpful with that though. He reached for Joey's mask and pulled it up and off his head.

"Are you alright?" Jack asked, sounding sincerely concerned.

"I-I-I'm fine," Joey murmured.

"Let's get this hood off you so you can breathe better."

"N-No, I'm okay like this. I can breathe fine," Joey's voice rose during the final syllables.

"Com'on over here," Jack said as he pulled Joey to the edge of the retaining wall close to the ladder, closer to the crowd gathered on shore, and closer to the photographer.

Joey grabbed onto the ladder rail to steady himself. Even though he was alive and well and uninjured, he was also exhausted from the long dive. He didn't know how he was going to get out of this mess though. He made one mistake, but he was able to get himself out of the cave alive, and with plenty of air left in the safety tank he had borrowed. He didn't deserve all this attention. He certainly didn't want it.

How did the press even find out anyway? How did they get to the spring so fast? When Joey's mother saw this headline, and it wasn't a matter of if but definitely when, Joey couldn't even imagine what her reaction would be. He might as well start packing and looking for another place to live.

Joey stood in the water next to the retaining wall, holding himself up by the ladder, trying to calm himself and prevent a panic attack from ensuing over the attention he was getting. That's all he would need, for everyone to see him having a panic attack after being pulled out of the cave by Jack Johnson.

Joey watched as Jack clipped the tow ropes of the DPVs to the other rail of the ladder so they wouldn't drift away. Jack then began to unclip Joey's sidemount tanks to remove them. Joey pushed him off and went to work on removing the tanks himself. Jack was being stubborn though and kept trying to remain in control, remain the hero.

"Let me help you, boy. You're barely functional after what you've been through." Jack said loud enough for everyone to hear.

Jack was sure playing it up. While Joey removed his right tank, Jack unclipped and removed the left tank. Then Jack tried to get Joey's hood off again. The photographer had apparently gotten all the photos he wanted and had stopped clicking away. The camera was hanging at his side from a strap around his neck. Seeing that, Joey finally conceded, if for nothing else than to get Jack away from him.

He pulled the hood off himself. As the hood cleared his face, he saw the photographer reach for the camera hanging at his side and point it toward him. Joey immediately looked down so the only thing the photographer could get in his lens was the top of Joey's head. Joey kept his head down and his face away from the camera lens.

"Com'on son, let's get you outta the water," Jack said as he grasped Joey's upper arm. Jack started leading Joey along the retaining wall toward the gently sloping white sand beach entrance 20 feet away. The retaining wall was only about three and a half feet tall, and Joey usually hopped up on top of it. Jack wasn't going to allow that this time. They walked to the end of the retaining wall and Jack grabbed Joey under both his arms and directed him up the slope out of the water.

"I'm fine! I can walk on my own!" Joey cried out as he tried to shake Jack off, unsuccessfully.

Once out of the water the photographer became disinterested in them, pulled out a small notepad, and started scribbling in it.

The ambulance crew rushed over to Joey and took over from Jack.

"We've got this from here, sir! Thanks for bringing him out alive," the taller of the two medics said to Jack.

"I'm just thankful I was able to find him still alive and bring him out safely. I'd much rather rescue someone than recover a body." Jack responded loudly as he handed Joey over.

With one crew member on each side of Joey they led him to the back of the ambulance and sat him in front of the open doors on the large shiny diamond tread rear bumper. They stood in front of him pulling out a bunch of equipment that was designed to make sure an injured person was not in life threatening danger.

"I'm okay, really! I don't need any help."

"We've got to do a quick exam, just to make sure. You understand, don't you," said the tall one. It was more of a statement than a question.

"Sure, I guess," Joey replied as he thought it was more likely to cover their butts.

The quiet medic placed some sort of monitor on his index finger and spoke for the first time.

"This is just a sensor to monitor the oxygen levels in your blood."

"I need to give you a small poke to get a drop of blood so we can check your blood sugar. Is that okay?" asked the tall medic.

"Sure, sure." Joey agreed to everything at this point. He just wanted to get it over with and get out of there.

As the medics were doing their jobs Joey noticed the photographer had his camera in hand again and was trying to snap some photos of Joey sitting at the back of the ambulance. Joey kept his head down and shifted so the quiet medic was positioned between him and the camera. The photographer either took enough photos or tired of his unsuccessful attempts at getting a better picture of Joey and brought the camera down to his side again. He turned and walked toward Jack.

Joey could hear Jack telling his version of events to the photographer.

"I had just arrived at the park and was setting up my scuba equipment to go continue some exploration I've been doing in here when the victim's dive buddy came out of the cave and said the victim was still stuck in the cave somewhere. I tried to calm him down and get details of what had happened and where he thought his buddy was. He told me they had been scootering back in the Trash Room, that's an area of the cave about 3000 feet back under an old sinkhole where people used to dump trash. They were on their way out when they missed a turn on the main line and headed into a smaller side passage. This was a small sidemount size passage I found a few years back and should be considered a very advanced passage. I almost pulled out the line I placed in there. I'm glad I didn't because it helped them find their way back to the main line."

"Anyway, the buddy told me the passage got silted out, but he managed to back out using the line I had placed there, and he found the main line. He waited about 15 minutes to see if the victim would exit, but he never saw him. He said the silt cloud kept getting bigger and bigger. So he decided to exit the cave and try to get help."

"I quickly assembled my equipment and got in the water. I scootered into the cave as quickly as I could and found the victim several hundred feet back pushing his DPV in front of him. He was so disoriented and confused he wasn't even using the DPV to get himself out faster. He was also very low on air. I could hear him crying through his regulator. I handed him the regulator from my second tank to breathe from, but he pushed it away. I had to force him to take the regulator so he wouldn't run out of air and drown. I then grabbed his arm and pulled him out to the cavern to do a decompression stop."

"When we got to the beginning of the main line, he was so weak he couldn't even get his decompression tank off the line. I had to retrieve it for him, open the valve, and hand him the regulator. I then stayed with him until his decompression obligation was done. I even made him stay a few extra minutes because I'm sure he was stressed, and when the body is stressed, it requires more decompression than under normal circumstances."

Joey couldn't believe what he was hearing. None of that was true. Jack had come up to him when he was only about 200 feet from the opening. Joey was swimming because he was ascending up the chimney. No one in their right mind scooters up the chimney. Ascending that quickly would certainly get someone bent. Joey only refused Jack's regulator because he had plenty of air left in the safety tank, and Jack didn't force him to take it. Joey never breathed from it. And he was definitely not crying! He also didn't get his decompression tank because Jack wouldn't let him, not because he was so weak. And Joey was the one who decided to extend his decompression stop, not Jack. Jack wasn't even looking at Joey's dive computers.

All of those thoughts rushed through Joey's mind as he contemplated running over to the photographer or reporter or whatever he was and telling him the facts. Joey wanted to tell him exactly what had happened.

Joey tried to stand up, but the quiet medic held him down. She was still taking vital signs and listening to his lungs and heart, and he couldn't get away just yet. But even so, who would the reporter believe?

The real course of events was uneventful and boring. Jack's version was much more exciting and newsworthy. Even if Joey could tell the reporter what really happened, he would likely brush it off as Joey still being confused and disoriented and print Jack's version anyway. Because drama sells. And that is exactly what happened. Jack's version was printed.

8

CAVE DIVER RESCUED FROM JACKSON BLUE SPRING! HERO JACK JOHNSON SAVES ANOTHER!

That was the headline Joey woke up to the following day. Fortunately, it had only made the Jackson County newspaper and not the local paper in Santa Rosa Beach, where Joey lived. Joey's parents weren't likely to see the news…yet… Joey only saw it because there was talk about it on the social media sites he frequented. Otherwise, he wouldn't have known about it either.

He searched for the story and once he found it, he quickly scrolled through it on his phone. There were a couple of photos taken at Blue Spring Park, but because Joey had kept his head down, none where he could be recognized. All anyone could see in the photos was the top of his head. No names were mentioned other than Jack's. And lots of quotes of things Jack said and about his heroism. The reporter hadn't bothered to print Joey's name. Instead, Joey was simply referred to as "a cave diver." This was good, Joey thought. He preferred to remain anonymous. His mother might still give him grief over the incident, but at least she wouldn't know it was him.

Throwing on a t-shirt, Joey stepped out of his room and walked across the hall to the bathroom. He could smell the odor of bacon coming from the kitchen. After splashing some cool water on his face, he headed to the kitchen where his mother was preparing eggs and bacon for his father's breakfast. She still hadn't spoken to Joey since she found the cave DPV certification card he received in the mail. And she still wasn't offering to make him breakfast. This morning was no different.

Joey's father hadn't come out to the kitchen yet, so Joey had time to scan the local paper. Even though Joey's name hadn't made the story, and he wasn't recognizable in the photographs, he still wanted to see if there was a chance his father might find out about the incident. Any negative news about cave diving was not accepted well by his parents, especially his mother.

He grabbed the newspaper from where it was sitting next to his father's place setting. His mother glared at him and appeared as if she was going to reprimand him for taking his father's paper but then she looked back at the stove without saying a word. Joey sat down with the paper and slowly flipped through the pages.

There was nothing about his incident on the front page, but because this had happened in a small town almost an hour and a half away, he hadn't expected to find anything there. He was more concerned that they may have picked up the story a few pages in. His father was the type of person who read the entire paper front to back. He couldn't imagine what would happen if his father ever decided to give up print for online news. He would never leave the table!

Joey scanned the pages quickly. Any story about anything happening in an underwater cave to a cave diver would be of special interest to Joey's parents. He wanted to prepare himself for any fallout that might occur.

Joey's mother turned toward him and looked like she was about to say something again. She was probably curious as to why Joey was flipping through the paper. This wasn't something he usually did. But then she apparently remembered she wasn't speaking to him. Her mouth had opened as if she was about to speak, and then quickly closed as she turned around to face the stove again.

After he finished flipping through the newspaper, Joey neatly folded it and returned it to the table next to his father's place setting exactly as it had been. He poured himself a glass of orange juice, grabbed a package of pop tarts out of the cupboard, and headed to his room. His mother didn't like Joey eating in his bedroom but since she hadn't been speaking to him there wasn't anything she could do about it. Back in his room, Joey fired up his laptop and scrolled through his feeds to see what, if anything, was being said about his incident on social media.

* * *

Two hours later, Joey shut his laptop and threw himself on his bed. He was wiped out from pouring over post after post by countless cave divers Monday morning quarterbacking the dive from the day before. None of them were there. None of them had any accurate details. Yet, every single one of them had an opinion on what could have been done differently to avoid what happened.

Mike hadn't told anyone what happened other than when he

surfaced and found Jack at the park getting ready for a dive. And, according to Mike, he hadn't said very much. All he claimed to have told Jack was that his buddy was stuck back in the cave near the Trash Room, and he needed help. No other information was provided. Shortly after Joey surfaced and was deemed uninjured by the ambulance crew, Mike quietly slipped away.

Being an even more private person than Joey, Mike didn't want anything to do with the local news or the commotion that had been created. Joey had stolen a glance when he surfaced and noticed Mike standing by the pavilion, away from the crowd and the fuss. As Joey was walking out of the water, he noticed Mike was staying out of the way, quietly packing up his scuba equipment, and preparing to make a quick getaway. Joey didn't fault him. He wished he could do the same. Because of this, he also knew that Mike hadn't said anything about the dive to anyone.

Just to be sure, Joey sent a text to Mike to see how he was doing.

Joey: *How ru doing today?*

Mike: *Good. Still shaken up but good. U?*

J: *Physically good. Mentally not so much. Just spent the last couple hrs reading all the talk about our dive.*

M: *Saw a bunch of it this am. Everyone has an opinion.*

J: *I know I don't have to ask but u didn't tell anyone about it?*

M: *Of course not!*

J: *So everyone is just doing their usual speculation.*

M: *Yep.*

J: *Thanks. TTYL*

M: *TTYL*

Well, that confirmed it. Mike hadn't said anything. And Joey definitely hadn't said anything. Yet, there were all sorts of "theories" as to what had happened. Fortunately, neither Joey's nor Mike's names had made it onto social media. No one seemed to know that information. Usually, if it was known, people would at least allude to knowing so they could inflate their self-importance as being someone in the know. That wasn't happening just yet.

The big rumor circulating was that the diver (meaning Joey) had a medical event during the dive and had to be dragged out, weak and unable to swim.

I heard he's diabetic and had low blood sugar. That's why he was confused and disoriented.

His buddy should never have left him in the cave. What if Jack hadn't shown up when he did. He would have died.

I think he did the right thing. If he couldn't provide help there's no point in making 2 victims.

It's a good thing for this guy that Jack happened to be there. Otherwise it would certainly have been a body recovery.

The comments went on and on like that. The most common story circulating on social media was that the two divers had been on a dive with their DPVs in the cave. They got separated, and one diver panicked and left his buddy behind in the cave. This diver surfaced and saw Jack getting ready for a dive. He yelled for help and Jack quickly got in the water and went looking for the missing diver.

Jack found the missing diver more than a thousand feet inside the cave motionless, confused, and disoriented. The diver was almost out of air in his scuba tanks. When Jack attempted to share his air by offering his second regulator, the confused diver rejected it. Jack had to coax the diver into taking his regulator and then pulled the diver out through several hundred feet of passage.

When they reached the beginning of the gold line, the diver was so weak and disoriented that Jack had to retrieve his oxygen decompression tank and carry it for him until they reached 20 feet of depth. Jack then opened the valve and had to convince the disoriented diver to breathe from it. Jack stayed with the diver and made him pad his decompression stop by staying an additional 5 minutes to make sure he didn't get bent. Jack finally pulled him out of the cave to the surface.

At the surface, the diver was so weak he could barely stand and couldn't hold his head up. He had to practically be carried out of the water to the back of the ambulance where they assessed him. The ambulance crew did a full assessment of the diver, determined his blood sugar was low and gave him juice and snacks to get it back to normal. They wanted to transport him to the hospital for further evaluation, but he refused. They released him from their care half an hour after he had surfaced.

The circulating story had Jack Johnson written all over it. Jack made a couple of other rescues during the previous year. This story sounded very similar to those rescues. Could Jack have really set things up to boost his reputation among cave divers?

* * *

Jack moved to the area several years earlier and did some exploration in the local caves. He built a reputation for himself. Then talk of Jack's explorations fizzled out. Joey just figured it was because there was no more exploration to be done. After all, the caves had been explored decades earlier. The exploration being done currently didn't result in much more previously undiscovered passage.

Rumors started popping up that Jack wasn't the big explorer he made himself out to be. The virgin passages he claimed were actually found by other divers that didn't live in the area. And when their visit was over Jack went in to continue the exploration they had begun, claiming the finds himself. Probably even removing the line arrows they had left behind. Joey didn't know if this was true or not. Like many others, Joey looked up to Jack and his accomplishments. He not only respected Jack, but he also idolized him. Joey didn't want to believe the rumors.

Then earlier in the year Jack rescued those two students from the same cave Joey had been diving. The story was similar. The instructor surfaced and saw Jack getting ready for a dive. The instructor told Jack he had gotten separated from his students in a tunnel that was too small and had gotten too silty for him to follow. He didn't know if his students were still alive or not. Jack rushed into the cave to go find them, which he did almost immediately. He then led them to the gold line and out of the cave to safety.

This was Jack's first rescue and it made him an instant hero in the cave diving community. The rumors about Jack suddenly fell silent. Usually, incidents like these ended in fatalities. This would have been a double fatality had Jack not been there and rescued them.

Prior to that incident there had only been one documented rescue from a cave. It happened years earlier, before Jack had moved into the area, in a different cave but in the same town of Marianna, Florida. The diver had been exploring a newly found cave known as the Bat Guano cave. Several bats lived in the dry opening to the cave and used it as a restroom of sorts. Getting in and out of this cave was not fun. It wasn't a cave Joey had any desire to dive.

The cave diver was diving in the cave alone and ended up lost. Before he could find his way out, he breathed his tanks empty. During his search for the exit, he had been fortunate enough to have found an air-filled chamber in the cave. When he saw his air supply was getting low, he headed to the air chamber and was able to climb out of the water onto a ledge. He spent the night on that ledge.

The next day, after he had been reported overdue from his dive, another cave diver entered the cave to look for the body. The recovery diver followed the line that had been placed in the cave by the missing diver. He eventually found the air-filled chamber. He ascended and popped his head above the surface only to hear the words, "Are you looking for a dead diver?" This almost caused him to soil his drysuit with his own guano.

After a brief exchange and making sure the once thought to be dead diver was okay, he slid into the water and the two exited the cave with the rescued diver breathing from one of his rescuer's tanks. It was an amazing rescue, one that was still talked about more than 10 years later.

It seemed like Jack's rescues were gaining the same notoriety. Joey had met Jack several times while out cave diving. Jack was personable enough. He was quick to speak with others, always very friendly. Even offering to dive with anyone interested.

"How are y'all doing? What's your dive plan?" Jack would ask, sounding earnest.

Joey would always excitedly tell Jack about where they were planning on going.

"Well, next time y'all ought to check out King's Canyon. It's one of the most beautiful places in this cave. And it's not too far back. I'd be happy to take you there some day."

Joey couldn't believe Jack was offering advice on where to go and even offering to dive with him. Being a new cave diver, Joey was star-struck. He was proud to be able to say he knew Jack. And he certainly hoped to be able to dive with Jack at some point once he was no longer so intimidated by the thought of it. Joey feared that the excitement of diving with Jack would be so great he would breathe through the air in his tanks too quickly to make it very far into the cave.

Joey had run into Jack enough times that Jack had begun to recognize Joey and call him by name.

"How ya doin', Joey? Got a good dive planned today?"

Joey thought it was cool to be known by someone so experienced, so well-known among cave divers, and someone considered a hero. After what Jack had just done to him, Joey wasn't so sure how he felt about that anymore.

9

Three days later discussions about Joey's incident were still going strong on the social media sites. Joey's name hadn't been brought into it yet, but some people were claiming to know who the victim was. They were referring to Joey as a victim. At least they weren't posting his name online, but Joey was certain his name was being passed on from diver to diver in DMs. Joey was also certain they knew he was the one involved. After what he had seen he wouldn't put it past Jack to intentionally let it slip that it was Joey.

So far, the news hadn't made it to Lindsey. And Joey hadn't told her either. He knew he was going to have to, especially since it had become the most discussed thing on the cave diving social media sites. If people knew it was him, it would get back to her. He hadn't told Lindsey about the incident because he knew she would be upset at him for doing such a stupid thing and almost getting himself killed.

Lindsey knew Joey was cave diving that weekend. He had told her he and Mike were heading to Jackson Blue to do a dive.

"Well, y'all be careful. Don't push things, Joey. I know you want to get in there and see as much as you can. But remember, the cave will always be there."

Lindsey had a couple more years' experience cave diving than

Joey and she was always watching out for him. Part of the reason was because she knew he tended to push the limits sometimes…well, usually…

"Don't go scooterin' where you haven't been yet. The farthest you should scooter in the cave is the Hall of the Mountain King area. We've only been beyond that area that one time together and don't know the passage well enough to scooter back there," she cautioned him.

Even though Lindsey had specifically told him not to scooter beyond the Mountain King area, Joey rationalized what they had planned. He had been to the Trash Room before and the passage looked straightforward.

And that area wasn't even half the distance of the main passage in Jackson Blue. They were only planning on going about 2400 feet in from the entrance. He had heard the end of the gold line was about 4900 feet back, and the passage continued from there lined with regular cave line for another few hundred feet.

A bit of a reach that Joey was sure wouldn't go over well with Lindsey. And this was why he hadn't told her. But he no longer had a choice. She had been right, again, and he had gotten himself into a situation that resulted in what appeared to be a rescue involving an ambulance and the press, and Jack Johnson.

Lindsey was off work that evening and they had planned on hanging out after Joey got done with his classes for the day. It was Thursday so he had a full schedule that day with two classes after work. He had to figure out how to tell Lindsey that he was the diver Jack was claiming to have rescued. And he had to figure out an excuse for why he didn't tell her about it the day it happened, five days earlier. Truth be told, he was surprised she hadn't questioned him about it yet. She certainly must have already read about it online.

The one thing in Joey's favor was that Lindsey had her own secrets. Like the one from the night at Eddy Spring two years earlier. She had been behaving strangely that evening. Joey never did find out why. And they had never discussed it. It was just one of those things that was left unspoken.

Was that worth bringing up if Lindsey got mad at Joey for not telling her about the incident during Saturday's dive? It had been left unspoken for a reason. And Joey didn't know if he really wanted to discuss what happened that evening. It might be better to leave it unspoken. He would have to give that some thought before meeting with Lindsey after class.

Joey thought about reaching out to some friends to see if they had heard who the diver from Saturday's incident was, but he dismissed that idea. If they knew it was him that would be awkward and strange. The only person he felt comfortable discussing it with was Mike, and Mike had made it clear he didn't want to discuss it. Mike wasn't well known within the cave diving community, and he wanted to keep it that way. Unfortunately, Joey was not so unknown.

Because Joey was dating one of the hottest cave divers in Florida, anonymity wasn't something that was easy to maintain. Almost everyone in the cave diving community knew Lindsey, or at least knew of her. So they all knew who Joey was by association. That may be why Lindsey still hadn't heard about it. Anyone who knew her probably expected that she would already know and not bother to reach out to her to tell her that her boyfriend was almost killed while cave diving and had to be rescued by Jack Johnson.

Joey knew if that was the case his luck wouldn't hold out for long. He decided to tell Lindsey about the dive that evening and let the pieces fall where they may. Their relationship was established enough that he wasn't concerned about that. He just didn't want to hear the reprimand for doing something he already knew was stupid to do. Something that Lindsey had explicitly warned him not to do. The dreaded I told you so.

* * *

That evening after his second class, Joey headed straight to Lindsey's house. They had planned to go grab a late dinner and hang out on the beach for a while. Joey had decided he would tell Lindsey while they were at the beach. That would give them plenty of time to discuss it and Lindsey plenty of time to let Joey know how stupid he had been to plan such a dive.

And that's exactly what happened.

"Lindsey, I-I-I need to talk to you about something." Joey's stuttering had improved as his confidence grew since he started cave diving and dating Lindsey. But it still crept back in whenever he got nervous about something, like telling Lindsey about his screw up.

"Y-You remember the dive Mike and I had planned for last weekend?"

"Of course, sweetie, the one where you weren't supposed to scooter any farther than the King's area?"

Oh crap! She must already know something, thought Joey.

"Yeah, th-th-that one." Joey stammered. "W-Well, w-we didn't stick to the p-plan."

Lindsey started to say something, but Joey cut her off.

"Let me finish," he said. "I know you said we shouldn't scooter that far back, but you and I had already been to the Trash Room, and it seemed like a straightforward passage. What could go wrong?"

By this point Joey was running his words together. Lindsey stood in front of him with her arms folded across her chest. He thought he could see her foot tapping but he was afraid to look away from her face to confirm that.

He then recounted his mistake of not paying enough attention to the gold line and scootering off of it.

"Mike and I scootered to the Trash Room and spent about 20 minutes swimming around looking at everything. Since Mike hadn't been back there, I took the lead on the way in and the way out." Joey paused for a moment, but Lindsey didn't say anything.

"On the way out, I wasn't paying enough attention to where I was going, and I scootered into a side tunnel somewhere in the area of the traffic light."

Still no response from Lindsey. Joey was beginning to get worried. He'd much rather have her yelling at him than giving him the silent treatment, like his mother had been doing.

"This side tunnel gets small quick, and I-I-I ended up getting stuck in it." Another pause. "I did get free."

"Oh really??" Lindsey finally said something, even if it was sarcasm.

Joey dropped his head and continued. Lindsey was no longer

tapping her foot.

"It took me a while to get free and I had to cut my stage tank off. Then I couldn't find it in the silt. But I did find someone else's safety tank that had been staged at the traffic light, which was a miracle because one of my sidemount tanks was empty and the other one only had 200 psi left in it."

"Joey, how could you be so careless?? No, not careless. Reckless!" Lindsey yelled. "You almost got yourself killed!"

Joey was relieved Lindsey had finally said something. He didn't like Lindsey yelling at him, but it was better than her not saying anything.

"I-I-I know. It was stupid and I shouldn't have done it. I let Mike convince me it was okay because I had already been there with you."

"Don't blame this on Mike! You know better! Going back to a section of cave on a DPV that you've only been to once is not smart! Actually, it's stupid! You can't learn a passage in one dive! It takes several dives to be able to see everything. And even then you haven't seen everything."

"I-I know. I'm sorry."

"I don't want an apology, Joey! I want to know that I won't have to worry about you doing something so reckless again! And I won't have to worry about reading online that your body was pulled out of a cave. Cuz maybe next time you won't be so lucky and you'll end up dead."

"Y-You definitely don't. That's the last time I do something like that. I know I was lucky to get out of there alive."

"Who all knows about this?"

"Besides Mike and Jack, and now you, no one that I know of

for certain. No names have been posted on the forums besides Jack's. But people are posting that they know who was on the dive. I don't know if they really do. If they do, then a lot of people might already know. You know how some cave divers are."

"Yeah, I do. If it hasn't gotten out, you can count on it getting out eventually. And people are so taken in by Jack Johnson's reputation that they will believe his version before they believe you."

"I know. And I don't know what to do about it."

"Well, you can't say anything. No one will believe you anyway and they'll just twist your words around to fit their narrative. Leave it be and it will eventually go away."

"I sure hope so."

And that was it. Lindsey had gotten upset but not nearly as upset as Joey had expected. After Lindsey had finished reprimanding Joey, he told her about his ascent up the chimney fissure and seeing Jack's light in front of him. He recounted exactly what had happened. Lindsey had already read the public, or rather Jack's, version of events online. And still she hadn't mentioned it to him.

"I'm not really surprised at how he made himself out to be the hero. Even his previous rescues sounded a little far-fetched to me," Lindsey responded. "What I can't believe is how different his story is. He didn't just stretch the truth a little. He fabricated a completely different story. And then he spread rumors that you were having a medical emergency. That's just bein' a snake in the grass!"

"I know. And I don't know what to do about it. My name

will eventually get out. People will think I'm an incompetent diver. Worse yet, they'll think I'm not safe to dive with because I might have a medical emergency on a dive."

"We'll figure something out, sweetie. I'm not going to let people think you're a danger to them, or to yourself. But next time you need to tell me sooner! I read about it and wondered if you were involved and when you would tell me."

"I should have told you the day it happened. I was hoping it would blow over first. I'm sorry."

Joey had expected Lindsey to be upset with him. Instead, she was upset with Jack Johnson and the lies he was spreading. After Joey had told her the real version of events, Lindsey had forgotten about the error in judgement Joey had made and focused her attention on Jack Johnson. This scared Joey a little. After what had happened two years earlier Joey wasn't sure how he felt about Lindsey's response.

10

Joey's name as the latest Jack Johnson rescue was eventually made public. Someone casually mentioned in one of the social media threads about the incident that they had heard the diver rescued by Jack Johnson was dating "a really hot chick". Everyone knew that was Joey Simmons.

Joey hated it when they referred to Lindsey by her looks only. Lindsey was so much more than that. She was an intelligent, capable person, who just happened to be extremely attractive. That was just the mentality he was facing, though.

Once his name got out, the speculation as to what really occurred began. The first theory they went with was the low blood sugar.

He was probably so weak and disoriented because he had low blood sugar.

He was too weak to even swim out and get his own deco tank.

He couldn't even stand up when he got to the surface. Jack had to hold him up to keep him from falling back into the water and drowning.

Dude couldn't even walk to the ambulance from the water. The medics had to strap him onto a backboard in the water and carry him.

I heard he was so bad he spent a night in the hospital.

It really got out of control. Not only were they going with Jack's story, but they were also embellishing it and creating new details. Details that only made Jack look like a much bigger hero. Joey was tempted to post the factual details so the speculation and rumors would stop but Lindsey talked him out of it.

"Sweetie, it's best not to say anything. Like they say a guilty dog barks the loudest. If you say anything everyone's just gonna think you're covering something up."

Joey decided Lindsey was right. It was best to stay out of it. For all anyone knew, Joey wasn't even following the discussions online and had no idea about the stories going around. It was best to pretend he didn't know about it and go on with his life as if nothing had happened.

And, really, nothing had happened. Joey made a mistake. He survived the dive and learned from the mistake. There was no medical event. There was no rescue. There was nothing to get worked up over. Hopefully all the online chatter would eventually go away.

* * *

The following weekend Joey and Lindsey were at Jackson Blue preparing for a dive. Lindsey wanted Joey to show her the tunnel he had gotten stuck in. He also needed to retrieve the stage tank he had left in there. Joey was certain he would be able to find the tunnel. He had to swim back to the traffic light once he got free from where he had gotten trapped, so it had to be before that. And he knew it was to the right as he was exiting. He also thought it was directly in line with the gold line right before it split in two at the traffic light as they were heading out.

The gold line at the traffic light is the fourth T on the main guideline of the cave. At 1900 feet penetration distance from the cave opening, the gold line splits. The options when heading farther from the entrance into the cave are to go straight or take a sharp left. Most divers take the sharp left because it's an easier area to get through. Both paths go through restrictions, but the restriction going straight is a bit smaller than the one on the path to the left. The two lines meet back up a couple hundred feet later at the traffic light and the line then angles to the right slightly.

Heading out, the line at the traffic light splits with one line making a sharp left and the other a slight left. The one that heads to the far left is the one that goes through the smaller restriction and joins back up straight into the third T at 1900 feet. The other line, the one on the right, is angled about 15-20 degrees to the left. If you're not too familiar with the passage, it's easy to miss the slight turn in the line and continue along the wall to the right. This is exactly what happened to Joey.

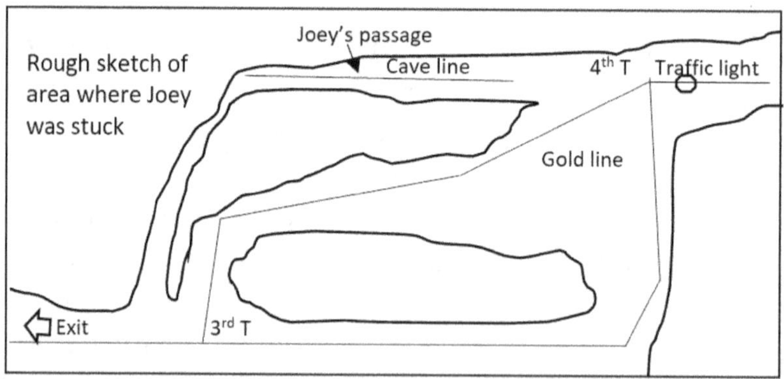

Joey and Lindsey planned to scooter to the traffic light, clip the DPVs onto the line, run a line from a small spool straight from the gold line to the wall on the right, and follow it to the small tunnel where Joey had gotten stuck. That should put them right on top of the cave line in that passage and eventually lead them to Joey's stage tank.

The reason for running a line from the gold line to the white line in the small tunnel was to ensure they always had a continuous line back out to the opening of the cave – one of the main rules of cave diving. This way if they found themselves in a silt-out, as Joey had the previous weekend, they had a continuous guideline to follow all the way out to the surface. The line they would place from the main gold line to the white cave line in the side passage was called a jump line.

Joey hadn't run a jump line the previous weekend but that was because he hadn't intended on jumping off the gold line during that dive. Fortunately, the room where all this happened was large enough and the water flow was strong enough that Joey was able to see the traffic light when he got back to the end of the cave line in the small tunnel even though it was about 30 feet away. This allowed him to be able to get back to the gold line, which was continuous all the way to within 100 feet from the opening of the cave. If the visibility in that room had been disturbed, the outcome could have been very different.

Lindsey and Joey were setting up their equipment at one of the green metal picnic tables under the pavilion at Blue Spring Park when another vehicle with a couple of cave divers arrived and parked next to Joey's car. Joey had been hoping they would have the park and the cave to themselves. After all the discussion and speculation that had been going on the past week, he just wanted to do a nice leisurely dive with his girlfriend and try not to think about any of it.

That was not likely to happen with other divers around. The divers that pulled up were sure to know about Joey's incident. They probably even knew Joey was the diver involved. They would either ask him about it or there would be awkward silence the entire time. Joey wasn't sure which would be better. He sped up his equipment assembly so he could get in the water and try to avoid finding out.

"Slow down, sweetie. What's your rush?" Lindsey asked Joey.

Joey glanced over at the truck that had just arrived and back at Lindsey.

"Oh, I get it. Don't worry, sweetie, if they say anything I'll handle it."

Joey wasn't sure whether to be relieved or concerned about Lindsey's response. He had already witnessed Lindsey reprimand know-it-all divers after the first dive they ever did together at Morrison Spring. The two divers walked away in shame. Joey knew if these guys said anything they were sure to get an earful from Lindsey.

The new arrivals sat in their truck for several minutes while Joey and Lindsey continued to set up their equipment. Joey could hear muffled talking coming from the cab of the truck, but he couldn't make out any of the words. He turned back to their equipment, placed all four of their sidemount tanks on a truck cart and wheeled it to the edge of the water. He lined up the tanks on top of the retaining wall with the valves hanging over the edge just a few inches above the smooth surface of the clear water.

Lindsey followed with her DPV and lowered it into the water near the ladder, clipping the tow line to the same rail Jack had clipped his and Joey's DPV to the week before. Joey returned to the pavilion and loaded their stage and decompression tanks on the truck cart and lined those up next to the sidemount tanks while Lindsey followed with his DPV and placed it in the water next to hers.

The divers were still in the truck talking. Joey started to feel the panic creep up inside him. *Were they talking about him and the rescue? Were they just avoiding him?* Either way, at least Joey didn't have to talk to them or answer any questions. But the panic was there just below the surface screaming to get out. Joey pictured himself on a dive and concentrated on his breathing, willing the anxiety away.

After a minute, Joey returned to the pavilion where Lindsey was already gathering the plastic tubs that held their equipment and putting them away in the trunk of Joey's car. The only things left were their undergarments and drysuits, which they quickly put on so they could get in the water and out of the heat.

The drysuits were nice once in the 69 F degree water, especially on longer dives. They were miserable to wear in the heat of the Florida summers, which lasted from April through the end of October. Joey always started sweating the moment he pulled the undergarments on.

Once they were dressed and their suits sealed, they walked to the dive board platform that had been constructed directly over the entrance to the cave and jumped into the water. The cool water felt good on Joey's head, the only part of him besides his hands that got wet. They floated on the surface of the water enjoying the feeling of weightlessness and the coolness of the water as the heat from their drysuits dissipated. After a few minutes they swam toward their tanks and DPVs and to where it was shallow enough to stand.

Suddenly Joey had a flashback to the previous weekend of Jack pulling on his arm up the slope of the basin and toward the cinderblock retaining wall. He thought he even heard the digital sounds of a camera and its shutter opening and closing in rapid succession. He dropped his head so no one could see his face.

"Joey, what's wrong?" Lindsey's voice broke Joey out of his daze.

"Um, nothing. I'm okay. I was just thinking about last weekend."

"Are you sure you're up for this dive, sweetie?"

"Yeah, definitely." Joey paused for a moment. "I need to do this."

They clipped their tanks into position onto the D-rings on their harnesses, clipped the tow ropes of their DPVs to the D-rings on their crotch straps, and discussed the dive plan one final time.

"You take the lead. When we get to the traffic light, we'll clip our DPVs and stage tanks to the line. You'll then run a jump line to where you think the passage is. Once you tie the jump line to the permanent cave line give me the okay signal and I'll head into the passage to look for your stage tank," Lindsey laid out the plan.

They had decided that Lindsey would be the one to retrieve the stage tank. Joey had already gotten stuck in there once. The water movement in underwater caves slowly wears away at the floors, ceilings, and walls, making the tunnels bigger. But there was no reason to think the cave had gotten any bigger in only a week's time. This was a process that took centuries to make a difference. Lindsey was a bit smaller than Joey so it wasn't as likely that she would get stuck in the restriction. She also had a lot more experience than Joey, both as a diver and a cave diver.

Just as they finished going over the dive plan, Joey heard a car door slam shut. He glanced toward the parking lot just beyond the pavilion and saw the two divers that had arrived earlier exiting the truck. Coincidence or planned? Joey didn't know, and at this point he didn't care, or at least tried not to care. He and Lindsey were about to begin their dive so those guys could talk about him to their hearts' content.

Joey returned his focus to Lindsey and agreed to the plan. He and Lindsey submerged to begin their dive into the darkness of the cave.

11

Once submerged, Lindsey and Joey individually went through a final mental checklist of their equipment and the dive plan. They signaled to each other that they were ready and squeezed the triggers on their DPVs and let themselves be whisked into the darkness of the cave. Joey took the lead with the trip to the traffic light lasting 15 minutes. Joey thought he did well handling the turns, the low ceilings, and the restrictions, especially considering he hadn't been scootering very long.

When they arrived at the traffic light, they clipped their DPVs and stage tanks to the gold line. Joey deployed his jump spool, looped the end of the line on the spool around the gold line, and turned so he was facing away from the gold line and in the direction it was heading before it split off at the T. He flicked his fin tips to get himself going and the water current grabbed and pushed him directly to the white cave line leading into the tunnel where he had gotten stuck a week earlier. The line was tied off to a rocky protrusion jutting up from the floor. From there it disappeared into the small tunnel.

Joey wrapped the line from his jump spool around the permanent cave line and clipped it back on itself using a double ender bolt snap. He pointed his primary dive light into the tunnel. He hadn't had much of a chance to look at it the weekend before. He had passed the traffic light and headed straight into it at close to 200 feet per minute. Maybe five seconds had passed from the time he passed the light to when he got stuck. And seconds after that, the tunnel had filled with silt completely obscuring the visibility around Joey.

The ceiling in the room they were in dropped down as it got closer to the wall on Joey's right. About five feet to the left of the wall, the ceiling dipped down and back up. There wasn't a true left wall to this small tunnel. The ceiling just dipped down enough to create the appearance, or rather feeling, of a wall.

Joey allowed himself to descend to the floor so he could see how close the ceiling got to the floor. Close enough. Maybe four or five inches. There was no way Joey would have been able to slide to his left and slip under it even if he had known at the time that there wasn't a wall to his left. There wasn't enough clearance between the ceiling and the floor for anyone to pass through, but Joey could see the main passage through the narrow space between the floor and ceiling.

Turning his attention back down the tunnel, Joey could make out a dark shadow almost beyond the reach of his light beam. He squinted to try to make out the shape. He thought about moving forward a few more feet but quickly pushed that thought out of his mind. Getting stuck in this tunnel once was more than enough. And he didn't want to stir up the silt and make it impossible for Lindsey to go in and retrieve the stage tank.

The stage tank! That must be what that shadow was. Joey could make out the curved bottom of the tank once it occurred to him what it could be. It was pretty far in the small tunnel, maybe 50 feet. And there wasn't much room on either side of the tank. Joey couldn't believe he had made it that far into the tunnel. He could see why he had gotten stuck though. He was surprised he was able to get himself unstuck and back out after seeing just how small the space was.

Joey felt a squeeze on his calf and almost jumped forward into the tiny passage plugging it up again. Then he realized it must be Lindsey trying to get his attention. He also realized he was breathing faster than usual. He signaled to Lindsey to hold her position by extending a closed fist in her direction. He took a moment to regain control of his breathing rate. They were more than 2000 feet back in the cave and Lindsey still had to retrieve the stage tank. Joey didn't want to breathe through the air in his tanks and have to turn back and exit before they did what they had come to do.

Once he slowed his breathing rate down, Joey kicked his fins to move back out of the way. He didn't move though. He tried kicking a little harder and moved a couple inches backwards, but then he was pushed forward to where he had been. The water current was too strong, and he wasn't able to do an effective enough back kick to overcome it. He hadn't noticed the current being that strong the weekend before, but then again, there was so much going on inside his head that a hurricane could have blown through and he probably wouldn't have noticed it.

Joey carefully reached down to the uneven floor below him with his right hand and tested the strength of the limestone to make sure he wouldn't break anything. It seemed solid, so he applied more pressure and pushed himself backwards. He tested another area with his left hand and pushed himself back even more. He did this a couple more times until he was alongside Lindsey and able to look at her face.

Lindsey formed the okay signal and held her hand in front of Joey's face, asking him if he was alright. Joey returned the signal to let her know he was fine. Lindsey then pointed at herself, then into the small tunnel, followed by another okay signal to communicate that she was going to go into the tunnel.

Joey watched Lindsey slowly and gracefully move away from him into the tiny space. The tunnel immediately began swallowing her up with its walls and ceiling. It looked small with Lindsey in it. Joey couldn't imagine how it must have looked with him in it. Probably like a big turd clogging up the waste line of a public toilet. At least that's what Joey felt like as he thought about his stupid mistake. He felt the anxiety returning and the panic beginning to rise. He almost reached forward to grab Lindsey by the ankle and pull her back. He wanted to forget the stage tank. It wasn't worth the risk. He could work a few extra shifts at the restaurant and buy a new tank and regulator.

He stopped himself just short of touching her ankle, and instead focused on remaining calm. Joey reminded himself that Lindsey was a very careful and experienced diver. And she was intentionally going into this passage, not blowing into it at 200 feet per minute on a DPV like Joey had. And if Joey was able to get out of it with no visibility, then Lindsey would certainly be able to get out of it.

The walls of the tunnel quickly closed in on Lindsey until the wall on the right was almost touching her right tank and the ceiling on the left was almost touching her left tank. She had less than an inch clearance on each side. Joey didn't know if she would be able to reach the stage tank or not. He didn't know how he had gotten so far into the passage with the stage tank clipped onto him. He felt the panic starting to come back.

Joey closed his eyes for a moment and concentrated on breathing. Once he had regained a slow rhythmic pattern, he opened his eyes. He watched Lindsey's fins move slightly as she tried to move forward. She then twisted her body so the left side was lower than the right and he watched her left tank slide into the small space below the ceiling that formed the left wall. This allowed her to move forward a couple more feet.

Almost as quickly as she had gotten there, Lindsey began moving backwards toward Joey. There was a little bit of silt in the water, but it only made the visibility hazy. And even that didn't last long because the water flow was clearing it out quickly. Lindsey continued to slowly back up along the small tunnel, getting closer and closer to Joey. Joey backed up a few feet to give her space to turn around.

As Lindsey backed up alongside Joey, he saw the stage tank she was holding by the valve with her right hand. Joey reached forward to take the tank from her and allow her to reposition herself. The plan was for Lindsey to carry the additional stage tank because Joey had never done a dive with more than one stage. They quickly realized they had forgotten one minor detail in their plan. Joey had cut both bungee cords that had held the bolt snaps that were used to clip the stage tank to the D-rings on the harness. The bungee cords were too short to tie the cut ends into knots and still be long enough to stretch to the attachment points. And Joey had removed the bolt snaps from his harness D-rings after the dive. They were sitting in a toolbox in the trunk of his car.

It looked like they might have to leave the tank there and come back for it the next day. Joey carried the tank back along the jump spool line to the gold line and had another realization. Without bolt snaps he wouldn't be able to secure the tank to the gold line so it wouldn't be pushed off somewhere by the water current. They might have to tuck it back into the small passage for the night.

Lindsey appeared beside Joey, rolling the jump line onto the spool. She removed the looped end from the gold line. Instead of securing the looped end of the line with the double ender and clipping it to the spool, Lindsey shoved the spooled line into her thigh pocket. She then reached for the stage tank Joey was holding. The bungee cord that had been around the valve of the tank was gone. It must have snapped off when Joey cut it. The longer bungee cord that was attached lower on the tank body with a hose clamp was still there.

Joey watched as Lindsey removed one of her cutting tools from her forearm and cut the bungee cord as close to the tank as she could. That left her with a section long enough to tie into a loop around the tank valve. Once that was done, she clipped one end of the double ender to the newly formed loop, wrapping the bungee around the head of the double ender a few times to make sure it was secure. She then clipped the other end of the double ender to the gold line. Joey thought that's where it would stay until they could return with more bungee cord and bolt snaps to repair the rigging. Lindsey had something else in mind.

With the stage tank secured to the gold line Lindsey grabbed the stage tank she had brought with her and mounted it to her harness. She then grabbed the tank she had just retrieved and clipped the double ender to a D-ring located on the lower back of her harness. Joey had breathed about a third of the air in it the previous week so the bottom of the tank was floating about a foot and a half above Lindsey's back. He wondered how that was going to work with some of the lower areas of the cave they had to pass through to exit.

Lindsey waved her hand in front of Joey's face to get his attention. He snapped out of his thoughts and realized he should have been getting his own stage tank mounted to his harness while Lindsey was working on hers. He quickly grabbed his tank and got it secured in place. He then unclipped his DPV from the gold line and clipped the tow rope bolt snap to a D-ring on his crotch strap. Lindsey did the same with her DPV.

Lindsey pointed at Joey and then in the direction of the exit. Joey gave her the okay signal, pointed his DPV parallel to the gold line away from the traffic light, and squeezed the throttle trigger. The white path was only a few feet away and Joey focused on that rather than the gold line. He kept the gold line in his peripheral vision until it disappeared into the ceiling above him. He continued to follow the white path, turned left with it, and saw the gold line drop back down into view just before the Rabbit Hole restriction. He let go of the trigger and allowed the current to carry him through the restriction.

On the other side of the Rabbit Hole restriction was a large silt mound that rose about eight feet up from the floor. Once through the Rabbit Hole Joey angled his DPV up to avoid running it into the silty floor. He squeezed the trigger and steered toward the right to continue following the gold line.

As he was ascending up the slope, Joey stole a glance back toward the Rabbit Hole to make sure Lindsey was behind him and was going to be able to get through with the additional floaty stage tank. He saw the glow from her dive light pouring out of the Rabbit Hole restriction. He also noticed a white line with a marble on the end tied just outside another hole about five feet to the left of the Rabbit Hole restriction. The marble was from a hair tie. It was placed on the loop of dive reels and acted as a stop to keep the line from being pulled through the guide on the reel. Joey wondered if that was the other end of the tunnel he had gotten stuck in.

He looked back toward the Rabbit Hole just as the front end of the Lindsey's DPV came into view. Joey continued to watch as Lindsey gracefully scootered through the Rabbit Hole without touching the sides or stirring up the sand on the bottom. Unlike Joey, she hadn't let off the trigger to maneuver through the restriction. As her body emerged from the Rabbit Hole, he noticed the quickly modified stage tank was lying flat above her legs. The forward motion of the DPV was enough to keep the floaty bottom pushed down against her legs.

Joey began to turn back toward the exit just as the nose of his DPV crashed into the silty bottom of the cave. He had only glanced away for a few seconds to watch for Lindsey, but it had been enough to cause him to forget the sloped bottom and he hadn't adjusted his course of travel enough to clear the top.

Immediately releasing the trigger, Joey pulled up on the DPV to get it out of the mud. Along with it came a large cloud of sediment, filling the empty, previously clear, space in the water above it. Joey maintained a visual of the gold line beyond the growing silt cloud and kicked his fins a few times to push himself past the silt cloud. When he got beyond it, he dropped down and formed a circle with his index finger and thumb around the line. He was on the line and knew he could get himself out as long as he maintained contact with it. And because they had planned their air reserves to allow them to swim out from the farthest point of their dive, he had plenty of air to swim out.

His main concern was Lindsey. She had been behind him when he crashed into the bottom and would end up in the silt cloud. As Joey turned back to look for Lindsey, the silt cloud slowly began surrounding him. The current was pushing the silt on top of him. Joey thought about moving through the silt cloud to get on the back side of it, but he was concerned he might run into Lindsey as she was making her way out. He also didn't think it would be a good idea to be on the far end of the silt cloud from the cave exit.

He flicked his fins a few times to move away from the growing cloud and give himself space to be able to look around the room. The room was a decent size so the silt shouldn't affect the visibility in the entire room.

Just as Joey got far enough back from the silt cloud to look around, he saw Lindsey's dive light to his left. He also heard the quiet whir of her DPV. *Why was she scootering in a silt out??*

Joey looked around and noticed the visibility in the rest of the room was clear. He glanced back and saw the passage behind him, the one heading out, was clear and he could easily see the gold line. He let go of the gold line and added some air into his buoyancy compensator so he could ascend a few feet. Once he was about six feet above the dark silty bottom, he noticed that the silt cloud he had created wasn't all that big compared to the rest of the room. It was maybe 10 feet in diameter and the room they were in was at least 50 feet wide, over 100 feet long, and about 20 feet tall. Lindsey had seen the silt cloud and steered around it.

No longer hearing the whir of Lindsey's DPV, Joey looked back toward Lindsey and found her right beside him again. He sheepishly shrugged his shoulders and pulled his DPV around so it was facing toward the exit again. He squeezed the trigger and followed the gold line through the passage, careful to keep his eyes straight where he was going so he wouldn't crash into the bottom again.

12

The rest of the dive went without further issues. Lindsey and Joey made it back to the decompression tanks they had left at the beginning of the gold line, grabbed them, and headed to the Deco Room to do their decompression stop. After twelve minutes at 20 feet of depth breathing oxygen, they began their slow ascent out of the opening back to the surface.

Just as they crested the top of the sandy slope Joey noticed a couple of pairs of legs in drysuits standing on the sandy bottom of the spring basin. They were facing the retaining wall. Joey glanced at his dive computer. They had been in the water for an hour and 20 minutes! Were these the same divers that had gotten out of the car as Joey and Lindsey were beginning their dive? Did they do a short dive or were they just now getting ready to begin their dive? An hour and 20 minutes was a long time to get set up for a dive, thought Joey.

Joey wanted to turn and head back into the cave. He didn't want to face these guys. Not now that it was known he was Jack Johnson's latest rescue victim. Victim. Joey hated that word. The only thing he considered himself a victim of was Jack's inflated ego.

Lindsey kept swimming toward the retaining wall. Joey couldn't leave her there alone. She had told him she would deal with it if they said anything, and he knew she could and would. But he didn't want her to have to bail him out. Not again. He could defend himself.

Fighting the urge to turn and run, Joey continued to swim beside Lindsey. They moved to the left of the legs. Joey watched Lindsey hover in place as she removed both stage tanks, clipped them together, and set them on the white sandy bottom. She unclipped the DPV tow rope from her harness next and clipped it to the tanks she had just set down.

Joey followed suit and removed his stage tank and clipped the DPV tow rope to it, all while hovering in place a foot above the sand. He wasn't as good a diver as Lindsey, but he had come a long way over the previous two years. The two remained hovering in the water and started to unclip the sidemount tanks from their harnesses.

Once all the tanks were removed and resting on the bottom of the basin below them, Lindsey and Joey stood up. Joey thought he had heard the muffled talking of the divers next to them while he and Lindsey were removing their tanks, but there was no talking when their heads broke the surface. Joey stole a glance to his right, where the divers were standing, just as their heads dropped below the surface of the water. Joey again didn't know if this was coincidence or planned but his anxiety began creeping back up.

Joey and Lindsey retrieved their tanks and DPVs from where they had left them and set them on the grass adjacent to the retaining wall. They got out and quickly stripped their drysuits and undergarments off so they wouldn't get overheated. After breaking down their equipment and loading everything in the car, Joey and Lindsey did a final search of the area to make sure they hadn't left anything behind. Just as they were getting into Joey's car, he saw the divers surface in front of the dive platform. Perfect timing again. At least Joey wouldn't have to be there when they exited the water.

"Let's stop and get our tanks filled at Cave Masters before we head to lunch," Lindsey suggested as Joey started his car and began to pull away from the pavilion.

Joey wanted to avoid the shop because he didn't want to chance running into other cave divers. And he didn't want to expose himself to any comments from the shop staff either.

"I'm really hungry, Linds. Can we just get them filled at your shop?"

"Sweetie, you know our air banks are only filled to 3300 psi. The cave shop can fill the tanks to 3600."

"I-I'm okay with that," Joey replied.

"Well, I'd rather get a little more breathing gas in the tanks. Besides, you can't hide from the world forever."

"I-I'm not…"

"Yes, you are! I know you and I know you don't like confrontations, but you can't change your life because of one little incident. If you hide, the rumors will only get worse. If you go about things like you normally do people will stop talking. They're only talking to see if they can get a rise out of you. Changing the way you do things is exactly what they want."

Joey realized there was no way he was going to win this argument. Worse yet, he knew Lindsey was right, as usual. He drove to the dive shop hoping no one else would be there. And hoping the staff would just fill their tanks and they could get to lunch without any confrontations.

Thankfully, no other customers were at the dive shop and the tank monkey, a common nickname for dive shop employees, filled their tanks and got them on their way without any mention of Joey's dive the previous week.

"What cave were y'all divin'?" asked Danny, the tank monkey.

"We went diving in Jackson Blue, back to the Trash Room," Lindsey answered.

"I can't wait to get cave certified so I can go see that part of the cave," replied Danny. "I'm only cavern certified right now. But I have my intro cave class scheduled next month."

"That's cool. You'll really like it. The cavern at Jackson Blue is amazing but it gets even better. There's so much to see."

Lindsey and Danny kept up the small talk while the tanks were being filled. Danny sure was a talkative one. Lindsey could barely get a word in with him. Joey sat down in the shade and drank from a cold water bottle he had pulled out of their cooler.

Once the tanks were filled, Joey and Danny loaded them into the trunk of the car. Joey paid for the fills and pulled out of the parking lot just as the other divers they had seen at Jackson Blue were pulling in. Relieved they had just missed them again, Joey drove up the road, glancing into his rearview mirror and watching the divers get out of their truck laughing at something. Probably him.

Joey drove toward the interstate at the edge of town where the Mexican restaurant they usually went to was located. The thought of some special tableside prepared guacamole and sizzling fajitas was making Joey's mouth water. He was starving by the time they got to the restaurant. Fortunately, the lunch rush was over and there were plenty of available tables. The hostess sat them in a booth located near the back of the restaurant and brought them chips and salsa, which Joey immediately dug into while they placed their guacamole and drink orders and looked over the menus.

Joey didn't have to look at the menu. He already knew what he wanted because he always got the same thing. Lindsey decided on her usual meal as well, number 33 on the menu. They placed their orders and grazed on the chips and salsa, even getting a fresh basket of chips, and talked about the dive while they waited for their food to be served.

Suddenly, Joey heard a loud commotion behind him, coming from the front of the restaurant. He glanced over his shoulder and saw a group of men standing near the door waiting to be seated by the host. His anxiety came roaring back as he had flashbacks to a similar occurrence two years prior when Earl Hewitt came storming into the small Italian restaurant on the coast where Joey and Lindsey had their first official date.

Joey recognized a couple of the men that had just arrived. He had seen them a few times when cave diving, but he didn't know any of their names. They were talking about the dives they had done earlier in the day. They had rented a pontoon boat from a local waterfront campground and had been out on Merritt's Mill Pond diving Hole in the Wall and Twin Caves, the two other popular caves in the area that were only accessible by boat. That was why Joey and Lindsey hadn't seen them at Jackson Blue.

The restaurant had booths along both walls. There was a half wall that ran the length of the dining room splitting the room a third on one side and two-thirds on the other side. Joey and Lindsey were occupying a booth on the smaller side of the wall. On the larger side were some tables located along the length of the room in between booths lined up against both walls. The group was seated at one of those tables about midway back. They couldn't see Joey and Lindsey in their booth, but Joey and Lindsey could hear them clearly, especially with how loud they were talking.

The group of cave divers sat down, ordered a round of beer and looked over the menu. They were pretty quiet until the beer was served and their orders were placed. Then they began talking about the day's adventures. The conversation quickly turned to Joey and Lindsey. The center wall and the backs of the benches were tall enough, so they hadn't noticed the couple sitting only 10 feet away from them.

"Did you hear who was getting their tanks filled today at Cave Masters?" asked one of the guys that Joey didn't know.

"Yeah, Danny said that kid Joey and his girlfriend were diving JB. I can't believe he would dive there again after having to be rescued last weekend. Not even a week later."

"What I can't believe is that anyone would dive with him after he had a diabetic seizure and almost died. He's lucky Jack was there to pull him out of the cave and save his life."

Joey couldn't believe what he was hearing. Now the rumor was he had a seizure in the cave. *How could anyone survive a seizure underwater? Were they that stupid?*

"I didn't see Jack around today and Danny said he hadn't seen him either. Must be taking a day off from being a hero."

"Well, that kid's lucky he didn't have another issue today. If I were him, I would quit diving. It's not worth it. There are things you can do to be safer when cave diving but there's not much you can do to prevent a medical event."

Joey listened to the conversation in shock. It was worse than he thought. He had to say something. He wasn't about to let them go on thinking he was a helpless victim.

Joey began to stand up so he could walk over to the group of cave divers and give them a piece of his mind, but Lindsey grabbed his hand. He turned toward her, and she squeezed his hand tighter as she leaned across the table and whispered.

"Just let it be, sweetie. I know what they're saying bothers you, but they're just a bunch of jackasses. They idolize Jack Johnson and will believe anything he says. They won't believe you until the same thing happens to them and they become the focus of one of Jack's stories."

Joey sat back down, exasperated. He knew Lindsey was right but that didn't make him feel any better about the rumors being spread about him. While he was trying to come up with something he could do or say to show those guys that none of what Jack had said was true, the waiter brought the guacamole ingredients to the tableside and began to prepare the fresh guacamole for them.

After mixing all the ingredients together, the waiter left the guacamole on the table and returned a couple of minutes later with their meals. Joey's hunger took over his thoughts and by that time the group of divers had moved on to another topic.

* * *

Lindsey and Joey finished their food. They didn't talk about much else while they were eating. The group of divers was still talking loudly, and they were too distracting for Joey to try to hold a conversation. After paying the bill they quickly and quietly left the restaurant. The group of cave divers never noticed them. Once back in the car, Lindsey started back up.

"Sweetie, this will all blow over soon. I promise. You just need to have some patience."

"I-I-I know. It's just hard to deal with. I know I screwed up on that dive, but I didn't screw up like everyone thinks. And I wasn't rescued like everyone thinks."

"It'll all come out in the wash, Joe. You just wait and see."

Joey knew deep down that Lindsey was right. Well, kind of right. He knew it would blow over, but he certainly didn't think the truth would come out. Jack Johnson was too popular among cave divers, especially the newer cave divers. They all envied him for being able to go cave diving anytime he wanted. After the rescues started happening, Jack became even more popular. Who would believe that Jack, such an experienced cave diver, hadn't rescued Joey, someone who had only been cave diving a little more than a year?

Joey knew that trying to convince Jack's fanboys, the Jackasses, wasn't going to be effective. What he had to do was figure out how to get Jack to tell the truth about the incident. He had to come clean. Joey didn't have any idea how he would make that happen, though.

13

Joey wanted to go cave diving the following weekend, but Lindsey had to divemaster an open water diver class at Eddy Spring and Mike wasn't ready to head back into the caves just yet. He was still taking it pretty hard. Joey and Mike had talked about it during the week.

"I don't know if I'm cut out for cave diving, Joey."

"You're a good cave diver, Mike. We both screwed up thinking we could do that dive the way we planned it. Lindsey and I have discussed it a lot. We should have done a few dives to work up to that one. We should have learned the cave better before scootering all the way to the Trash Room."

"I know, Joey, but that's not it. I shouldn't have left you in the cave like that. I panicked and abandoned you."

"Mike, you did the right thing. If you had waited around until I got free, we probably would have both run out of air and died in there."

"You don't know that. I mean, I waited about 15 minutes but when I saw I was down to only my reserves I panicked. I was breathing so fast I wasn't even sure I was going to make it out before *I* ran out of air."

"That's what I'm saying, Mike. You made the right decision.

There was only one safety tank at the traffic light. There's no way that would have been enough to get both of us out. And it only had one regulator on it anyway. Can you imagine us trying to scooter out while buddy breathing? We've only practiced that once in our decompression class while stationary. Never while traveling through a cave going almost 200 feet per minute."

"I know you're right, Joey. I'm just not ready yet. I get anxiety just thinking about going back into a cave."

While Mike was dealing with his issues and Lindsey was busy assisting with a class, Joey had a choice to make. He could stay home and be bored, or he could go to Eddy Spring with Lindsey and be bored hovering in the water watching the class she was supervising. He could always sign out the key to the grate in the Eddy Spring cave and take a peek beyond it. Ever since finding that body he had wanted to see what was so special beyond the grate that someone had lost his life back there.

Lindsey wouldn't go for that, though. Not him going back there alone, without a buddy. Without her there to watch over him. That would be something they would have to plan together one day. And that's something Joey definitely wanted to do.

The only way Joey was going to be able to cave dive that weekend was if he went to Jackson Blue by himself and didn't tell Lindsey until after the dive. Or at all. He decided he would head to Marianna and do a very conservative cave dive. No DPV. Only in the main passage on the gold line. And rather than dive his usual rule of thirds - using one third of his air for penetration, one third for exit, and one third in reserve for emergencies – he would use the rule of fourths. That would leave him with half of his starting air pressure in reserve. As it was, he and Lindsey usually planned their dives using the rule of thirds and subtracting another 100-200 psi from the penetration pressure. Using the rule of fourths just meant subtracting an 300 psi. He wished he had known about the rule of thirds two years earlier.

It had been a couple of years since he went diving alone. He recalled that experience with a shudder. The first time he went diving alone in a cave he ran out of air just inside the cave entrance and 50 feet below the surface. It didn't help that he only had one tank on his back. It was a miracle he had made it back to the surface and didn't get bent.

This would be different, though, Joey told himself. He was trained and knew how to plan dives better. Well, except for that dive a couple weeks earlier with Mike.

Besides using a more conservative air management plan, Joey also had other advantages with the dive he was planning over the one from two years prior. Two years prior Joey had never been inside the cave at Eddy Spring, or any cave for that matter. He currently had several dozen dives in Jackson Blue and was very familiar with the first 1000 feet of the cave.

Another advantage was the attributes of the caves. Even though he didn't know it at the time, the floor in the Eddy Spring Cave was covered with silt that was several inches thick. There was very little silt in the first 1000 feet of Jackson Blue. In fact, the main passage in Jackson Blue had almost no silt in it. It was mostly clean, hard limestone surface.

Eddy Spring also has a grate 300 feet in that's meant to keep open water divers from penetrating farther into the cave. That's where he found the dead body on that first dive. There was no grate in Jackson Blue, so he didn't have to worry about finding any dead bodies trapped behind one.

Joey justified to himself that there was no reason for him not to dive Jackson Blue alone. He had worked through a plan and minimized all the risks he could think of. He would take a leisurely swim in the main passage, stop and turn the dive when his air pressure reached 2700 psi in each tank, and let the current in the cave push him back out to the opening. He might not even have any decompression obligation for a dive like that. But, just in case, Joey would bring his oxygen decompression tank with him. Just in case…

14

Saturday morning arrived and Joey was up and out of bed early. He wanted to get out of the house before his parents woke up and questioned him about his plans for the weekend. He had never been a very good liar. Mainly because he had a big tell that he couldn't control.

He wasn't stuttering as much as he used to but when he was stressed it still crept back in. Joey had tried various techniques to control it, but so far nothing had worked. So he found avoidance was usually the best option. He left his parents a note on the kitchen counter telling them he was hanging out with friends and would be home in time for dinner. He grabbed a couple of packages of pop tarts on his way out the door.

An hour and a half later he pulled up to the gate at Blue Spring Recreational Area where Jackson Blue Spring was located. He had an annual pass that allowed him unlimited access to the park. All he had to do was call Cave Masters on his way there and as he was leaving to sign in and out. When he called that morning, Danny answered, talking loudly over the sound of the compressor that Joey could hear in the background.

"Good morning, Cave Masters, how can I help you?"

Joey couldn't help but think how corny that name was. Sure,

the shop catered mainly to cave divers because that was all there was to dive in the area, but they could have come up with a better name for it.

"Y-Y-Yeah, this is Joey Simmons. I-I'm calling to sign into Jackson Blue."

"Alright, hold on a minute while I get the sign-in sheet pulled up on the computer. You're the first one signing in today." After about 20 seconds had passed, Danny returned to the phone. "Alright, you said your name is Joey Simon?"

"Uh, n-n-no, it's Simmons. Joey Simmons."

"Oh yeah, Joey! Sorry 'bout that. The compressor is runnin' and I can hardly hear a thing. You have an annual pass, right?"

"Um, yeah. You should have me on the list."

"Yeah, I see your name there. And who's your dive buddy today? Is Miss Lindsey with you?"

Joey almost swerved off the road when Danny asked him that. He had seen other divers diving Jackson Blue alone before. He didn't think a buddy was a requirement. Joey didn't know how to respond. He wasn't sure if he should tell Danny he was diving alone or if he should make up a story and tell him his dive buddy would be calling in a little bit.

"Uh-uh-uh, h-he should be stopping by to sign in in a little bit. Lindsey had to work." Joey decided it would be best to let Danny think he had a dive buddy on the way. Maybe Danny would assume the next diver or divers to sign in were diving with Joey.

"Alright, no problem. Have a good dive! And don't forget to let us know you're done when you come by for fills after your dive."

That was nice of Danny to assume he would be getting his tanks filled there later, Joey thought. Just Danny being Danny, the perpetual salesman. Normally Joey would get his tanks filled at the dive shop in Destin where Lindsey worked. But since he hadn't told Lindsey about this dive, he *would* have to get them filled at Cave Masters. And risk running into more divers that would be talking about him behind his back.

Joey began to reconsider his decision to go cave diving that day. He was already there, though. He had driven more than an hour to get there. Might as well stick to the plan.

Cave divers had 24-hour access to the park every day of the year so they could cave dive anytime they wanted. Well, as long as they called the dive shop to sign in before they closed for the day. Non-divers were on a more limited schedule. The park was only open for them from Memorial Day to Labor Day and then, only from 11am to 5pm. This meant Joey was the only one at the park for the next hour and a half, unless other cave divers showed up. Joey might even be able to get out of there before it got too busy.

He quickly unloaded his equipment from the trunk of his car onto one of the green steel mesh picnic tables located under the pavilion closest to the water. During the summer months cave divers were supposed to set up under the other pavilion. It was even marked for cave divers. But there wasn't anyone else at the park. And even during the times Joey had been there during open park hours no one seemed to pay attention to the sign. People showed up and claimed whatever tables they could and paid no attention to signs.

Joey set up his equipment and rolled the tanks to the water's edge on his collapsible cart. Without a DPV and a stage tank it went much faster. He stowed the tubs in his trunk and prepared to get into his drysuit. Even though it wasn't even 10 am he could already feel the temperature creeping up. It was going to be another hot one in sunny Florida.

Once he was in his drysuit with everything he didn't need for the dive secured in the trunk of his car Joey approached the dive platform located directly over the entrance to the cave. He stood there and stared down into the clear water, watching the eel grass that had encroached on the entrance being blown around by the current. Joey couldn't be sure, but it looked like the flow had increased since the weekend before. That meant it would be more difficult to swim against, but he would also exit the cave much faster with the help of the current.

Joey glanced around the park one last time. It was nice to be the only one there. The park was surrounded by conifers on the land side and cypress trees in the water. The spring basin was almost perfectly round except for the side that led to the pond, or what used to be a spring run before a dam was built. The county had recently installed a floating dock across that side.

The dock must have been about 200 feet long. The plan had been to create a floating bridge from one side to the other, but that had been changed at the last minute. Joey had heard the state had prohibited that from happening because it would have prevented anything coming out of the spring onto the surface from being able to float downstream and might change the ecosystem. So the county left one of the sections out in the middle.

Joey could see eel grass that had come loose piled up against the floating dock on both sides. He supposed it was a good thing a section had been left out. Otherwise, the entire spring basin might be covered with eel grass. That would mean no natural daylight pouring into the opening of the cave. While it might look cool to exit under a ceiling of eel grass, that would take away one of the best features of the cave – the sight of the opening from inside the cavern. It was quite an amazing view.

Beyond the floating dock, an area of cypress trees began. There were a couple of old stumps in the immediate basin, but those trees had been long gone. Joey was amazed that any tree could grow rooted in the water. But there they majestically stood on both sides of the pond with Spanish moss hanging from their branches like fancy boas. On the far side from where Joey stood was a copse of cypress trees. By the time Joey exited from his dive there would be several boats anchored among them so the occupants could enjoy the shade they provided.

That was the next thing Joey wanted to buy – a small Jon boat or canoe so he and Lindsey could spend more time exploring the other caves on the Mill Pond. He really enjoyed Jackson Blue but there was so much more to be seen. Not just on the pond but also along the banks of the Chipola River, the main river that meandered through Jackson County.

He had been diving in Twin Cave and Hole in the Wall Cave during his training dives. Even after he completed his training, he, Lindsey, and a couple of other friends that were also cave divers had rented a pontoon boat from the campground on a few occasions to go dive in those caves. But they couldn't afford to do that very often, so they mainly went to Jackson Blue. It would be nice to be able to explore those caves as well.

Joey looked down the pond and marveled at the beauty of the waterway surrounded on both sides by cypress trees and Spanish moss. He could almost see the old wooden dock that had been built by cave divers among some cypress trees about 50 feet to the east of the opening to Twin Cave. He definitely wanted to get back there soon.

Snapping himself back to the present moment, Joey focused on the dive he was about to do. He had a solid, conservative plan. He would spend an hour on this dive and be on his way shortly after the park opened. But only if he stopped his mind from wandering and got in the water. With that thought he took one last look down the pond and stepped off the concrete dock, falling to the water's smooth surface five feet below.

15

After floating at the surface of the cool, crisp, clear water just above the cave entrance for a couple of minutes, Joey swam around the concrete platform to the shallows where his tanks were waiting for him on the grass just beyond the cinder block retaining wall. He pulled one tank off the wall and quickly clipped it onto his BC harness. He did the same with the second tank and followed up by snugging the valves in place with the bungee cords attached to the harness just under his armpits. He went through a mental checklist of his scuba equipment and pre-dive tasks. Everything was in order. It was time to sink or swim. Maybe that wasn't such a good analogy, Joey thought as his head dropped below the surface of the water.

Hovering in a horizontal position about a foot above the sandy bottom, Joey pulled his tanks up into his armpits to get them to the appropriate position and once again went through a mental checklist of everything. The tanks felt good. The position of his body in the water felt good. Joey felt good. He was ready for this dive, alone, into the darkness beyond the cavern zone that was illuminated by the daylight streaming in from the sun above.

Joey rotated his body while remaining in the same location above the sand, much like a helicopter rotor, only not quite as fast. He stopped his rotation once he was facing the direction of the opening to the cave. With his feet positioned above his bent knees, he flicked the tips of his fins together so they almost touched. This small movement of his calf and foot muscles was enough to propel him several feet forward toward the dark opening.

As soon as he came around the edge of the concrete structure positioned over the opening, he could see the long, thick eel grass that had anchored itself to the sandy bottom directly in front of the cave. The eel grass was slowly swaying back and forth, reacting to the flow of water coming from the cave. The flow was constant. The swaying was similar to leaves on a tree in the wind, only much slower, because these leaves were at least three feet long and had the thickness of the water to contend with.

Joey flicked his fins again and propelled himself in front of the opening. He felt the blast of water coming from inside the cave hit him and push him slightly to his right. He flicked his right fin only this time to affect another helicopter turn so he could face into the current. Once he was facing into the current, and the opening it was coming from, Joey flicked his fins again while exhausting the excess air from his BC and his drysuit to make himself negatively buoyant.

He dropped to the rocky bottom below him and grabbed onto an old hardened concrete bag that sat at the opening, probably from decades prior. He used this to anchor himself against the flow and prevent it from pushing him into the dancing eel grass behind him. He then injected just enough air into his drysuit to relieve the squeeze that had formed with the higher pressure he was exposed to 15 feet below the surface. This also had the effect of making him neutrally buoyant. With that done, Joey flicked both fins a third time while he simultaneously pulled himself past the concrete bag and pushed off of it.

This effort got him 10 feet inside the cavern opening and above a large rock. He reached down and anchored himself to this rock. He unclipped his primary line reel from a D ring located on the back of his harness and turned the stop screw counterclockwise to release the lock on the spool. He pulled a couple of feet of cave line out and wrapped it around this rock, running the reel through the large loop at the end of the line. He pulled the line taut and wrapped it twice more around the rock, securing his primary tie off.

Joey flicked his fins and pushed off the rock again allowing the line to unspool from the reel but keeping some tension on it. He arrived at the next rock about 10 feet in front of him. From there he pushed off to a rocky protrusion another 10 feet ahead. This was where he had remained on a decompression stop for 38 minutes with Jack Johnson a couple of weeks earlier. Joey felt a chill run through him.

At that location he wrapped the line around the protrusion twice and then looped it over itself, creating what was called a line lock. This was designed to keep the tension on the line. Loose lines didn't stay anchored.

Joey turned toward his left to face the restriction 15 feet away that connected the Deco Room to the Rock Garden Room. It was in this restriction that the strength of the water current increased, and Joey would really need to focus to get through it without expending too much effort.

* * *

When Joey had first finished his intro cave class, he and Lindsey did his first post-graduation dive at Jackson Blue. Even though he had done fairly well during class, something had changed. Or rather, Joey wasn't as focused as he should have been. That first dive in Jackson Blue as an intro cave diver hadn't gone much differently than his first dive in Morrison Spring with Lindsey almost a year earlier.

While Lindsey gracefully penetrated the cave with a combination of finning and pulling, Joey fought the water current every inch of the way. By the time they reached the beginning of the gold line, 100 feet inside the opening, Joey had reached his turn pressure on both tanks, and they had to turn around and exit. They hadn't even left the daylight illuminated cavern zone. Joey was beyond disappointed. They exited the cave and surfaced.

"Sweetie, you're tryin' too hard," Lindsey said to Joey as soon as their heads broke the surface and she spit her regulator out of her mouth. "You need to focus on the cave and where the water is moving and stay away from there. If you swim right down the middle of the passage, you're going to be fighting the current the entire time and that only increases your breathin' rate."

"I-I don't know what happened," Joey replied. "I-I-I did so much better in class. I never reached turn pressure that soon into the dive, even when I was leading the dive."

"Well, you were focused on what you had been taught by Adam. And you were doing exactly what he told you to do," Lindsey continued, referring to Adam Mitchell, Joey's cave instructor. "It's common for a new cave diver to forget the little things taught in class on the first few dives out of class. It

can be overwhelming and it's easy to get sidetracked."

"Alright, I'll do better next time. I-I-I hope…"

"Well, let's try again now."

Joey quickly glanced at the pressure gauges on his tanks. At the intro cave level, he was only allowed to penetrate using one sixth of his air, leaving one sixth for exit and four sixths, or two thirds, for emergencies. This was meant to not only limit penetration distance into the cave, but also to give newer cave divers more time to deal with any issues that might come up during the dive.

They had started the dive with 3600 psi in each tank. Joey had breathed 600 psi from one tank and 500 psi from the other tank by the time they arrived at the beginning of the gold line. Fortunately, the flow helped them exit the cave much more quickly and he only used 200 psi more from one tank. So he had 2900 psi in one and 3000 psi in the other. Joey did a quick calculation in his head and determined he could only breathe 400 psi from each tank before having to turn.

"I-I think we should get out and go get our tanks topped off. I-I only have 400 psi usable for penetration. I barely got to the gold line with 600 psi usable."

"You'll be fine, sweetie," Lindsey replied. "Just follow closely behind me and focus on what you're doing. You might just surprise yourself."

Joey protested, but Lindsey insisted they try it. With resignation, Joey agreed, even though he thought it was a waste of time. He doubted he would make it even halfway to the gold line. They dropped underwater and Joey lined up directly behind Lindsey. He watched as she gracefully moved through the water as if there wasn't any current fighting to keep them out. He focused on what she was doing and tried his best to mimic her motions.

Instead of swimming down the center of the passage, Lindsey stayed low and to the right of the cavern. She moved along the perimeter of the Deco

Room, a route that was at least three times longer in distance than swimming straight to the restriction, but somehow, they arrived at the restriction much more quickly than they had when Joey was in the lead.

Right before the restriction, to the right of it, was a large light colored, almost white, limestone boulder sticking out of the floor. Joey watched as Lindsey swam over the edge of it and dropped to the floor of the restriction four feet below. She grabbed a cinder block that was laying there and pulled herself past it and to the right. Joey mimicked her every move. Surprisingly, he found himself out of the current as soon as he was out of the opening of the restriction.

Lindsey continued hugging the right side of the cave. Joey noticed there was a sandy path just below them. This was the only place in the cavern that didn't have the white limestone this cave was known for exposed. There was almost no current in that area either.

Before he knew it, they were at the beginning of the gold line. Joey glanced at his pressure gauges and he had only used 400 psi from the one tank he was breathing from! He still had 400 psi in the other tank available to use.

Lindsey looked toward Joey and formed her thumb and forefinger into a circle, asking him if he was okay. Joey returned the okay signal and watched as Lindsey rotated in place and continued swimming deeper into the cave. Joey looked at his pressure gauges again to make sure he hadn't misread them. He couldn't believe he had made it to the gold line breathing only about one-third the air that he had breathed on the first dive.

* * *

That was a little more than one year earlier. Joey had learned a lot since that time and had become a much better diver. Maybe not the best diver, as evidenced by his incident two weekends earlier, but still a better diver than he had been. It no longer took 400 psi to get to the beginning of the gold line. He could get there barely using 100 psi from one tank. His breathing rate was almost as good as Lindsey's.

Joey passed through the restriction and pulled himself to the right side of the cavern, so he was hovering over the white sandy bottom. Lindsey had told Joey after that dive the previous year that there was sand there because there was very little water flow in that spot.

"Think about it, sweetie. If there was flow there, it would blow the sand out and expose the limestone below it. Just like the water flow has exposed all the rest of the surface in the cavern. This area hardly has any current, so the sand stays put. Anytime you're in a high flow cave, just look for the sandy bottom and swim over that."

It made perfect sense to Joey. As he passed over the limestone formations that were directly in line with the restriction, he felt the current dissipate and he was able to hover over the sand and maintain his position with little effort. At this point, he just swam over the sandy path without having to touch the cave and pull himself along. Once he arrived at the gold line, he unclipped his oxygen decompression tank from his harness and secured it to the gold line.

He couldn't breathe pure oxygen any deeper than 20 feet of depth, and at the gold line at 35 feet of depth he was too deep to breathe it. Most other divers left their decompression tanks on the floor of the Deco Room. Joey had been taught the same thing but changed his practice with another lesson from Lindsey after his first post-graduation cave dive.

"Sweetie, can I make a suggestion?" Lindsey had asked even though Joey knew she was going to make a suggestion whether he wanted it or not.

"Sure."

"I prefer to stage my decompression tank farther inside the cave, near the beginning of the gold line. I know it's too deep to breathe from it there and it's common to see deco tanks strewn about in the Deco Room. But I've also seen some of the locals dive into the cavern from the dive platform and surface into one of the air pockets on the ceiling. One time I saw one dive down from the air pocket to one of the tanks lying on the floor and try to breathe from it. My concern is they will open the valve and leave it open. If the second stage regulator gets dropped just right, it could cause it to purge all the oxygen out of the tank. Then we'd be stuck doing our decompression stop without it."

Again, Lindsey's logic made perfect sense. Joey no longer left his decompression tank in the Deco Room. And since that day, Joey had witnessed someone doing exactly what Lindsey had described. He was happy he had listened to her and started taking his decompression tank farther into the cave, even after getting chastised by some of his cave diving buddies for not leaving it in the Deco Room. And if someone without any scuba tanks could make it back to his decompression tank 100 feet inside the cave opening and 35 feet deep, they could have it!

Once the decompression tank was clipped to the gold line, Joey followed the line into the cave. He went through another mental checklist he had created for himself. This one incorporated techniques Lindsey had taught him during their many dives together.

About 20 feet after the beginning of the gold line the floor of the cave dropped down like a funnel. At this point, Lindsey had advised Joey to drop just below the gold line because he would be out of the current there. Looking forward, about 50 feet ahead, he could see the gold line disappear over the top of a shelf jutting out of the right wall of the cave. The rocks forming this shelf blocked the water flow below the gold line so positioning himself below the line meant being out of the current again.

At the shelf he would have to rise in the water column to get around it, but he could then shift to the left and use another large boulder to block the water flow from hitting him directly. Joey slipped to his left as he approached it. This was about the end of the cavern zone, the daylit section of the cave.

Even so, at this point Joey was 200 feet from the opening and the only way he was going to see any daylight was by shielding the beam from his dive light with his free hand and giving his eyes a few seconds to adjust to the darkness. Then he would be able to make out the pinpoint light coming from the opening.

The cavern diving rule of staying within the daylight zone didn't make a whole lot of sense when that was what was considered daylight. Joey supposed that if he were to have a light failure, he would still be able to get out from that point as long as the visibility in the cavern wasn't obscured by silt. It still didn't make sense. He was a cave diver, though, so it didn't apply to him anymore.

Joey ascended over the next boulder right into the current. This was one of the few places in the cave where there was nothing to hide behind to get out of the flow. As Joey swam over this boulder, he glanced up at the large air pocket just above him. The air pocket measured about 8 feet long by 3 feet wide and was at least 2 feet deep from the ceiling to the surface of the water. This air pocket was formed by the breathing exhaust bubbles from divers ascending up the chimney fissure and passing below it, which was every diver who went in and out of this cave.

Joey had stuck his head into the air pocket on a few occasions previously. While he did that, he looked at his dive computer to see if the depth had zeroed out. It hadn't. The depth reading was 35 feet. That confirmed for Joey that this was air from divers' exhaust bubbles, and it likely only had about 16% oxygen content in it. And unlike the air boxes at Eddy Spring, no one was coming into Jackson Blue with a scuba tank to refresh the air in this air pocket.

Continuing past the air pocket, Joey descended along the slope of the floor. He pointed his light at the gold line and watched it disappear into the fissure crack known as the chimney. This is where Joey had encountered Jack on his way out from being stuck back near the Trash Room. Joey shuddered at the thought and pushed back the anxiety that started to form again. He certainly didn't want a repeat of that.

Dropping into the chimney fissure, Joey inflated his drysuit with more air to relieve the squeeze and pinched his nose while gently blowing to equalize the pressure in his ears. The top end of the fissure was at 45 feet of depth, and it bottomed out at 85 feet of depth in a large room, the one where you could fit a couple of semitrucks side by side.

Joey arrived at the bottom of the fissure and continued following the gold line through the large room. The wall on the right gave way to another large passage, increasing the size of the room by almost 50 percent. That was called Young's Siphon because it led back to the funnel area in the Rock Garden room just beyond the beginning of the gold line. So if you turned to go down that tunnel, the current would be pushing you into it. The bad part was that the connection between Young's Siphon and the Rock Garden room was on the small side and required unclipping a tank to get through it.

To the left of Young's Siphon was another tunnel named the Parallel Line passage because it paralleled the main passage and joined back with it at the top of the first breakdown. Opposite the large opening in the semi-truck room was a dark sandy slope that went from the floor at 85 feet of depth up to a smaller tunnel near the ceiling at about 70 feet of depth. This tunnel also ran parallel to the main passage and joined back to the main passage at the top of the first breakdown a little past the Parallel Line passage. This was the Squirrel Tunnel, so named because of its small size. The Squirrel Tunnel was where the instructor lost his students, and the location of Jack's first rescue.

* * *

Apparently, the instructor meant to take the students to another, larger offshoot, one located adjacent to the bottom of the chimney fissure, named the Horseshoe Circuit. They had gone to the Squirrel Tunnel instead, with the students in the lead and the instructor following. Because there is very little flow in that tunnel, even when the current is up, there is a bit of sand and silt on the bottom. And because the tunnel was significantly smaller, it was fairly easy to disturb the silt and obscure the visibility. This was exactly what happened.

The students, being students, didn't have the most finesse in the water and they disturbed the silt. The tunnel continued to get smaller and the instructor, who was following from behind, couldn't see a thing. In fact, he couldn't see the passage at all and couldn't get through the restriction that the students had already pushed through.

The instructor backed out and, not being as familiar with the cave as he should have been, he didn't know to look for the students at the top of the first breakdown. Instead, he headed out of the cave to call for help.

Jack Johnson happened to be preparing for a dive in Jackson Blue, as usual. He got in the water and clipped his tanks on in record time and was off into the cave to search for the students. About 15 minutes later Jack surfaced with the two students alive. This was the first time two cave divers had been rescued after being lost in a cave. It was also Jack's first rescue, and he instantly became a celebrity.

* * *

Joey continued past this area of converging tunnels to the beginning of the first breakdown just 50 feet farther in. He ascended over the large boulders that once used to be part of the ceiling and shifted to the right to stay as much out of the current as he could. The tunnel was about 30 feet wide. Actually, because the Parallel Line passage joined it at this point, it was much wider. But if you measured from the left wall to the line that denotes the Parallel Line passage, it was about 30 feet.

Joey slowly swam to the right side of the gold line, shining his dive light around the cave taking everything in. He had been in this area many times before but had never fully appreciated it and its beauty. Being alone, he had no one else to keep an eye on so he could devote most of his attention to the cave.

On the left side, just beyond where the lost students had supposedly emerged from the Squirrel Tunnel was Chicken Head Rock. Joey couldn't help but think it was such a cool looking formation. He glanced up at the fissure above and behind it, where it had probably fallen from. Joey had always wanted to go check out that fissure. *Maybe…* He quickly pushed that thought aside. *Stick to the plan, Joe!*

Joey turned his attention back to the cave in front of him. The tunnel narrowed a bit at this point, and in turn, the current picked up. Joey hugged the right wall to stay out of the current as much as possible. One hundred fifty feet later he arrived at the second breakdown. This breakdown had created a couple of restrictions, and the current was definitely stronger. Joey had to pull himself up over the boulders to get over the top of the breakdown. About 50 feet later he pulled himself across another boulder and back down to floor level. This was where the current really kicked ass.

The room widened again but a little more than 100 feet ahead was the first gold line T in the cave system. Divers could choose to go to the right or to the left at this point. That also meant water was flowing from both sides into the passage where Joey was located. This explained the increase in strength of the current.

Joey hugged the right side of the tunnel as much as he could. There was some dark sand along the edges that told him the current wasn't as strong there. The issue was that the ceiling also dropped down not allowing for much clearance above the sandy bottom. Joey glanced at his pressure gauges to make sure he still had plenty of air before having to turn around and head out. He had reached turn pressure on one tank just after Chicken Head Rock and he still had 300 psi left in the other tank before having to begin his exit.

He continued hugging the right side until it curved back toward the center. The left side did the same thing creating a bottleneck and leaving divers a 15-foot-wide area to pass through. This was where the current strengthened even more and Joey had to pull himself along the bottom. About 40 feet later he came to the gold line T. He glanced at his pressure gauge – still 100 psi left. *Should he continue for a few more minutes? Or should he turn as planned at the T?*

As tempting as it was to continue, Joey decided against it. He had planned to turn at the T, and he was going to stick to that plan. If he were with Lindsey, she would have made him turn. Joey rotated his body to face the way he had come and, in the distance, he saw a dive light coming toward him. He had flashbacks to seeing Jack at the top of the fissure chimney and his breathing rate increased. He saw a small alcove about 30 feet in front of him, just to the right and before the bottleneck. He darted toward it, the current helping him.

Once he was in the alcove, and out of sight of the approaching diver, Joey shielded the head of his dive light to block the light from escaping. He remained hidden in the alcove, being pushed into the wall by the current, and watched as the DPV with the initials JJ on the side went by, with Jack Johnson behind it. Joey watched as Jack took the right-side passage at the T and disappeared into the darkness beyond. Seeing Jack in the cave again caused Joey's anxiety level to rise substantially.

Joey felt a tightness in his chest and his breathing rate got even faster. The regulator he was breathing from didn't seem to be keeping up with Joey's demand for air. Joey really wanted to be on the surface at that moment rather than breathing through a regulator. He wasn't that far from the opening, but his breathing rate was more than twice what it normally was. And this time he didn't have a safety tank to help him get out.

16

As soon as Jack had disappeared from his sight, Joey removed his hand from his dive light and grabbed onto a protrusion from the wall beside him. He closed his eyes and focused on slowing his breathing. After what seemed like an eternity, his respiratory rate began to slow down. The bubbles were no longer escaping the exhaust port continuously like they had been. He remained motionless for another minute to work on slowing his breathing rate even more.

Once his breathing was somewhat under control, Joey opened his eyes and pushed himself off the wall toward the gold line. He couldn't believe his breathing rate had increased as much as it had just because Jack Johnson had scootered by.

Joey was usually calm while diving, at least he had become that way. He hadn't always been relaxed and calm during dives. The more training he received, and the more experience he got, the more relaxed he was on dives. There wasn't much that could faze him at this point. He even kept his cool a couple weeks prior when he had gotten stuck in that restriction. While he had gotten a little anxious, he hadn't felt the way he was feeling at the moment in more than a year.

It had to be because of what Jack had done to him. Joey was still upset over that ordeal. Other cave divers were talking about him, and not just the ones at the restaurant. This was no thanks to Jack and his agenda to be *the* hero. Joey had to do something about it.

Joey formed the okay signal with his thumb and forefinger around the gold line to make sure he didn't stray from it. He then closed his eyes for a few seconds and let the current carry him out while he focused on slowing his breathing. He felt a calmness envelope him. Just as he was about to open his eyes, he felt a line arrow on the line. He knew it was the line arrow marking 800 feet from the opening. That meant the second breakdown was just 20 feet ahead.

He opened his eyes and saw the large boulders from the breakdown in front of him. He took in a breath and flicked his fins to direct himself over the top of the boulders and above the second breakdown. The current pushed him quickly over the boulders. It almost felt like he was riding behind his DPV. He flicked his fins again to change direction, so he was no longer heading toward the ceiling but was gliding just under it. A few seconds later he flicked his fins once more to direct himself toward the opening between the ceiling and the large rocks on the floor denoting the other end of the breakdown.

The current pushed him through, and he had to kick a couple of times to redirect his body and keep from crashing into the floor on the other side of the breakdown. He had about 400 feet from that point before he would have to adjust his direction of travel again. Joey relaxed and let the current carry him out as he swept his light across the cave in front of him, scanning the rock formations surrounding him. A couple hundred feet later he saw Chicken Head Rock again.

Joey decided to take a closer look at that formation and the fissure above it. He had been past it plenty of times with Lindsey and Mike, but they had never stopped to give it a close examination. Joey swam toward the large formation and noticed that he could actually swim around the back side of it. He glanced back at the gold line to make sure it was still visible from where he was. It was about 20 feet away. A little farther than Joey was used to going from the line, but this was the main passage and conditions were good. He should be okay.

Swimming behind the rock formation, Joey came out on the other side. Because he had been out of sight of the gold line, he quickly looked for it but couldn't see it. He felt a slight panic as he wondered if he had gotten into another passage unintentionally. He looked again and finally saw the outline of the line almost perfectly blended into the background of the cave. He felt a sigh of relief escape his lungs. Maybe this wasn't such a good idea, he thought as he turned back around to face the formation.

Joey reached down, and with his index finger tested a small protrusion on the floor to make sure it wasn't fragile. When he confirmed it was solid, he held on to keep the current from pushing him away.

The formation was amazing. It really did look like the head of a chicken, even this close to it. Joey was positioned about ten feet in front of it, looking up at the head and beak. As he was examining the formation, he caught a glimpse of some cave line on the wall behind it that appeared to be going up into the fissure. He pulled himself around the formation to get a better look. As he got closer, he saw the line was tied to a protrusion on the wall behind Chicken Head Rock and went straight up into a hole in the ceiling.

Joey had never noticed the line there before. As he looked up into the fissure, he could see how the Chicken Head Rock puzzle piece fit up there. At some point, hundreds, maybe even thousands, of years prior, this huge rock had come crashing down from above and situated itself where it has remained since.

Joey considered following the line up into the fissure. In order to safely do so, as he was trained, he would have to swim back to the gold line and tie off the line from one of his jump spools and secure the other end to the line going up into the fissure. He glanced at his pressure gauges. He still had 2000 psi in one tank and 1900 psi in the other. And he was only about 500 feet from the opening. Joey asked himself, *Should I do it?*

He started to reach for one of his jump spools but stopped himself just before unclipping it. This wasn't part of the dive plan. And this was his first solo cave dive. Diverging from the plan wouldn't be the smartest thing to do. But he was so close to the exit. *What harm would it do?*

Joey thought back to getting stuck in the small tunnel near the traffic light and reluctantly let go of the protrusion he had been holding onto. He kicked his fins a couple times to get his body positioned so he was facing toward the exit again. That fissure would always be there next time. Besides, Jack was in the cave and he didn't want to risk running into him again.

Joey allowed the current to carry him toward the exit. As he was being carried along the passage, he glanced back at the new line he had discovered and thought, *I will definitely check you out next time!* Just as he turned his head back toward the direction he was heading, Joey smacked his head on the ceiling. He reached out and pushed himself back and saw he was at the end of the first breakdown.

Instead of paying attention to where he was going and maneuvering himself to go through the opening to the right of the gold line, he had been too busy daydreaming again and smacked right into the ceiling where it dropped down. Fortunately, he wasn't going very fast and didn't hurt anything but his ego. It was a good thing he hadn't been racing his DPV through the passage.

Joey dropped down past the fallen rocks and entered the large room that was at the bottom of the chimney fissure. He glanced at his dive computer and noted he had 4 minutes of decompression at 10 feet of depth. *Good thing the decompression tank is waiting at the beginning of the gold line!* As he approached the middle of the room where he could jump to the left to the Parallel Line passage or to the right to the Squirrel Tunnel, where the instructor had lost his students, Joey noticed a new line cutting across the passage up to the Squirrel Tunnel. He hadn't seen any other divers along the way so they must have gone in there shortly before Joey had gotten to their jump line. Joey wondered who it might be. It seemed this cave had gotten busy in the past hour.

Reaching the bottom of the chimney fissure, Joey stopped so he could begin his slow ascent up the slope. The gold line angled up through the fissure at about a 45-degree slope. Joey slowly glided just above the line, letting air escape from his drysuit and BC so he wouldn't ascend too quickly. About two thirds of the way up he saw a light coming from above. Joey felt his breathing rate increase. *Another diver must be heading in,* thought Joey as he began to have flashbacks to two weeks earlier. He decided to leave the line and instead of following its 45-degree slope, he ascended straight up the fissure so he wouldn't have to come face to face with the diver heading in.

As he ascended above the ledge at the top of the fissure, he saw the beam projecting from the diver's light. He also heard the soft whir of the motor of the DPV the diver was using. His breathing rate increased even more, and he felt a tightness in his chest again. Joey looked down at the gold line but it was too far below to grab onto so he could close his eyes and try to calm himself. Instead, he moved to his right over the ledge and settled on the limestone floor below him.

Joey tensed as he waited for the diver to approach him and hold out his other regulator like Jack had done two weeks prior. Maybe it was Jack again. Maybe he had come out through Young's Siphon and back around toward the chimney fissure. But that didn't make any sense.

Instead of approaching Joey with his regulator held out, the diver coming at him moved his light in a circle, the universal dive light signal for okay, which, just like the hand signal, could be a question or a response. It was also sometimes used as a hand wave among cave divers passing each other. Joey hesitantly returned the signal by moving his light in a circle as he let out the breath he was holding and relaxed a little. It wasn't Jack, and the diver wasn't holding out a regulator.

The diver zoomed down the chimney fissure without slowing and disappeared into the darkness. Joey remained where he was for a moment and collected himself. He didn't know why suddenly every time he passed another diver he became so anxious. He couldn't go on almost having a panic attack every time he was cave diving and saw a light coming at him. And he certainly didn't want to quit cave diving.

Joey took a breath and ascended a few inches off the shelf he had been resting on. He flicked his fins together to begin the forward momentum and the current came in behind him and carried him toward the opening. As he floated over the large white boulder that sat below the air pocket, he shielded his dive light so he could look for the glow from the cave opening. A few seconds later, his eyes adjusted to the darkness, he saw the blue pinpoint light straight ahead. As he continued to glide toward it the light grew larger. Joey decided to turn off his dive light and float out enveloped by the darkness of the cave.

As he was slowly carried out by the current, Joey saw the outline of the grim reaper sign that was anchored in the center of the room even with the beginning of the gold line. He still had to retrieve his decompression tank from the gold line. Maybe turning off his light hadn't been such a great idea.

Joey looked toward the left where the gold line was located and surprisingly his eyes had adjusted to the darkness enough that he could see the outline of his decompression tank. He scanned around to see if any of the other divers in the cave had placed their decompression tanks nearby, but Joey only saw the one tank.

He descended to the gold line, which was about seven feet below, and reached down to unclip his decompression tank from the line. At this point the light streaming in was enough for him to make out the shapes of the passage and rocks. And for the first time he really looked at the shape of the opening.

Joey didn't think he had ever seen something so beautiful. The water had a deep blue color to it, apparently due to the high magnesium content. This was also how Jackson Blue got its name. That and because it was located in Jackson County. Many of the counties in Florida had their own blue springs.

Joey glanced at his dive computer. Fortunately, the LED display was bright enough to read it without a light. His decompression obligation had dropped to three minutes. By the time he got into the Deco Room, where it would be safe to breathe the oxygen in the tank he had just retrieved, he knew he would only have two minutes of decompression. That would be two minutes breathing the oxygen, or four minutes if he continued to breathe the air in his sidemount tanks. Not even worth switching to the oxygen tank. But better to have it and not need it than not have it and wish he did.

Five minutes later Joey was surfacing next to the retaining wall, the same place Jack had brought him. Actually, the same place Joey always surfaced. For some reason, everything to do with cave diving now reminded Joey of the day he had encountered Jack at the top of the chimney fissure. Joey wondered how long it would be before that was just a distant memory and he didn't associate everything about cave diving with Jack Johnson and his lies.

Joey shook the thought out of his head and looked around the park. The first thing he noticed was Jack Johnson's truck parked right next to his car. *He would have to park right there!* There was a van on the other side of Jack's truck that Joey didn't recognize. He didn't see any other vehicles nearby.

The lifeguards for the swimmers were running around getting ready for the day. The first of the locals were setting up lawn chairs and beach towels on the grass surrounding the spring basin. Joey looked up the hill beyond the concession building and saw a line of cars coming through the entrance. It was about to get crowded.

He quickly unclipped his tanks and placed them on the grass above the retaining wall. He then pulled himself up to the top of the wall onto the grass. He grabbed his decompression tank and carried it up the gentle grassy slope from the spring basin to his car. He was thankful the slope here wasn't as bad as at Eddy Spring. He still had flashbacks about that night with Earl and the wheelbarrow…and the dead diver.

Reaching into his drysuit thigh pocket he retrieved the valet key clipped to a small D-ring and unlocked the trunk. He placed the decompression tank inside and unzipped his drysuit. He felt the pressure from the suit relieve itself as fresh air made its way inside, and sweat stained air made its way out.

He pulled the top half of the drysuit off and tucked the sleeves into the suspenders built into the suit. He then pulled off his thick undergarment shirt. *That felt much better!* he thought. His t shirt was soaked from sweat but he had a fresh one in the car to change into after he retrieved his sidemount tanks.

After most dives Joey stripped down to his shorts before getting the rest of his equipment from the water's edge, but with all the people starting to show up he didn't want to leave the tanks unattended for very long. Joey pulled the collapsible cart out of the trunk and carried it to the water. He unfolded it and set it next to the tanks. After loading the tanks onto the cart, he pulled them back up the slope to the car and loaded them into the trunk next to the decompression tank.

He could finally strip down and get more comfortable. He stripped off the drysuit and undergarments and stood behind his car air drying as best he could while looking around the park. He sure enjoyed it much more during the winter months when it wasn't so warm, and when divers were the only ones with access to the park. Unfortunately, Florida winters only lasted two to three months. The remaining nine to ten months were its summer.

Snapping himself out of his thoughts he grabbed a fresh set of clothes from the back seat of his car and headed to the restrooms to change. A few minutes later he exited the restrooms and saw the same truck belonging to the divers who had been there the day he and Lindsey were retrieving his stage tank. They were still sitting in the truck. Maybe Joey could get into his car and leave before they exited.

Just as he approached his car the driver's side window slid open and the driver called out to him, "Hey, aren't you Joey Simmons?"

Joey froze in place. It was about to happen. He was finally going to be confronted and questioned by other cave divers about his "rescue". Joey thought about lying and saying no but rethought that. The cave diving community was too small for him to get away with that.

"Y-Yeah, I-I'm Joey," he responded as he started moving toward the trunk of his car to toss in his sweat-soaked clothes.

"You have a few minutes to talk?"

"I-I'm kind of in a hurry," Joey responded as he popped

open the trunk of his car and dropped his clothes inside.

"It won't take long. We just wanted to ask you a few questions about what happened with you a couple weeks ago and with Jack Johnson."

Joey's shoulders slumped down. He slammed the trunk lid and turned toward the divers. *Might as well just get it over with,* he thought.

"S-sure, I-I guess," Joey said.

17

An hour later Joey was still sitting at one of the metal picnic tables under the pavilion talking to the two divers from the truck. The conversation hadn't gone in the direction he thought it would. These guys weren't interested in poking fun at Joey or chastising him for the rumors that he was diving as a diabetic. These guys were the students who had been separated from their instructor and brought out by Jack Johnson. They were Jack's first rescues.

Their names were Jim and Gary. Joey had seen them every so often when he was out diving and had no idea they were the ones Jack had rescued the year before. Or at least that was how the public story went. Joey had just learned that the real story wasn't much different than his own.

"So, we were working on our full cave class and planned a dive in JB," Jim said.

"The plan was to head into the cave, down the chimney, and jump off the gold line to the Horseshoe Circuit. You know, the first jump to the left at the very bottom of the chimney," Gary continued.

Jim jumped back in. "The problem started when we chose the wrong passage to jump to. Because the Horseshoe Circuit is kind of hidden in the corner, we missed it and instead ran a jump line from the gold line up to the cave line tied on the ceiling across from the Parallel Line passage."

"Yeah, Jim was leading and totally missed the jump," Gary cut in.

"Dude! Seriously?!? I signaled you and you confirmed the jump. If you knew it was the wrong one, you should have told me!"

Jim and Gary both laughed. Apparently, they were used to ribbing each other over the mistakes they made while cave diving.

"Anyway," continued Jim, "I ran the jump spool line from the gold line to the line on the ceiling and continued. Our instructor followed behind."

"Your instructor didn't try to stop you from doing the wrong jump?" Joey asked.

"Not at all. We just kept going. The passage didn't look like what he had described but being new cave divers, and still students, I thought we must just not have understood his briefing very well," Jim replied.

"Have you been in that passage yet, Joey?" Gary asked.

"Yeah, Lindsey and I went through it a while back. I was glad to see it came out in the main passage at the top of the first breakdown. After we got to the other end of the line I turned around and saw nothing but silt. I was really happy we didn't have to go back through it!" Joey answered.

"Yeah, it got really silty for us too. In fact, I didn't even see most of the passage because I was following Jim the silt monster here." Gary laughed and ducked away as Jim tried to punch his arm.

"I'd like to see you do any better going through that passage in backmounted double tanks!" Jim retorted.

"Wait! You guys went through there in doubles??" Joey exclaimed.

"Yeah, somehow we pushed through there in doubles," replied Gary. "I don't know how we fit! I barely squeezed through, and I remember wondering how our instructor was going to follow us in there because he was a little bigger than us."

"So what happened next? How did Jack find you?" asked Joey.

"So, we also came to the end of the line and hovered there looking back into the silt waiting for our instructor to pop out after us," replied Jim. "But he never did."

"I tried to question Jim about the situation we were in, but our underwater communication wasn't the greatest back then. We only knew the basic hand signals," said Gary. "I pulled out my wetnotes and wrote 'what do we do?' on them."

"Neither of us wanted to go back into the silt we had just stirred up. We couldn't see a thing when we stuck our heads in there," jumped in Jim. "So I pulled out one of my safety spools and tied it to the end of the line in that passage and started heading away from it and the silt."

"We thought the instructor was doing a lost buddy drill with us," Gary added, referring to a drill required in cave training in which the student discovers his buddy missing, usually the instructor, and has to carry out certain steps to try to find the buddy.

"Gary saw what I was doing and also pulled out his safety

spool and tied it onto the line next to mine. We then spoked out away from the silted-out passage looking for signs of our instructor."

"I was just coming up on the gold line when I saw a dive light heading toward us from the right," Gary said. "Jim was to my left, so I signaled him and directed his attention to the diver approaching us."

"I swam toward Gary thinking it was our instructor revealing himself to cut the drill. As I approached Gary, I noticed the diver had a DPV."

"Once we saw the DPV we knew it wasn't our instructor. I signaled to Jim again and focused my light beam on the gold line that was about 5 feet ahead of us at this point."

"That's when the diver on the DPV stopped in front of us and signaled us to follow him."

"We still didn't know who it was at this point," Gary added.

"We signaled no to him thinking we had to stay put and wait for our instructor. The diver tried to get us to follow him again."

"He finally pulled out his own wetnotes and wrote something like follow me out, your instructor is on the surface waiting for you."

"We were both shocked at that," added Jim. "I mean, why would our instructor leave us in the cave?"

"So we followed this diver to the Deco Room, did a quick safety stop, and surfaced with him," Gary said.

"So wait! Ya'll weren't lost and panicked in the cave in the silt?" asked Joey.

"Not at all," both Jim and Gary said in unison, then both yelled, "Jinx! You owe me a coke!" and broke out in laughter.

When the laughter died down, "Sorry about that! We've been together a long time and this happens regularly. It's still funny for some reason," Gary said while still chuckling.

Jim continued the story.

"We thought we were in the middle of a drill. At first, when Jack came up to us on his DPV and tried to get us to follow him, we thought it was a test to see if we would do the right thing. After about five minutes we finally decided, drill or no drill, we weren't getting anywhere arguing with this guy so why not follow him. If it was a drill, our instructor would reveal himself and end it."

Joey couldn't believe what he had just learned. Jack's first rescue wasn't a rescue after all. Jim and Gary were oblivious to what was going on with their instructor and they were still in drill mode. They had even found the gold line and were just about to tie their safety spools onto it when Jack showed up. Jack didn't even give them the opportunity to spool their safety spools back up. When they finally gave in to Jack's demands, they dropped their spools on the floor in the middle of the passage and followed him out.

Joey had heard from another diver a few weeks after that incident that he had been diving Jackson Blue that day and was scootering out and saw a couple of spools laying on the floor of the first breakdown just a few feet from the gold line. Neither of them had thought anything of it. But now it made sense. Jack had found Jim and Gary, made them follow him out, and then took credit for rescuing them. He had embellished the story of the rescue quite a bit, just like he did with Joey's encounter with him. According to Jack, Jim and Gary were on the verge of tears when he found them. Joey was surprised that hadn't been said about him. At least, he hadn't read anything on the social media sites to that extent.

After Jim and Gary finished recounting what had happened to them, they asked Joey about his rescue.

"So, did your rescue really happen the way it's being reported online, or is there more to it?" Gary asked.

"Yeah, did Jack really rescue you, or were you doing fine on your own?" added Jim.

Joey recounted his story to his two new friends. He started by admitting the mistake he made by scootering in a passage he wasn't very familiar with. He told them about unintentionally scootering off the gold line into a small side tunnel and getting stuck for almost 45 minutes. He told them how he thought he was going to die in the cave until he remembered the safety tank he had seen by the traffic light. If it wasn't for that safety tank he would have died in there. And then he told them how Jack had done the exact same thing to him as he had done to them. Only worse, instead of having someone else like Jim and Gary's instructor to blame for the mishap in the cave, Jack told everyone Joey had a medical emergency in the cave.

Jim and Gary sat there, opposite Joey, with their jaws dropped in disbelief. What had happened to them was one thing. They were still student cave divers, new to the activity, and with their cave diving instructor. And Jack already had a bit of a reputation for being a great cave diver and cave explorer. Everyone envied Jack for being able to devote his time to doing nothing but cave diving.

After Jack became an instant hero for rescuing them, they

didn't know what to do or say. One thing working for them was no one knew anything about them. They were still students and, even though their names had been revealed, a year later no one remembered who they were or what happened to them.

While it still bothered them a little that everyone thought they had been rescued, the fact that very few people even knew it was them, and even those people likely didn't remember, made it easier for them to sweep it under the rug and ignore the attention that incident got.

With Joey, it was different. He was known in the cave diving community. More by association with Lindsey than on his own merit, but known, nonetheless. And there was no one else involved with this to shift the attention away from him.

While Jack had supposedly rescued other divers after Gary and Jim, those weren't discussed as much because the victims weren't cave divers and the rescues occurred in the cavern zone of the cave. There just wasn't as much glory to those stories. Then Joey's rescue happened, and word was it happened more than 1000 feet inside the cave.

When news of Joey's rescue came about, Jim and Gary admitted to being happy and relieved to hear that Jack had rescued someone for real this time. That meant their story would likely not be spoken about as much. Then they got to thinking about what had happened to them and began to wonder if the subsequent rescues were real or if they were more exaggerations, like their own.

The week prior when they saw Joey and Lindsey at Jackson Blue, they sat in their truck discussing whether they should approach Joey to ask him about his rescue.

"We wanted to talk to you about it but didn't know how you would react," said Jim.

"Yeah, if your rescue was real, we didn't want to make things worse by approaching you," added Gary.

"But the more we talked about it, the more we realized it probably wasn't quite the way it was being discussed online. The main reason being that if you really had an issue with diabetes why would you and Lindsey be cave diving less than a week later."

"That didn't make sense to us," said Gary.

"By the time we came to that conclusion, you and Lindsey had already started your dive," Jim continued.

"And then when y'all came out as we were getting ready to dive, we thought about hanging around to talk to you. We talked about it while you and Lindsey were removing your tanks and decided it wasn't the place or time and we would catch up with you another day."

"And here we are," said Jim.

Joey was still in disbelief. The week before he had stressed himself out because of these guys. And here they were sitting at a table together under the pavilion becoming fast friends.

"So, does anyone else know the real story about your rescue," asked Joey.

"Of course!" replied Gary. "We've told several people. But that's as far as it will go. Jack has too good of a reputation and everyone is afraid to say anything negative about him."

"So we just continue on with our dives," Jim added. "It's not like many people even associate us with that. But we have a feeling that won't be the case with your rescue."

"And we'd like to help set the record straight somehow. We don't know how, but if you come up with anything, we will be behind you 100%."

Joey was relieved to know he had someone willing to back him up besides Lindsey. Divers who had experienced something similar to what he had experienced. Granted, he did almost die in the cave, and they hadn't. But they didn't need to be rescued any more than Joey did. Now he just had to figure out how he could use their story and their help to clear his name and disassociate it from Jack Johnson. That's where Lindsey would come in.

PART 2

18

Lindsey

Lindsey was certain to be upset with Joey when she found out he had gone cave diving alone. It didn't matter that he had planned it meticulously and completed the dive with no issues. She loved Joey and didn't want to see him get hurt. But somehow, he seemed to often find himself in situations in which he put himself at risk. Trouble seemed to always find Joey and Joey welcomed it with open arms. As far as Lindsey was concerned, it was pure luck that Joey hadn't gotten himself hurt, or killed, yet.

Joey's mother had taken to Lindsey when they first met. If not for that, it would have been unlikely that Joey would have been able to continue cave diving, at least as long as he was still living with his parents. And if he wanted to stay in school and get a degree, he had to keep living with them for another couple years. There was no way he could afford to live on his own while working and going to school, especially since a large chunk of his earnings went toward cave diving.

As it was, Joey had to keep his cave diving activities discreet when it came to Mrs. Simmons. She knew he went cave diving, but as long as it wasn't discussed in front of her, she could push it to the back of her mind. Lindsey was sure she still worried about Joey, but at least this way she didn't nag at Joey everyday about it.

Lindsey had just finished assisting one of the shop's scuba

instructors with checkout dives at Eddy Spring for the new open water scuba divers. She was anxious to get her equipment loaded into her car and get back to Santa Rosa Beach. She was worried about Joey.

She had tried calling him when she had a few minutes during her surface interval between dives but he didn't answer his phone. That was not normal for Joey. She checked his status on the various social media sites he was active on, and he hadn't been online for more than 4 hours at that time. That was really unusual for Joey. There was nothing more she could do, though. She had responsibilities and had to get back to the class. She sent Joey a quick DM asking what he was up to and put her phone away in her car.

After the final dive of the day, Lindsey grabbed her phone to check for messages, but Joey still hadn't responded. She checked a couple of the social media sites again – 6 hours since he had been active. Something was definitely wrong. He hadn't mentioned anything about going diving while she was assisting with the class. But maybe Mike had contacted him first thing that morning and they decided to meet at Jackson Blue.

Joey usually uploaded a couple of pictures to Snapchat and Instagram of his tanks near the water or himself and Mike or Lindsey with the spring basin as a backdrop. He had stopped doing that two weeks earlier, for obvious reasons. He should have messaged her to let her know his plans, though. He always did that and then sent her a DM right before he was about to get in the water and another one after he got out. Something must be wrong.

After loading her scuba equipment into the trunk of her car, Lindsey ducked into the changing rooms. She peeled off her wetsuit, dried off, and quickly pulled a pair of shorts and a tank top on. She then headed to the picnic table on the other side of the Grande Vista Chalet to check in with Sheila, the instructor. Sheila was just finishing briefing the students with the plans for the next day's dives and reminding them what time to meet her at the St. Andrews Jetties in

Panama City Beach.

Lindsey liked working with Sheila. Most of the instructors at the shop did all the checkout dives at Eddy Spring or Morrison Spring. Sheila liked to start at the springs on the first day to ease the students into the world of open water diving. She liked to finish the class at the jetties, though, so they could get a taste of saltwater diving and the vastness of the open ocean. That was something neither Lindsey, nor Joey, had experienced during their open water scuba classes.

Lindsey had her first saltwater diving experience with some friends about a month after she finished her class. It was not the best experience. Her friends hadn't been diving much longer than she had and were almost as clueless as she was. She hadn't added any additional weight to counteract the increased buoyancy characteristics of saltwater and ended up having a runaway ascent toward the end of the dive in the middle of the channel. She was lucky she didn't get run over by a boat!

When she first met Joey, she knew he hadn't been on a saltwater dive during his class. He had done his training through the dive shop she worked at, and she knew the instructor he had wasn't one of the ones who bothered to head to the jetties. Lindsey invited Joey for his first dive at the jetties the day after they did their first dive together at Morrison Spring. She made sure to talk to him about the differences in buoyancy control and the need for 2-3 pounds more in saltwater. And while they had issues on that dive, it wasn't because Joey was underweighted.

When Sheila finished her debrief, she turned to Lindsey.

"I don't have anything else for you, Linds."

Lindsey quickly glanced around the area to make sure neither she nor any of the students had left any equipment lying around.

"Looks like everything is gathered up. I'll see you at the jetties in the morning, Sheila."

Lindsey headed to her car and checked her messages and Joey's socials again. Still nothing. She pressed the quick dial icon for Joey on her phone and listened as it rang. She could hear the theme from Jaws, Joey's ringtone, playing in her mind. After four rings she heard Joey's voicemail.

"Hey sweetie, calling to let you know I'm done with the open water class at Eddy Spring. I DM'ed you earlier but haven't heard anything back, obviously..." Lindsey let a touch of sarcasm slip out with that last word. "Call me."

She pressed the end call icon and set her phone on the passenger seat. Her concern was growing even more. She didn't know if she should head home or head toward Marianna to see if Joey was at Jackson Blue. It was doubtful he would have gone diving anywhere else. If she drove to Marianna and he wasn't there, then she would be adding almost two hours of driving for nothing.

Lindsey sat in her car for a moment while she tried to decide whether to drive to Marianna or home. An idea came to her. She snatched her phone back up and found the quick dial icon for Cave Masters. After a couple of rings, she heard Danny on the other end.

"Good afternoon, Cave Masters, how can I help you?"

"Hey, Danny, how are ya, hon? This is Lindsey Carter."

"Oh hi, Miss Lindsey," Lindsey could almost hear Danny blushing over the phone. She knew he had a huge crush on her. He was a good-looking kid and very nice, but even if she wasn't with Joey, he was only 17! "I'm good. How are you doing? I was surprised when Joey called to sign in this morning for a dive and you weren't signing in with him."

So he had gone to Jackson Blue without telling her. Lindsey could feel the heat rising up from her neck. She took a deep breath and slowly let it escape through her nostrils.

"Oh, I had to divemaster an open water class at Eddy Spring today and couldn't make it. I tried to call Joey earlier, but he didn't pick up. Has he checked out yet?"

"He hasn't called or come by for fills yet. But a couple of other cave divers, Gary and Jim, I don't know if you know them or not, also signed in. They might be yapping it up. You know how cave divers can be when they get together."

"Yeah, they just start talkin' 'bout the caves and lose track of time," Lindsey replied. "Do…"

"Oh wait! I think I see Joey's car coming down the street right now. Yeah, that's him. You want to hold on?"

Lindsey felt a sense of relief at hearing that Joey was driving toward the dive shop and apparently not hurt…or worse…

"No, hon, that's alright. I don't want to keep your line tied up in case anyone else wants to sign in or out. I'll just call him in about half an hour once he's done there."

"Okeedokee, you want me to tell him you called?" Danny asked.

"No, don't bother, hon. He'll just get worried wondering why I called. I'll just talk to him in a bit. Thanks, sweetie."

Danny let out an uncontrolled giggle. "No problem. Will you be over this way diving next weekend?"

"Most likely, hon. I've got the weekend free, so I don't see why not. Anyway, I'll talk to you later." Lindsey replied quickly, anxious to get off the phone before Danny said anything else and Joey pulled into the parking lot.

So he went cave diving without telling her. At least he was alive. She was definitely relieved about that, but she was also a bit upset that he hadn't told her his plans. That could only mean he was up to no good.

And who were Gary and Jim? She hadn't heard of those guys before. Maybe new divers? Maybe from out of the area? Joey still should have let her know he was going diving, especially if he was diving with two guys he didn't even know. And how did he meet them? Were they insta-buddies from one of the cave diving Facebook groups?

So many questions Lindsey had for Joey. And he better have some good answers. She just had to figure out how she was going to approach him.

19

Joey

Joey pulled into the Cave Masters parking lot. He saw Danny standing outside by the tank fill station hoses talking on the cordless phone. Danny waved at him, and Joey waved back. Joey turned the car so he could back in right in front of the fill hoses. By the time he exited the car Danny was off the phone.

"How ya doing, Joey?" Danny called out. "Did you have a good dive?"

Danny was always excited to talk to cave divers about their dives. Since he hadn't completed his cave training yet, he was living vicariously through them.

"Yeah, it was a good dive," Joey replied.

"Cool! How far back did ya go?" Danny asked.

That was always the question. It seemed people were only interested in knowing how far back a cave diver went on a dive. They didn't seem to care about the rest of the dive. Joey had been like that at first as well. Lindsey had taught him to enjoy the journey – the entire dive – not just the goal.

* * *

"Lots of divers don't even see the beauty on the way to the back of the cave because they're so focused on getting to the back," Lindsey told him one day. "There's even a cave diver who's done hundreds of dives in Jackson Blue and never

noticed Chicken Head Rock!"

Joey couldn't believe that. Chicken Head Rock was a very obvious formation and a large one. It stood about 10 feet tall and was right in the main passage.

"The reason he never noticed it was because he was always scooterin' back, reachin' his turn point, and scooterin' out. He wasn't lookin' around," Lindsey continued. "Ya have to look around and learn the cave, sweetie."

Joey was glad he had learned that lesson early. He had seen a lot of beautiful formations and passages in the front end of the caves he'd been diving in. And he knew the passages quite well.

* * *

"I didn't go too far back," Joey told Danny. "I just wanted to do a slow, relaxing dive. Swam to the first T and turned around. I didn't even bring a stage tank with me."

Danny looked at Joey incredulously. "No way! Haven't you been back to the Trash Room already? Isn't that more than twice as far in? And don't you have a DPV?"

"Yeah, but sometimes it's nice to just take things slow and look around. Otherwise, you miss a lot of the beauty of the cave. Lindsey taught mc that carly on."

"Wow! I don't know if I'll be able to do that once I have my cave diving cert. I can't wait to see what the Trash Room looks like. And what the cave looks like beyond that."

"It'll still be there when you're ready for it, Danny. The trash in the Trash Room has been there for decades. It's been almost 30 years since Sheck first found it and marked it on his map and it's all still there. Don't rush things," Joey urged. "You'll enjoy it a lot more that way."

"Yeah, we'll see," Danny half-heartedly replied, then quickly changed the subject. "So you just need your sidemount tanks filled today?"

"Yeah, that's it," Joey replied. "My deco stop was so short I didn't even use my oxygen tank."

Danny shook his head as he grabbed the sidemount tanks out of the trunk of Joey's car and set them in the water bath used to help absorb some of the heat from the scuba tanks as they were being filled.

While Danny was filling the tanks, Gary and Jim pulled up to get their tanks filled.

"Hey guys!" Joey called out. "Long time no see."

Gary and Jim laughed in unison.

"Yeah, imagine running into you here," said Jim.

"Hey guys!" called out Danny from the fill station. "Good dive? How far back did you get?"

Joey shook his head. Maybe Danny would learn one day. Or maybe not…

After Gary and Jim pulled their tanks out of the back of the truck and left them with Danny, the three of them sat at a picnic table next to the fill station sipping water and talking more about what had happened to all three of them, trying to come up with a plan to deal with it. Joey knew he would have to get Lindsey involved at some point, but he still wanted to have the beginnings of some kind of a plan before bringing her into it.

Danny finished filling all the tanks and loaded them back into Joey's car and Gary's truck. He then brought over the bills for each of them.

"Y'all paying today or keeping it on a tab for the weekend?" Danny asked.

"I'll pay now," Joey responded. He didn't like to run a tab for too long otherwise it might get out of control. The longest he was okay running a tab was for a weekend of diving and he didn't think he would be back the next day. He also didn't want Lindsey to find out if she was with him the day he ended up paying for it.

"We're coming back tomorrow so we'll keep a running tab," replied Jim.

"Oh, hey Joey," Danny said, "Miss Lindsey called earlier looking for you. She was a little worried because you hadn't called or DM'ed her after your dive. This was right as you were driving up the road so she knows you're okay, but you might want to give her a call soon."

Joey's jaw dropped. *Why was Lindsey calling Cave Masters looking for me?* he thought. She was supposed to be divemastering a class.

Gary and Jim must have noticed the look on Joey's face because they both started hooting and singing "Ooooooooo!!! You're in trouble!"

They weren't wrong.

Joey reached for his phone, but it wasn't in his pocket. He suddenly realized he had never pulled it out of the trunk after the dive. He had been so distracted talking to Gary and Jim it had slipped his mind. He jumped up and ran to the car. Reaching around his equipment he found the phone wedged inside the lining on the side of the trunk where he had placed it that morning. He unlocked it and saw several notifications. Lindsey had called him twice and sent a few DMs. *This was not good!*

"I have to go guys!" Joey cried out. "He slammed the trunk shut and jumped into the driver's seat. He started the car and peeled out of the parking lot. He would call Lindsey as soon as he got onto the interstate.

"I guess he's running a tab after all," Danny commented to Gary and Jim.

20

Lindsey

Lindsey pulled into her driveway about an hour later. She hadn't bothered to call Joey on the drive home. She wanted to be face to face when she confronted him about his escapades while she was at Eddy Spring. She thought about how that was going to go down on her drive home.

It wasn't that she minded Joey cave diving without her. He usually went diving with Mike whenever she was busy working at the shop or assisting an instructor with a class. It was that he hadn't told her he was going diving and hadn't DM'ed her at all throughout the day. Joey always DM'ed right before he stowed his phone in the car and then right after he got out of the water.

The day he had gotten stuck in the cave the post-dive message had been a little late, for obvious reasons. Lindsey hadn't thought anything of it because it wasn't unusual for Joey and Mike to get caught up talking about the dive and Joey forgetting to DM her right away. But he always sent her a message. Lindsey couldn't figure out why this day was different.

Suddenly, it came to her. Joey had been talking about doing a solo dive for some time. Lindsey didn't think Joey had enough experience to do it at the time and told him so. Joey tried to convince her otherwise, unsuccessfully.

"But Lindsey, Mike isn't always available to dive when you're working."

"Well, that's no reason to dive alone, Joey," Lindsey replied. "Just because you don't have a buddy available doesn't mean you should solo dive."

"I just want to work on skills. I'm still new to this and I need as much time as I can working on my skills," Joey pleaded.

"You can come to Eddy Spring and practice your skills there while I'm with a class. You don't need to be in a cave to practice them."

"But…"

"But nothing. Nothing you say is going to convince me solo diving in a cave is a good idea. At least not right now at your experience level," Lindsey interrupted.

Joey had given up trying to change her mind. He knew he wasn't going to convince her otherwise. Yet, he went alone anyway. Well, maybe, thought Lindsey. Danny did mention there were other divers signed in. Maybe Joey went diving with them. But if that was the case, why hadn't he message her like he usually did?

Lindsey decided she wasn't going to bring it up just yet. She wanted to give Joey an opportunity to confess without her confronting him. Confess… She had already passed judgment without knowing the details. Well, it was Joey…

She wouldn't give him longer than that evening to say something. She wasn't the type of person to let things go for too long. She liked to confront things head on. And after being together more than two years, Joey knew that about her. He was supposed to come by later. She would see how things played out.

Her phone rang as she was exiting her car. She looked at the screen and saw it was Joey calling. This might be interesting.

21

Joey

Joey drove through town on the way to the interstate. He knew he had to call Lindsey but wasn't sure how he was going to handle it. He knew he had messed up. He should have told her he was going diving. Or he should have at least checked his phone throughout the day. Instead, he got caught up talking to Gary and Jim and let it slip by him. And now he had to face the consequences.

He came to a stop at a red light. Tapping on the steering wheel he tried to come up with some excuse. He was drawing a blank, though. He just had to tell her the truth. Lindsey would end up finding out eventually anyway. And he would be better off coming clean than being caught in a lie. At least at this point he was only guilty of omission. If he lied to her, that would be so much worse.

The light turned green, and traffic started moving. Joey unlocked his phone and set it on the seat beside him as he slowly accelerated. The onramp to the interstate was after the next light. He would call her as soon as he was on it.

"Hey Siri, call Lindsey," Joey said a couple minutes later after he had merged into the light traffic on interstate 10.

He saw the phone app come up on his screen and tapped the speaker button to put it into handsfree mode. He heard the phone ringing a few seconds later.

Two rings.

Three rings.

"Hey sweetie, whatcha doin'?" Lindsey answered.

"H-H-Hey, babe, just driving home," Joey replied.

Hmmmmm, Lindsey thought, *his nervous stuttering is back.*

"Oh yeah? Where've you been all day?" she asked, deciding maybe she didn't need to be face to face with him after all. The stuttering gave him away.

"W-W-Well, I-I-I have a confession to make," Joey said.

"Oh…" started Lindsey.

"I…" continued Joey at the same time.

Lindsey decided to let Joey continue. "Go ahead, sweetie."

"Th-This morning I-I decided to go diving." Joey paused to give Lindsey an opportunity to respond. She didn't say anything.

"I called Mike, but he wasn't in the mood. Actually, I don't think he'll be cave diving anytime soon. He's still messed up after what happened to us."

"M-hmm" Lindsey replied.

"So I thought I might find some other divers that would let me tag along." Joey said.

He hadn't planned on telling her that, because it wasn't true, but it suddenly came to him. He wouldn't tell her he was diving with anyone else but at least he could say he had intended on it. Then the guilt got the best of him.

"Actually, that's not true." He paused. "I drove to Jackson Blue with the intention of diving alone," Joey confessed.

"Hmmmmm…."

Why wasn't she saying anything? Joey wondered. It was so much worse when she didn't say anything.

"I know we've talked about it before. But after what happened a couple weeks ago. I mean, I essentially did a solo dive then. I got myself unstuck and scootered out on my own." Joey was talking so fast his words were running together. "So I thought I would do a nice, easy dive to the first T and back. No DPV. No stage. Just swim in and swim out."

Still no response.

"Lindsey? You still there?" Joey asked.

"Yeah, I'm here," Lindsey replied deadpan.

"A-A-Are you mad at me?"

Another moment of silence.

"I'm not mad at you, Joe. I'm disappointed. And not even because you went diving alone. You're a grown man. You can do what you want. I don't want to be like your mother and try to keep you from doing things you like to do."

"Well…"

"Let me finish." Lindsey cut him off.

"Sorry."

"I had wanted to do this face to face because I wasn't sure you were even going to tell me the truth. So the fact that you came clean right away is a good thing."

Wait! What did she just say? Joey asked himself. *She already knew?* Lindsey had called the dive shop and talked to Danny. So she knew Joey was there. But she couldn't have known he was diving alone. Not even Danny knew that until after he had gotten there to get his tanks filled.

"What bothers me is that you didn't tell me your plans and then you didn't answer your phone or respond to my messages all day." Lindsey continued. "I feel like you were intentionally avoiding me. I was worried sick about you. I couldn't get done with the class and out of there fast enough this afternoon."

Joey waited for Lindsey to continue but all he heard was silence from the phone. After about 30 seconds Joey decided to respond.

"I-I-I know I should have called you, or at least sent a message to let you know what I was doing. And I should have checked my phone after the dive. But I swear I wasn't avoiding you!" Joey responded. "I put my phone in its usual spot in the trunk and I didn't get it out of there until Danny said you had called."

"Wait, what did you just say?" Lindsey interrupted.

"I swear I wasn't avoiding you."

"No, not that. The part about Danny."

"I didn't get my phone out of the trunk until Danny said you had called."

That little punk! thought Lindsey. She had told him not to tell Joey about her call so he wouldn't worry about her, and he had said something anyway. She would deal with him later.

"So you knew I knew you were in Marianna then?" Lindsey asked.

"All I knew was that you had called the shop looking for me. So I knew Danny had told you I was there. But I was planning on telling you about my day even before Danny said anything."

"How can I believe you?"

"First, because it's the truth. But also, when you hear what I learned today, you'll know for sure I was going to tell you."

"Go on…"

"This is better done in person," Joey replied. "I'm about 35 minutes from home. I'm going to jump in the shower and change clothes, and I'll head over to your place right after that. It's 4:25 now. I should be there by 5:30."

"This better be good, mister."

22

Lindsey & Joey

A little over an hour later, Kona, Lindsey's McNab, started barking to alert her of outside activity. Sometimes it seemed barking at every little noise was the only thing that girl was good for. Lindsey looked out the window and saw Joey's car pulling into the driveway. Right on time.

"You be a good girl," Lindsey said as she gave Kona a rub on her head.

She then grabbed her purse and headed out the door. She had a feeling the conversation she was about to have with Joey would be better spoken away from the prying ears of her parents.

Lindsey opened the passenger door and got in. Once she had the door closed and her seatbelt buckled, she turned to Joey.

"Let's go to the beach," she told him.

Without saying a word, Joey backed out of the driveway and headed toward the beach. Lindsey loved the beach. She couldn't think of anything better than the smell of the gulf carried on shore by the breeze, especially at this time of evening when the sun was about to set, and the air was cooling off. If she had to have a deep conversation with Joey, it usually happened at the beach. That was a precedent that was unintentionally set a couple years earlier before they had even kissed the first time. That first conversation about what had happened to Joey at Eddy Spring not long after he had gotten his scuba certification.

Since then, every time they had to have a serious discussion, Lindsey suggested they go to the beach. The calmness along with the sound of the surf breaking as it approached the shoreline helped her clear her mind. And Lindsey had a feeling she was going to need something to have a calming effect on her when she spoke to Joey.

About 20 minutes later Joey pulled into the parking lot of a public access entrance for the beach. It was the same one they had gone to two years prior when Lindsey first learned about Earl. Lindsey opened her door and unbuckled her seatbelt simultaneously and stepped out of the car while Joey turned the key in the ignition to shut off the engine. Lindsey walked toward the beach, kicked off her flip flops, and stepped onto the warm sand. The feeling of the sand against the bottom of her feet and between her toes always relaxed her.

As Joey walked up behind Lindsey, he could see her shoulders relax only seconds after she stepped barefoot onto the sand. He approached her, kicked off his flip flops, and stepped onto the sand next to her. Lindsey wanted to reach out and take his hand, but she didn't want him to think he was quite out of the woods yet. She wanted to hear his explanation.

"So, what…"

"I'm sorry…"

They both started at the same time.

"Go ahead," Lindsey said.

"I-I'm sorry I didn't tell you I was going diving today," Joey began.

Lindsey wanted to say something, but she restrained herself. Better to let Joey explain himself. Instead, she started slowly walking on the sand toward the water. Joey followed alongside her.

"I hadn't planned on diving with you working and Mike not ready to dive just yet." Joey paused.

Lindsey remained silent.

"Like I told you on the phone, I thought maybe I could do a solo dive. Just to the first T. I've done that dive dozens of times. Maybe a hundred times. And yes, I was tempted to go beyond the first T once I got there, but I didn't. I stopped and swam out. Even though I hadn't reached my turn pressure in my tanks yet."

She still wasn't ready to respond.

"The dive actually went really well. It was peaceful. The only time I got stressed was when I saw Jack scootering into the cave right after I had turned to head out."

Lindsey stopped walking and turned toward Joey.

"Wait! You saw Jack Johnson while you were diving alone?" Lindsey asked.

"Yeah, and I got really anxious. At first, when I only saw the light, my breathing rate went up a little. But when I recognized it was Jack, the anxiety really jumped. I thought I was going to overbreathe my regulator. But I held onto the wall next to me and closed my eyes and concentrated on slowing down my breathing. After a couple of minutes, I was breathing normally again and continued swimming out." Joey continued. "I came across another diver in the same spot where Jack came up to me a couple weeks ago. I started to get anxious again. It wasn't so bad that time. I guess because I knew Jack was already in the cave behind me."

"I didn't even switch to breathing from my oxygen tank because I only had 4 minutes of decompression without it. So I relaxed in the Deco Room watching all the fish swimming around, and then slowly exited and surfaced."

"I'm glad you had a good dive," Lindsey replied as she started walking alongside the water. "But you still haven't explained why you didn't bother calling or messaging me."

"Well, by the time I thought about it you were already in the middle of divemastering your class. I didn't want to send you a message saying I was going on a solo cave dive and have you be worried about me during your surface interval. I had planned on telling you tonight." Joey told her.

Lindsey stopped and turned toward Joey again.

"And what if something had happened to you? I'm certain you didn't tell your parents what you were doing. Did you at least tell Mike?"

"U-U-Um, no." Joey replied and hung his head down.

"So no one knew your plans. No one knew what you were doing. You're lucky nothing did happen."

Joey hadn't thought about that. In the past he had always told Lindsey when he was diving with Mike. It was something she had requested of him the first time he went cave diving without her. Joey thought Lindsey was being a little clingy, but he now realized she was only being concerned. She just wanted him to check in and check out so she could know he was safe.

"I think I understand where you're coming from now." Joey told her. "I promise I won't do it again."

"You better not, mister! I love you too much and I don't want to be worrying about whether you've come out of the cave alright or not." Lindsey replied as she took another step forward. "Now, what's this you said you have to tell me? Who are Gary and Jim?"

23

Lindsey & Joey

Lindsey and Joey continued walking barefoot on the beach. The water from the surf would reach them occasionally and rise above their ankles. It felt good on the hot summer evening.

"Gary and Jim are a couple of divers I ran into at Jackson Blue. Do you remember those two divers we saw last week in the blue pickup truck?" Joey asked.

"Yes, I didn't recognize them, though."

"That's Gary and Jim."

"Okay, and?"

"Well, Gary and Jim also happen to be the two students that were rescued by Jack last year. Allegedly rescued."

Lindsey stopped walking and faced Joey.

"What do you mean allegedly rescued?"

"According to them, the story Jack tells isn't the way things actually happened."

Twenty minutes later, Joey finished telling Lindsey about Gary and Jim and how they hadn't actually been rescued but rather just led out like Joey had been.

"So these guys had no clue their instructor had left them in the cave? They were just going about their business doing a lost buddy drill when Jack showed up and made them follow him?" Lindsey clarified with Joey.

"According to them, that's exactly what happened. And I don't see any reason for them to lie about it. No one knows who they are. All they know is that two students were rescued during a cave dive that happened during their class. Because they were students, no one even remembers their names." Joey responded. "And after what happened with me, I tend to believe their story."

"So Jack Johnson just happens to be at the right place at the right time, really doesn't do anything, but sets it all up to look like he's this big hero."

"That appears to be the case. I just don't get what his angle is. Why even bother? What does it do for him?" Joey asked in frustration.

Lindsey grabbed Joey's hand and started walking. "Awww, sweetie, sometimes you're so innocent and naïve. It's to feed his ego. He just wants the popularity and fame."

"But he already has that, doesn't he?" Joey asked. "I mean, people look up to him. They respect him. Before all this I would have given anything to be able to say I did a dive with Jack Johnson."

"Yeah, and a lot of the newer cave divers feel the same way. They all worship Jack. According to his reputation, he's such a great diver. He does a lot of exploration and is pushing limits all the time. But other than seeing him pass by on a DPV, have you ever seen him actually diving? Has anyone?" Lindsey resumed walking along the beach.

"Now that you mention it, I only ever see him diving alone," Joey responded.

"Exactly! So who has witnessed this greatness of his? Who can vouch for what a great diver Jack Johnson is and what great accomplishments he's made? I've even heard the occasional whisper from other cave divers questioning just how good of a diver he is."

"Why have you never told me this before?"

"Well, it's just rumors, sweetie, and I don't like to gossip all that much. And other than never seeing Jack diving with anyone else, I don't have any proof that he's not a good diver."

"So you think he just saw these opportunities with Gary and Jim, a couple of students, and with me, a fairly new cave diver, and maybe even the other rescues he supposedly made, and he made it look like he rescued us to boost his ego and reputation?"

"Well, we have three divers for sure who were supposedly rescued that didn't even know they were being rescued while it happened. What else could it be?" Lindsey replied as she turned around and started walking along the water back toward Joey's car.

"So what do we do?" asked Joey. "How do we get the truth out? No one is going to believe any of us. Even if there are three of us claiming the same thing."

"There's not much we can do, sweetie. Even if we start telling others the truth, most of them won't believe it. They'll just think you're making excuses for needing to be rescued."

"But I didn't need to be rescued!" Joey cried in frustration.

"I know it. And you know it. And I think Gary and Jim probably know it now too. But that's not enough. We need to catch Jack in the act. He needs to claim he rescued someone who has a bigger and better reputation in the cave diving community than you or Gary or Jim. It has to be someone that others respect and believe. And that someone has to be willing to play along and let Jack think he's rescuing him."

"Who do you know that would be willing to do that?" Joey asked.

"I'm gonna have to think about that. Jack has a lot of jackasses that blindly worship him. Even some of the cave divers that have been around for a while respect Jack and don't question his claims. Whoever it is, we have to approach it carefully, so it doesn't come back on us."

Joey didn't know what Lindsey had in mind, but he wasn't so sure it would be a good idea. When Lindsey became upset over something someone did, the consequences could end up bad. Joey had personally witnessed that.

24

Joey

Joey decided to head to Eddy Spring with Lindsey the following day. The class was supposed to go to the St. Andrews Jetties but a storm out in the gulf had made surface conditions rough, so they went with plan B. Joey would watch over the class in the water and maybe even head into the cave to see the grate on the other side of the Opera Room. He hadn't been back there since he found the dead body beyond the grate two years earlier, shortly after he had finished his scuba training.

That had been Joey's first dive into a cave. He had only meant to go far enough to test his new-to-him dive light. But he couldn't help himself. He had to continue into the darkness beyond to see what was there. He knew lots of open water divers ventured into the Eddy Spring cave and thought it would be okay. And he did make it out alive, both times he went back there, but barely.

This time he decided he would deploy the cave line from his primary reel. There was a large pipe half buried in the floor leading from the opening where he could ascend directly to the surface all the way back to the Opera Room and beyond the grate into the recesses of the cave, but his own cave line just felt safer. That's how he was trained, and he didn't think it was a good idea to deviate from that practice, especially in a cave as silty as Eddy Spring.

Joey even thought about getting the key to the lock on the grate from the dive shop and finally seeing what was beyond it. He decided against that. He preferred to go back there with someone else, particularly Lindsey. Maybe if she got done with her divemaster duties early enough she would be willing to do a quick dive beyond the grate.

With that in mind, Joey loaded Lindsey's sidemount tanks and both of their oxygen decompression tanks into the trunk of his car. He knew the grate was more than 100 feet deep and, according to the map on the wall of the dive shop, the cave beyond was even deeper. They would definitely have a decompression obligation if they went back there.

Sunday morning Lindsey and Joey arrived at Eddy Spring about 20 minutes before the students. On the hour-long ride from Santa Rosa Beach, Joey had told Lindsey part of his plan for the day.

"S-S-So I was thinking I would swim b-back to the Opera Room and check out the grate leading to the rest of the cave," Joey stuttered. He hated that whenever he got nervous he started stuttering. It made it difficult to keep things from Lindsey.

"Oh…." Lindsey bit her bottom lip. Joey was sure she was suspicious of his true intentions by the way she had said that.

"W-Well, I haven't been back there since, well, you know," Joey continued. "The times I've come up here with you were always while you had classes. And I wasn't ready to do that kind of dive alone again. B-B-But after my experience in Jackson Blue yesterday I think I can do it. I-It's only 300 feet back. And I'm guaranteed not to run into Jack Johnson here."

"Alright, sweetie, I think that's a good idea. You should confront your fears, as long as it's in a controlled environment. And there's not much more of a controlled environment than Eddy Spring." Lindsey replied.

Joey couldn't believe what he was hearing. He was almost certain she would try to talk him out of it. Maybe it wouldn't be so difficult to talk her into doing a dive beyond the grate with him later that afternoon. The rest of the drive Joey told Lindsey what his plan was for his dive. She gave him some suggestions but otherwise she was just fine with what he had planned.

When they arrived at the scuba park, they parked to the right of the Grande Vista Chalet near the large yellow chains that kept the cars from getting too close to the chalet, and to the water. The chalet was a lodge built on stilts that contained five guest suites. Under the chalet was a large fake fireplace, like those found in ski chalets, only this one was a scuba tank fill station rather than an actual fireplace.

Lindsey lifted her bag of dive equipment from the trunk. She carried it across the grass and under the chalet where she placed it on a picnic table located near the fake fireplace. They then walked across the dirt road to the dive shop to wait for the instructor and students.

Lindsey grabbed a sign-in sheet and began filling in the class information at the top while Joey stood in front of the map of the Eddy Spring cave and memorized the passages. It was one thing to see a two-dimensional map compared to actually diving inside the cave. But with some basic knowledge of the lay of the land, Joey could at least have some idea of where they were in the cave, that was if Lindsey was agreeable to doing a dive there.

Joey still hadn't mentioned it to her. And she hadn't seen that he had loaded her sidemount and decompression tanks along with his. He had conveniently camouflaged them under their dive equipment. He thought his scheme was about to be revealed when Lindsey pulled her dive bag out, but she was too busy looking around to notice.

Once all the students arrived, signed in, and paid their entry fees, they all headed back to the picnic table under the chalet. The students set their rental equipment on and around the table so they could set it up. Joey decided to keep his distance from the class and set up his equipment right behind his car. It was a hot day, and he would have preferred to be under the shade of the chalet, but it was already getting crowded under there. Besides, he had a little bit of shade from the tall pine at the end of the parking area.

While Lindsey set up her equipment and attended to the students, Joey finished setting his up, and then carried his sidemount tanks down the steep hill to the spring basin. He tried using his truck cart at Eddy once, but the hill was too much for him. It was much easier to carry one tank at a time up and down the slope.

He lowered the tanks into the water to the side of the stair platform and clipped them onto the small loops of rope that were left there for that purpose. With his tanks and regulators set up and in the water, Joey decided to take a quick dip to cool off. He was diving in his drysuit but he could dry off with a towel before putting on his undergarments and suit. And he would be much more comfortable after submerging in the 68 F degree water.

After cooling off in the water, Joey dried himself, quickly changed into his undergarments, and pulled his drysuit up over them. Once he was zipped into the drysuit, he grabbed the rest of his scuba equipment and hurried down the hill to the water. He would put on his BC and harness once he was back in the cool spring water.

Joey glanced toward the chalet and saw Lindsey and Sheila talking to each other. They must be going over the dive plan. The students were already dressed in their wetsuits and at various stages of putting on their BCs and tanks. By the time Joey finished putting on his own equipment and clipping on his sidemount tanks, the students should be getting in the water to begin the fourth dive of their class. Technically, that was the last dive of the class and they would all be certified, if they passed. Joey knew Sheila liked to have the students do one additional dive just for fun so they could see what it was like to dive without the stress of having to do any skills demonstration.

The class would probably be done by 1pm. Plenty of time to hopefully convince Lindsey to do a dive beyond the grate and still leave at a reasonable hour. Joey placed his dive equipment on the edge of the platform near his tanks and walked down the steps into the water. He felt the coolness of the water through his drysuit and undergarments as the pressure squeezed them tightly around his body. He grabbed the handrail and pulled himself around it toward the shallows where he could stand near his tanks.

Joey donned his BC, dive computers, and fins. He grabbed one tank at a time and clipped it in place on the harness, routing and connecting the inflator hoses to the BC and drysuit and routing the regulator hoses around his neck. Just as he finished getting his equipment and tanks situated, Lindsey and the class of students arrived at the platform. Lindsey glanced down at him, smiled and winked.

"Have fun!" she called out. "But don't stay back there too long. Watch your deco!" she warned.

"I won't be back there long. I don't plan on having any decompression obligation, so maybe half an hour at most," he replied.

Joey thought Lindsey sounded a little strange. Worried maybe. She had nothing to be worried about. This dive was going to be much easier than the one he had done the previous day in Jackson Blue. It was a third the distance. There was a string of lights that led to the Opera Room and went around the perimeter of the room. There weren't any tunnels off of the main one. And he was running a line on this dive. He would be fine.

Joey dropped his head under the surface of the water and swam toward the manmade metal cavern that was set between the steps and the entrance to the cave. The visibility hadn't quite recovered from the training activities the day before and there were already a couple of classes in the water, so Joey had 15 feet of visibility at best. But he knew this spring basin pretty well. He had done a lot of dives in it when he first got certified. That is, until he discovered Morrison Spring just down the road.

Once at the top of the chimney-like opening to the cave, Joey angled his head down into it and started slowly descending alongside the rope that was anchored to the bottom and held to a large white buoy on the surface above it. He recalled how he had regularly used the rope to help himself descend and ascend in the chimney. This caused him to smile, the movement in his cheek muscles broke the seal of the mask on his face and allowed some water to seep in. Joey exhaled through his nose to clear the water out of his mask as he continued his descent.

At the bottom, he looked to the right and saw the grim reaper sign against the far wall. He decided he would tie the beginning of his primary reel line to one of the posts of the sign. It wasn't exactly in open water, meaning it didn't have a direct ascent to the surface from that location, but it was close enough.

Joey swam to the sign, noted the three skeleton divers lying at the grim reaper's feet, and felt a shudder move through his body. He recalled his last experiences in this cave from two years earlier. *Maybe this isn't a good idea after all*, he thought. Then he pushed that thought aside. This was something he needed to do.

He unclipped his primary reel from a D-ring on the back of his harness, unlocked the stop, and pulled at the loop at the end of the cave line. He ran the line around the right leg of the sign and pushed the reel through the loop, securing the line to the sign. Joey turned to his right and looked at the restriction in front of him. It looked bigger than he remembered. It actually didn't look like much of a restriction. *I guess that's what experience does to perception*, Joey thought. He flicked his fins and began his journey into the darkness beyond.

25

Lindsey

Lindsey had been worried about Joey. Ever since the incident at Jackson Blue involving Jack Johnson, he had been distracted. His mind was always some place else. This solo diving thing was really concerning. He had brought it up before but never pushed the subject too much. Now he was going off and doing it without even telling her. Joey had never done anything like that before. At least not that Lindsey was aware.

She was glad he had agreed to accompany her to Eddy Spring that day. With him being nearby, she would be less worried. On the way up he had mentioned wanting to go back to the Opera Room and look at the grate while she was busy with the class. She didn't like the idea but there wasn't much she could do to prevent him from doing it. Besides, open water divers went back there all the time. Joey was a trained cave diver, and a good one. He had come a long way since he first started diving a couple of years earlier.

Lindsey watched out of the corner of her eye as Joey carried his tanks to the water from the car. She couldn't get done with this class soon enough. Apparently, it was also obvious to Sheila.

"You alright, Linds?" Sheila asked.

"Yeah, I'm okay."

"Ya sure? You look like you're a thousand miles away."

Lindsey stopped setting up her equipment and stood and faced Sheila. They had worked together for a few years and even spent some time together outside of dive shop activities on several occasions. Lindsey felt comfortable talking to her.

"Well, it's just…I'm worried about Joey. Remember I told you about the incident he had in the cave a couple weeks ago?" Lindsey bit down on her bottom lip.

"Yeah, I still don't know how y'all can stand to go into those caves. You're crazy, girl!"

"I know. You've told me that before. Anyway, Joey's been acting strange since then, distracted all the time. I know the whole situation messed with his head, you know, with Jack Johnson claiming he rescued him and all. But he can't seem to move on from it." Lindsey blurted out, then remembering they were in the middle of a scuba park on a busy summer weekend, she glanced around to see if anyone had overheard. Everyone seemed to be busy with setting up for their dives and paying no attention to the conversation.

"Ya gotta give him some time, hon." Sheila looked around at her students. "It's only been a couple weeks. It'll take him a lot longer than that to process things. In the meantime, we should schedule a spa day. Just the two of us getting pampered all day, girl."

"I know it's only been a couple weeks. But he did a solo dive yesterday at Jackson Blue and didn't tell me until afterwards. And right now, he's getting ready to go back to the Opera Room by himself." Lindsey responded, ignoring the suggestion of a spa day.

"That's crazy! Doing a solo cave dive yesterday. What was he thinking?" Shiela turned away from the students and looked back at Lindsey with a concerned look on her face. "You shouldn't worry about him today, though, Linds. You know everyone goes back to the Opera Room at least once. And by everyone, I mean brand new open water divers that have no business being back there. Even I've been back there. And you know how I feel about cave diving. Joey is a trained cave diver. He'll be fine."

"I know he has the training and skill to do it. What I'm worried about is his mental state. He shouldn't be doing these dives while he's still messed up about this whole thing."

"Com'on, Linds, he'll be fine. Let's talk about this later. We've got to get these students in the water so mama can pop open a beer at lunch!" Shiela ordered as she turned back to her students.

Well, she wasn't any help, Lindsey thought. While Sheila was a really good open water instructor, she wasn't the type of person Lindsey would typically hang out with. Sure, they had gotten together every now and then, but they weren't exactly best friends forever. Sheila liked spa days and hanging out on the beach drinking beer. Lindsey preferred to be doing something productive. And yes, cave diving was productive. Or at least it was relaxing for Lindsey. Except right now, it was anything but.

Lindsey glanced down the hill toward the water and found Joey standing in the shallows next to the stair platform. He had one tank clipped on and was grabbing the other tank from the rope that was tied to the platform. If she hurried, she might get in the water just as he was about to start his dive.

26

Lindsey

Lindsey was glad she had managed to see Joey before he began his dive. And to give him that final warning about not staying too long. She knew it was a fairly easy dive for a cave diver. He had plenty of air in his tanks. And he said he was going to deploy a line. But he hadn't been in that cave in two years. And the last time he was in there, he was pulling out a dead body he had found beyond the grate.

During their conversation on the ride to Eddy Spring, she had encouraged Joey to go ahead and do this dive. She really did think it would be therapeutic. But that didn't mean she wasn't going to worry about him and how it might affect him. He had his ghosts to confront, literally. She just wished she could be there with him. Just in case.

On the other hand, this was probably something he needed to do on his own since the only times he had been in there hadn't gone so well. Lindsey knew she had to step back and stop being so protective of Joey. She just couldn't help herself.

"Lindsey! Linds?" Sheila was calling her loudly. "Earth to Lindsey! You okay, girl?"

"Oh, yeah, I'm fine," Lindsey replied. "Sorry, I was just thinking about Joey and the dive he's about to do."

Sheila looked back at the group of six students floating in the water behind her doing their last-minute buddy checks.

"You sure your head's in the game, Linds? This is dive four and they did great yesterday. I can handle these last two dives without you," Sheila offered.

"No, I'm good. I'm sorry. There's just a lot going on. But I'll set it aside so I can help you. It's not like I even have my cave equipment with me so I can join Joey anyway. I'll be good," Lindsey said as she stepped into the water.

"Alright, but if you decide you need to break away just signal me and let me know you're heading off. It'll just be between you and me." Sheila winked as she said that last part.

It's not like Lindsey got paid to assist with these classes. Not exactly, anyway. She did get free tank fills and a bigger discount on dive equipment. Divemasters were supposed to assist a certain number of classes each year. Lindsey did more than her share. And she was also the shop manager, so she had more leeway than the other divemasters. But the shop owner wouldn't be all that happy if she heard Lindsey had skipped out on a class she had committed to. So Sheila was being very generous with that offer. Lindsey wasn't one to shirk her responsibilities, though. She pushed the thought of Joey diving in the cave alone to the back of her mind and focused on the class.

Sheila, Lindsey, and the students watched as another class pushed off the concrete slab below them and began their tour of the spring basin. When that class was clear of the slab, Sheila's group descended below the surface to it. Lindsey made sure the students positioned themselves in a semi-circle around the edge of the slab facing Sheila.

Lindsey's job was to hover above and behind them watching to make sure they didn't have any issues. If one of them had an issue while Sheila was working with another student, Lindsey was supposed to attend to that diver and make sure he or she stayed safe. If Sheila was working with the entire class, she would focus on the distressed diver while Lindsey supervised the rest of the group. There always had to be one of them keeping an eye on the students.

Lindsey positioned herself so she was able to keep an eye on both the students and the top of the chimney leading to the cave entrance. Usually, Lindsey was positioned right behind the students, which would have required her to turn her head to the left to see the cave entrance. Sheila noticed the change but let it go. She knew Lindsey would do her job and keep the students safe. And if she needed to also keep an eye on the cave entrance, that was okay. Sheila knew Lindsey could do both.

The students only had a couple of skills to complete on this dive. Most of the dive would be spent swimming around the basin practicing their buoyancy control. Lindsey hovered just above the heads of the students so she could keep an eye on them and watch as Sheila tested each student individually on the remaining skills. About fifteen minutes later Sheila finished the skills testing and signaled Lindsey to begin the tour. Lindsey would swim in front and lead the students around the basin while Sheila followed behind to observe them.

Lindsey slowly started swimming toward the top of the chimney. She flicked her fins a couple of times then changed her mind. She usually went the other way first. She had to get Joey out of her mind and concentrate on the class. Besides, Joey wouldn't be ascending the chimney at this point anyway. It was too soon.

Lindsey led the students to the right away from the chimney around the metal man-made cavern that had been placed there years earlier by the previous owners. She was certain Sheila would question her choice of route later, but she would also understand. Lindsey continued around the metal cavern and took the students around the perimeter of the spring basin. About 10 minutes later they swam over the top of the chimney. This was actually part of the tour and not a detour because of Joey.

Sheila liked to do a fifth dive with her students even though it wasn't required by standards. This was mainly to allow them to experience a real dive without any skills. Usually the last two dives were at the jetties, when the weather permitted. The jetties allowed the students to experience the difference in buoyancy control in saltwater versus freshwater. It also gave them an opportunity to see the marine life that lived among the rocks forming the jetties. There were fish in Eddy Spring, but they weren't native to it. The jetties also allowed the students to be able to dive to 60 feet of depth, the limit for the open water certification.

When conditions weren't favorable, Sheila returned to Eddy Spring with the students and made sure the fifth dive involved descending to the bottom of the chimney. If they couldn't experience saltwater and marine life, at least they would be able to experience a dive to a little deeper depth. While they couldn't get to 60 feet of depth at Eddy Spring without going into the cave, the bottom of the chimney was 50 feet deep, so they got close.

Lindsey stopped at the top of the chimney and looked down to see if she could recognize Joey among the divers. Just below her and the class was another class making their way down the rope. And right below them was a diver in sidemount configuration. Lindsey recognized Joey by his hood. He had customized it with some goofy gamer stuff on top that made him easy to distinguish from other divers.

Joey was ascending as the other class was descending right on top of him. Lindsey saw the fins of the students whacking Joey from all sides. Well, at least he had made it out of the cave, Lindsey thought with a smile.

27

Joey

Joey let the line from his reel feed out as he proceeded into the cave through the restriction at the opening. The daylight behind him faded as he moved deeper into the darkness. Usually, he welcomed the enveloping darkness of the cave. This time he felt apprehensive. Things just didn't feel right. Joey put the feeling off to his prior experiences in Eddy Spring and continued into the cave. He swam slowly and cut the darkness with his light, shining it around the tunnel. It looked so different on this dive than it had two years earlier.

The last time he was in this cave, he had a large halogen pistol grip light. It hardly produced any light at all. The yellowish beam, if it could even be called a beam, barely punched two feet through the water. The string lights that ran along the pipe on the floor produced more illumination than that old light. Joey had hung that old thing from a nail on his bedroom wall as a reminder of what he had done with it.

The light he had purchased for his cave diving classes was much brighter. By that point LED technology was just starting to make its way into the scuba diving world. He had gotten himself a 1200 lumen LED canister light, meaning the battery canister was separate from the light head that he held, and they were connected by a power cable. He had the battery canister clipped to the back of his BC at the bottom of the rails on the butt plate and had an extra-long cable on it so the light head could be held with his arm extended.

The light head was much lighter with the battery being separate, so he didn't get tired from holding out his arm. It also allowed for a much larger battery with a much longer burn time for the light. In addition to being so bright, the light would stay on for about four hours. That came in handy when doing a couple of dives back to back like he usually did on the weekends.

There was so much more to this cave than Joey had seen in the two times he had done this dive before. He remembered being able to see the wall to his right. It was only a couple feet away, so it was easy to see, even with the halogen light he used back then. But he couldn't see the wall to the left on those dives. With his LED light he had no problem seeing it. And Joey was surprised to learn that it was only about six feet away from him. This tunnel was not as wide as he had thought.

He scanned the left wall and saw some nooks here and there, but he could easily see they didn't penetrate beyond the wall very far, maybe a foot or two. He also noticed there were several air pockets on the ceiling above him. Some of these air pockets were a decent size.

Just as Joey was about to ascend and look into one of the air pockets someone appeared above him as if out of nowhere. The diver popped up into a large air pocket just ahead of Joey and stuck his head out of the water. He was a thin, lanky man wearing nothing but speedos and a monofin! Joey couldn't believe his eyes. Since losing weight, Joey could no longer dive in the springs in just a swimsuit and t-shirt. This guy had no fat on him whatsoever. Joey didn't know how he wasn't freezing.

Then Joey noticed something else strange about the diver. He didn't have a scuba tank with him! Joey was at least halfway to the Opera Room, 150 feet, and this guy was doing a breath hold dive this far back! Well, kind of a breath hold dive. He appeared to be taking a breath from the air pocket before proceeding even farther into the cave. Joey thought this guy had to be crazy. Those air pockets only contained 16% oxygen, not enough to breathe and keep one's senses for long.

Joey sped up his pace as he continued to reel out line and follow the practically naked diver. He was curious to see how far the guy would go into the cave. He was moving a lot faster than Joey was.

A couple minutes later Joey saw the walls of the tunnel get farther apart from each other. Just beyond that he saw the outline of the airbox. It was about 30 feet ahead and to the left. This was the second of two airboxes in this spring. One was in the spring basin not far from where many open water scuba classes knelt and did their skills. This second one was in the Opera Room.

An employee of the scuba park went and replenished the air in the airboxes every morning from a couple of scuba tanks to make sure the oxygen content stayed as close to 21% as possible. Lots of divers that visited Eddy Spring would pop their heads up into the airboxes to talk to each other, so the staff liked to make sure the air was safe to do that.

As Joey got closer to the airbox in the Opera Room he noticed a couple of skinny legs with a monofin at the end of them sticking out from beneath it. The breath hold diver had swum all the way back to the Opera Room with no scuba tank! 300 feet! *That was incredible!* And he still had to swim back out.

Just as Joey had that thought, the monofin moved back and the diver popped his head down and out of the airbox. He looked at Joey, smiled and waved, then took off back up the tunnel toward the opening. Joey hoped he made it back. He didn't want to have to drag another dead body out of this cave.

Joey turned his attention back to the Opera Room. He swept his light slowly from the left to the right, examining the walls of the room. He saw all sorts of nooks and dark spaces. Joey wondered if any of them went anywhere. He decided he would check out the grate first. Then he might examine those areas more closely afterward.

He remembered the grate was under a shelf on the wall and the pipe on the floor passed beneath it. Joey moved back to the pipe and wrapped the line from his reel around one of the spikes holding it in place on the floor to keep the line from sweeping across the room as he turned to head toward the grate.

He continued to reel out the line and swam toward the grate. As he approached it, he felt himself tensing and noticed his breathing rate getting faster. The last time he had been to the grate he had found a dead body beyond it. *What are the chances of that happening again?* he thought.

Just in case, Joey descended closer to the floor careful not to disturb the layer of silt on it. He dropped his head a little more and shined his light ahead toward the grate. He could see the "Larry and Matt were here" sign still propped up to the left of it. He visually scanned the area but didn't see anything beyond the grate this time. He continued slowly swimming toward it, stopping every few seconds to give it a better look.

When he was about ten feet away, he could feel the flow of the water coming from the grate and pushing against him. He kicked a little more often and with a little more effort to counteract the force of the current. A few seconds later he reached the grate and grabbed onto it with his left hand, the one with the light strapped on top of it. No dead bodies…that he could see. He locked the spool of the reel to keep the line from pulling out and gently placed it on the coarse sand in front of him. He grabbed the grate with his right hand. He then pushed his left hand through one of the squarish openings in the grate and lit up the passage beyond it with his light.

The tunnel got smaller pretty quickly. It was much smaller than the tunnel leading from the opening to the Opera Room. Joey estimated it to be about three feet tall at the farthest end that he could see. And the walls narrowed as well. He could easily touch both walls at the same time if he were on that side of the grate.

Joey pulled his light back and shined it around the grate, looking for the padlock. It was in the same place he remembered it being. He gave it a tug. It remained locked. Joey shook the grate back and forth, but it didn't budge. He still had no idea how the dead diver he had found had gotten beyond the grate without having a key to the lock. That wasn't the only question Joey had about those times that would likely forever remain unanswered.

Joey snapped himself out of his daydreaming and checked the time on his dive computer. About 15 minutes had passed. He still had a couple of minutes before he started to accumulate a decompression obligation. He checked the pressure gauges on his tanks. He still had plenty of breathing gas as well. He grabbed the reel, unlocked the spool, and started to reel the line back on as he allowed the current coming from the other side of the grate to push him backwards. Once he had enough room, he spun himself around so the grate was behind him.

The thought of swimming the perimeter of the Opera Room to check out the other openings he had seen entered Joey's mind. He thought better of that idea. He was close to having to head out so he wouldn't accumulate a decompression obligation. He would have to save that exploration for another day.

Turning back to the exit, this would be the first time Joey was actually going to see the passage as he exited the cave. Both times previously, he had a few silt clouds he had to contend with on his way out. Unfortunately, they were silt clouds he had created. He had come a long way since that time and could move through the water, and through low silty cave passages, without disturbing any of the silt on the floor.

Joey continued to spool the line onto his reel as he followed the tunnel back out. He glanced at his dive computer and saw he was 85 feet deep and the amount of time until he would start accumulating a decompression obligation had extended itself. As he swam out of the cave and got shallower, his no decompression limit would continue to extend itself. He knew he wouldn't come close to having a decompression obligation by the time he got back to the chimney.

Just as he passed from the Opera Room to the tunnel leading out Joey noticed a light ahead. He was too far from the opening for that to be the natural daylight of the sun. Some other divers must be heading to the Opera Room. He hoped it was another cave diver, or at least a cavern diver, and that the silt on the floor wasn't being stirred up.

As Joey continued his exit while reeling up the cave line back onto the spool, the light ahead became two lights. There were at least two divers heading in. One of the rules of diving was that the exiting diver or divers always had the right of way because they had less air in their tanks, and they could be having an issue that required them to get out as quickly as possible. But this was a rule that only cavern and cave divers were familiar with.

Joey flashed his light up above the divers quickly to see if he could tell what type of scuba configuration they were using. Unfortunately, he saw a single tank on each of their backs. That meant the chances of them being trained to dive in a cave weren't very high. So they weren't likely to stop and move to the side to let Joey by. And they weren't likely to even realize Joey was reeling the line back up that he had deployed on his way to the Opera Room.

The divers were positioned so they straddled the pipe on the floor, one diver on each side of it. Joey's line ran directly alongside the pipe so that meant he would have to swim in between the divers to get through. Rather than try to deal with that, Joey stopped moving and held himself in place while he waited for the divers to reach him and swim past on their way to the Opera Room.

When they were about five feet in front of Joey, they both stopped, and their fins dropped down into the silt creating two large silt clouds behind them. Joey felt his shoulders drop in frustration. *So much for seeing the tunnel on his way out this time.* Joey waited for them to continue past him, but they just knelt on the floor in front of him waiting for him to pass. The problem was they were shoulder to shoulder and the line from his reel was directly below their shoulders.

Joey raised his reel up and shined his light on it, then traced the line toward them to try to communicate that his line was beneath them. They didn't understand. Joey considered barreling through in between them but decided to not be that guy. Instead, he moved to his right, toward the far wall, carefully guiding the line just above the silty floor, trying not to disturb it. As soon as he was against the wall, the two divers kicked their feet off the floor and started quickly finning to continue toward the Opera Room. Joey was left surrounded by silt, the visibility in the tunnel completely obliterated. Luckily, he had the reel in his hand and the line led out to the opening.

He began reeling the line in again, putting tension on it so he could follow it through the visibility obscuring silt. Joey couldn't see anything, so he closed his eyes. It always relaxed him to do that when the visibility was bad. He opened them every few seconds to see if the silt had cleared, but it hadn't gotten any better. They had come in finning like that the entire way.

A little more than a minute later, Joey felt something against his head. He reached up and felt the ceiling of the cave. He must be at the restriction at the opening, he thought. He ducked his head down, flicked his fins together, and opened his eyes. He could see the glow from the daylight overhead penetrating through the silt cloud. Joey felt the reel hit something. He reached forward and found one of the posts of the grim reaper sign. He opened his eyes again and saw that the visibility was finally much better. Reaching down, he grabbed the end of the loop around the signpost and pulled it out so he could pass his primary reel through it and unlock it from where it was anchored. That done, he turned to his left and swam toward the bottom of the chimney.

Just as he was about to pass from the overhead of the cavern into the chimney, he saw the speedo wearing breath hold diver again, heading back into the cave. Joey signaled him with his light and waved his finger back and forth in the universal signal for no. Then he covered the mask over his eyes to indicate the visibility in there was not good. The diver signaled back okay with his index finger and thumb in a circle and turned to the left instead, toward a small alcove in the cavern. He popped up into an air pocket and his head disappeared into the air pond above making him look like a headless body hanging from the ceiling.

Joey shook his head in disbelief and turned back toward the chimney. He reached the rope and slowly ascended beside it. When he was about 25 feet deep, just below where he would stop for three minutes to do a safety stop before surfacing, he saw several pairs of fins drop down all around him. Then he felt someone crashing onto his back. Suddenly Joey remembered why he had stopped coming to Eddy Spring to dive when Lindsey was with a class.

28

Joey

Joey managed to get past the group of open water students and their instructor and up to twenty feet to do his safety stop. As he was trying to get through the class of divers, he thought he recognized Lindsey above them with Sheila and their class. By the time he ascended to 20 feet of depth, they were no longer there. Joey watched the divers around him for the next three minutes, occasionally glancing at his dive computer, as he hovered at 20 feet to off gas the nitrogen that had built up in his body. About two minutes into his safety stop, the monofin diver zoomed past him back up to the surface, waving and smiling as he went by.

Once the final minute had passed, Joey began swimming the same way he had seen Lindsey and the class go. He knew Sheila liked to do the first part of the debrief floating on the surface so he might still catch them in the water. Maybe he could sneak up behind Lindsey and surprise her, he thought deviously.

Ascending alongside the metal cavern so he could swim over it toward where Lindsey and the class should be, Joey slowly let air out of his BC so he wouldn't ascend too quickly. He cleared the top of the manmade cavern just in time to see Lindsey's pink fins strapped to her feet five feet below the surface of the water. He watched her finning her way back toward the steps behind her.

Dammit! he thought. They were already making their way to the steps and there was no way he would be able to get behind her before she got to them. But at least she hadn't exited the water yet.

Joey flicked his fins a couple times to propel himself through the water toward the steps. He reached the side of the platform as Lindsey was pulling off her fins and stepping onto the bottom step. He popped his head out of the water only five feet away from her just as she was turning around to ascend the steps. She turned toward him, and a huge smile formed on her face. That smile was what had made Joey fall in love with Lindsey. Such a genuine, caring smile.

29

Lindsey

Lindsey saw Joey pop his head up above the surface as she was turning around on the steps. *What a relief!* she thought. She didn't know why she had been so worried about him. Joey was a very capable diver, a very capable *cave* diver. But his history with Eddy Spring could have affected him psychologically. She worried about that. But he had made it back and looked fine.

"Lindsey. Hey Linds!" Sheila called out.

Lindsey snapped her attention back to the class and looked up at Sheila standing on the platform at the top of the steps.

"What's up Sheil?" she called back.

"Just making sure you're still with us." Sheila said as she waved her hand in a wide circle back toward the grassy hill behind her.

Lindsey looked around and noticed she was the only one left in the water. The students had already exited and were making their way back up to their picnic table. *How long was I zoned out?* Lindsey thought to herself. She was starting to act like Joey.

"Y-yeah, I'm good." Lindsey turned to Joey. "See you in a few, sweetie," then started climbing up the steps toward Sheila.

"Well, you look much more relaxed than you did before the dive. That's for sure!" Sheila put her hand on Lindsey's shoulder as she glanced over at Joey who was still in the water getting his tanks unclipped from his harness.

"I feel much better." Lindsey reached up and grabbed Sheila's hand. "Sorry I've been such a goofball this morning."

"Don't be!" Sheila interrupted her. "I completely understand. At least Joey's fine and done with his dive. I can handle this last dive without you if you want to get a dive in with your boo. They're certified at this point anyway and they all did great." Sheila said referring to the students.

"Ya know," Lindsey smiled as she looked back at Joey, "I think I'll take you up on that if you're really sure. I think it would be good for us."

"You got it girl!" Sheila hugged Lindsey. "Now let's catch up to the students and get these tanks off our backs!"

30

Joey

Joey pretended he wasn't listening, but he heard the entire conversation between Lindsey and Sheila. He knew Lindsey had been a little worried, but he didn't realize she was so worried she was distracted from the class. That wasn't like Lindsey at all. Usually, she was in complete control of everything.

He unclipped the second tank from his harness and placed it on the platform next to the equipment he had already placed there. Joey pulled himself around the railing toward the end of the steps and began to climb out of the water. Once on the platform, he leaned over to grab his fins, mask, and hood. He'd come back to get the tanks once he removed his BC.

Joey stood back up and almost walked right into Lindsey. She must have quickly removed her BC and tank and rushed back down to meet him. Lindsey put her arms around him and gave him a kiss as they stood on the platform. Nothing obscene. Just lips to lips for a few seconds. But it embarrassed Joey a little.

"Hey!" Joey cried out after Lindsey released him. "What was that all about?"

"Oh nothin'." Lindsey took Joey's hand in hers and started walking toward the grass. "I was just a little worried about you and I'm happy to see you out safe and sound."

"I knew you were concerned, but I didn't think you were this worried. It's only Eddy Spring. It's no big deal!"

"And that's why I was so worried, mister!" Lindsey chastised with a big frown as she snatched Joey's fins, mask, and hood from his hands. "A cave is a cave. They're all just as dangerous as the next one if you don't respect them."

"Okay, you're right." Joey began removing his BC as they walked up the hill. "I guess I wasn't respecting it as much as I should. Especially considering my history here."

"Yeah, that's another thing that had me worried! You haven't been back in there since…well, you know." Lindsey set the equipment she was carrying on top of the roof of the car.

"I know." Joey paused. "So…I heard Sheila telling you she could handle the last dive on her own."

"Yeah." Lindsey walked around to the gas tank door and popped it open to retrieve Joey's keys.

"W-What do you think about doing a dive in the cave?" Joey took the key from her and unlocked the trunk.

"You mean back to the Opera Room? Didn't you just do that?"

"N-No. I-I mean back beyond the grate." Joey held his breath for a moment. When Lindsey didn't respond he continued. "I've always wondered what it's like back there. We could sign out the key to the lock and do a short dive. J-Just to see what's back there."

Lindsey stood in front of Joey with a pensive look on her face. He started to get a sinking feeling that she was going to decline. He'd have to plan to come back another day if he wanted to see the cave. He just wasn't sure he wanted to do it alone. The memories of his experiences and what he had seen beyond the grate were a little unnerving.

"Sure, let's do it!" Lindsey interrupted Joey's thoughts. "Oh, but I don't have my cave diving equipment with me." The corners of her mouth turned down into a big pout. That was the second look that had made Joey fall in love with Lindsey.

31

Joey

Joey went back to the platform to grab his tanks so he could get them filled for the next dive. He left the tanks lying on the ground next to the chalet fireplace fill station and headed into the dive shop to purchase a couple of fill tickets and sign out the key to the lock on the grate. By the time he returned his tanks were already being filled. Lindsey had spoken to the tank monkey and gotten him to begin filling them before Joey got back with the tickets. That was one of the perks of being there at least once a month assisting with classes.

While Joey was in the shop getting the fill tickets, Lindsey grabbed her dive equipment and began to set it up for their dive. This would be a new experience for her as well. Lindsey had never been beyond the grate at Eddy Spring. She had been diving at Eddy Spring lots of times over the years, probably well over a hundred, and she had been back to the Opera Room at least a couple dozen times. This would be her first time going beyond that room.

Lindsey went to change from her wetsuit to her drysuit while Joey carried her tanks down the hill to the platform and set them in the water hanging from the ropes. By the time he had both of Lindsey's tanks and his and her oxygen decompression tanks in the water his tanks were filled and ready to be carried down the hill. With all the tanks hanging from the ropes off the side of the platform, Lindsey and Joey sat at a picnic table to discuss the dive plan.

"I don't like the idea of locking ourselves on the other side of that grate. I don't want to be fumbling with a lock if we have a situation that requires us to get out quickly," Lindsey said.

"I completely agree. So how do we do this without having a bunch of open water divers who are checking out the Opera Room follow us back in there?"

"Good question." Lindsey pulled her hair loop out and redid her ponytail. "I suppose we can dummy lock it."

"Dummy lock it?" Joey asked with a quizzical look.

"Yeah, we put the lock where it usually is except we only hang it from the swinging part of the grate. Not the fixed part. That way it looks like it's locked. It will at least keep the honest people honest."

"That might work.".

"It will have to. Like I said, I don't like the idea of locking ourselves in the cave. At least it will look like it's locked. If anyone bothers to try the grate, they'll figure out it isn't locked, but I'd rather take that chance than risk delaying a quick exit if we need it."

"Okay, so we'll get on the other side of the grate, dummy lock it closed, and continue into the cave." Joey picked up his BC and examined it. "I've never noticed a line when I've looked through the grate. I wish I had remembered to look more closely this morning when I was back there."

"Yeah, I don't know how far back the line begins. Probably just around the first corner. I'm sure they just didn't want the line visible from the Opera Room. I can't blame them."

"So one primary reel will be enough, you think."

"I think so. I've never heard of anyone mentioning needing two reels here or at any other cave."

"Alright, I don't imagine we'll get more than maybe 10 minutes of penetration beyond the grate at those depths. I've looked at the map and it looks like the cave keeps getting deeper the farther in you are." Joey placed his BC back on the table. "We'll turn when we get to turn pressure. Or rather, when I get to turn pressure," Joey said sheepishly.

Lindsey had the advantage of having more experience than Joey as both a diver and a cave diver. Even though Joey's breathing rate had gotten much better, he still couldn't match Lindsey's. She also had smaller lungs so each breath she took required about three-fourths as much volume as Joey's breaths. At least, that's what Joey liked to tell himself. He teased her about her girly lungs, which was actually a compliment in the scuba diving world. Any diver, man or woman, would love to have girly lungs. It meant requiring less air during each breath, which meant longer dives.

"Oh! One more thing. I don't like taking the oxygen tanks so deep, but I don't like the idea of leaving them out in the open where someone might take them," Lindsey added. "We need to bring them in with us and clip them to the line on the other side of the grate. In fact, we should clip them where they can't even be seen from the Opera Room. There will be enough curiosity from anyone who might go back there and see the cave line going through the grate into the cave."

"I hadn't thought about that," Joey replied. "Yeah, that's a good idea. We're not bringing stage tanks so there shouldn't be any mix up and accidental breathing of the oxygen at that depth."

"Even if we did have stage tanks, we always need to verify and confirm, mister. You know that." Lindsey was always being the teacher.

"Yes ma'am." Joey dropped his head.

With the plan set, they both stood up, put on their BCs, grabbed their fins, masks, and hoods, and started heading down the hill toward the water. As they were walking down the hill, Lindsey reached over and took Joey's hand in hers. Joey glanced around, a little embarrassed at having to hold hands as they were getting ready to go do a dive in the cave, but he didn't dare pull his hand away. He had done that once before and hadn't heard the end of it from Lindsey.

As they neared the platform, Lindsey released Joey's hand and

Joey slowed down to let her walk in front of him. The platform was wide enough for them to walk side by side, but there were divers exiting the water.

"Hey, y'all forgot your tanks," one of them called out.

"Oh sugar," Lindsey responded, "no we didn't. They're right there in the water. We're diving sidemount."

The diver looked back at the tanks hanging off the ropes in the water and back at Lindsey wide-eyed.

"Are y'all going in the cave?" he asked incredulously.

"Yeah, we're heading back there," Lindsey replied.

"What do you see back there? Is it scary?"

"Wet rocks," Joey replied, "They're the scariest thing you've ever seen!"

Lindsey smacked him on the arm.

"Ignore him! We see lots of beautiful formations. The water has done an amazing job carving the walls and ceiling in the caves," Lindsey cut in. "It's not scary for us. But we've had a lot of training and experience diving in the caves around here. There are a lot of rules we have to follow to make the dive safe."

Lindsey was always so good with the newer divers. She always took the time to talk to them and explain things, even when she had a heavy tank on her back, which thankfully she didn't at the moment. The people asking the questions never seemed to notice those things though.

"Wow! I'd like to go check that out some day!" replied the new diver.

"Well, just make sure you get the proper training before going into an overhead environment. There are a lot of risks involved and you need to learn how to reduce those risks."

"I will. Do you teach that stuff?"

Were they ever going to get in the water? Joey thought to himself.

"No, hon, I'm only a divemaster. But there are plenty of good instructors in this area that can teach cavern diving. You can either ask your instructor or ask inside the shop. Either one should be able to help you." Lindsey looked around, probably looking to see if she saw an instructor who taught cavern diving to direct the diver to. Apparently, she didn't. "Well, we've got to get going on our dive. Good luck and be safe!"

Finally! Joey thought. Lindsey had much more patience than he did. When new divers stopped and asked him questions, he usually grunted a couple of short responses like wet rocks, and that was enough for them to get the hint that he wasn't very social. Lindsey, on the other hand, would stand and talk to another diver for 15 minutes, even with a set of double tanks on her back. That was almost 100 pounds of weight! Not much less than Lindsey's total body weight. Joey's back started hurting just thinking about it.

Lindsey and Joey stepped into the water and pulled themselves around the railing to where their tanks were hanging. As they clipped the tanks onto their harnesses, they reviewed the dive plan one final time. Joey was going to carry the key since he had experience unlocking and locking that lock before. It had been a couple of years, and hopefully they had replaced the lock since then. Joey remembered it didn't close very easily the last time.

Once they were set up, they descended and faced each other to make sure nothing was out of sorts. Then they both turned and started swimming toward the chimney side by side. Lindsey reached across and took Joey's hand in hers again. Joey glanced around quickly to see if anyone was watching them.

Joey led them around the side of the metal cavern away from the scuba classes and other divers. He didn't notice any bubbles rising out of the chimney. He was hopeful there weren't any classes at the bottom doing skills. When they reached the chimney, Joey looked down into it and the only person he saw was the nearly naked monofin diver heading back up from another breath hold dive. They waited for him to ascend past them, then Joey gave Lindsey the okay signal and she finally let go of his hand and returned it.

They began their descent to the bottom of the chimney and the entrance to the cave. Once there, Joey looked into the large area just inside the overhang of the wall. He didn't see any divers in there either. Had they managed to get lucky and have the cave to themselves?

He flicked his fins together and propelled himself toward the grim reaper sign as he unclipped his primary reel from the rear D ring where it was hanging. He secured the line around the same signpost as he had earlier that morning and reached back to flip the power switch on his light. The bright LED lamp came to life and sent a beam far into the darkness of the tunnel in front of him. He glanced back at Lindsey and saw she had also switched on her light.

Joey began swimming into the cave slowly, careful not to stir up any silt as he passed through the restriction at the entrance. The visibility was a little hazy, but Joey blew that off to his earlier encounter with the single tank divers. About 30 feet past the restriction, he wrapped the line around one of the metal spikes holding the large pipe in place on the floor. That way if someone messed with the line outside the restriction, they still had this tie off to keep the line in place. With the pipe they really didn't need the line to help lead them out of the cave, although it was easier to hold onto the line if the visibility was disturbed than to hold onto the pipe.

As they went farther into the cave, the visibility began to get even hazier. Joey noticed his light was no longer penetrating the darkness as far as it had just moments earlier. As he progressed into the cave, the visibility got even worse. He thought back to the single tank divers entering the cave as he was leaving it earlier and the silt clouds they had left, but that had been more than hour earlier. The visibility should have cleared more by this time. Of course, more divers might have gone back to the Opera Room since then.

Joey glanced back at Lindsey. She held her bent index finger up in the sign of the question mark. Joey shrugged his shoulders. He decided he would continue into the silt. There was sufficient flow coming out of the cave that it should clear quickly. Maybe the visibility was only obscured for a few feet.

Joey felt three knots pass by on the line on his reel as he continued farther into the cave and let the line off his reel. He had knots tied every ten feet. He had done that in case he should ever find passage without line in it. The knots would make it easier to survey the passage. Although Joey wasn't sure how to survey. This was just something he had read on the internet. He wanted to be prepared, nonetheless. In the meantime, it helped to know how far he had swum in situations like the current one.

The visibility was still bad, actually worse than it had been. Joey could feel slight tension on the line from his reel, likely caused by Lindsey maintaining contact with it. He was a little surprised Lindsey hadn't caught up to him and signaled him to turn around. The conditions in the cave were definitely not something under which they should be penetrating deeper into it.

Joey felt Lindsey's hand slide along his leg and torso and up to the back of his arm. She grabbed his arm and pushed it, the contact signal meaning move forward. Joey wondered why Lindsey wanted to keep going. Then it hit him. She was concerned that there were open water divers on the other side of the silt and that they would need help.

Joey had a flashback to his experience in this very passage from two years earlier. He remembered the panic he had felt. Suddenly, an urgency took over and he hastened his movement into the cave toward the Opera Room. A few feet later he felt something in front of him, and it was moving.

32

Lindsey

Typically, Lindsey wouldn't push into a silted area, but she knew open water divers regularly swam back to the Opera Room and usually created some silt as they were swimming through the tunnel. It wasn't their fault, completely.

Open water divers weren't typically trained how to do modified frog kicks, a finning method that minimized the amount of silt stirred up. As they moved along the tunnel kicking up and down with their fins, the way open water divers were taught, it was impossible to not silt out the smaller tunnels. Lindsey also knew the visibility shouldn't be too bad and shouldn't last too long. The water current did a good job at moving it along and clearing things out of the tunnel.

She followed the line until she felt Joey's leg next to her arm. She slid her hand along his body until she came to his arm. Grabbing the back of it, she pushed forward, communicating to him to keep going. Joey had apparently understood because he suddenly began moving much faster into the cave, almost too fast. She wondered if he was having flashbacks to his dives in the cave two years earlier and beginning to panic.

Then Joey suddenly stopped moving forward and Lindsey crashed into him. *Why would he go from swimming so fast to suddenly stopping?* Lindsey thought. Then it occurred to her. Whoever was making all this silt must be coming out of the cave. Just as that thought popped into her head, Lindsey felt Joey push forcefully back against her. At this point, she was right next to him, shoulder to shoulder.

Lindsey slid her hand along the cave line until she felt the hard curved outline of the primary reel Joey was spooling the line from against her hand. The visibility was much worse. She couldn't see even a slight bit of illumination from either of their dive lights. Usually, there was a little bit of a glow. But the silt was so thick that it completely swallowed the bright beams.

She felt Joey reach back and take her hand in his. She then felt his fingers against her palm. They were wiggling around. It felt like he was crossing them and uncrossing them. Crossed fingers meant you were entangled in the line, and she knew that wasn't the case with Joey. Then she remembered they had gotten into the habit of crossing and uncrossing their fingers to communicate dive buddy.

This was a signal they had come up with on a dive vacation together with some friends. In open water ocean diving it was easy to get separated and out of sight from each other, so they had come up with the crossed and uncrossed fingers sign to ask each other where their dive buddies were. But she knew Joey wasn't asking her where her dive buddy was. Then it occurred to her. He might be trying to tell her there was a diver ahead.

Lindsey grabbed Joey's hand as she quickly moved around him so she was in front. She didn't want to lose contact with Joey and the cave line he had in his hand. While she knew there weren't any tunnels to the side of this main one that she could get lost in, it was still comforting to know she was in contact with a line that led back to the exit of the cave. Especially in the zero visibility conditions they were in.

With her other hand Lindsey grabbed the hose where it connected to the regulator in her mouth and held tight. If the diver in the silt ahead of them was panicked, there was a chance there would be some arm flailing and her regulator could get knocked from her mouth. She wanted to avoid that.

Lindsey felt Joey tugging her back. She resisted and pulled harder.

He finally gave in, and she felt him letting line out of the reel so they could move forward. Lindsey hoped the visibility would begin to clear a little, but she didn't expect that to happen. She felt Joey grab onto the shoulder strap on her harness. But he wasn't trying to hold her back this time. Instead, he was holding onto her so she wouldn't get separated from him. Putting all of her trust in him to not let go of her and not lose contact with the cave line, she released her grip on his hand and started feeling around in front of her for the diver Joey had supposedly encountered.

She didn't feel anything right away. Joey must have scared the diver off when they bumped into each other. She didn't know how long that diver had been in the cave, or if there was more than one diver, but she knew she had to find the diver quickly. The last depth reading she had seen on her dive computer was 76 feet. That meant they were breathing about 3.5 times the amount of air than they did on the surface. She and Joey had plenty of air in their larger volume double sidemount tanks. If this was an open water diver, the only air would be in a single 80 cubic foot tank. And coming out of the cave from the Opera Room would mean there wasn't much air left in that tank. Lindsey was pretty certain she would have to hand one of her regulators to the diver in front of them to get that diver out.

She moved forward quickly, keeping a firm grip on the regulator in her mouth with her right hand and extending her left hand ahead, sweeping it back and forth in case the diver wasn't directly in front of her. She felt Joey's hand on her harness as she moved forward. She hoped he still had hold of the reel with the line that led back to the chimney and the surface above.

After sweeping her left arm back and forth four or five times, Lindsey would reach down and feel for the large pipe on the floor to make sure she was still heading in the right direction. She should have felt the other diver by now, she thought to herself.

Then the back of her hand knocked into something fleshy in front of her. She quickly rotated her hand and grabbed onto what felt like someone's upper arm. She was thankful she hadn't knocked her hand against the regulator and knocked it out of the diver's mouth. With that thought she tightened her grip on her own regulator. She then gently squeezed the other diver's arm a couple of times trying to communicate reassurance and hoping the diver would understand.

Lindsey felt a hand on the back of her left hand. The diver was grabbing her hand and trying to move it in between the two of them. Lindsey let go of the arm and grasped the hand and gave it a couple of gentle squeezes just like she had with the arm. The diver squeezed back tightly. *That's good,* Lindsey thought, *this diver is not in a complete fit of panic.* Had the diver been panicked it's unlikely there would be any communication.

Lindsey wanted to ask the diver if there was anyone else in the cave, but she didn't know how to do that. They still couldn't see anything and the finger crossing thing was not universally known. It was just something she and Joey had come up with. It was rare for an open water diver to go back to the Opera Room alone, though, well, except in Joey's case. Chances were there was someone else in the cave. Lindsey couldn't leave the cave knowing there was probably another diver needing help.

Rotating her body around so Joey would be on her left and the distressed diver on her right, Lindsey pulled the diver across toward Joey. She kept her hand low to the bottom so she wouldn't knock it into Joey's regulator and hoped to run it into the reel in Joey's hand. Fortunately, that's exactly what happened. Lindsey felt the hard edge of the reel against the back of her hand. She had to somehow figure out how to transfer the diver's hand to Joey and take the reel from him so she could continue toward the Opera Room and look for the other diver.

Taking a chance, Lindsey released her grip on her regulator and brought her right hand down to the diver's wrist. Once she had the wrist in her hand, she released her grip of the diver's hand with her left hand and reached for Joey's right arm, the one holding onto her harness. She found his bicep, grabbed it, and squeezed several times while pushing it away from herself. Joey didn't release his grip on her harness at first, probably because he was being protective and didn't want to let go of her. Lindsey kept pushing his arm away and Joey finally relented and let go of her harness.

Sliding her hand along his arm she found his hand and grabbed it. She then pushed his hand toward the hand of the other diver. Once she was assured that Joey had the diver's hand in his, Lindsey grabbed the reel and jiggled it. Joey quickly let go this time. As Lindsey moved the reel away from him, letting out some line, she could feel tension on it from where Joey was still maintaining contact with the line. Joey could exit the cave with the diver while Lindsey continued deeper into the cave. Hopefully, she would find the other diver, if there was one, still alive and just needing to be led out.

Lindsey felt the diver she had transferred to Joey slide past in front of her as Joey began pulling back. She hoped Joey was prepared to donate one of his regulators. She could hear the shortened breaths that are delivered by an unbalanced first stage regulator when the pressure in the tank was getting low. And there was only one place that could be coming from. Both she and Joey were using balanced first stage regulators.

She knew Joey would recognize the sound for what it was. They had both heard it before on a recreational boat diving trip. The regulator belonging to one of the divers on that trip had started making that same noise and that diver ended up having to do an emergency ascent to the surface. Joey and Lindsey had discussed it later that day over lunch.

Suddenly Lindsey no longer heard the clipped breathing. She still heard the unsynchronized exhalation bubbles from two separate divers though. Joey must have donated his long-hosed regulator to the diver. Lindsey let out a sigh of relief and turned her focus to finding the other diver in the cave. She quickly swam forward, farther into the cave, while letting more line out from the reel. She desperately hoped that she would find a diver to rescue and not a body to recover.

33

Joey

Joey followed behind Lindsey, letting the line off his reel as quickly as he could while still maintaining some tension so his fins wouldn't get entangled. Suddenly Lindsey stopped. Joey would have crashed into her if he hadn't slammed the reel in his left hand into the thick silt on the floor to stop himself. Normally, he wouldn't do that, but the visibility was already non-existent. Pushing his reel into the silt wasn't going to make it any worse. It couldn't get any worse.

He held onto Lindsey's harness as tightly as he could with his right hand. She was depending on him to maintain their contact with the continuous line leading back to the opening of the cave. Joey was all too familiar with being in this passage without any visibility and no cave line. He didn't want to find himself in that situation again, especially with two, possibly three, additional divers.

Lindsey started rotating her body back toward him. Joey thought she must have decided to turn around and leave. *But what about the diver he had encountered?* Maybe the diver was dead. *Not again!* Joey thought. He might never dive Eddy Spring again if that's how this was going to end up.

Then Joey felt Lindsey push against the reel in his hand. Next, he felt her hand on his right arm. She squeezed his arm repeatedly. *Did she want him to let go of her harness?* he thought. Joey didn't feel comfortable doing that, but Lindsey kept squeezing his arm. He finally released his grip and started reaching for Lindsey's arm. Before he could find it, Lindsey had slid her hand down along his arm and grabbed his hand. She pulled his hand toward her. Joey began to think that maybe Lindsey wanted him in front of her for some reason. Until he felt another hand. She must have found the other diver and was holding on with her other hand. Lindsey pushed their hands together and pulled back her hand. Joey held on tightly to this unknown diver, who was thankfully alive.

Next Joey felt the reel in his left hand start to jiggle. Lindsey must have wanted the reel. That only made sense since she would be coming out behind him and the other diver. Joey released the reel, careful to maintain contact with the line by making the okay sign with his thumb and index finger around it. He began finning backwards and pulling the other diver along to give Lindsey room to reel the line back onto the spool as they made their way to the opening.

Suddenly, Joey heard shortened breaths directly in front of him matching up to the other diver's inhalations. He had heard that sound before. That diver was about to have an empty scuba tank. Joey quickly wrapped his arm around the line to keep from losing contact with it and grabbed his long-hosed regulator from his mouth. He thrust it down toward his other hand, and the hand of the diver he was holding on to. He hoped the diver would understand to take the regulator and start breathing from it.

Joey felt the regulator being pulled away. A few seconds later all he heard were normal breathing sounds, fast but normal rather than clipped like they had been. He reached for his short-hosed regulator that was hanging around his neck and placed it in his mouth. He had to get them out of there. His tanks still had a lot of air in them, but he could hear the other diver quickly breathing the pressure down.

Joey pulled his arm back around the line and circled his fingers around it. He then rotated his body to the left, pushing the other diver in a wide circle so they could swim out side by side. There was no point in trying to get the other diver to make contact with the line as that diver likely never had any kind of training on using a guideline in a cave.

They swam quickly, Joey keeping his eyes closed most of the time so he wouldn't begin to panic. Having his eyes closed sent the message to his brain that he shouldn't be able to see. Completely opposite of the message that was sent to his brain when his eyes were open. Keeping his eyes open in zero visibility still brought him anxiety.

He opened his eyes every 15 seconds or so to see if the visibility was clearing. He was starting to see the glow from his light, but the visibility was still bad. The third time he opened his eyes he could finally see his hand on the line in front of him. Another few seconds should do it. He closed his eyes again and reopened them about 10 seconds later. He could not only see his hand on the line, but he could also see a faint light ahead. They were close to the opening.

Joey looked to his right at the diver he was holding onto. The diver looked back at him, eyes bugged out behind the mask lenses. *This diver was going to bolt to the surface as soon as it came into view*, Joey thought. Joey had to be prepared for it and make the diver do a slow ascent. Joey didn't know how long the diver had been back in the Opera Room and whether there would be a decompression obligation to contend with. He didn't hear any audible alarms coming from a dive computer, but the diver might not even have a dive computer. Joey didn't have time to look for one.

Now that he was almost out of the cave Joey felt comfortable releasing hold of the line. He had to grab onto the diver and make sure he didn't let an uncontrolled ascent to the surface happen. After everything he and Lindsey just went through to save this diver, he didn't want to have to deal with a lung expansion injury. That happened when a diver bolted for the surface without breathing properly and the air in the lungs expanded and popped the alveoli. Basically, the lungs blew up like a bubble gum bubble.

Joey grabbed the BC of the diver and wrapped his hand around the shoulder strap. He made sure he had a firm grip on it. He tried to pull his other hand from the diver's hand, but the diver wasn't letting go. That was fine. The diver would probably let go once they got to the rope leading up the chimney. That's when Joey would grab the rope and hold them both at depth.

They reached the restriction and Joey pushed the diver forward so they were staggered as they went through it. The diver saw the rope and started kicking hard to get to it, at the same time releasing Joey's hand just as Joey had predicted. Joey let himself be dragged to the rope as he held tightly onto the BC.

Once they were at the rope Joey grabbed onto the metal rod embedded in the bottom of the chimney and gripped it hard. Just as expected the diver grabbed the rope and tried to climb up it. All that did was pull the buoy 50 feet above about a foot below the surface before the force of the buoy's buoyancy kept it from coming any deeper. Joey continued to hold onto the diver and the metal rod thinking to himself, *this is not going to be a fun ascent!*

34

Lindsey

Lindsey continued toward the Opera Room desperately hoping to find a diver needing help. The visibility wasn't getting any better as she moved forward. She could hear the low hum of the reel as it spun out line below her. She was glad she had insisted they run a guideline into the cave. Joey had suggested they didn't need one until the grate because of the pipe, but with no visibility, and a diver possibly in distress, the line was definitely going to be helpful.

As Lindsey continued into the cave, the visibility seemed to clear a little. It had cleared at least enough for her to see the glow from her dive light at that point. She tried to look at her dive computer to read the depth, but the visibility wasn't improved enough for that.

Then Lindsey thought she heard something. It sounded like whining. She stopped moving and held her breath for a moment to see if she could hear it again. A few seconds later she heard the same noise. This time it sounded more like whimpering, or maybe crying. Lindsey immediately started moving quickly toward the Opera Room. It was a good thing the pipe was on the floor otherwise she wouldn't be sure what direction she was heading.

She couldn't tell for certain where the sound was coming from. That was impossible underwater. Sound underwater came from all directions. Nature's surround sound. But it had to be somewhere in front of her. She hadn't passed anyone else in the tunnel behind her.

Lindsey heard the crying again. This time it was louder,

confirming she was heading in the right direction. The farther she went the more the visibility cleared. She could now see the outline of the beam from her dive light and not just a glow. She began sweeping her light back and forth, not hoping to see anything, but rather hoping to attract the attention of the diver that was in the cave crying. The person was obviously under distress.

Another look at her dive computer revealed that she was at 90 feet of depth. She had to be in the Opera Room. Had those divers really messed up the visibility so much that they blew out the entire room? Lindsey decided to move away from the pipe. Open water divers were more likely to stay along the pipe. Some of them ventured away from it to the airbox but this diver wasn't in the airbox. If that was the case Lindsey wouldn't hear the crying. A sound made above the surface would have to be really loud to carry underwater.

As Lindsey moved to her left, away from the pipe, the visibility cleared even more. She saw the outline of the airbox about 10 feet in front of her. That meant the diver had to be behind her, possibly by the grate. The crying continued in a rhythmic fashion, almost like the sound a train makes as it's departing the station, only a much higher pitch.

Lindsey turned to her right and swam toward the far wall of the Opera Room, careful to keep tension on the 300 feet of line between her and the opening to the cave. She reached the wall and began to follow it to the right toward the grate. The water beyond the grate would still be clear so it was likely the open water diver would be holding onto the grate and waiting for the silt in the room to clear. The problem with that was that the diver was still moving and creating more silt. It wasn't going to clear anytime soon. And the air in that diver's tank was limited. There probably wasn't enough in it to make it out of the cave.

Hastening her movement, Lindsey darted forward, keeping her left hand on the wall beside her and holding her right hand, the one with the reel in it, in front of her face. When she did encounter the distressed diver, she didn't need her regulator knocked out of her mouth or her mask torn from her face. While those were both situations she could deal with, she didn't have time for anything like that to happen. She had to get to the diver, hand the diver her long-hosed regulator and hope it was accepted, and get them heading out of the cave quickly.

She hoped the diver would remain calm, but given the crying she was still hearing, she doubted that would be the case. Panicked divers were dangerous. They have only one thing on their minds – survival. Unfortunately, that usually meant full on thrashing and panic. The best way to approach those divers was from behind. But Lindsey could only see a few inches in front of her. By the time she could figure out which way the diver was facing Lindsey would be too close to choose a safe approach.

As Lindsey moved along the wall of the Opera Room, she could hear exhaust bubbles matching up with the crying. Even though the sound was coming from all around her, she knew she was getting closer if she could hear the bubbles. Lindsey slowed her pace. She didn't want to swim full speed into the diver and make the situation even worse. She decided to hold the reel with her left hand so she could grab her long-hosed regulator with her right hand and hold it in front of her. Lindsey was beginning to hear that same clipped breathing. Another unbalanced regulator.

It was only a matter of a few breaths before the distressed diver would no longer be able to pull a breath from the regulator. Lindsey not only had to reach the diver before that time, but she also had to communicate to the diver, in limited visibility, to accept Lindsey's regulator and follow her out of the cave through even worse visibility.

The visibility continued to clear. Lindsey was getting closer to the grate. Maybe they would have enough visibility to get through this smoothly. Lindsey slowly moved forward into the clearing water, keeping her right hand with the regulator in front of her face.

Movement below her grabbed Lindsey's attention. She glanced down and saw the outline of a fin moving up and down in and out of the silt, with larger plumes of silt clouds popping up and moving away toward her right with the flow of water.

Lindsey followed the outline of the fin toward where the leg should have been. It was buried in more silt, though. She contemplated reaching out, touching the fin, and following it up to the leg but she didn't want to spook the diver. She thought better of that idea and decided to try to get the diver's attention another way.

Moving to her left with her shoulder against the wall, Lindsey began sweeping the beam of the dive light strapped onto the back of her left hand in front of her, hoping to get the attention of the diver. As she moved forward, she started to make out a larger mass of something, probably the diver's BC based on its position relative to where Lindsey had seen the fin. Lindsey moved the beam of her dive light so it was focused on the mass and then followed the mass up toward where the head should be.

Suddenly, the mass jumped away just as Lindsey heard what sounded like a muffled scream. The silt got worse, swallowing the little visibility there had been. Lindsey stopped moving and held still, her left hand in front of her.

Listening…

Waiting…

The rhythmic crying resumed, only a little faster this time. The train gaining speed as it got farther from the station. Lindsey inched forward, sweeping the light beam, searching for another outline. The visibility began to clear again with the help of the water current coming from beyond the grate. A moment later the water was completely clear to her left. Lindsey could see the edge of the grate a few inches from her shoulder. She followed the outline of the grate to the far end. There she saw a hand grasping onto the rebar so tightly the knuckles were white. Lindsey followed the outline of the arm to the right and came face to face with the distressed diver.

35

Joey

With all his might, Joey was holding onto the metal pin with his left hand and the open water diver with his right hand. The diver was kicking and pulling, trying to climb the rope up to the surface. Joey knew if he let him go chances were very high that he would suffer an overexpansion injury, or in lay terms - pop a lung. He had to calm the diver and convince him to make a slow ascent.

Joey pulled hard, bringing the diver down next to him. He rotated the diver around trying to get them face to face. Joey had learned in his rescue diver course to always try to look into the other diver's face. The eyes told a lot about the state of mind. Joey didn't need to see this diver's eyes to know his state of mind. He was in a full-on panic. But sometimes eye-to-eye contact helped calm a person down.

As Joey was trying to rotate the diver so they were facing each other, the diver appeared to realize there was someone else next to him. He turned toward Joey and tried to bring his fists down hard on Joey's head. Had they been standing on the grassy hill next to the spring basin, he might have knocked Joey out. But water slows things down. It's difficult to get enough momentum to punch someone underwater, regardless of what Hollywood would like everyone to think.

Joey was able to deflect the punches. And with the diver's focus now on fighting Joey instead of trying to get to the surface, Joey was able to release his grip on the metal pin with his left hand and grab the diver's right hand with it. At first, the diver struggled and tried to break free. Joey held on tight though and kept turning the diver to face him. The diver finally relented and looked at Joey. That was enough to calm him a little, at least momentarily.

Keeping a tight grip on the BC with his right hand, Joey released the diver's hand and made the okay signal in front of the diver's face. He did it with forcefulness, though, thrusting his hand in front of the diver as if commanding him to be okay. It seemed to work because the diver finally stopped moving completely.

With this new calm, Joey grabbed the diver's left arm and pulled his wrist to where he could look at the dive computer display. He examined the numbers on the face of the computer. It wasn't a dive computer Joey was familiar with, but they were all fairly similar and he was able to quickly decipher the numbers.

The diver hadn't violated his no decompression limits yet, or NDL as divers referred to it. According to the dive computer, they had 2 minutes before that happened. Joey had to begin ascending soon. Overstaying the limit meant doing a much longer stop while hovering midwater at 15 feet. Joey wasn't sure if he could keep the diver a mere 15 feet below the surface for 3 minutes, let alone longer.

Even though safety stops were recommended and not mandatory, a safety stop under these circumstances was necessary. Joey hadn't scrolled through the dive computer screens to extract the other data. He was certain the diver had made it to the Opera Room, which would put him at a maximum depth of just over 100 feet. And he had been on this dive for 37 minutes according to the display. That wasn't a long time. Most of Joey's dives were at least an hour longer than that. But those were planned decompression dives with minimal exertion.

With all the exertion the diver had made just in the time Joey had encountered him, Joey knew it was important to allow enough time for the nitrogen built up in his body to off gas. And the only way to do that was to remain at a shallow depth long enough for the bubbles to escape before they got too big.

Joey thrust the okay signal in front of the diver's face a second time. He wanted to communicate the necessity for the diver to remain calm. The diver finally returned the signal with his right hand. Communication! That meant the diver was calming down. Now all Joey had to do was keep him calm. No small task.

Hand signals weren't going to do. Joey needed to communicate the plan to the diver. He took the diver's hand and placed it around the rope and squeezed it, communicating to him to hold on tight. He glanced back at the dive computer – still reading 2 minutes until a decompression obligation.

Reaching into his right thigh pocket, Joey found his wetnotes and pulled them out while still holding onto the diver with his left hand. This is where it got tricky. Joey needed both hands to write his instructions to the diver. Which meant he had to let go of the BC. The diver appeared calm…at the moment. That could quickly change once Joey was no longer holding onto him.

Prepared to reach out and grab the diver again if he began to bolt to the surface, Joey released his grip on the BC and grabbed the wetnotes with his left hand. He quickly flipped them open and pulled out the pencil while maintaining eye contact with the diver. Joey quickly jotted on the page:

Must do safety stop

He held up the page in front of the diver's eyes and watched as he read the words. The diver turned his head toward Joey and nodded. Joey made the okay signal and thrust it in front of him. The diver returned the signal.

Joey turned back to the wetnotes and continued in his sloppy underwater writing:

Slow ascent 3 mins
@ 15' Lots of air

He held up the page in front of the diver's eyes and watched as he read the words. The diver turned his head toward Joey and nodded. Joey made the okay signal and thrust it in front of him. The diver returned the signal.

He held the page back in front of the diver and thrust it in place again. He then tapped on the words "Lots of air" and smacked his tanks to accentuate that part. He wanted the diver to be confident that they wouldn't breathe through all the air. Speaking of which, Joey decided he better check his gauges to make sure he wasn't lying to this guy.

Joey grabbed his left tank gauge first, the one he was breathing from. The gauge read 2600 psi. He had started with just over 3000 psi. That's as high as they filled tanks at Eddy Spring, even the steel tanks Joey was diving. He had plenty of air to get the diver to the surface and then come back down for another hour in the cave.

Next he grabbed the gauge on the first stage of his right sidemount tank. *Wow!* Joey thought. That gauge read 1200 psi. Joey had never even breathed from that regulator other than to test it before the dive. This diver had just breathed 1800 psi of air. That was equivalent to about three-fourths of an aluminum 80 cf foot tank, the typical tank most recreational scuba divers used. And only about 10 minutes had passed since Joey had donated that regulator to the diver.

Suddenly Joey remembered they had limited time to begin their ascent. He grabbed the diver's right wrist and looked at the dive computer display. He watched the 1-minute NDL readout transform to a 0. Time to get going up the rope toward the surface.

36

Lindsey

Lindsey immediately thrusted the regulator in her right hand toward the diver in front of her. The diver snatched it out of Lindsey's hand and pulled it back to begin breathing from it…but forgot to remove the regulator already in her mouth first. The mouthpiece of Lindsey's regulator hit the purge button on the front of the other regulator and a burst of bubbles escaped from the exhaust holes. Lindsey watched as the diver tried to take in another breath, but there was nothing left in the tank.

Making sure the diver still had a hold of her regulator, Lindsey reached out and grabbed the regulator in the diver's mouth and yanked it out. This could have gone one of two ways. The diver could have taken a big breath of water and drowned right there in front of her or the diver could have taken Lindsey's regulator and started breathing from it.

Lindsey knew the more likely option was the first, but the diver was panicked, and she didn't know how else to get the diver to breathe from the regulator she had provided. And if Lindsey didn't do something quickly, the diver was likely to knock Lindsey's regulator out of her mouth and then Lindsey wouldn't have anything to breathe either.

Fortunately, the diver was aware of the working regulator and began breathing from it, upside down, but still breathing from it. *It's a good thing I bought these good regs last month!* Lindsey thought to herself.

Usually breathing regulators upside down meant poor breathing quality and mouthfuls of water. Even though they weren't meant to be used upside down, the higher end regulators minimized issues and could easily be breathed while upside down. They weren't the most comfortable in that position, and it was more difficult to pull a breath from, but they still breathed better than most rental regulators. And more importantly, they would keep you alive.

Lindsey was out of regulators to donate, and she didn't think she would be able to convince this diver to remove the regulator and put it back right side up. That was fine. As long as everyone remained breathing it didn't matter how that was accomplished.

Now that they were tethered by Lindsey's long-hosed regulator, Lindsey could try to communicate with the diver. She looked into the diver's eyes and saw the widest, most bugged out eyes she had ever seen. And Lindsey had seen quite a few in her time as a divemaster. She also noticed for the first time that this diver was female. Wetsuits and hoods make it difficult to differentiate underwater. Lindsey was hoping that dealing with another woman would help her make a connection with this diver. Sometimes men's egos could make them less willing to accept help from a woman. At this point, anything would help.

Lindsey reached out and put her hand over the hand that was gripping the grate and gently squeezed it a couple of times. The girl's other hand had a death grip on the hose leading to the regulator in her mouth.

As soon as Lindsey squeezed her hand, she released her grip on the grate and grabbed Lindsey's hand. Lindsey took it and gave it another reassuring squeeze. This girl was placing her confidence in Lindsey. She took the girl's hand and moved it to the back of her arm hoping the girl would hold onto that for a moment. Lindsey needed both of her hands to secure the line and reel to the grate. It would have to stay in the cave for the time being. There was no way she would be able to reel the line out while also guiding this girl out of the cave through the silt that was sure to be even thicker.

The girl complied and Lindsey quickly pushed the reel through one of the openings in the grate, around a piece of rebar and back out. She looped the reel around its own line, locked it to keep it from spooling out, and clipped it back onto the line. She tested the tension on the cave line to make sure it wasn't too loose.

With that done, Lindsey grabbed the girl's hand and held it tightly in hers with all her fingers except the index and thumb. She needed those to okay the line as they made their way out with no visibility. Her right arm would be stretched out in front of her with her right hand protecting her head from any unseen obstructions they might encounter. She slowly brought their hands down to the guideline and formed a circle around it with her index finger and thumb and then nodded to the girl and pointed toward the exit.

They began moving side by side slowly following the guideline out of the cave. Lindsey quickly glanced at her dive computer to note the time. She had been on this dive only 12 minutes. It seemed so much longer than that. She and Joey had encountered the other diver quickly about halfway to the Opera Room. And then she had made it to the Opera Room in about a minute after leaving Joey with the other diver. It seemed like hours had passed.

Lindsey wanted to look at the girl's dive computer, if she even had one. Lindsey hadn't noticed if there was one on her left wrist. And that wrist was attached to the hand that had a death grip on the regulator hose. It didn't matter at this point anyway. She would try to get a look at it once they were at the bottom of the chimney.

Instead, Lindsey looked at her pressure gauges. She still had 3100 psi in her left tank. Fortunately, these tanks had been filled at Cave Masters in Marianna and were topped off at 3600 psi. She looked at her right tank and saw there was still 2800 psi in that one. The girl was breathing fast, but not too fast. Lindsey had plenty of air for both of them to make it out of the cave.

Within a few seconds of beginning their way out they encountered a large silt cloud that completely obscured the visibility. The girl stopped moving and held back. Lindsey tried to coax her forward, but the girl didn't want to go into the silt. Lindsey knew they had at least 100 feet of silted cave to get through before it started to clear. And even then, the visibility wouldn't be great. There was no way to go around it, even if she rerouted the cave line. Then she had an idea.

Lindsey turned toward the girl and gave her the okay signal. The girl shook her head no. *Poor girl,* thought Lindsey. She reached out with her right hand and held the girl's right hand in both of hers. Lindsey gently squeezed and looked into her eyes. Lindsey then pulled her right hand up and swept it over her mask from top to bottom hoping the girl's open water scuba instructor had used that hand signal to communicate to the students to close their eyes. The girl shook her head no.

What am I going to do? Lindsey thought. They had to get through this silt to get out of the cave. And the silt wasn't going to dissipate any time soon. Lindsey squeezed the girl's hand again and held it tight while she swept her other hand down over her mask again and tried to look as pleading as she could with a scuba mask on her face.

The girl slowly closed her eyes. Lindsey squeezed her hand a couple more times, offering more reassurance. She remained motionless for several more seconds to make sure the girl was keeping her eyes closed. When she didn't see the girl try to open her eyes, Lindsey moved back to her position facing toward the exit. She squeezed the girl's hand one more time and they disappeared into the silt.

37

Joey

Joey began his ascent up the rope toward the surface holding tightly onto the BC of the diver in front of him with his right hand. The diver kept his right hand wrapped around the hose of the donated regulator and the left on the rope between them. He slid his left hand up the rope quickly and pulled up. Joey held onto the rope with his left hand and pulled them down. The diver wasn't trying to bolt to the surface like he had been earlier, but he was still trying to ascend too quickly.

Getting right in his face, Joey almost touched his mask to the other diver's mask. He glared into his eyes as he knocked the diver's left hand off the rope. The diver's eyes got wide again, and Joey thought he was about to take off toward the surface. Joey hated to let him go but he wasn't sure what else he could do. And he didn't want to risk himself getting hurt and end up having two victims for emergency services to deal with.

Fortunately, the diver didn't bolt to the surface and began to calm down a little. Joey watched his eyes get back to a semi-normal size. The diver reached for the rope and Joey swatted his hand away before he was able to grab onto it. Joey took the diver's left hand and was about to place it on his own harness when he thought better of it. Joey might be able to overpower him but, just in case, he didn't want the diver holding onto him if he decided to try to bolt toward the surface again. Instead, Joey directed the hand to the diver's own

BC and made him grab the front edge of it. This would at least keep that hand occupied and hopefully away from the rope.

With that done, Joey resumed a slow ascent. The diver was finning aggressively but couldn't overpower Joey's grip on the rope between them. They slowly made their way toward the surface.

Once they were even with the top edge of the chimney, Joey slowed even more. He knew that ledge was about 25 feet below the surface. Another 10 feet and they would have to stop for at least 3 minutes. Joey tried to get a look at the diver's dive computer, but it was on his left wrist facing the other direction. He would look at it once they reached 15 feet of depth.

At 20 feet, the diver began to kick even harder. Joey pulled down on the diver until he was in front of him where he could look into his eyes again. Once they were eye to eye, the diver calmed down. Joey decided they would remain in that position until they finally reached the surface. He glanced at his dive computer and saw they were 17 feet deep. *Close enough!* Joey thought. He stopped their ascent and brought his left hand up the rope so it was in front of the diver's face, twisting his wrist so the diver could see the computer display.

Joey then nodded his head toward the diver's left wrist. He wanted to get a look at it and see if there was a decompression obligation or just a safety stop. But he didn't want to let go of the diver or the rope to do so. The diver just stared at Joey. Joey wiggled his left wrist back and forth and nodded his chin toward the diver's computer. The diver finally got the message and slowly opened his fingers and released his grip on the regulator hose. He glanced at the dive computer but looked as confused as Joey had that first time he ascended this chimney with a dive computer he had rented from the dive shop. The diver positioned his wrist so Joey could see the display.

The computer read 2:43 minutes remaining on the safety stop. That meant they had begun their ascent before exceeding his no decompression limits. That definitely made things simpler. Joey let out a breath he hadn't realized he was holding. He nodded at the diver and released his grip on the diver's BC to give him a reassuring pat on the arm, then grabbed the BC again.

Joey watched the countdown of the safety stop. When the 3 minutes passed, he looked at the diver and saw he was relatively calm. Joey decided to extend the safety stop by a couple of minutes. With the exertion and panic the diver had experienced on the dive, it could only help. And he didn't yet seem to be aware that 3 minutes had passed.

After another 2 minutes, Joey resumed their ascent to the surface. The diver appeared completely calm and slowly began finning with Joey. They eased up the rope and a minute later broke the surface. As soon as their heads were above water, the diver spit his regulator out and began thrashing his arms and kicking his legs wildly. *He had done so well,* Joey thought.

Joey pushed himself away from the thrashing diver and created some distance between them, just as he had learned in his rescue diver class. If he stayed close to the panicked diver, he was likely to get pushed underwater as the diver tried to climb out of the water on top of him. Joey knew the panicked diver would eventually tire out and at that point he would be able to move in and help him back to the steps and out of the water.

About three minutes later, the diver, finally exhausted, grabbed onto the large white buoy next to him, just like Joey had done that first time two years earlier. Joey called to him.

"Are you going to stay calm now?"

The diver looked at Joey like he was seeing him for the first time. It was as if he hadn't realized Joey had been there with him for the past 15 minutes.

"Um, yeah, I think I'm okay now," he cried.

"Okay, listen to me. I know you're exhausted. You've exerted a lot of energy and you're stressed. I want you to reach for your BC inflator and orally inflate your BC. That will help you float. You got that?"

"Y-Yeah."

The diver slowly released his grip on the buoy with his left hand and felt for his inflator hose. Once he found it, he brought it to his mouth and blew into it.

"Nothing's happening," he said.

"That's because you didn't press the exhaust button. Press the button on the end of the power inflator and then blow into it."

The diver did as he was told and this time his BC began filling with air and squeezing his torso. But as soon as he pulled his mouth away from the inflator Joey could hear the air whooshing back out.

"You have to let go of the button before you pull your mouth away otherwise all the air you blew in will just come back out," Joey said, exasperated, his patience wearing thin.

The diver tried again. He pressed the exhaust button and blew into the mouthpiece. He then released the button before pulling his mouth away.

"Like that?" he asked Joey.

"Exactly! Now do that a couple more times."

The diver continued to orally inflate his BC until he couldn't blow anymore air into it.

"I think that's all it will take," he told Joey, a little out of breath.

"Okay, just relax a minute," Joey told him. "My name is Joey. What's yours?"

"Alex."

Joey thought about asking Alex if he had a dive buddy in the cave with him, but he didn't want Alex to start panicking again. Instead, he decided to get Alex to the steps and out of the water before he began questioning him.

"Okay, Alex, I want you to let go of the buoy. You have enough air in your BC that you'll float just fine. Lean back so you're looking up at the sky and I'll come around behind you and start pulling you to the steps. You can kick with your fins a little if you want to help but I don't want you to do anything else. Do you understand?"

Alex nodded. He then slowly released his grip on the buoy and leaned back so he was floating face up on the surface. Joey swam a wide circle around him, remaining just out of reach, until he was about five feet behind him.

"Okay, Alex, I'm directly behind you now. In a few seconds you're going to feel me pulling on your tank valve. Just relax and float there while I pull you to the steps."

"Okay," Alex exhaled.

Joey swam toward Alex and stretched for his tank valve just behind and below his head. He grabbed the valve and began swimming backwards toward the steps about 100 feet behind them while pulling Alex with him. Joey remained on alert and ready to push off of Alex in case he started thrashing again.

"You doing okay, Alex?"

"Y-Yeah, I'm okay."

"Good, you're doing great," Joey reassured him.

About five minutes later Joey felt the railing of the steps against the back of his head. He turned his head and saw the steps were to his left. He rotated his body, grabbed the railing and pulled himself to the steps.

"Okay, Alex, there's a railing to our left. Reach out with your right hand and grab it."

Alex reached out and found the smooth round surface of the railing and grabbed onto it. Joey let go of the tank valve and moved to the other side of the steps.

"Alex, I need to take my tanks off. Just hang out there holding onto the railing while I move around to the shallows and clip my tanks to the ropes. Then I'll be back to help you get out of the water."

Alex nodded and remained where he was, his breathing rate a little fast, but not quite hyperventilating…yet. Joey pulled himself around the railing and along the steps to the platform where the water was shallow enough to stand. He kept his attention on Alex to make sure he didn't drop back underwater. Once Joey was able to stand on the bottom with his head still above the surface, he quickly unclipped his tanks and hung them on the ropes attached to the platform. Next, he pulled his fins and mask off and placed them on the platform above the tanks, watching Alex the entire time. With that done, Joey pulled himself back around the railing to where Alex was still waiting.

"Alex, I'm going to pull your fins off so you can climb up the steps."

"Okay."

Joey reached down and unclipped the heel straps and tugged the fins from Alex's feet.

"Do you want to get out with your BC on or would you rather take it off here in the water?"

"I can get out with it on."

"Okay, go ahead and turn around and let's get out of the water."

Alex rotated his body and faced the steps and the platform. He placed his feet on the bottom step and stood up, maintaining his hold on the railing. Alex and Joey both slowly climbed up the steps to the platform.

"Let's get up to one of the picnic tables and get that thing off you," Joey said.

They walked across the platform onto the grassy slope and climbed up the steep hill stopping at the first unoccupied table they came to. Fortunately, it was already late in the day and most of the scuba classes had finished, and the students were gone. Joey helped Alex pull the BC off and placed it with the tank lying on its side on the table.

"Have a seat on the bench," Joey directed Alex.

Joey sat down beside Alex.

"First, I want to let you know my girlfriend is still in the cave, so if you have a buddy in there, he's in good hands. She has a lot more experience than I do."

"Oh my god! Oh my god! Oh my god!" Alex yelled as he jumped up and started to grab his BC and empty tank. "Emily is still in the cave! We have to go back in and get her!"

Joey grabbed his arm and pulled him back.

"First, you aren't going anywhere! You ran out of air in there and have an empty tank."

"But we have to help Em…"

"I already told you my girlfriend, Lindsey, is in there looking for Emily. The Opera Room isn't that big. I'm sure she's found Emily by now. There's nothing we can do. Especially you. You couldn't even help yourself."

Joey was being a little harsh, maybe too harsh, but he had to convince Alex he couldn't go back into that cave.

Alex tried to shove Joey aside, but Joey held onto his arm tightly and pulled him away from the picnic table.

"Listen to me!" he yelled at Alex. "Emily is in good hands. Let Lindsey deal with it. You'll only get in the way and cause more problems."

Alex sat down, defeated, and dropped his face into his hands. Joey let him have a moment. While he had never left behind a friend on a dive, he had more than his share of bad dives and thought he knew how Alex might be feeling. Little did he know that at some point in the future he would completely rethink that sentiment. There was no feeling in the world like leaving behind a friend on a dive.

After a few minutes, Alex raised his head and looked at Joey, his eyes shiny and red, streaks of tears marking his cheeks.

"So what happened in there?" Joey asked.

"W-We, me and Emily, went back to the Opera Room. It was my idea. Em wasn't too excited about it. She tried to talk me out of it, but I kept insisting we could do it safely. I know some other divers from my open water class that have been back there, and they had a great time. Emily thought it was a bad idea all around. But she finally gave in to me and agreed to go."

Alex stopped for a moment and buried his face in his hands again. Joey reached out and placed a hand on his shoulder and just stood there giving Alex time to deal with his grief.

"Everything was going fine. We got in the water and swam to the top of the opening and began our descent. We had already been down there during our open water class with our instructor, so we knew what it looked like at the bottom. Our instructor had even taken us over to the sign just inside the entrance. We thought it was kind of funny at the time."

"We dropped down and saw the sign again. I think Em was having second thoughts because she grabbed onto the rope and just knelt beside it and wouldn't let go. I had to take her other hand and pull her away from it. She finally let go and followed me."

"We started into the tunnel, following the lights next to the pipe. We even had our own lights I bought just for this dive. They were small lights, but they did a pretty good job lighting up the tunnel. We got back to the Opera Room. It looked so awesome. The lights strung up around the walls gave it a spooky look. We kept following the lights and the pipe and came to the grate with the lock on it."

"We looked in beyond the grate. It looked so cool back there. If it wasn't for the grate being there, I would have kept going. I think Em would have too. She didn't seem afraid anymore. She actually looked a little excited about it."

"We finally decided it was time to turn around and get out of there. That's when we noticed we couldn't see a thing behind us. The dirt on the floor had all come up and made it so we couldn't see anything at all."

"I grabbed onto one of those metal bars around the pipe with my right hand and grabbed Em's hand with my other hand. She wouldn't move away from the grate, though. She had grabbed onto it and refused to let go. I pulled her arm as hard as I could, but she wouldn't budge. She just knelt there and started to cry."

"I looked at my air gauge and saw I only had 300 psi left. Em doesn't breathe as fast as me, so I figured she had a few hundred more. I decided to head out by myself and call for help. I hated leaving her there, but I knew I didn't have much air left and wasn't sure I even had enough to get out. And I guess I didn't. I left Em in there to die!" Alex buried his face in his hands again and slumped over on the bench.

"Listen to me! I told you my girlfriend, Lindsey, is in there looking for Em. She hasn't come out yet so I'm guessing she found her and they're making their way out. Lindsey had more air in her tanks than I did, and she also breathes less than I do so they have plenty of air to make it out. Em's going to be okay. The best we can do is wait here and watch for their bubbles to come up the chimney."

Alex lay on the bench crying into his hands. Nothing was going to calm him until he saw Emily on the surface alive and well. Joey stood up. He wanted to get his tanks and equipment from the platform while they waited. He turned toward the water and noticed someone standing in the shallows gearing up on the opposite side of the platform from where his tanks were hanging. Joey couldn't tell who it was because he had his head down, clipping on his tanks. Then the diver picked his head up and looked toward Joey and Alex.

It was Jack Johnson.

38

Joey

As soon as Joey recognized Jack Johnson, his stomach turned. *What was he doing here?* Joey quickly turned toward Alex.

"Stay right here! Don't move! I'm going down to get my tanks."

Joey turned and began running down the steep hill toward the water. Just as he reached the platform Jack's head submerged under the surface. Joey ran onto the platform hoping to be able to jump in the water and cut him off. His wet boots slid on the slick platform and his feet flew out from under him landing Joey flat on his back on the hard metal surface.

He went down so hard his head smacked onto the platform and he momentarily saw stars. Joey lay there gathering his wits. He slowly raised his head and felt a sharp, deep pain where it had hit the metal surface. A moment later, Joey raised his shoulders and propped himself up on his elbows. He was just in time to see Jack's bubbles hit the surface around the large white buoy floating over the chimney. It was too late.

How had he not noticed Jack when he surfaced with Alex, Joey asked himself. He had to have been in the water already by that time. Joey must have been so focused on Alex he didn't even notice Jack on the other side of the platform.

Oh crap! Jack was sure to have heard Alex yelling about Emily still being in the cave. Joey didn't know if Jack had heard that Lindsey was also in there, but Joey hadn't exactly been whispering it. Jack was heading into the cave to claim another rescue.

The visibility was zero in there. If Lindsey found Emily, which Joey was certain she had, Jack would only make their exit all the more difficult in those conditions. *Dammit! Why didn't I slow down when I got to the platform. That thing is so slippery!* Joey chastised himself.

There was nothing he could do about it. Jack was down the chimney and likely in the cave already. Even if Joey had his tanks on, a fourth diver in a reduced visibility environment would only complicate things. He hoped no one ended up getting hurt because of this. If Lindsey or Emily were hurt, Jack would likely blame it on them.

Joey sat up and rubbed the back of his head. He could already feel it starting to swell. He was going to have a goose egg there later. He grabbed the railing next to him and hoisted himself to a standing position. The quick movement brought about a wave of dizziness and nausea. Joey held onto the railing to steady himself and hoped for the feeling to pass.

About 30 seconds later, after the dizziness and nausea were gone, Joey decided to leave his tanks in the water and grabbed his fins and mask instead. He would get the tanks later. He looked up the hill toward Alex and saw he was still lying on the bench with his face in his hands. Joey looked back toward the large buoy and waited to see bubbles reappear around it.

39

Lindsey

Lindsey and the diver slowly continued through the silt. Lindsey also had her eyes closed. It was calming to swim along in the darkness with no visual stimulation. Lindsey did open her eyes every minute or so to see if the silt was clearing at all. Unfortunately, the diver with her was creating more silt with her knees and fins as she practically crawled along the floor of the cave.

It was slow moving because the diver wasn't swimming. Lindsey had to drag her along as they followed the line toward the opening. Every few feet the girl would get caught up on one of the metal brackets holding the pipe in place and Lindsey would have to help her get over it and continue their exit. Lindsey tried to get her to rise off the bottom and float above the pipe, but she wouldn't comply. Unfortunately, this also meant her fins were dragging through the muck on the floor of the tunnel and making the silt hanging in the water worse.

Lindsey had plenty of air in her tanks. That wasn't her concern. Her concern was a decompression obligation. Once they reached the rope leading to the surface, Lindsey didn't know if she would be able to keep this girl from ascending too quickly. That wouldn't be good if there was no decompression obligation. But if they did have to do a decompression stop, the result would be much worse.

Lindsey tried to get a glimpse of her dive computer, but the silt was too thick. Even with it pressed against her mask she couldn't read the numbers. She could only see a faint glow. If she didn't end up having a decompression obligation, she still had no idea how long the girl had been back in the Opera Room at 100 feet depth. The chances of her having a decompression obligation were very strong.

As they made their way through the passage, Lindsey was certain they had already moved out of the Opera Room and into the tunnel leading out. Lindsey thought she felt movement on the guideline. It wasn't from the girl next to her. It felt like someone was ahead coming toward them. *Had Joey gotten the other diver to the surface and come back into the cave?* Lindsey wondered. She hoped not. The visibility was still completely blown out and it was difficult enough to deal with one other diver in the conditions they were in. Adding a third diver would only complicate the situation.

Joey should know better. But Lindsey also knew Joey would be worried about her, especially since they were taking so long to exit. She would have to deal with it when the time came. For now, she had to focus on getting this girl out of the cave. She tried to kick harder to get them moving faster but it was no use with the girl dragging her legs and fins along the bottom. All Lindsey was doing was increasing her own breathing rate and wasting precious air that she might need to breathe before they were able to surface.

Lindsey resigned herself to moving slowly, inch by inch, pulling the girl along beside her. The movement on the line felt like it was getting closer. Someone was coming toward them. *Dammit, Joey! You know better!* Lindsey screamed at him in her head. She felt like screaming it through her regulator, but she knew all the girl would hear was unintelligible screaming and that would put her back into a bigger panic.

The line movement kept getting closer and closer. Lindsey estimated whoever it was had to be no farther than 30 feet ahead. She and Joey had practiced bump and go exits in the cave several times. This was a technique designed to get two divers out of a cave quickly in zero visibility. The diver in front swam with closed eyes while slowly counting to ten before stopping. The diver behind would also count to ten but remain in place. Once the second diver got to ten, he or she, they swapped roles, would begin swimming forward until bumping into the diver in front. Then the drill would start over.

During those drills they would come across a line arrow about every three cycles. The line arrows were placed on the line every hundred feet to mark the distance from the opening. That meant they were swimming about 30-35 feet each cycle. The movement Lindsey was feeling was similar to the movement she felt on the line when Joey was behind her and just beginning to swim toward her.

A few seconds later the line movement felt similar to what it felt like on the count of five, or 15 feet of distance. Lindsey decided to stop and wait for Joey to reach her. There was no point in them bumping into each other head on while both moving toward each other. She placed her right hand in front of her face and waited.

3, 2, 1…

Lindsey felt a hand bump into her right hand. Rather than pull back, the hand grasped hers and held tight. This wasn't Joey's hand though. Lindsey was certain of that. This hand had large rings on several fingers. There were at least three rings. Maybe more. This person was squeezing her hand tight, and the rings were cutting into her fingers. Lindsey tried to pull back, but he wouldn't release her hand. At least, Lindsey thought it was a he based on the size of his hand. It was either a he or a very large she. Either way, it was a strong person.

She felt his other hand slide down the guideline and grab her left wrist. He actually grabbed both her wrist and the wrist of the girl next to her. He had his hand clamped around both of their wrists. He then started pulling back on both of them hard. Lindsey wasn't sure how he was doing this, but he was swimming backwards and pulling them after him. And they were moving much faster than she had been moving with the girl.

Suddenly, Lindsey could hear the girl next to her begin to scream into her regulator. This brute had made her panic return. Lindsey had done so well to keep the girl calm and now she was going into a full-on panic. Lindsey wanted to reach over to her and try to reassure her, but the brute also had her right hand locked tight in his other hand. She couldn't even make sure that the girl still had her long-hosed regulator in her mouth. Well, as long as she continued to scream Lindsey knew she had air in her lungs.

By this point Lindsey had opened her eyes. She still couldn't see anything but the faint glow from what was probably the brute's dive light on the back of his hand. Lindsey could feel the hard metal of the Goodman handle that held the dive light in place on top of his hand against her palm. Lindsey started to fin faster. She figured as long as they were moving faster out of the cave she could assist. The faster they got out of the tunnel, the sooner she would be able to see and maybe get this brute to let go of them.

A few minutes later, the visibility began to clear a little more. Lindsey could now make out the outline of the diver in front of her. She couldn't recognize him. The visibility wasn't that good. But she could see the outline of his head and the mask on his face. She could also see the regulator in his mouth. It was a Poseidon. There were very few divers Lindsey knew of that used Poseidon regulators. And one of them was Jack Johnson.

40

Lindsey

Lindsey couldn't believe it. What were the chances of Jack Johnson being at Eddy Spring the same day she and Joey were there, and a couple of open water divers decided to foolishly go back to the Opera Room and get themselves into trouble? Jack must have seen Joey and the other diver surface. And once he encountered the silt, he would know there was trouble ahead.

The situation had been under control. Lindsey had been concerned about how things would go once they got to the rope at the bottom of the chimney. But she was dealing with the situation in the cave just fine without the help of anyone else, especially Jack Johnson.

All Jack had done was cause the girl next to her to begin panicking again. At least when Lindsey had encountered her, they had clear water coming from beyond the grate. When Jack bumped into them, they were still in zero visibility conditions. This girl had no clue what was going on. All she knew was that someone, or something, had just come up to them and started yanking them through the silt. The calmness Lindsey had worked so hard to get from her was completely gone.

Lindsey could feel the girl struggling next to her. She tried to move her hand up to the girl's wrist to get a better grip on her, but Jack was squeezing both their wrists too tightly. His grip was hurting Lindsey's wrist, which was sandwiched in between Jack's grip and the girl's wrist. Lindsey was certain the girl's wrist hurt even more. Maybe that was what she was crying about. Lindsey rethought that. The cry coming from her was a panicked cry not a cry from pain.

As Jack continued to pull them out from the cave, he was also moving them faster than the water current, which meant they were beginning to move away from the thick silt into water that had better visibility. Lindsey could see through the mask lenses on Jack's face and see his eyes. *It was Jack Johnson, alright.* She recognized those beady eyes anywhere. He wasn't looking back at her. He was just staring vacantly ahead of him, but strangely also a look of determination like she had never seen before.

She tried to wiggle her right hand free from his grasp, but that only caused him to tighten his grip, hurting it as well. Lindsey relaxed her right hand and hoped Jack would loosen his grip on it. She was already starting to feel the circulation in her fingers stop because of how tightly he was squeezing them. After about a minute she felt the grip on her right hand loosen and she started to regain some feeling in her fingers. She was careful not to fight his grip for fear he would clamp down on her again.

Unfortunately, his grip on her left wrist, and the girl's right wrist, didn't loosen up at all. While it felt like the fingers of her left hand had fallen asleep, Lindsey was thankful he had a tight grip because the girl was still struggling to get loose. That was part of the problem. Jack's tight grip on her wrist with the girl struggling to get her wrist loose only made the loss of feeling in her hand worse.

The visibility was clearing even more. Lindsey could see beyond Jack's head. She could also see the beam of light from the dive light she had strapped to the back of her left hand. That was another problem. Jack's grip was also placing pressure on the dive light and the handle was digging into the back of her hand. She tried to wiggle her hand to get the light to fall off but that only caused Jack to tighten his grip on both of their wrists, so she immediately stopped.

Lindsey looked into Jack's mask again. The look in his eyes hadn't changed. All she saw was that vacant stare. It was like he didn't even see her. She looked past his head and saw a glimmer of light behind Jack. Lindsey hoped that was the natural daylight dropping down into the cave and not another diver coming in to complicate things.

As they got closer to the light Lindsey saw it was daylight penetrating the opening of the cave. They were almost out! Maybe once they got to the rope Jack would let go of her hand and wrist. If he held onto them for much longer, she might lose some function in them due to nerve impingement and loss of blood circulation. He was holding on that tightly.

They finally arrived at the restriction near the opening of the cave. Jack flew through the restriction backwards like he had done it a thousand times. Then they came to a hard stop. Well, Lindsey and the girl did. Jack was still pulling but the girl was stuck against a rocky outcropping coming from the side of the tunnel. And Lindsey felt like her arms were about to be yanked out of their sockets.

Lindsey pulled back as hard as she could. She knew that would only cause Jack to tighten his grip but maybe he would understand that they were stuck on the inside of the restriction, and he needed to stop swimming backwards.

At first, Jack only doubled his effort to pull back. Lindsey looked into his eyes and saw the same blank stare. He wasn't understanding what was going on. Then suddenly something snapped, and he looked toward the girl. He must have noticed she was stuck because he pulled both of them to his left, their right, away from the outcropping. As soon as the girl cleared it and was in the opening of the restriction, Jack yanked them through.

Lindsey and the girl were forced through the tight space shoulder to shoulder. Lindsey could feel the wall on her side scraping against her right shoulder and then heard the tank on her right side clank against the rocky wall as it scraped through and squeezed against her like a vise. Once the bottom of the tank cleared the restriction, Lindsey felt the tank vise release and she and the girl popped out into the large, open cavern next to the grim reaper sign. Lindsey glanced at the sign and shuddered. There were almost two more divers added to the fatality list at Eddy Spring. It was a good thing she and Joey had been there when they were.

41

Joey

Five minutes had passed, and Joey still hadn't seen any bubbles around the buoy. Lindsey should have been out of the cave by this time. They had almost made it to the Opera Room when Joey encountered Alex and started leading him out. It shouldn't have taken that long for Lindsey to find Emily and lead her out. It was only 300 feet from the grate to the bottom of the chimney.

Under normal conditions that should only take about five or six minutes to swim. With a panicked, untrained diver it might take two to three times that amount of time. It had already been 20 minutes since he and Alex had surfaced.

Joey looked back up the hill toward Alex. He hadn't moved from his position on the bench. The kid was in shock. He probably thought he had killed Emily by leaving her behind. That must have been how Mike had felt leaving Joey behind when he got stuck in Jackson Blue. He hadn't really talked to Mike since that incident. He had tried but Mike always claimed to be busy and unable to talk. Mike also hadn't been cave diving again since that day. Joey was beginning to understand why. He would have to make a better effort at reaching out to Mike and talking to him. He had to convince Mike he didn't blame him for leaving him in the cave.

Suddenly, Joey heard a burst of bubbles from behind. He turned around and saw a flurry of bubbles a few feet away from the buoy. That had to be Lindsey and Emily, and probably Jack Johnson, as well. Considering how many bubbles he saw, it had to be three divers.

Joey decided to run around the edge of the spring basin and get as close to the buoy as he could. Maybe he could see down into the chimney. He carefully stepped off the platform and ran to the left, following the shoreline until he was just over the entrance to the cave. He tried to look down into the chimney but the reflection of the sun off the surface didn't allow him to see anything.

He remembered he was still holding his fins and mask. He quickly jumped into the water and strapped his fins on his feet, dropping the mask as he did so. He managed to snatch the mask back up before it sank out of reach. He slipped it on his head with the mask over his forehead. He finished strapping the fins on and lowered the mask down over his eyes as he kicked his way toward the buoy.

About halfway there he got the mask situated and dropped his face into the water just as he was passing over the edge of the chimney. He saw three divers 50 feet below him. He recognized Lindsey in her sidemount kit to the right of a diver with a single tank on her back, who was most likely Emily. There was a third diver, one in sidemount, in front of them facing them. That had to be Jack. And Jack was holding onto both of Lindsey's arms. It was difficult to tell from 50 feet up, but it looked like Lindsey was holding onto Emily's hand.

Joey watched as Emily tried to bolt for the surface. She was thrashing her left arm and both legs wildly. It looked like Jack had a firm grip on both Lindsey and Emily with his right hand. Emily was just a flag flapping in the wind tied down by her right arm.

Joey continued to watch from 50 feet above, completely helpless. He should have been getting his tanks on so he could descend down the chimney and help them instead of floating above watching.

42

Lindsey

No sooner had they passed through the restriction, Lindsey was looking at the grim reaper sign and the girl began thrashing wildly trying to bolt to the surface. Lindsey looked at her and noticed her long-hosed regulator was still in the girl's mouth. At least she was still breathing. Lindsey tried to reach for her with her right hand, but Jack clamped down even more forcefully on it. Her hand was going to be bruised.

Jack kept leading them toward the rope that held the buoy in place on the surface. The closer they got to the rope the more the girl thrashed. Lindsey wasn't sure if Jack was going to be able to keep her at depth. But the girl was still breathing from Lindsey's long-hosed regulator. She would get seven feet up and the regulator would either tear out of her mouth or she would pull Lindsey with her.

Lindsey could hold her own. She wasn't a weakling. She regularly moved around the 40-50 lbs scuba tanks in the fill station at the dive shop as well as at Eddy Spring when she was assisting with classes. But she didn't know if she would have the strength to overpower a diver in a full-on panic. For the first time, Lindsey was thankful Jack was there.

Then she rethought that. The girl had been calm on their way out of the cave. It wasn't until Jack arrived that she began to panic again.

It didn't matter at that point. All that mattered was trying to keep the girl from bolting to the surface because that would most definitely lead to her suffering significant injuries, maybe even death.

When they got to the rope, the girl thrashed even more wildly. The only thing keeping her down was Jack holding both of their wrists against the rocky bottom. The girl was flapping around like a flag in a hurricane.

Jack finally released his grip on Lindsey's right hand so he could grab the rope beside him. With her right hand free, Lindsey reached over and tried to grab the girl's free hand. It took her a few attempts, but she finally grabbed it and held on tight. The girl kept trying to thrash around. Lindsey managed to intertwine her fingers with the girl's fingers and began gently squeezing her hand. After several squeezes, the girl finally began to slow down her thrashing. Lindsey thought her actions might have been reassuring to the girl. Or maybe the girl was just getting exhausted. Either way, the result was the same.

Lindsey wanted Jack to release his grip on her left wrist so she could try to put her arm around the girl and comfort her, but he wasn't releasing it. If anything, his grip was even tighter than it had been. Instead, Lindsey gently rotated the girl's left wrist just enough so she could see the display on the dive computer mounted on her wrist. She couldn't get a good enough look at it to read the numbers, but she could tell the numbers were flashing. Just as Lindsey had feared, the girl had been underwater long enough to have exceeded the no decompression limits. They would have to ascend to 15 feet depth and stay there until her decompression obligation cleared. Maybe she could get her to move off the rope to a shallower area where they could rest on the bottom of the spring basin. She'd have to somehow convince Jack of that though.

Looking back at Jack, Lindsey noticed he was no longer looking their way. He was focused on the rope beside him. Jack had started to allow them to ascend along the rope. She looked back down and noticed they had ascended almost ten feet from the bottom. She looked at her backup dive computer on her right wrist and saw they were 38 feet deep. The girl was still relatively calm, at least compared to how she had been only moments earlier.

Lindsey hoped Jack realized the girl had a decompression obligation and planned on stopping to allow her to off gas the nitrogen that had built up in her body. She remembered Joey telling her that Jack had let him stay at his decompression stop longer than necessary so maybe he would.

Lindsey looked at the girl and made eye contact with her. She then gently squeezed her hand. The girl squeezed back. At least she was calm enough to respond. Lindsey slowly pulled her hand away from the girl's and held up her index finger signaling her to wait. She then pulled up the pressure gauge on her right tank, the one the girl was breathing from. She still had 500 psi in that tank. Not much. She would have to see how long of a decompression stop she had to do to determine if it was enough. She didn't bother looking at the pressure gauge on her left tank. She knew she had plenty of air for herself.

Slowly placing her hand around the girl's wrist, Lindsey rotated her arm so the dive computer display was facing her. Lindsey was thankful she was a divemaster and familiar with a multitude of dive computers. The dive computer the girl was wearing was one she was very familiar with.

She looked at the flashing numbers. The number under stop depth, the depth they would have to stop before continuing the ascent to the surface, was flashing 10. *That was good,* Lindsey thought. If it had been flashing 20 or 30 that would have meant multiple decompression stops and Lindsey didn't think the girl would calmly get through that.

She looked at the time to surface number next to the number 10. That number was 7, meaning they would have to stay at 10 feet for at least 7 minutes before continuing to the surface. That was going to be tough. Lindsey didn't know if the girl could remain calm for that long. And she didn't know if she had enough air to last that long, either. She would have to deal with that when the time came. Jack must have full tanks. He could donate his long-hosed regulator.

Lindsey looked at Jack. He was still focused on the rope and his own dive computer. He was letting the rope slip a foot at a time to allow them to ascend slowly. She tried to get his attention to let him know the girl had a decompression obligation. He was so focused on what he was doing he didn't notice her waving her hand in front of his face. Lindsey looked at her dive computer again and saw they were at 24 feet of depth. She wanted to stop at 15 feet to give them a buffer. Decompression models allowed for that.

The depth readout on her computer slowly reduced by a foot at a time as Jack eased them up the rope. When they reached 17 feet, Lindsey tried to get his attention again. Jack still didn't look away from the rope and his own dive computer. She finally decided to tap him on the head, even though she actually felt like knocking him upside the head.

Jack's head snapped around toward Lindsey as soon as she tapped him on the top of the head. He glared at her like he was angry. Lindsey ignored the look and directed his attention to the girl's dive computer. She tapped the display of the computer and gave him the hand signal to stop and hold, slicing her hand palm down in front of his face and then making a fist.

A look of realization flashed across Jack's eyes. He looked back at his dive computer. Lindsey took the opportunity to look at her own dive computer. They had just arrived at 15 feet. Just as she was about to signal Jack, she saw him grip the rope firmly. Lindsey immediately turned toward the girl and grabbed her free hand and squeezed it reassuringly again. They looked into each other's eyes and Lindsey squeezed again. This was going to be a long seven minutes.

43

Joey

Joey floated at the surface watching the three divers 50 feet below as he continued to feel helpless. It looked like Lindsey was struggling to get her hand free from Jack. If Jack let them both go, they would likely shoot to the surface. That would not only result in a definite injury for Emily, but Lindsey might also get hurt. Joey cursed himself for not thinking ahead and having his tanks clipped onto his harness.

Jack suddenly released Lindsey's right hand and grabbed onto the rope. His other hand still holding Lindsey's and Emily's arms together. Joey watched as Lindsey swung around to face Emily and tried to grab her free hand. She finally got it in her grasp and about 30 seconds later Emily stopped thrashing so much.

Good for Lindsey! Joey knew Lindsey was an excellent divemaster and had a knack for being able to keep students and divers calm, but this was an extreme situation and she had still managed to do it. Lindsey and Emily remained facing each other as Jack slowly led them up the rope toward the surface, toward Joey.

Joey watched them get closer as they slowly ascended up the rope. He watched as Lindsey let go of the girl's hand and looked at her right tank pressure gauge. He knew she had to be worried about whether there was enough air to get Emily safely to the surface. Then he watched as Lindsey looked at Emily's dive computer. He couldn't be certain, but it looked like Lindsey's body had stiffened. That wasn't good.

Joey continued to watch the scene play out below him, feeling more and more helpless the closer they got. He couldn't descend to help them underwater, but at least he could be on the surface to lend a hand when they got there. And from the way Lindsey had reacted after she had looked at the pressure gauge and dive computer, they might need help.

Lindsey was waving her hand in front of Jack's face. He didn't seem to be responding though. Joey watched as Lindsey tapped Jack on the head and his head snapped toward her. Joey jumped when he saw that rapid movement. But the trio suddenly stopped, probably about 15 feet below him. Emily must have a decompression obligation. That made sense since Alex was only a minute from having one himself and he had been underwater a lot less time than she had.

Joey watched Lindsey grab Emily's hand and look at her. Lindsey was doing her magic again. Maybe she could keep Emily calm long enough for them to do whatever decompression obligation she had.

Then he watched as Jack pulled his long-hosed regulator from around his neck and jerked the regulator Emily had been breathing from out of her mouth. Jack tried to force his regulator into Emily's mouth, but she was already thrashing again, this time causing Lindsey to get thrashed around, as well.

44

Lindsey

Lindsey had been so busy looking at the girl, trying to keep her calm, she hadn't noticed Jack pulling his long-hosed regulator from around his neck. What she did notice was him jerking her own long-hosed regulator from the girl's mouth and trying to force his into her mouth. But by that time, the girl was thrashing again.

Lindsey tried to squeeze her hand to calm her and get her to take the new regulator, but she wasn't paying attention. She was thrashing wildly and taking Lindsey along with her now that she had a grip of Lindsey's free hand.

Lindsey could kill Jack for doing what he just did. How could he yank the regulator out of the mouth of a diver that had just been in a panic? *He was such an idiot!* How had he managed to rescue anyone before this?

Lindsey was able to get her right hand free from the girl. She snatched the regulator from Jack's hand and thrusted it in front of the girl's mask so that it was the only thing the girl could see. The girl immediately reached up and grabbed it with her free hand and shoved it in her mouth. Lindsey kept her hand over the purge button and pressed it as soon as the regulator was in her mouth. If she hadn't done that the girl would have gotten a mouthful, and possibly a lungful, of water. Not only was the girl not in the right frame of mind to remember to purge the regulator herself, but she also probably wasn't familiar with Poseidon regulators and the fact that the purge buttons on them were on the side and not in front like most regulators.

As soon as Lindsey was certain the girl was breathing from the regulator, she turned toward Jack and smacked him hard on his mask. She smacked him so hard that she knew he was going to have a mark on his face in the outline of the mask. Maybe it would even leave a bruise. He deserved it for what he was doing to this poor girl.

Lindsey turned back toward the girl, grabbed her hand, and looked into her eyes. Lindsey squeezed her hand several times to let her know she would be okay. Lindsey also kept an eye on Jack. She wasn't going to let him do anything else stupid. If she had to, she would elbow him right in the bridge of his nose.

Rotating her wrist so she could see her dive computer display, Lindsey saw that they had about four more minutes before they could ascend to the surface. She would double check that against the girl's dive computer when they were down to a minute remaining.

Looking back at Jack, Lindsey glared at him. He glared back, unfazed by her. *This guy is a sociopath,* she thought. He has no clue what's going on. He just had to have the girl breathing from his regulator. She could already hear him on the surface talking about how he had rescued another diver. Well, he wasn't going to get away with it this time.

45

Joey

Joey watched in helpless amazement from 15 feet above. He couldn't believe what he had just witnessed. Why would Jack just pull Emily's regulator out of her mouth? The regulator she was breathing from was still fully functional.

Then he watched in surprise as Lindsey snatched the regulator from his hand and placed it against Emily's mask. Emily reached for it and brought it to her mouth, fortunately purging the water out of it before taking a breath. Then he watched as his girlfriend of two years punched Jack Johnson in the face.

He anxiously waited for Jack to retaliate. Instead, Jack reached for the rope and grabbed it tightly. Joey couldn't believe Lindsey had just gotten away with punching Jack Johnson. When they reached the surface, it was going to be very interesting. He was glad he was there because he had a feeling he would be needed.

46

Lindsey

When they had one minute left on the girl's decompression obligation according to Lindsey's dive computer, Lindsey rotated the girl's wrist to get a look at her dive computer display and confirm. Time left at 10 feet read one minute. Lindsey was torn between padding the decompression stop a few more minutes because the girl had been exerting so much energy thrashing around or going directly to the surface and getting her to a safe place.

She looked into the girl's eyes and saw that they were starting to get wide again. Lindsey decided they would have to take their chances and ascend at the end of the minute. The decompression models were on the conservative side anyway, especially on the dive computers made for recreational divers, so the girl should be okay.

Once the minute passed and the girl's dive computer displayed "DECO CLEAR" Lindsey tapped Jack on the head again. He flinched and then glared at her as she gave him the thumb up signal. Rather than resuming their ascent he looked away from her and held tightly onto the rope.

Lindsey looked back at the girl. She was seconds away from going into panic mode and thrashing around again. She could see it in her eyes. Lindsey tapped Jack harder, and this time practically punched him in his mask when she shoved her fist with her thumb up right in front of his eyes. He flinched even more but looked away again, refusing to ascend. Lindsey would have ascended with the girl without him, but he still had a strong grip on their wrists. She tried to twist her wrist out of his grasp but that only made him clamp down even tighter.

Just as Lindsey was turning her head to check on the girl, the girl began thrashing again. Maybe that would convince Jack to begin ascending, she thought. Instead, he yanked them both down closer to him. The girl was thrashing so much her free arm and legs were swinging into both Lindsey and Jack.

During one of the wild swings, the girl's arm smacked against Lindsey's mask and knocked it crooked on her face. Water immediately rushed into the mask and temporarily caused Lindsey to not be able to see anything. She tried to straighten the mask on her face, but she kept feeling the girl's arm smack into her head. Lindsey hated opening her eyes underwater without a mask on because it burned whenever she did.

Lindsey took a deep breath and held it. She then forced her eyes open. After the initial shock of the burning passed, she tried to focus her vision. Everything remained distorted but at least she could make out the girl's arm swinging wildly in front of her. Lindsey watched and dodged it as she one-handedly straightened the mask back over her eyes. She then let the breath she had been holding out through her nose, forcing the water still inside the mask to escape under the skirt sealing the mask to her face. The water level in the mask dropped just below her eyes. She blinked several times to relieve the burning and clear her vision again. She then took another breath and forced it out of her nose, clearing the remainder of the water out of the mask. She blinked several more times to try to get some relief.

With her vision restored, Lindsey turned her attention back on the girl. She seemed to be tiring sooner than she had earlier. Lindsey reached out and grabbed the girl's free hand and squeezed it hard. The girl struggled to pull away, but Lindsey held on tight and kept squeezing. The girl finally looked at Lindsey and her thrashing started to slow. Lindsey pulled the girl closer while remaining focused on her eyes.

With the girl finally calm again, Lindsey looked at Jack. He hadn't moved. He remained anchored to the line by his right hand and held on tight to the girls with his left hand, not even looking at them. Lindsey slowly released the girl's hand and tapped Jack on the head again. Just as he turned his head to look up at her, Lindsey slammed her right elbow hard into his mask. She watched in amusement as blood immediately started rising up the lenses.

47

Joey

Joey waited impatiently on the surface for them to ascend. *Why weren't they moving??* They were just hovering 15 feet below him. Jack hadn't even responded to Lindsey punching him in the face. He wondered whether the girl actually had a decompression obligation or if Jack was just prolonging things to try to make himself look better. Joey considered swimming back to his tanks to get them on so he could descend underwater to help, but he was afraid they would surface while he was gone.

Five minutes had passed when Joey saw Lindsey look at her dive computer and then Emily's dive computer. Lindsey tapped Jack on the head and gave him the thumb up signal indicating she was ready to surface. Jack turned away, ignoring her.

Suddenly, Emily began to thrash her free arm and legs again. Joey watched as her arm smacked Lindsey in the head several times, almost knocking the mask completely off Lindsey's face. Then Lindsey reached for her mask. It must have been knocked off. That was going to piss Lindsey off for sure. Not at the girl, but at Jack for not ascending when she told him to. And when Lindsey was angry, you didn't want to be the focus of her anger. She was a petite girl, but her anger matched that of a giant.

Joey watched helplessly as his girlfriend had to deal with a panicked diver and an uncooperative sociopath at the same time. When it looked like Lindsey got the mask situated properly on her face, she grabbed Emily's free hand and held it. Joey watched as Emily eventually began to slow her movements and calm down. Lindsey and Emily remained face to face for what seemed like forever to Joey.

Then Joey watched as Lindsey released Emily's hand and tapped Jack on the head again. Apparently, she was going to try again to get him to ascend. Just as Jack was turning his head to look at her, Lindsey planted her tiny, bony elbow right in the middle of his face. Joey flinched at that. She had never elbowed him in the face, but he had gotten elbowed in the ribs a few times when they play wrestled. Those never felt good and always knocked the wind out of Joey. He was certain Jack was seeing stars after that blow to his face and his ego.

48

Lindsey

Jack released his grip on the girls' wrists so he could flood his mask and clear the blood out. As soon as her wrist was free Lindsey grabbed hold of the girl and pulled her away from Jack and began finning as fast as she could while hitting the power inflator button on her BC to get them to the surface. The girl had been breathing from Jack's regulator and the hose that tethered it to his tank was only 7 feet long. That meant the girl would have to release the regulator and ascend the last ten feet without one in her mouth.

Lindsey still had her long-hosed regulator available, and it still had between 100 and 200 psi of air in it. The issue was getting the girl to take it as Lindsey was trying to get them both to the surface. It was only ten feet. The girl would probably be screaming, which was a good thing. She just needed to get her to the surface before she tried to take in a breath.

Lindsey felt a hand clamp over her ankle and pull her down. *You bastard!!!* she screamed into her regulator. Although she was certain all he would hear were garbled grunts. Lindsey and the girl were yanked back down. Fortunately, they hadn't ascended enough for the girl to get the regulator ripped out of her mouth. When they got on the same level as Jack, she saw that he had one leg wrapped around the rope to hold himself at that depth and had grabbed both their ankles and pulled them down.

Jack looked angry. Lindsey could see a vein on his forehead

popping out from under the mask skirt. And there was a red glow coming from the mask. *Well, that was probably from the blood*, she thought with a snicker. Lindsey faced Jack and brought her hand up in front of his face, causing him to flinch away from her again. But all she was doing this time was giving him a different finger up signal.

Lindsey watched as Jack's leg began sliding along the rope. She still had air in her BC, making her positively buoyant. He was having trouble holding them down. Lindsey slyly reached for the power inflator button and tapped it a few times to get more air in her BC. She watched as the rope slid several more inches through his leg.

Jack couldn't grab onto the rope with either hand because one was holding her, and the other was holding the girl. Lindsey thought about inflating the girl's BC but then remembered she didn't have any air left in her tank. Or did she? They had ascended more than 80 feet, meaning any air they had in their BCs and hoses would expand by at least 3.5 times.

Lindsey's hand shot across to the girl's power inflator and she squeezed the button hard. She felt a short surge of air move through the hose before it stopped. It wasn't much but every little bit helped. And this little bit did. Lindsey watched as the rope continued sliding faster along Jack's leg. *I hope you get rope burn, you bastard!* she thought as they started moving quickly toward the surface.

49

Joey

Joey watched the events unfold below him, still helpless to offer any assistance. Immediately after Lindsey had elbowed Jack in the face, she grabbed Emily and began swimming toward Joey on the surface. They ascended a few feet. It looked, to Joey, like their fins were even with Jack's head. Then he watched Jack release the rope and grab both girls by the ankles as he wrapped one leg around the rope. Lindsey and Emily were yanked away from Joey back to where they had been at 15 feet of depth.

Turning to look at the platform where his tanks were hanging, Joey again contemplated heading to get them. They were too far though. It would take him 10 minutes to swim to the tanks and back plus another couple of minutes to get the tanks clipped on enough to descend below the surface. That was too much time.

Or was it? Jack seemed intent on keeping the girls at 15 feet for a while. Maybe Joey would have time. Just as Joey was about to swim to retrieve his tanks, he saw the three divers below him begin to ascend again. The rope was slipping through Jack's leg. He wasn't able to keep them at depth any longer.

Joey finally understood what was happening when he watched Lindsey reach across to Emily and grab her power inflator. Lindsey had inflated her own BC and was trying to use the little bit of remaining air in Emily's hoses to give Emily's BC some positive buoyancy. And it was working!

50

Lindsey & Joey

As they were finally ascending toward the surface, Lindsey looked up and noticed for the first time that Joey was floating just above them. When she got close enough to touch him, Lindsey grabbed his ankle and tried to pull herself to the surface even more, hoping Joey would be buoyant enough to not be pulled underwater.

***

Joey watched Lindsey reach up and grab his ankle. She began pulling him down, or rather, pulling herself up. Joey grabbed his own inflator as he took in a deep breath, covered the mouthpiece with his mouth, and pressed the exhaust button as he forcefully exhaled into his BC.

He then turned his attention back to Lindsey and Emily. They were almost within reach. Joey stretched his arms out trying to get her attention so she could reach up and grab his hands.

***

Lindsey felt Joey being pulled down into the water for a moment before he rose back up taking her and the girl with him. She risked a glance at Jack and noticed the rope was sliding through his leg even faster. The momentum was too great. He wasn't going to be able to stop them.

She turned back toward Joey and pulled herself up even harder. She released his ankle and reached up for his BC. If she could grab onto one of the straps, she could make it to the surface. Instead, she felt Joey grab her hand and begin to pull her up even faster.

A few seconds later Lindsey's head broke the surface. Two seconds after that, the girl's head broke the surface. Jack was still below them holding onto their ankles, struggling to pull them back down.

"Kick girl! Kick with all your might!" Lindsey screamed as she started kicking at Jack herself.

Jack finally released his grip on the girls' ankles. As soon as Lindsey felt her ankle free, she began kicking back away from the buoy and pulling the girl with her. But Jack broke the surface before they moved very far, grabbed the valve on the girl's tank, and pulled her toward him.

"What the hell are y'all doing?" Jack yelled at them. "I'm trying my darndest to get you back to the surface safely and all y'all do is struggle and fight me!"

Lindsey was preparing to go on a tirade against Jack when she heard someone call from behind her.

"Are y'all aight?" someone on shore called out. "We have tha ambulance comin'. They shud be 'ere in about 5 minits."

Lindsey turned her head and saw a crowd had gathered on the banks of the spring basin.

"We're alright now," Jack called out. "I managed to find these girls lost in a silt out and bring 'em back out. I'm gonna get 'em over to the steps now. Just give me a minute."

Lindsey glared at Jack. Not only was he trying to claim rescuing this girl, but he was trying to claim Lindsey as one of his rescue victims. She finally knew exactly how Joey had felt.

PART 3

51

Joey and Lindsey sat across from Alex and Emily in a booth in the back corner of a diner in Ponce de Leon. It was the same diner where Joey and Lindsey had eaten their first meal together. It hadn't really been a date. It had happened after their first dive together at Morrison Spring where Joey had made a fool of himself in front of Lindsey. And Lindsey had still suggested they go to lunch together.

Earlier at Eddy Spring, at some point while Joey was looking down at Lindsey, Emily, and Jack Johnson, a crowd had formed on shore near the entrance to the cave. Joey was so focused on what was happening 15 feet below him that he hadn't noticed. Alex had though, and he had pulled himself from his self-pity and joined the crowd.

"I could just barely make the three of you out underwater from the shore," Alex told the others. "I saw the bubbles coming to the surface and saw dark areas below it. I couldn't tell what was going on though. I was really hoping that Em was part of the dark shadows I was seeing," he continued as he pulled her in close to him with his arm wrapped around her shoulders.

"I'm just glad y'all are both okay," Lindsey said. "That could have ended up so much worse."

Once the girls and Jack had surfaced, Jack immediately took back control of the situation. Everyone on shore began clapping and whooping and hollering their appreciation for him. Jack's reputation was well known, not just in Marianna, but in most of the southeast.

Everyone on shore assumed if Jack was there, he must have rescued more divers in trouble.

The ambulance arrived and the medics checked Alex and Emily's vital signs while asking them several questions. Both were fine and exhibited no signs of decompression sickness, so they were told to hydrate, rest, and stay out of the water for a couple of days. And they were to call the Divers' Alert Network, DAN for short, and go to the nearest hospital if they started to feel any differently than they were feeling at that time.

Since neither of their dive computers showed a decompression violation, they didn't think they would have any issues. To be on the safe side they were going to abide by the recommendations of the ambulance crew. All four divers had opted out of ordering sodas and instead had large cups of ice water on the table between them.

"I'm so glad the two of you started your dive into the cave when you did. If you hadn't I think we'd both be dead in there," Emily remarked.

Joey shuddered as he had flashbacks to when he had found a dead body beyond the grate in Eddy Spring and had to drag it out.

"Are you cold?" the waitress asked as she approached the table to take their food order. "I can shut that fan off."

"No, I'm fine," Joey responded. "You can leave it on. Thanks."

The waitress took their orders and disappeared into the kitchen.

"Well, we did find you and you did make it out alive with nothing but a few bruises," Lindsey remarked as she looked at Emily's right wrist and rubbed her own left wrist where Jack had held a tight grip on them.

"What's the deal with that guy?" Emily asked. "I know I was on the verge of panic the entire time. If it wasn't for you, Lindsey, I don't think I would have made it out of there alive."

Lindsey reached across the table, took Emily's hand in hers, and gave it a gentle squeeze.

"That right there!" Emily exclaimed. "That's what kept me calm.

Then that guy shows up and grabs the two of us. It just pushed me over the edge, and I couldn't help myself. If it wasn't for you, I would have probably drowned in that cave."

"Well… There's a little history there," Lindsey replied.

"Yeah, he claimed rescuing me about a month ago," Joey cut in.

"What??" Emily and Alex said in unison.

"Well, I was on a dive over in Marianna in Jackson Blue with a buddy of mine," Joey began.

About 15 minutes later, Joey concluded his story, ending it with showing them the headline on his phone from the local newspaper in Marianna with Jack claiming to have rescued a cave diver, including a large full color photograph of Jack standing in the water next to Joey, who fortunately, was not recognizable because he had kept his face down and away from the camera.

Alex and Emily sat across from him with their jaws dropped in shock.

"After seeing what he did today, I can only imagine what he would have done if I hadn't cooperated with him that day," Joey added.

"How do you think he even knew something was going on today?" Alex asked.

"I think he was already in the water when we surfaced and got to the steps. You were in shock, and I was so focused on you, we didn't even notice him there. He must have overheard us talking." Joey explained. "And then when you started yelling about Emily, he definitely heard all of that. He knew something was going on in the cave. That and when he found the line from my reel going into the cave and then encountered the silt in the tunnel, it wasn't hard to figure out."

"He's an opportunist," Lindsey added. "He did this with Joey. Before that, with a couple of other divers that we know. And now with us today."

Emily and Alex sat there in disbelief at what they were hearing.

"Just wait. It will be all over the local papers tomorrow. I guarantee Jack Johnson somehow got the news to them about his latest rescue," Lindsey continued.

Just then the waitress brought out two of their orders and set them on the table. She disappeared into the kitchen and came out a few seconds later with the other two orders. The group ate in silence. They were all ravenous after the experience they had just shared. When they were finished, they all sat back holding their bellies.

"I didn't realize how hungry I was," Emily said.

"Yeah, well, you did exert a lot of energy on that dive!" Lindsey remarked and laughed.

The rest of the group joined in on the laughter.

52

Lindsey

The next day Lindsey woke up early and grabbed her phone. She immediately pulled up Google and typed the words eddy spring rescue into the search bar. The first few results were from two years prior about the missing diver that was never found, the one Joey had pulled out of the cave for Earl Hewitt. The fourth result was dated that morning and had Jack Johnson's name at the forefront. Lindsey clicked on the link.

LOCAL HERO SAVES 2 MORE DIVERS!

Local hero, Jack Johnson, saved 2 more divers, this time at Eddy Spring, located just outside of Ponce de Leon, FL. These rescues happened only one month after Johnson saved a diver from the depths of the head spring at Blue Springs Recreational Park in Marianna, FL.

Johnson happened to be getting ready for a dive at Eddy Spring, allegedly preparing to look for signs of the body of the diver who disappeared after having been last seen there 2 years ago. Johnson was already in the water getting his oxygen tanks on when he saw 2 other divers come to the surface crying about their girlfriends who were still in the cave. One of them happened to be the diver he rescued last month.

Johnson grabbed his oxygen tanks and rushed to the entrance of the cave. He descended into the dark opening and immediately encountered blackout conditions. He knew he only had minutes, possibly only seconds, to find the girls and affect a rescue before it turned into a recovery.

"Rescues are one of the most dangerous things you can do in cave diving," Johnson said. "The victims are always panicked. I didn't think about my own safety, though. All that was on my mind was finding those girls and getting them out alive."

The girls were fortunate to have Johnson at the spring preparing for a dive at that moment. Had he not been, they would have certainly perished inside the cave, maybe never to be found again.

Readers may recall that another diver was reported missing from Eddy Spring about 2 years ago and a body has never turned up.

Lindsey couldn't believe what she had just read. Jack Johnson was taking full credit for the rescue. Actually, who was she kidding? She did believe it. This was now the third confirmed time this had happened. Lindsey quickly scanned a couple more news articles about the incident, and they all said basically the same thing. The story must have been shared among the papers and changed just enough to make them unique to each source.

Lindsey sent Joey a text message.

Have u read the news stories about the rescue yesterday?

Joey responded immediately.

Ya doesnt surprise me. Same that happened 2 me Jim & Gary. He even mentioned me to the reporter.

L: *Come by the shop when u get off work*

J: *Already planning 2*

Lindsey didn't have to ask Joey to come by the shop. He always did anyway. She wanted to make sure he did this time as well. She wasn't sure why. She didn't have anything in particular to say to him. But she wasn't going to just let this go. Maybe by the time he got to the shop she would have a plan.

53

Lindsey & Joey

A little after five, Lindsey heard the chimes from the door to the shop. She looked up and saw Joey walking in. He didn't look very happy. She ran out from behind the counter and rushed over to him.

"What's going on, sweetie?"

"Just a bad day. The cave diving groups have been blowing up over this latest Jack Johnson rescue. All the Jackasses are praising him up and down for another job well done. Several people have even dropped my name into the conversation implying I was one of the divers that had to be rescued again."

Lindsey already knew all this. Mondays were typically slow at the shop until around 6 when everyone who had rented scuba equipment and scuba tanks over the weekend stopped in to drop them off. She spent most of the day doing paperwork. She had gotten pretty efficient at it and that left her with lots of free time. Free time to spend browsing the social media forums and groups.

"Well don't go borrowin' trouble, sweetie. We'll figure somethin' out," Lindsey tried to console him.

Truth be told, she had no idea how to deal with this. Her name had also popped into the discussions and people were calling her and Joey the perfect pair for each other and predicting that they would both die in a cave together within a year. Either Joey hadn't seen those comments, or he was trying to protect Lindsey from them.

Lindsey wrapped her arms around Joey and held him tight. He

hugged her back, and they remained that way for several minutes until the door chime sounded again.

"Am I interrupting you two love birds?"

"Oh no, Roger, we just haven't seen each other all day. Bringing back your rentals?"

"I am. I'll drop them in the back for you. Do I owe you anything?" Roger asked.

"Nope, you're all paid up. Picking it up again in a couple weeks?"

"You know me! I have to eventually get my own equipment though. This rental stuff is getting expensive."

"You can always finance some equipment through us, Rog. You know we finance here. It will be the same as if you're renting it except after a couple of years the equipment will be yours and you can keep it at home. We even throw in a free service each year."

"I know. I know. You've told me this several times. I'm just not sure exactly what I want. I'll give it some more thought. See you in a couple," he yelled back as he walked out the door.

Lindsey walked behind the counter and logged the rental return into the computer program she had already pulled up on the screen. Then she turned to Joey.

"We'll figure something out, sweetie. That sociopath can't keep doing this and getting away with it. The Jackasses will eventually begin to figure it out. They can't all be that gullible."

Joey thought about what Lindsey said. She was right. Besides, what could they do about it? If they posted anything in response it would only draw them into unwinnable internet arguments and those who did believe the rescues were real would become more convinced of their legitimacy. It was best to keep quiet.

An hour and a half later Lindsey was shutting off most of the lights in the shop, leaving only a couple on for security. Joey stepped out of the shop while Lindsey set the alarm and quickly followed him and locked the door.

"What do you want to do for dinner?" Lindsey asked Joey.

"How about we go to that little place down the road? We haven't been there in a while."

"Okay, I'll follow you," Lindsey replied.

They each got into their cars and drove the short distance to the restaurant, one of their favorite places.

Lindsey and Joey were sitting in their booth sipping their sodas waiting for the burgers they ordered to be brought out. Joey was telling Lindsey about his day at work.

"It was a tough day. Typical Monday. Everyone rushes in first thing with their sick dogs and cats. The worst part are the ones that should have gone to emergency care over the weekend but put it off because they didn't want to pay the emergency fees. We ended up having to euthanize six dogs today. It was heartbreaking. Only one of the families even bothered to stay in the exam room when we did it. I felt so bad for those dogs." Joey was practically crying as he was telling Lindsey about it.

"Things finally started to slow down after lunch. That's when I had some time to get on the socials and started reading all the crap on there. Then…"

Just then the door to the restaurant slammed open. Joey had déjà vu. This was just like when Earl came barreling into the Italian restaurant where Joey and Lindsey had their first date. Only this time it wasn't Earl. It was Jack Johnson.

Another man followed Jack in. *Strange.* Joey had never seen anyone with Jack. Joey recognized the man from the dive sites but didn't know his name. They must have been diving one of the caves in the area earlier in the day. Maybe Ebro or Line Eater. Or maybe they had been over near Judges Spring on Holmes Creek.

Lindsey turned around to see what had caused Joey to stop talking midsentence and saw Jack and his buddy. She quickly turned back to Joey and grabbed his hands.

"Just ignore them, sweetie."

Joey faced Lindsey. "I feel like going up to him and punching him out."

"I know, sweetie, but it won't do a bit of good. You know how he is. He thinks the sun comes up just to hear him crow."

That softened Joey a bit. He always loved it when Lindsey interjected her cute southernisms into the conversation. She didn't do it intentionally. It was the way she had been brought up. Probably learned most of them from her grandmother. But it always had the same effect on Joey.

"You're right," he replied. He glanced back at Jack and they made eye contact. It looked like Jack was glaring at Joey with hatred so intense Joey thought Jack wanted to stomp over to their booth, pull him out of it, and beat him to death.

Instead, Jack smiled, although the smile didn't reach into his eyes, and slowly walked toward their booth with his friend. As he got closer, Joey noticed that his nose had a cut across the bridge and looked a little crooked, like he had been in a boxing match…with an elbow.

"How y'all doing today?" Jack asked from the end of their booth as he carefully rubbed his nose. "Y'all doin' okay after that little incident yesterday? How are your little buddies?"

He actually sounded sincere and like he really cared but his eyes told a different story. The hatred remained in them, even with the smile hanging just below.

"We're doing just fine," Lindsey replied. "No thanks to you."

Jack's hand shot up to his chest over his heart like he had been wounded.

"Whaddya mean darlin'? If it wasn't for me, you'd probably be dead in that cave at Eddy Spring."

This time it was Joey who reached across the table and grabbed Lindsey's hands and squeezed them tight. She had been about to let loose on Jack but then stopped herself.

"Well, aren't you precious," Lindsey retorted. It wasn't meant as a question, or a compliment.

"I'll let y'all get back to it. Me and Jonathon just came in for a quick bite after some exploration we did up the road in Ebro. You wouldn't believe the passage we found today! Sadly, we had to pull the line out cuz it's far too dangerous for anyone else to go into. Well, y'all stay safe. Don't get yourselves into any more predicaments y'all can't get yourselves out of. I'm not *always* close by."

Joey started to get up to go after Jack and give him a piece of his mind. Lindsey reached out and grabbed his hands just as he was about to slide out of the end of the booth and stand up. Joey looked back at her. Lindsey looked just as upset, if not more so, than Joey felt. But at least she had the sense to keep calm in a public place.

Joey felt his anger subside a bit, but still thought about slashing the tires on Jack's truck when they left. That would be too obvious, though. He was going to have to come up with something to put Jack Johnson in his place.

54

Joey

Lindsey and Joey finished their burgers and opted to skip any of the southern sweets offered on the menu. As much as Joey would have liked one, he had been doing a good job of keeping his weight down. And he really didn't want to spend any more time that close to Jack Johnson.

As they walked back to their cars they passed by Jack's truck. He looked at the oversized tires that had to cost several hundred dollars each. Joey put his hand in his pocket and felt the smoothness of his pocketknife. He could do it so quickly. No one would even see. Once again, he thought better of it. Whatever he did would have to be better than that.

As soon as they got back to their cars Lindsey went on a tirade.

"The nerve of him!" she yelled.

Joey stood there quietly and watched. He knew better than to try to calm her down, or to say anything at all. Lindsey just had to get it out of her system and then she would be her usual calm, logical self. It was rare she got like this, but occasionally someone would anger her enough for her to lose her composure.

"I can't believe he's still going on about rescuing us. After what happened! And did you notice his nose? I must have broken it when I slammed my elbow into his face. I should have hit him harder and knocked him out and left him at the bottom of the chimney to drown."

Joey had more flashbacks. This time to the look on Lindsey's face two years earlier during the Earl thing. He pushed those out of his mind.

"I think he actually believes he rescued us. He probably thinks when I elbowed him it was accidental. He must be living in his own little fantasy world."

Then she yelled out a long guttural grunt. She was about done, thought Joey. He waited a few more seconds just to be sure. When Lindsey didn't say anything, Joey took a step toward her, wrapped his arms around her and held her tight. He felt the stiffness leave her body as she melted into his arms and wrapped her own arms around him. They stood there for a few minutes holding each other.

"Let's get out of here," Lindsey said. "Let's go for a walk on the beach. I need to clear my head."

Joey walked Lindsey to the driver's side of her car to open the door for her. Lindsey stopped as they rounded the back of the car.

"Doesn't that truck over there belong to that sociopath?" she asked Joey.

"U-U-Um, I think it might," he replied, fearful for what was coming next.

"Give me your pocketknife," Lindsey demanded.

"For what?"

"Just give it to me!" she insisted.

"Not until you tell me what you're going to do with it, Linds!"

Lindsey stood in front of Joey with her hand out waiting for Joey to hand over the knife.

"Listen, we just ran into him inside the diner. If he comes out and finds his tire stabbed flat or scratches on the side of the truck, he's going to know it was us. That's just going to make things worse. Just leave it be. He'll get what's coming to him," Joey pleaded.

He couldn't blame Lindsey for what she wanted to do. He had the same thought both in the restaurant and as he walked past Jack's truck. He couldn't believe he was the one talking sense into Lindsey.

Usually it was the other way around. But Jack Johnson had gotten so deep under Lindsey's skin that it was making her irrational. Joey didn't like seeing her this way. He had to figure out a way to put an end to all of this before it was too late.

55

Joey

The gossip on the internet only got worse as the week went on. Joey had hoped it would die down and people would get tired of it. But with Jack claiming two rescues only a month apart, of a couple of cave divers that were dating each other, it kept the chatter in full force. Not only that, but Lindsey had a slow week at work and was able to spend more time than usual on social media reading all the comments.

Every evening when Joey stopped by after work Lindsey had gotten more and more angry at Jack Johnson over what she had read earlier in the day. The discussions went from merely praising Jack for his amazing efforts to denigrating Lindsey and Joey openly. People were posting that neither Lindsey nor Joey should be cave diving. They were not only a danger to themselves, but also a danger to others who might be cave diving in the same cave as them, as well as a danger to those like Jack who would eventually have to go into a cave to recover their bodies.

Joey was upset about it, even more so than when he was the sole focus of the internet chatter. Part of it was Joey's concern about how Lindsey was taking all the information. He was so focused on trying to calm her down that he didn't have time to be upset about it himself. He cringed every time he went to see Lindsey after work because he knew she was going to be livid with the new things that had been posted earlier in the day. Something had to be done about the situation, but Joey hadn't yet come up with a plan.

The weekend was approaching, and Lindsey had it off since she had worked the previous one assisting with a class. Joey was concerned she would want to go cave diving like they usually did on her weekends off. He wanted to go but he didn't want to run into any of the characters that had been posting derogatory stuff about them online.

On Thursday, Lindsey finally brought up the subject of diving that weekend.

"Do you want to go dive Jackson Blue this weekend or would you rather rent a boat and hit one of the other caves on the pond?" Lindsey asked.

"I don't know, Linds. I think maybe we should keep a low profile until all this blows over."

"No way, mister! I'm not hiding from any of those Jackasses! If we alter our lives because of them then they've won," she retorted. "So what is it? Should I see if there are any boats available to rent?"

Joey thought about that. There was a better chance of running into other cave divers if they rented a boat than if they took their chances at Jackson Blue. At least at Jackson Blue they could keep their distance from other cave divers and get in and out of the park quickly. If they rented a boat, they would be more likely to be stuck with other cave divers on the small docks built near the entrances to the caves on the pond. And Joey knew he wasn't going to be able to talk Lindsey out of diving. He wished he had already saved enough money to buy a Jon boat so they could head out to one of the remote river caves in the area. There was a much less likely chance of running into anyone at one of those.

"Let's head to Jackson Blue," he responded defeatedly.

"Sounds good to me. I'll fill our tanks right now and top them off tomorrow after they've cooled down. I'll fill a couple of stage tanks too."

The weekend was going to be interesting. Joey hoped that they'd be lucky enough that Jack wouldn't be there. Maybe he'd be back at Ebro pushing more passage too dangerous for anyone else like the previous weekend. Then, Joey had an idea. He quickly pulled out his phone and started typing a DM.

After having met Jim and Gary a couple weeks earlier, they had started to become good friends. They created a chat group and chatted almost every day. Most of the messages were funny memes or gifs they each found and shared with the others. But there was also discussion about Jack Johnson and his rescues.

The past few days their chat had been very active with all of the ongoing chatter on the social media sites. Jim would find something in one of the Facebook groups and share a screenshot. Then Gary would find something else in another group and share a screenshot. Joey mainly reacted to the screenshots with the open mouth emoji. He had already seen most of the comments being made.

Jim and Gary were probably relieved that the kind of talk that was occurring about Joey and Lindsey hadn't happened with their "rescue". Joey clicked into the chat and shot off a message.

Joey: *Yall diving this weekend?*
Gary was the first to respond: *Yep! JB. U?*
Joey: *I wanted 2 keep a low profile til all blew over but Linds wants 2 dive*
Jim: *Want 2 meet & hang b4 & after dive?*
Joey: *Thats what I was hoping. Force in #s*
Gary: *We got u covered bro. Wut time?*
Joey: *We shud b there by 9*
Jim: *CU then*
Gary: *CU then*

The last two messages came through almost simultaneously. The funny thing was Jim and Gary were probably together during that entire discussion. Unless they were working, they usually were.

At least with four of them hanging out before and after the dive it was less likely that anyone would bother them. People were brave when they were sitting at home behind a keyboard or hiding behind their phones, but when it came to face-to-face confrontations, they typically kept to themselves and whispered about you. Joey had already encountered one of the divers that had shitposted about him and the guy just turned away without saying a word.

The only thing Joey had to worry about was whether or not Jack Johnson would show up. There was no telling what Lindsey might say or do if she ran into Jack out there. There was no telling how Joey, himself, might react to seeing Jack in a place with just other cave divers around.

56

Joey

The socials' chatter seemed to die down on Friday. Joey was certain it was by no means over. This was just the typical routine. Discussions would be hot and heavy during the week when all were supposed to be at work but were avoiding their duties and gossiping online instead. Then the weekend approached, and they started getting ready for it – prepping their equipment, getting tanks filled, going over dive plans. Over the weekend they were all underwater diving during the day and hanging out drinking beer in the evenings. Social media was usually quiet during those times, at least among scuba divers.

Joey was hoping this would mean Lindsey was in a better mood when he showed up after work. With nothing new posted that day, she shouldn't have anything to be upset about except the things she had already gotten upset about earlier in the week.

Joey walked into the shop and stood at the front of the store watching Lindsey finishing with a customer. She appeared to be in a good mood. But then again, she always appeared that way with customers. As soon as they walked out the door her mood could change completely.

Lindsey packaged up the customer's new scuba equipment and handed it to her. When the customer turned around to head out of the shop, Lindsey turned toward Joey and gave him a big smile. *Phew!* he thought, *Linds is in a better mood!* Joey walked up to her and gave her a hug and kiss as the chime to the door rang out. He turned toward the door, but it was just the customer leaving.

"How was your day, sweetie?" Lindsey asked.

"Not bad today. Pretty slow. It's Friday so we didn't have any surgeries scheduled this morning. And it must have been a good day for all the dogs and cats in the area because we only had a few people come in. Nothing serious though. A few vaccinations. And one cat that had a string hanging out its butt."

"Ewwww!!! How did the string get there??"

"The cat ate it. That's what happened. And you can't just pull it out because that can do some serious damage. Doc Hadfield had to sedate the cat to get it out. How was your day?"

"It's been busy. Lots of people coming in to get last-minute things for the weekend. A few people stopped by to pick up their rental equipment for the weekend already. I did manage to get our tanks topped off for tomorrow, though. Want to help me load them in the car?"

At that moment the door chimed and a customer walked in.

"I'll get them in the car while you take care of Rhonda." Joey told Lindsey when he saw Rhonda, a regular at the shop, coming in to pick up some tanks for the weekend.

Joey headed into the compressor room and found their sidemount, stage, and decompression tanks all lying in a neat pile on the floor against the wall. He placed the decompression and stage tanks to the side so he could grab the sidemount tanks, which were on the bottom, and load them into the trunk of his car first.

Twenty minutes later and four trips between the compressor room and the parking lot, Joey came back into the shop and its cool air conditioning. Sweat stains formed in his pits and around his neckline. He found one of the AC vents and stood beneath it.

"I'm done with Rhonda and can help you with those tanks now," Lindsey said as she walked up behind him.

"You always have perfect timing," Joey laughed. "Everything's already loaded into my trunk."

"Yeah, well, it's funny how that works." Lindsey laughed back.

"I heard you and Rhonda going on and on about one thing or another. I think you kept her talking just so you wouldn't have to carry any of those tanks out to the car," Joey accused.

"You caught me!" Lindsey replied as she held her hands in the air like someone was pointing a gun at her and then busted out in laughter. Joey was happy to see Lindsey in such a good mood.

The rest of the evening went by quickly. Joey hung around until closing time to help Lindsey with all the customers coming in to pick up rental equipment for the weekend. He had been helping her out since before their first official date more than two years earlier. The owner of the store regularly joked that she had two employees for the price of one. Joey didn't mind working at the shop for free. It gave him extra time with Lindsey.

The owner had also comped Joey some classes for all the work he had done around the shop. He had gotten his Rescue Diver class and a few specialty classes for free. He knew it didn't cost the owner anything because the classes were already scheduled, and Joey just became an additional student in them. But, nevertheless, it was nice to not have to pay for those classes. That allowed Joey to buy more scuba equipment from the shop, which was probably the owner's plan all along.

Joey had even considered becoming a divemaster. The only thing holding him back was that he was having too much fun cave diving on the weekends. With a full-time job at the veterinary office during the week, plus the occasional shift at the restaurant a couple times a month, and taking classes after work, he hardly had any time for himself. That and he also didn't know if he had the patience to deal with students.

After the last customer left, Lindsey shut off the lights, set the alarm, and locked the front door. They walked toward their cars at the far end of the parking lot when they saw a truck pull into the lot.

Joey's heart sank as soon as he recognized the truck. It was Jack Johnson.

57

Joey

Jack stopped behind Joey and Lindsey's cars, blocking them in. Joey thought about pulling Lindsey over to the convenience store located next to the shop but when he saw the look on her face, he knew that wasn't going to happen. Instead, he grabbed her hand and tugged it toward him.

"Linds," he said, "stay calm." *Oh boy! That was a mistake!* Joey regretted the words as soon as they left his mouth.

Lindsey marched over to Jack's truck and yanked the driver's door open. Joey ran after her and watched as Jack recoiled in the seat, apparently afraid Lindsey might elbow him in the face again. That is, if she could. Jack owned one of those lifted trucks that were said to serve to compensate for certain diminutive qualities.

"What the hell are you doing at my shop? And blocking my car! You need to move that small penis mobile out of here right now!"

"Calm down, little lady!" Joey heard Jack say as he backed away.

That was now two men telling her to calm down. And little lady! What was Jack thinking?? Lindsey was going to be even angrier.

"Don't you tell me to calm down you sociopath! After all the lies you spread about me and Joey and then you have the nerve to come to my dive shop and block in our cars!" Lindsey continued to scream at him.

"Look! I didn't know this was your shop," Jack yelled back. "I was just stoppin' in to pick up some stuff. I'm not trying to block you in.

I was about to back my truck into that spot."

Jack pointed at one of the spaces behind Lindsey and Joey.

"Well, we're closed for the day! Go buy your crap somewhere else! You're not welcome here!" Lindsey said, this time in a much lower voice.

Joey winced. Lindsey only spoke like that when she was really angry. He hadn't seen her do that very often, fortunately, and only one time was it directed at him. But Joey quickly learned that when she did that, he had to give her space and let her calm down on her own.

Jack reached out for his door handle to shut the door, but Lindsey pushed the door and caused it to slam shut. Apparently, it slammed into Jack's hand because Joey saw Jack pull his hand back as a look of pain came over his face. Jack turned and glared at Lindsey as he put the truck in drive and tore out of the parking lot, leaving a streak of rubber from his expensive, oversized tires on the asphalt.

Joey stood back and watched Lindsey. He wanted to go to her and put his arms around her, but he was also afraid she wasn't ready for that and that she might swing at him without realizing it was him. He knew she would never hurt him intentionally, but right now she was so angry Joey wasn't sure what she might do.

About a minute later, Joey saw Lindsey's shoulders relax and watched as she turned toward him. She ran to him and put her arms around him and started crying her eyes out. All of this was really getting to her, Joey thought. He was certainly stressed over everything that was being said online but it was tearing Lindsey apart.

They stood in the parking lot holding each other while Lindsey bawled for about five minutes. Finally, she stepped back, wiped her eyes, and looked up at Joey.

"I'm sorry for losing my temper like that. I don't know what's come over me," she whispered. "I've never had someone get to me like this. But that sociopath gets the better of me."

Joey took her back into his arms and held her again. He didn't know what to say. All he knew to do was to hold her and try to provide emotional support. After another minute Lindsey pulled back and wiped her eyes.

"Alright, let's get out of here before that sociopath decides to come back. I'm liable to kill him if I see him again this weekend."

Joey understood exactly how Lindsey felt. He felt the same way. If Lindsey hadn't rushed over to Jack's truck as quickly as she had, it might have been Joey pulling Jack out of the truck and beating the crap out of him. And Joey didn't think Lindsey would have been able to stop him.

Joey's thoughts turned to the weekend. They were diving at Jackson Blue the next day. Jack might be diving Ebro again this weekend. For him to be down along the coast he had to be there. But there was also a chance they might see him in Marianna. There was nowhere else in the area to get his tanks filled so he would have to do it in the morning in Marianna. Which meant he might just stay in on the Mill Pond to dive. Joey didn't know what he would do if Jack showed up the next day while they were getting ready to dive. Then he remembered Jim and Gary were going to be there.

Strength in numbers.

58

Joey

At 7:30 the next morning, Joey arrived at Lindsey's house to pick her up. She came out to the car in a better mood than he had left her the night before.

"Ready to relieve some stress in the cave?" she asked as she buckled her seatbelt across her lap.

"Yep," Joey tersely replied, still nervous about who they might encounter and what might be said after everything that had been happening on the social media sites the past week.

As he drove north on 331, Joey contemplated bringing up the topic of Jack Johnson with Lindsey. Considering the way she had reacted the night before in the dive shop parking lot, Joey expected much worse if he showed up at the park before or after their dive. At least in the parking lot there hadn't been anyone else around. It was a beautiful Saturday morning and there were bound to be several cave divers at the park. If anyone witnessed Lindsey losing her temper with Jack Johnson, the chatter in the social media groups would only get worse.

When they merged onto I-10 25 minutes later, Joey still hadn't gotten the nerve up to say anything. He knew it was a sore subject with Lindsey and would likely only lead to them having an argument. And he didn't want to go on a dive with her after an argument. That was no state of mind to be in while cave diving.

Lindsey sat in the seat next to him singing along to the latest country music hit playing on the radio. Joey wasn't sure how she could like that kind of music. He supposed it was okay, but he much preferred the styles of rock and roll, particularly rock and roll from the 70s and 80s. He knew that was considered ancient, old-fashioned music by his peers but that was all he had listened to growing up. His parents played it in the car all the time and he had grown up liking it.

As they approached exit 136, the first exit leading to Marianna, Joey lowered the volume on the radio.

"Hey!" Lindsey cried out. "I was listening to that."

"I have to call Cave Masters to sign us in to the park," Joey replied.

"Oh, that's right. I guess we're almost there. I'll call them."

Lindsey grabbed her phone from the center console and hit the Cave Masters quick dial icon. She hit the speaker button and waited for it to ring. The phone rang four times before going to voicemail.

"Danny must be swamped and have the compressors going so he can't hear the phone. We're going to have to stop there to sign in," Lindsey said as she tapped the end call icon and turned up the volume on the radio.

Joey stiffened in his seat. If they were swamped that meant there would be lots of cave divers there getting ready for the day of cave diving. He regretted waiting until they were almost in Marianna and not calling at 8 o'clock when the shop opened. As they were driving over the railroad tracks and approaching Lafayette Street, the main street in Marianna, Joey lowered the volume on the radio again.

"Try giving them another call. Maybe Danny will pick up this time," Joey suggested.

"Let's just stop in. It'll only take a minute."

"There might not even be anywhere to park if they're that busy. Try him again," Joey pleaded.

Lindsey relented and unlocked the phone she was still holding and went through the motions of calling Cave Masters. A few seconds later the phone started ringing again. After four rings, Joey heard the familiar Cave Masters' voice message:

Thanks for calling Cave Masters, where you can find everything and anything you need to cave dive. Our hours are from 8 to 6, 7 days a week. If you're hearing this message during those hours, it's because we're busy attending to other customers. Either leave a message or get yourself down here and hang out with us!

Lindsey ended the call again.

"Wait!" Joey cried out. "You could just leave a message."

"I'd rather not do that. They might not get to their messages until later this afternoon and then, technically, we won't be signed in. Just head over." Lindsey said as she turned the radio volume back up.

As they sat at the red light waiting to turn onto Hwy 71 from Lafayette Street, Joey tried one last time, lowering the radio volume and pleadingly looking at Lindsey.

"Oh, okay!" she said, exasperated.

She unlocked her phone and called Cave Masters a third time, fully expecting it to go to voicemail again. This would be the last time because they were less than five minutes away. The phone rang three times, and then suddenly.

"Cave Masters, how can I help you? Umm…good morning!" came the familiar voice of Danny. "Sorry about that, we've been swamped over here. It seems everyone decided to go cave diving this morning. I've been non-stop since before we even opened!"

"Hey Danny, it's Lindsey Carter."

"Oh hey, Miss Lindsey! Sorry for talking your ear off. I guess I should have at least waited to find out who it was before letting all that information out. I really wish they'd hire some more help, at least for the weekends. Whatcha need?"

This guy went on and on. He almost never shut up. Joey didn't know how he got any work done when he was always talking. He probably wasn't even that busy. He was just busy running his mouth.

"Joey Simmons and I are headed to Jackson Blue to dive. Can you sign us in, pretty please?" Lindsey asked in the sweetest, southern belle accent Joey had ever heard. That was one of the first things he had noticed about her, and she seemed to know how to use it to get what she wanted.

"Oh sure thing!" Danny replied. Joey could almost see him blushing over the phone. "Will I get to see you after the dive for fills?"

Joey was almost jealous. But Danny was a 17-year-old kid working a low paying job. Sure, that wasn't much younger than Joey but at that age, four years was quite a big difference in the dating scene. Besides, he knew Lindsey loved him and wasn't about to leave him for Danny.

"We might just do that, sweetie," Lindsey continued, laying the accent on heavy.

"Alrighty, then. Got y'all signed in," Danny giggled probably because Lindsey had called him sweetie.

Lindsey ended the call as they drove past the shop. There were at least half a dozen trucks and vans in the parking lot. It looked like it was going to be a busy day at the park. Hopefully some of them were going to rent boats at the campground.

Joey turned onto Blue Spring Road and drove the last couple of miles to the park entrance. Less than five minutes and they would be at the park. Joey wished they had left earlier as he silently hoped they had beat the crowds, but doubtful of it. Things might get interesting.

59

Joey

Joey turned off Blue Spring Road into the entrance to Blue Spring Recreational Area. The park hadn't opened for the swimmers yet, so the gate was locked. Joey put the car into park and jumped out to enter the code into the keypad to open the gate. The gate unlocked and Joey pushed it open. Just as Joey was getting back into his car, Jim and Gary pulled up. He waved at them and pulled into the park. It was always a little bonus when someone you knew pulled in behind so they got stuck stopping to close the gate. Joey turned right a few hundred feet later and drove down the hill to park next to the disabled parking spaces leaving Jim and Gary to close the gate and make sure it was locked.

Joey looked down the hill and saw a couple of trucks already parked and some divers under one of the pavilions getting geared up. They were talking and laughing and none of them looked up toward his car. Joey didn't recognize any of the divers, but they were a little too far to clearly make out faces. Fortunately, neither of the trucks belonged to Jack Johnson.

Joey backed the car into a spot on the other side of the small lot near the far pavilion. He shut off the engine and looked at Lindsey. Her mood wasn't quite as bright as it had been earlier, but she didn't look upset or angry. He reached down to the floorboard to pull the trunk release, and they exited the car.

The group of divers under the other pavilion suddenly stopped talking. Joey saw one of them glance toward him and Lindsey. Joey looked at Lindsey and watched her shoulders tense. And then he felt his own shoulders get tense. He quickly walked to the back of the car and began pulling their scuba equipment from on top of the tanks and placed it on the metal picnic tables located under the pavilion.

The group under the other pavilion resumed their talking but in quieter tones. Joey couldn't tell what they were saying. Lindsey grabbed the oxygen tanks out of the back of the car and set them on the table next to the equipment.

"If you want to set up the regulators on those, I'll grab the rest of the tanks from the trunk and the scooters from the back seat," Joey said to Lindsey. The scooters, being as expensive as they were, rode seat belted into the back seat of the car. Anyone driving past them on the highway probably thought it strange when they saw long black tubes with seatbelts wrapped around them sticking up behind Joey and Lindsey.

Lindsey began digging through the pile of equipment on the table until she found the padded bags containing their regulators. She sorted through those until she found the bag containing their oxygen and stage regulators. Usually, Lindsey was talkative when they were setting up their equipment, but this morning she wasn't saying a word.

As they were getting ready, Joey heard a vehicle coming down the road behind them and turned to see who it was. He was relieved to see it was only Jim and Gary. And then he remembered they had been right behind him. They shouldn't have taken this long to get down to the parking lot. He saw another truck directly behind Gary's truck. He had seen that truck at the park before, but he couldn't remember who it belonged to. At least it wasn't Jack.

Gary backed in next to Joey and the two jumped out and walked toward them. The other truck pulled in next to the two trucks that belonged to the guys under the other pavilion.

"Hey guys! How are things this morning?" Jim called out.

"Not too bad so far," Joey mumbled as he nodded his head toward the other pavilion.

Jim and Gary both glanced toward the divers under the other pavilion as the divers that had arrived behind them exited their truck and joined the group. Jim and Gary turned back toward Joey and Lindsey. They both nodded an acknowledgement and scrunched up their faces. Apparently, they knew the other divers. They must be Jackasses.

Gary climbed into the bed of his truck and unstrapped the tanks from where they were tied down near the cab. He then pushed them toward Jim, who was waiting at the tailgate. That was the nice thing about having a truck. They didn't have to carry their tanks anywhere to set them up. They could do that on the tailgate and then haul them to the water on the truck cart that was also in the bed of Gary's truck.

"So what are y'all planning for your dive?" Gary asked.

Joey waited for Lindsey to respond but she didn't even turn around. She just continued to set up the regulators on the tanks.

"We're just going to head to Queen's Bypass," Joey answered. "We plan to scooter to the first jump to Queen's, leave the scooters on the line, and swim the circuit back to the Hall of the Mountain King. We might do the King's Canyon loop too. Depends on how we feel when we get there. We're going to leave that as an option."

"Sounds like a cool dive!" Jim said. "We haven't done Queen's Bypass yet. What's it like?"

"Not too bad," Joey responded. "Going in from that direction, there's one area that's fairly low. You wouldn't get through there in backmounted tanks, but it's easy in sidemount. The rest of it can easily be done in backmounted tanks. Although, you have to be on your game with your finning technique because it is silty back there and there's not a lot of height to the passage. It's really pretty, though."

"You think it would be okay if we followed you in there?" Gary asked. "We're just swimming so it would probably be a good 15 to 20 minutes after you start at the Queen's Bypass before we get there if we start our dives at the same time."

"So we definitely wouldn't get in your way!" Jim added.

"Yeah, sure," Joey replied. "I don't see a problem with that. What do you think, Linds?"

"Huh? What was that?" It was unusual for Lindsey to not be paying attention.

"Gary and Jim want to come in after us in Queen's Bypass. They're just swimming. You okay with that?"

"Oh, yeah, that's fine, guys. Are y'all planning on coming back on the main line or are y'all going to turn around and swim back through Queen's Bypass?"

"Well, based on what Joey said about the passage, I think we should come out on the main line, just in case, you know, cuz of Jim the silt monster." Gary laughed as Jim punched him in the arm.

"Alright, since we're both doing the same passage, we'll place the jump line in from the gold line to the Queen's Bypass line. When y'all get there y'all'll see our markers a few inches from the spool where it's looped around the Queen's line. Make sure y'all place markers on the jump line near ours. That way if we don't see y'all in the main passage when we're coming out, we'll know whether to pull our jump line or leave it in case y'all need it." That was the Lindsey Joey was used to.

"Thanks guys!" Gary and Jim said in unison.

As they finished setting up their equipment, the group under the other pavilion carried their tanks to the edge of the water and jumped into the basin from the dive platform located over the entrance to the cave. Lindsey, Joey, Jim, and Gary slowly continued to set up their equipment, taking their time to allow those guys to clip their tanks on and begin their dives. Jim and Gary asked more questions about Queen's Bypass while they set up their equipment.

When the Jackasses dropped below the surface, the tension that had been in the air surrounding the Jack "rescuees" almost immediately dissipated. Their chatter increased as they excitedly talked about the dives they were about to do. With the tanks and scooters at the water's edge, the guys disappeared into the men's room while Lindsey went into the women's room to change into undergarments. Ten minutes later they all emerged, carrying their street clothing, only to find another group of divers had arrived for the day.

Joey quickly scanned the parking lot. Still no sign of Jack Johnson's truck. At least he had that to be thankful for. The new groups of divers were still sitting in their trucks. With the glare of the sun shining off their windshields Joey couldn't quite make out who they were. The newcomers remained in their trucks as the four friends donned their drysuits and headed to the water. Joey had another déjà vu moment to when he had first met Jim and Gary. Only he had a feeling the newcomers weren't going to turn into more fast friends.

60

The dive went well for all four. Mostly… Lindsey and Joey scootered back to the first T and took the passage to the left. A couple hundred feet later they stopped and clipped their DPVs to the main line just under the crack in the ceiling that led to a small room above the main tunnel. Lindsey pulled one of her jump spools out of her thigh pocket and looped it onto the main line. She ran the line to the left, across the room down to the floor where she looped it around a large rock and continued under the low ceiling on that side. Joey remained on the main line watching her, waiting for her to signal that she had tied onto the Queen's Bypass line.

A minute later, Lindsey used her light beam to signal the okay signal back at Joey and he followed the jump line to join her on the permanent guideline leading to the Queen's passage. Lindsey took the lead.

Joey loved this area of the cave. The passage began with an ascent over a large rock mound and a squeeze between the mound breakdown and the ceiling. That was the one restriction in the tunnel that required sidemount configuration. A few feet after the restriction, they were in a relatively large but silty area and came to another T in the line. If they went right, they would end up in a dead-end that circled around. To the left was the continuation of the Queen's passage.

The tunnel started winding back and forth at that point, which was the fun part. A couple hundred feet after the T was another restriction, which was barely large enough for someone in backmounted tanks to pass through. The water flow picked up in this area, which was evidenced by the lack of silt on the floor. But this also made it possible to finger walk through this part of the tunnel. That's when you gently anchored to the bottom with the tips of your fingers and pulled yourself through.

The floor sloped down a couple of feet before coming back up and popping through what appeared to be a hole where it looked like a thin wall had once been. As Joey popped into the silty room just beyond the hole, he momentarily lost control of his buoyancy and started to descend toward the thick silty floor below. He quickly stuck a finger out to stop his fall and it sank into the silt and kept going until his fist was completely buried.

Joey grabbed his inflator hose with his other hand and sent a blast of air into his BC as he filled his lungs with air. Unfortunately, there was always a delayed response to those actions. Joey should have inflated his BC a bit before he got to the silty room. After about ten seconds, he felt himself begin to rise away from the floor. He had almost buried his body in the silt. He quickly exhaled to try to get neutrally buoyant and not hit the ceiling.

As he regained his neutral buoyancy, Joey flattened his hand and gently waved it over the area where it had penetrated the silty floor, hoping to smooth it out and eliminate any evidence of his sloppiness. He also hoped that the silt cloud he had created would be blown off by the water current before Jim and Gary reached this point in their dive.

Joey flicked his fins to move away from the scene of his crime. He looked around and took measure of the room he was in. He had been there a couple of times before but had never taken the time to really look at it. It was all low and silty, but the room was also wide. Joey had looked for possible leads to other tunnels along the sides of the room on his previous dives but hadn't been able to find any. With this area only being about 1500 feet from the opening to the cave, he hadn't really expected to.

This time, however, Joey thought he saw a promising lead to the left. He stopped to try to get a better look, careful to stay off the bottom, but he was too far from the edge of the room to really tell. He thought about signaling Lindsey to stop so he could take a look, then he remembered that Jim and Gary would be coming through soon. And the area between Joey and the lead he thought he saw was very silty and there wasn't much clearance between the floor and ceiling. He had already created a little bit of a silty mess. He was likely to blow out the visibility completely if he tried to check out the lead. So Joey made a mental note of where the lead he thought he saw was and continued following Lindsey along the guideline.

The farther into the cave they went, the closer the walls on either side became, and the taller the passage got. About 10 minutes after beginning this part of the dive, they came to another T in the line. Lindsey took the tunnel to the right and made the 90-degree turn. Joey followed. A couple of minutes later they emerged in one of the cross valleys of the Hall of the Mountain King.

As they were swimming through the small valley, Joey noticed lights ahead in front of Lindsey. He quickly got her attention by sweeping his light beam horizontally back and forth a couple of times. Lindsey looked back and Joey signaled for her to come back to him. While she might have questioned him on the surface, during a cave dive, signals weren't questioned unless they presented risk.

Lindsey glided back to Joey and held up the question mark signal. Joey closed his hand into a fist, indicating to her that he wanted her to hold position, then shielded his light so the light beam was trapped inside his palm. Lindsey did the same with her own dive light as she rotated so she was shoulder to shoulder with Joey and facing the same direction. They waited in the dark hearing nothing but the escape of their bubbles from their regulators as they exhaled.

Joey started to feel the heat from the dive light on his palm. It felt good in the 69-degree water. That water was not cold by any means, especially with a drysuit on, but the warmth still felt good.

The light Joey had seen just before signaling Lindsey finally appeared again. It was coming from the left, farther into the cave. Joey felt Lindsey nudge him on the arm, but he didn't move. He remained in place hoping Lindsey wouldn't unshield her light and give their presence away. Joey knew this had to be the group that began their dive about 30 minutes before they did.

Joey and Lindsey watched as the first diver appeared about 20 feet in front of them and 10 feet above them. He was swimming slowly, sweeping his light around the room. Just as he was passing the cross valley, another light came into view. A few seconds later the diver with the second light emerged into the Hall, also sweeping his light around the room. At one point the light beam swept right over Joey and Lindsey. Joey was certain the diver had seen them, but he hadn't react like he had. He just continued following the first diver through the passage.

Two more divers swam by as Lindsey and Joey remained hunkered down in their hiding spot. After the last diver passed, Joey slowly counted to thirty before uncupping his dive light and allowing the light beam to spill out into the small valley they were in. Lindsey did the same thing and turned to Joey. She gave him the okay signal in the form of a question. Joey returned it as an answer. As long as no one had come in and scootered the main line past this area while they were in Queen's Bypass, they shouldn't come across any other divers in the cave until they were on their way out.

Lindsey flicked her fins and glided back to her position in front of Joey. A moment later they arrived at the end of the line they were on. From that position, they could see the gold line about 12 feet ahead of them. Because they were both familiar with this part of the cave and knew the gold line was a continuous line back to the opening, through the area where they had left their DPVs, they swam the short gap from the Queen's Bypass line to the main line without running a jump line between. It was the only circumstance under which they would go from one guideline to another without connecting them with the line from a jump spool.

They swam 50 feet or so to the right, the cave exit side, and Lindsey stopped at the jump line to King's Canyon. She rotated to face Joey and circled the line leading to King's canyon and then illuminated her index finger which was bent into the question mark signal. Joey quickly checked his pressure gauges to make sure he had enough air in his tanks to do the loop. After verifying he was good to go, he circled his light on the floor in front of Lindsey indicating he wanted to swim King's Canyon.

Lindsey pulled a second jump spool from her pocket and gapped the short distance between the main line and the line to King's Canyon. Joey started getting excited and noticed his breathing rate had increased. This was one of his favorite places in Jackson Blue. He loved swimming through King's Canyon. It was one of the most beautiful areas in the cave.

The canyon was about 30 feet from floor to ceiling with a couple of areas that jutted out from both sides, almost forming a tall 8 with three circles and requiring sidemount divers to rotate sideways to get through the narrow areas while ascending or descending. The passage was only a couple of hundred feet long, but it was worth visiting even for that short of a distance.

They swam the 250 feet from the main line to the T that indicated they were at the bottom of King's Canyon. Going straight on the T didn't lead to anything special. It was the line that went straight up into the canyon that was special. They ascended up the line to the next T. Going right brought you to the end of the canyon, about 100 feet later, then back down and through a restriction to another low, silty passage that eventually popped out close to the second T on the gold line. That 100 feet wasn't quite as magnificent as what was waiting for them to the left.

Going to the left was what brought you through the most beautiful section of the canyon. Joey had brought his GoPro just for this part of the dive. He pulled it out of his pocket as they ascended and turned it on, ready to catch the swim through the canyon on video.

They began swimming to the left even farther into the cave. Joey held his GoPro in front of him. He had recently bought a small video light just for this purpose. It was one thing to get video with a dive light with a focused beam but completely different when using a video light.

Unfortunately, this video light wasn't bringing out the full effect of the canyon. The area was just too big and the light not powerful enough. Joey had been afraid that might be the case. He was saving up for a more powerful video light, but it would still be a few months before he could afford it.

A couple hundred feet later Lindsey reached the end of the King's Canyon line. She stopped and turned back toward Joey. She circled her light beam and then illuminated her closed fist, telling him to hold his position. She swam around the edge of the wall that had been to their left and Joey watched her go toward the gold line that was about 25 feet away. When Lindsey reached the gold line, she circled her light toward Joey and he followed.

Joey looked to the right at the floor. Thankfully, it looked smooth and undisturbed. That was the spot where he had crashed into the bottom after coming out from the Rabbit Hole when he and Lindsey went back to retrieve his abandoned stage tank. He circled his light toward Lindsey and they both faced the way the two arrows on the gold line below them were pointing. They let the current carry them toward their DPVs and the exit.

Six minutes later they arrived at the Hall of the Mountain King again and saw lights ahead. Joey momentarily stiffened and thought about hiding in the cross valley where they had hidden earlier but they were still about 50 feet from it. He looked around for somewhere else to hide. Then he remembered Gary and Jim. This had to be them, thought Joey.

He relaxed a little and continued half swimming, half riding the current over the large mounds that named the Mountain King room. As they came over the first mound Joey saw two divers coming out from the same cross valley that he and Lindsey had earlier. He immediately confirmed with relief that it was Gary and Jim. He could tell Gary's yellow-colored fins anywhere. He didn't know of any other cave divers that had yellow fins.

He waved at the guys as they passed by them. Gary and Jim waved back excitedly, flashing their lights in big circles. Apparently, they had enjoyed Queen's Bypass. Hopefully they hadn't encountered any silt along the way, thought Joey. Gary and Jim fell in behind Lindsey and Joey and the four of them continued out of the cave, stopping briefly at the King's Canyon jump to retrieve Lindsey's jump spool as Gary and Jim peered down the passage, probably wondering about King's Canyon.

The cave got a little smaller at this point resulting in the current getting stronger. They had to fin less and could let the current carry them out at a decent pace. As they were getting to the second T on the gold line, Joey saw more lights coming from the left side of the T. *This was a busy* place, he thought. He tensed up as his breathing rate increased. Then he remembered the divers that had arrived just before they got in the water. Must be them, he thought.

Lindsey went to the right side of the T as Joey and the guys followed. Joey saw the other divers' lights pop up over the breakdown just as he was swimming into the restriction in front of him. Joey didn't get a chance to see if he recognized them. He didn't even see how many were in the group.

Once they reached their DPVs, Jim signaled that he would retrieve the jump spool so Lindsey and Joey could continue out and get started on their decompression stops. The couple signaled agreement and took off out of the cave on their scooters. It only took about seven minutes for them to reach the bottom of the chimney fissure where they released the triggers and began their slow ascent up the fissure.

As they were ascending, Joey heard a loud creaking sound surrounding them, a sound like he had never heard inside a cave before. He scanned the area trying to figure out where it was coming from and what was causing it. As he was scanning, he saw another light appear above them, near the top of the fissure. And that's when he saw it. The ceiling above the fissure was moving! It was moving down, or rather, falling. And there was a diver directly beneath it!

61

Lindsey

Lindsey was slowly ascending up the chimney fissure reliving the dive in her mind. It had been a very good dive, very relaxing and exactly what she needed after the way the week had gone. Suddenly, she heard a loud creaking noise surrounding her. She had no idea what could be making such a horrible noise. Then she felt someone grab her ankle and pull her back and down.

She had flashbacks to the previous weekend when Jack Johnson had grabbed her ankle and pulled her away from the surface. She started thrashing her leg, trying to get Jack's hand off her. Only it couldn't be Jack. He was nowhere around that morning.

Lindsey turned back and saw Joey directly below her and felt him pulling her backwards with force. *What has gotten into him?* she thought. This was very out of character for Joey. Usually, he was very calm and communicated well. Compared to his initial experiences at Eddy Spring, before he had even received any cavern training, most situations were mild. But he seemed to be on edge this dive.

Joey kept pulling her back, and his other hand reached up and grabbed her arm. He pulled her down to the bottom of the chimney fissure and to the other side of where the ceiling ducked down. And he kept pulling her. She tried to get him to release her, but he had too tight of a grip on her.

A moment later, Lindsey felt a strong current of water pushing her back in the direction Joey was pulling her. *That wasn't right.* The current was coming from the opening to the cave, not farther in the cave like it should be. She looked behind her, toward the chimney fissure and saw a huge silt cloud engulfing the space. She could no longer see the gold line where it turned to go up the fissure. She couldn't even see the side of the ceiling nearest them. And the silt cloud was growing larger.

Lindsey turned back toward Joey, who by this time had released his grip on her leg, and she began kicking as fast and hard as she could while pushing him away from what was happening in the fissure. She quickly processed what was going on – the noise, the strong underwater wave, and the silt. The cave had just collapsed in front of them, blocking their exit.

62

Joey

Joey had grabbed Lindsey's ankle and started pulling her back. She initially tried to fight it, but he was able to grab one of her arms and pull her back by both. She only struggled against him for a few seconds. He had turned away from the falling ceiling as he was pulling her so he could swim harder and faster. By the time he turned around he couldn't believe his eyes.

Releasing Lindsey's leg, Joey turned and saw a huge silt cloud rapidly moving toward them. It was swallowing up the entire room. He could no longer see the chimney fissure. Actually, he couldn't see any of the walls on that side of the room. And the silt was quickly moving toward them.

Suddenly he felt Lindsey pushing him even farther back. He tried to do some backward finning to help her but soon realized that wasn't doing any good and let her continue to push him until he felt the wall behind him against his feet.

Joey looked around room. He saw Gary and Jim appearing through the restriction to the first breakdown. He swept his light rapidly back and forth toward them and then toward the growing silt cloud, then rapidly back and forth toward them. They stopped moving forward and aimed their lights at the silt cloud. Joey swore he could see their eyes grow wide, even from 80 feet away.

Jim and Gary turned around and headed back through the restriction to the first breakdown. Once through it, Joey watched them turn toward him, perch themselves on top of the breakdown, and focus their lights on the silt cloud.

With them hopefully at a safe distance, Joey looked back toward Lindsey and grabbed her hand. They hit the triggers on their scooters and zoomed along beside the wall, away from the silt cloud toward the back side of the room. The silt cloud had already encroached on the opening leading to the Horseshoe Circuit, their alternate way out of the cave. Although Joey wasn't sure he wanted to try to exit that way.

The Horseshoe Circuit tunnel was only about three feet tall in some places. If a cave collapse was happening, it might be happening in there too. But they couldn't stay in the cave forever. They didn't have enough air in their tanks to wait for anyone to come in and try to dig them out. If that was even possible. Not even Jack could save them from this. He wondered if this was how Gavin and Turner had felt in Indian Spring.

Then Joey remembered there was one other way out – Young's Siphon. The line in Young's Siphon went toward the Parallel Line passage and passed it, continuing for a couple hundred feet before ending just below a small restriction that led into the cavern about 40 feet from the beginning of the gold line. He looked toward that passage and saw the silt cloud had already enveloped it.

That was their best chance of getting out, but they would have to do it in zero visibility. Joey got Lindsey's attention and aimed his beam at where Young's Siphon was supposed to be. He then gave her the thumb up signal, indicating that was their exit. She responded with an okay signal and aimed her light beam toward Gary and Jim. The guys might not know about that option, so they'd have to get them and lead them out. Joey pulled his wetnotes out of his pocket and started to write on them as they made their way toward the other two divers.

When they got to Jim and Gary, Joey saw that they indeed had very wide eyes. They looked scared to death. Not that Joey wasn't also scared, but he had already experienced a few close calls. This was just the first one that wasn't caused by his own bad choices. Unless you count going cave diving that day a bad choice.

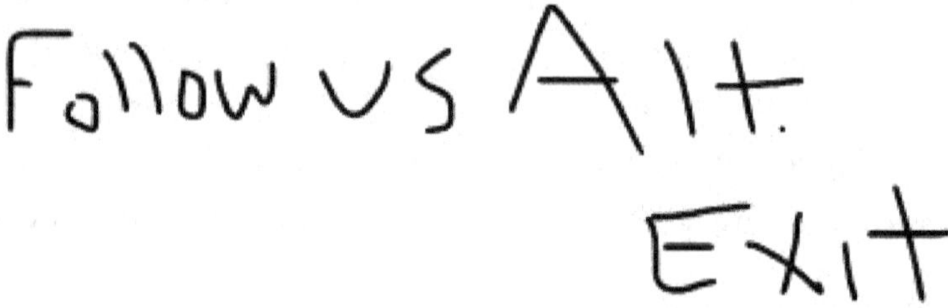

Joey showed Jim and Gary his note and they quickly nodded their heads in agreement. Joey started to swim deeper into the cave. The far side of the Parallel Line passage was just 30 feet away and Joey thought that would be the quickest way out, and possibly the way with the best visibility. Lindsey stopped him.

Lindsey signaled Joey to follow her into the silt. While they had a rule that they didn't question each other on dives, Joey felt this was one of the exceptions. Lindsey was wanting to take them into the silt, into zero visibility. He pointed toward the silt and covered his eyes, then pointed the other way as he removed his palm from over his mask. Lindsey remained insistent that they follow her. Joey thought about pulling his wetnotes out again but decided against it. Lindsey had more experience than him and was more familiar with the cave. He would trust her instinct.

The group of four divers made contact with the line and Lindsey clipped her DPV onto it. Joey did the same with his. It would be easier to leave them behind and retrieve them after everything had settled…if they could. Joey made sure Gary and Jim made it past the DPVs.

The group began swimming into the silt and toward the collapsed ceiling. Joey closed his eyes as the silt got thicker. A minute later, he felt Lindsey stop in front of him. He waited patiently until he felt the line being tugged to his left. Moving forward slowly, a couple seconds later he felt cave line looped onto the gold line in between the two cave line arrows marking Young's Siphon. It was leading to his left, into Young's Siphon. Joey finally understood.

The line in Young's Siphon was only 15 feet away from the gold line, the end tied onto a protrusion from the floor. It was much easier to find it in zero visibility from the gold line than if they had gone the way Joey initially wanted to go. Joey remembered the lost line drill his instructor had made him do during his cave diving class. It took place right in this passage.

The instructor had Joey and his class buddy swim to the end of the Parallel Lines guideline with a blacked-out mask. When they reached the end, they had to deploy a safety spool and find the gold line. The gold line was to the right of the end of the Parallel Lines guideline, about 40 feet away. The Young's Siphon guideline was directly across from the Parallel Lines guideline, but closer to the ceiling at that point. Neither Joey nor his buddy had found either line. In fact, they had both ended up going farther into Young's Siphon, away from both lines! Even though they were both familiar with the area and knew where the lines were located, once they no longer had a visual reference, they both went the wrong way.

Joey lightly held onto the jump line that Lindsey was spooling out and waited until he felt the movement on the line stop. He then moved slowly, off the gold line, but keeping one hand on the intersection of the two lines. When he felt Jim or Gary, he wasn't sure which one had taken position number 3, he took his hand and moved it onto the jump line and pulled him around so he was between Joey and Lindsey. He waited for the other to reach the line intersection so he could do the same. Joey would then take up the rear.

When Joey felt the second diver at the line intersection, he did the same thing and got him from the gold line to the jump line. Once he was there, Joey followed behind. He kept a loose hold of the jump line and swam the 15-foot lined gap until he felt the spool on the other end. He reached down with his other hand and traced the line to the permanent line it was looped around, made the transition, and continued along the passage following behind the other three divers. At least he hoped all three were still ahead of him.

The silt was thick in Young's Siphon as well. This didn't surprise Joey. He knew the chimney fissure was to his right through a very low, silty area. It made sense that the silt would quickly make it to this tunnel as well. Joey was hoping as they got farther into the tunnel the visibility would begin to clear.

Except it didn't. This was a siphon, as indicated by its name, because the water flow was moving in the same direction they were going. So it was pushing the silt into the tunnel, which was out toward the opening of the cave. It would be difficult to negotiate the restriction at the end of the line with no visibility. He wondered how Jim and Gary would handle it. *I may have screwed myself by putting them in between me and the exit,* Joey thought to himself. If they didn't get through, they would be blocking his egress.

Fortunately, the visibility did begin to clear after the area where the ceiling pinched down. The floor also sloped up and came within a foot of the ceiling about two-thirds of the way in. After that restriction, the silt was not as thick. Less than 100 feet and they would be at the restriction leading to the cavern. Out to safety, Joey hoped. As long as the entire entrance hadn't collapsed.

Gary suddenly stopped in front of Joey. Joey finally knew who was in front of him because the yellow fins really stood out, even in the silt. *Maybe there was something to getting bright colored scuba equipment,* thought Joey.

Lindsey must be at the restriction. It would take a few minutes for all of them to get through, so Joey settled into place to wait his turn. Less than a minute later Gary began moving forward again. Joey inched forward close behind him. The silt was getting thicker.

The yellow fins went vertical. Gary must be going through the restriction. That went quicker than he had expected. Joey saw why as he inched forward. Lindsey was backed up to the left of the line letting the guys go through first. And she was signaling Joey to go before her as well.

63

Lindsey

Lindsey was glad Joey hadn't argued with her when she directed him to go back into the silt. She understood why he wanted to go get to Young's Siphon from the Parallel Lines tunnel, but it would have been a lot more difficult to find the Young's Siphon line from that direction than it was from the gold line in the large room at the bottom of the chimney fissure. He only questioned her once then acquiesced to her request.

Once she was positive Joey understood what she wanted to do she took the lead so she could run the line from her safety spool connecting the gold line to the Young's Siphon line. She quickly deployed the safety spool line and easily found the beginning of the Young's Siphon line. She considered letting the others pass before continuing but she was concerned Jim and Gary might not move as fast if they weren't following someone, especially if they were unfamiliar with the passage.

Lindsey swam about 10 feet along the Young's Siphon line and stopped to feel for movement behind her. About 30 seconds passed before she felt the vibration of someone touching the guideline. The silt was already too thick for her to see any illumination, even from her own dive light.

As Lindsey began slowly moving forward again, she felt something hitting the tips of her fins, she hastened her pace a little. Every 20 feet or so she stopped so she could feel for the vibration in the line. She resumed moving when she felt it getting closer, moving slowly at first until she felt something hit her fin tips again. She kept this pace until she reached the part of the tunnel where the floor came within a foot of the ceiling.

As soon as she passed through that restriction the visibility cleared slightly. She still couldn't see very far but at least she could see the light beam coming from the dive light on her hand. She moved forward enough to give room to whoever had been behind her to get beyond the restriction and turned to watch for him. She hoped that Joey had let Gary and Jim get between them and Joey had taken up the rear.

Lindsey didn't know how comfortable Jim or Gary were with restrictions. They had gone through the Queen's Bypass, which had areas that came close to that low, but that was in good visibility. It was a different experience when you couldn't see very much, especially if you had never been in that area.

She watched as the first one made it through the restriction with no issues. It wasn't Joey so he must have taken the rear. *Good man,* she thought. As Jim or Gary got closer to her, she waved him by. That must be Jim, she thought, no yellow fins.

She waited for Gary to come through the restriction. She watched as his head popped through, then he stopped, and his head disappeared back into the silt. *Crap!* Lindsey thought. He was spooked by the restriction. But then she saw his head pop through again, this time a little more to his right, her left. He must have snagged on something when he first tried to pass through.

Gary emerged and Lindsey quickly moved past Jim and resumed the lead confident Joey would have no problem getting through. They were less than 100 feet from the end of the line but the restriction to the cavern wasn't the easiest to find. Once at the end of the line, you had to look up to see it. If you could even see it under the conditions they were in.

Lindsey reached the end of the line and looked up to where the restriction was supposed to be. She shined her light into it. Fortunately, she could see it and she could see the cavern beyond. It was already starting to get hazy but wasn't nearly as bad as it was in Young's Siphon. And the opening hadn't caved in.

Lindsey moved to the left of the line where there was more room for her and rotated her body so she could look at the rest of the group. Jim arrived a few seconds later and came to a stop at the end of the line. Lindsey signaled for him to remove his stage tank as there was no way he would fit through the restriction with it on. Then she pointed her light beam up into the small hole and gave Jim a thumb up signal.

After Jim removed his stage tank, he looked up and Lindsey could see his eyes getting wide. He looked at her and shook his head no. Lindsey pointed her light into the hole again and pointed at it and shook her hand. She then grabbed his upper arm and shoved him up toward it.

Jim reluctantly continued moving toward the restriction just over his head. Lindsey watched his head disappear through the hole, and then his shoulders. As Jim ascended into the hole he suddenly stopped moving. Lindsey watched him wiggle his body back and forth. He wiggled it a little more erratically as Lindsey came to the realization that he had just gotten stuck. Not only that but he had plugged their only exit.

Lindsey grabbed one of Jim's ankles and pulled back on it. He moved down easily so she knew he hadn't gotten himself wedged. He just needed to rotate his body to be able to fit through it the right way. She pushed his left leg, causing him to rotate to the left, then pushed him up. About 10 seconds later, Jim's fins disappeared through the small hole. Lindsey pushed his stage tank up through the hole and a few seconds later felt it being pulled out of her grasp.

That's when Gary appeared on the line. Lindsey went through the same motions with him as she had with Jim. Gary wasn't as hesitant to go through the restriction as Jim had been. He actually looked a little excited about being able to do it. He immediately pulled off his stage tank, handed it to Lindsey, went vertical, and began pushing through the restriction. Lindsey pushed his leg to rotate him into the proper orientation to get through the hole and Gary disappeared into the cavern above. She pushed his stage tank up into the hole and felt it being pulled from her hand.

Joey appeared out of the silt next. She signaled for him to go as well. Joey signaled back for her to go first. *That idiot!* she thought, *you better not argue with me right now!* Lindsey aimed her light into the restriction and grabbed Joey's arm and shoved him toward it. Fortunately, he didn't put up a fight. Lindsey and Joey had gone through this restriction a few times on previous dives, so she didn't have to force him into the correct orientation. He pulled his stage tank off and pushed it above him so it passed through the restriction first. He then quickly slid through, and she watched as he turned around to watch her pass through.

Lindsey, being the smallest of the group, easily passed through the hole. She could have gone through in any orientation and didn't even have to remove her stage tank. That was one of the advantages of being a petite girl. Once she got through, she saw that all three guys were waiting for her. She illuminated her right hand with her light and gave them the thumb up signal. Jim and Gary turned and began swimming toward the opening, which was only about 150 feet away. Visibility was hazy but Lindsey could see the daylight penetrating the cavern.

When Joey didn't turn to leave, Lindsey repeated the thumb up signal. Instead, Joey gave her the buddy signal, crossed fingers, and pointed into the cave, away from the exit. Lindsey looked at him as she tilted her head, wondering what he was trying to tell her. Then she remembered the diver they had seen as they were beginning their ascent up the chimney fissure. There could be someone stuck under the collapse.

Lindsey didn't know what they would be able to do. The piece of ceiling she had seen coming down was huge and must have weighed several tons. If anyone had survived the collapse, it wasn't likely she and Joey would be able to get them out from underneath it. But there was a chance the diver didn't get pinned down and was lost in the silt looking for the exit. Lindsey looked at the pressure gauges on her tanks. She still had plenty of air left. She looked at Joey, circled her light beam in front of him, and they started back into the cave, into the heavy silt, and into the darkness beyond.

64

Joey

Joey looked toward the cave opening one last time, expecting to see Jack Johnson scootering in to save the day. Only this time, it was a real situation with a diver truly needing help. There was no bright light beam rapidly heading toward them, though.

Joey turned back toward the gold line and circled it with his thumb and index finger and prepared to make his way into the silt. He wasn't sure if the diver he had seen had even survived but he had to at least try to help if there was the slightest chance. He quickly assessed the air reserves in his tanks. He had about 1800 psi in each sidemount tank and 1000 psi in his stage tank. That meant he could search for this other diver until his sidemount tanks reached 1200 psi. The chimney fissure was only 100 feet away, so that was plenty of air. He would reserve the stage tank for the diver in case it was needed.

He looked toward Lindsey and circled his light beam on the floor in front of her. She returned the signal and fell in place on the line behind Joey. Joey flicked his fins and disappeared into the silt. He felt the vibration of the line as Lindsey followed closely behind him.

They had begun on a section of the gold line that was in the middle of the room just over the restriction leading to Young's Siphon. About 10 feet later Joey felt the limestone shelf below the line as expected. He tugged up on the line slightly to allow his fingers room to remain circled around it without rubbing on the shelf the line rested on.

About 30 feet later the guideline wrapped around a protrusion from the shelf and angled down at about a 20-degree slope toward the top of the chimney fissure. The silt was even thicker in this area. Joey listened carefully for any more sounds like he had heard earlier right before the ceiling had collapsed. While he felt he needed to try to help anyone that might still be in the cave, he didn't want to become a victim of it, especially after having found a way around the collapse.

Joey continued following the guideline down the slope. He pictured the passage and the line in his mind. He should come to another line wrap and then it would slope down at an even steeper angle until it reached the bottom of the fissure, wrapped several times around a large rock, and turned slightly to the right and horizontal, leading into the large room they had been in when the collapse began.

Except that's not what Joey felt this time. About 20 feet after the last line wrap, Joey swam into a wall, or a large boulder. He wasn't certain as the silt was still preventing him from seeing anything. He felt Lindsey bump into him from behind. She found his arm, grabbed it, and pushed forward, the touch-contact signal for move forward.

Only Joey couldn't move forward. He reached down with his free hand for the line and tried to trace its route. The line seemed to lead into a very small crack. Then it came to Joey. He must have swum into the part of the ceiling that had collapsed. It had fallen onto the gold line.

Joey held onto the line with his left hand and stretched toward the right. The large boulder that had dislodged from the ceiling was wider than his reach. The bottom seemed to be resting on the silty slope that was to the right of the fissure opening. He tried to reach over the top of the boulder. He felt the top edge and stretched over the boulder in front of him. It felt like he could continue that way, but he would have to deploy a safety spool and anchor it around the gold line.

Before doing that, Joey checked the other side. He switched hands and held onto the gold line with his right hand and reached toward the left of the line. He felt the wall that he knew to be the left side of the fissure. He moved his hand down along the wall and immediately felt the bottom. He brushed his hand up along the wall until he couldn't stretch anymore. He slid back along the gold line as he continued to reach above himself, finally coming to the top edge of that wall. He continued to follow the top, which was the floor to the upper room and reached farther out from the gold line.

As Joey stretched his hand along the upper floor, he smacked his head on something. He brought his left hand up and hit something with the top of it. That wasn't right, he thought. There was at least 20 feet between the floor and the ceiling in that area, or at least there was supposed to be. Joey swept his arm around and felt limestone all around. He judged it to be about two and a half feet tall and 5 feet wide.

This must be another part of the ceiling that had collapsed, he thought. *It wasn't going to be easy to find anything as long as this silt remained.*

It seemed what was once a large room about 20 feet tall had turned into a two and a half foot tall room.

Joey moved back to the line where Lindsey had been waiting for him. He could see her face at that point. The silt seemed to be clearing a little. He pulled out his wetnotes and scribbled a message to her.

Ceiling parts all over
Line buried

He thrust the notes in front of her mask and waited. He watched as Lindsey started to do something and then thrusted her safety spool in front of him, pointed to it, and pointed to him. She then pointed at herself and to the right and pointed at Joey and to the left. Joey pulled his safety spool out and prepared to begin searching to the left while Lindsey searched to the right.

65

Lindsey

Lindsey had been moving along the line behind Joey in the thick silt. She felt him pulling the line up off the shelf, stop briefly at the line wrap, and then continue down toward the top of the chimney fissure. Then she swam right into his fins. She moved alongside him, grabbed the back of his arm, and pushed forward, communicating to him to keep going. Only he didn't move.

He must have found the diver, she thought. She tried to look around, but the silt was still too thick to see more than a couple of inches. She could barely make out Joey's left tank below her.

Lindsey let go of his arm and reached in front of her. Her knuckles hit a wall. That must be the collapsed ceiling, she thought. It had fallen into the fissure. She wondered if the fissure was completely blocked.

She felt Joey move to the right, away from her. *He must be looking for a way around the collapse.* Moving back to give him room Lindsey waited patiently, maintaining contact with the gold line while Joey searched the area in front of them.

The silt was slowly clearing. She still couldn't see the pieces of ceiling that had collapsed, but she was seeing more of Joey's outline in front of her. She estimated visibility had gotten to about two feet. She raised her hand above her head and could feel the water flowing by. That meant the passage wasn't completely blocked. If they waited a few more minutes, they might be able to see enough to assess the situation.

About three minutes later, Joey was in front of Lindsey facing her. He pulled out his wetnotes, wrote something on them, and placed them in front of her mask. Lindsey weighed their options. They could wait for the visibility to clear some more, or they could each deploy a safety spool and start looking. Lindsey opted for the latter.

She pulled her safety spool out of her pocket and signaled to Joey to do the same. Then signaled that she was going to go to the right, and he should go to the left. She watched to make sure Joey understood her hand signals as he retrieved his own safety spool out from his pocket.

Lindsey pulled a cave line arrow from its pigtail holder and placed it on the gold line in front of her, pointing out toward the exit. Not that they really needed it as the line was trapped underneath a piece of what used to be the ceiling, but she kept to procedure anyway. She looped the end of her safety spool line around the line arrow and moved to the right. She watched as Joey did the same with his safety line.

Lindsey pointed at Joey, then behind him, then gave him the okay signal. When he signaled okay back, she turned and began following the obstruction to the right. The cave passage must not be completely blocked because the current was slowly clearing out the silt hanging in the water as she made her way along the old ceiling that currently lay on the floor.

Several seconds later, Lindsey came to the end of the large boulder and followed it to the left, down the slope it was on. As she rounded the corner, she saw a dive light on the floor in front of her. It wasn't moving. The silt was still too thick to make anything else out. She didn't know if it was just a light that had been dropped or if there was a diver nearby.

66

Joey

Joey began spooling out his safety line as he moved in the opposite direction from Lindsey. He found the five-foot wide by two-and-a-half-foot tall area he had encountered a few minutes earlier and tried to swim into it. He got about a body length in before he ran into a blockage. He felt around, looking for continuing passage, or a trapped diver, but found neither. He backed out of the small tunnel and continued following the large boulder up above the small opening he had just vacated.

He thought back to his intro cave diver training and remembered doing the lost line drill in this very spot.

Joey's instructor, Adam had him wearing a blacked-out mask. Adam then moved Joey about 15 feet off the gold line and set him on the floor. Joey felt around until he found a protrusion from the limestone. Then, as he held onto the protrusion, he pulled his safety spool from his pocket and wrapped the end of the line around it several times. Once that was done, he began looking for the gold line.

Joey had thought he was facing toward the exit, meaning the gold line would be to his left. He rotated to the left and began swimming toward the line as he swept his free hand up and down, brushing his fingertips against the hard, rough floor, waiting to hook the gold line in his hand.

That didn't happen. He felt three knots on his safety spool, indicating he had swum 30 feet, and hadn't found the gold line. He was happy Adam had recommended tying knots every 10 feet on his safety spool line otherwise he wouldn't know how far he had gone. He turned around and spooled the line back up until he got back to where he had anchored it.

Joey rotated back the way he had come and settled in place. He tried to picture the cave in his mind. He must have turned too much to the left last time and was probably swimming parallel to the gold line. This time he rotated only a slight bit before he began his swim out while sweeping his hand and counting knots.

Three knots later and he had still come up empty. He did this five times before Adam stopped him and handed him his own mask. He swapped masks, cleared the water out of his mask, and looked at his instructor. Adam pointed the various directions Joey had swum while searching for the gold line. Every single one of them was in the opposite direction of the gold line!

Joey had no idea how he had continuously gone the wrong way. He thought he had oriented himself properly. Adam's words before the dive rang loud in his mind — You have the rest of your life to find the line! Joey finally understood that statement. Keep looking for the line until you find it. Because if you don't find it, you'll eventually run out of air and die right there in the cave.

67

Lindsey

Lindsey flicked her fins harder and darted toward the light in front of her. The silt continued to get less dense, and she was able to see the outline of an arm underneath the dive light when she was about five feet from it. She also saw the outline of the large boulder that had the arm pinned down. The corner of it had come down on top of the arm.

This is bad, she thought. If the diver was trapped underneath the boulder there was little that could be done. The diver might even already be dead. The boulder must weigh at least half a ton. Maybe more. She couldn't see exactly how large it was.

Flicking her fins again, Lindsey continued moving forward as she let out more line from her safety spool. She saw the edge of the boulder as she got closer to the light. Her head came even with the edge and on the opposite side she saw the rest of the diver. It looked like only the arm had gotten pinned beneath the boulder. Maybe the diver was still alive and there was hope for getting free and out of the cave.

Lindsey reached for the edge of the boulder and grabbed it. She tried to move it, but it didn't budge, not that she really thought it would. She pulled herself around the corner and came face to face with the trapped diver. She immediately recognized the Poseidon regulator in the diver's mouth.

68

Joey

It didn't take long for Joey to reach the top of the rock he was ascending next to. Part of the ceiling had fallen on top of the area where Joey had done his lost line drill in his class. He couldn't see how big of an area was affected, but from what he could see and feel, it felt significant.

Joey searched the area over the new floor of the cave. The silt was continuing to clear, and he could see farther around the room. The boulder was huge. While spooling out his safety line, he followed the perimeter of the boulder, counting knots as they slipped through his fingers.

The boulder appeared to be about 25 feet wide and close to 40 feet long! And based on his ascent from the small tunnel he had gone into, he estimated it to be four to six feet tall. If anyone was trapped under it, that person was never coming out. This area would become a grave.

After not finding any signs of a diver around the edges of the large boulder, Joey spooled up his safety line as he returned to the gold line. He would see if Lindsey had found anything, and if not, he would try searching over top of the boulder that had fallen on top of the gold line. He had at least determined that the ceiling had broken into more than one piece – the large boulder sitting on the shelf at the top of the chimney fissure and the boulder that came to rest on top of the gold line.

When he arrived back at the gold line, Lindsey wasn't there. Her safety line was still in place heading in the opposite direction from where Joey had been. Joey removed his safety spool from the gold line and stowed it in his pocket. He then followed Lindsey's safety line around this other boulder. The silt had cleared enough that he no longer had to maintain physical contact with the line.

Joey rounded the corner of the fallen boulder and saw Lindsey's motionless fin tips a few feet in front of him. He slowly swam toward them. As he got closer, he saw bubbles escaping her regulator as she exhaled. Joey thought about swimming around Lindsey to her right to let her know he was there and ask her if she had found anything, but he didn't want to get that far from her safety line in case the visibility started getting bad again.

Instead, Joey ascended above Lindsey, keeping his left hand on the fallen boulder, and swam over top of her. As he moved forward, Lindsey began moving backwards. When Lindsey moved, Joey noticed a second dive light below her. *That must belong to the diver I saw,* thought Joey, wondering if the diver was close by.

Joey tapped Lindsey on the leg to let her know he was there. She flinched and looked back at him. Joey gave her the okay signal with his thumb and forefinger. She shook her head from side to side. Joey felt anxiety creeping up inside him. *Does she mean something is wrong with her or something is wrong with the diver?* thought Joey.

Joey pointed at Lindsey and gave her the question mark signal, asking if she had an issue. She shook her head no again and pointed to something around the corner of the boulder. Joey pulled himself forward so he could look at what Lindsey was pointing at. He looked down and saw the top of a diver with his left arm disappearing underneath the boulder.

Bubbles were streaming up from around the diver's head. At least he was breathing, Joey thought. Joey pulled himself to the left over the top of the boulder and grabbed the edge that was just above the trapped diver. He pulled as hard as he could. It was no use. The boulder didn't budge. It was too large and too heavy.

Maybe they could dig the silt out from around the diver's arm and loosen it enough for him to pull his arm out, Joey thought. He moved back down next to Lindsey to communicate his idea. He descended in front of her instead. She had moved back a few feet from her previous position. As he approached the floor below, he glanced at the trapped diver. He immediately recognized the Poseidon regulator the diver was breathing from.

Jack Johnson.

69

Lindsey

Lindsey began backing away from Jack just as Joey approached from behind and tapped her leg. She hadn't expected that and was startled. She turned to face Joey and saw him asking if she was okay. She shook her head no. All she wanted to do was get out of there. No way was she going to help Jack Johnson. He didn't deserve to be rescued. And he would probably twist things around and claim he rescued Lindsey and Joey from the collapse.

When Joey asked for clarification on whether she was the one not okay, Lindsey shook her head again and pointed toward Jack. She watched as Joey moved forward to look at what she was pointing at. She moved back a couple more feet to give him room and to create more distance between her and Jack. She couldn't get far enough away from him.

She looked back up at Joey, but he had disappeared over the top of the fallen boulder. She just wanted to get out of the cave and leave Jack Johnson trapped under the boulder to suffer his demise. He deserved every bit of it.

But she couldn't leave Joey behind. She would let Joey do what he had to. She knew there was no way they beyond able to move the boulder and get Jack out of there.

After about a minute, Joey descended back down in front of her. She saw him look toward Jack and watched as his body stiffened. Then Joey moved back away from Jack. She didn't know if Joey would want to help Jack or not after he saw who it was. However, after seeing his response, maybe he would be on the same page as she was.

Lindsey knew it would be a tough decision for Joey to make. As much as he hated Jack and would have beat the crap out of him in the restaurant the other night, Joey was too kindhearted for his own good, even with people like Jack. But after what they had both been through, maybe this would be different. Maybe Joey would gladly follow her out of the cave and leave Jack trapped under the boulder breathing away the last of the air in his tanks.

70

Joey

Joey was torn. Why had he insisted they go look for the diver he had seen? Why hadn't he recognized it was Jack right before the collapse when they were at the bottom of the chimney fissure? There was no use questioning himself. They had found the diver, it was Jack, and Jack was trapped. Leaving him there was not an option. Joey couldn't do that. He would feel guilt for the rest of his life.

Joey turned to his left and began scooping out the sand around Jack's arm. He had to be careful. If he scooped out too much, the boulder could shift and slide down the slope on top of both of them. He scooped out a small trench the width of his hand alongside Jack's arm as far back as he could reach.

When he got his arm under the boulder about midway to his forearm, he felt a hard limestone floor. He moved his hand side to side and felt a ridge running perpendicular to his arm.

That was good and that was bad. It was good because the boulder was resting on this limestone shelf that had been buried beneath the sand. It was bad because Jack's arm was trapped beneath the boulder and the floor, probably crushed.

Joey turned to Jack and held his closed fist in front of Jack's face, telling him to hold his position. *Well, that was stupid,* thought Joey, *Jack was pinned down and couldn't do anything but hold his position.* Joey moved around the corner of the boulder to where Jack's hand was sticking out of the other side. Lindsey was on the opposite side of the hand waiting on him.

Lindsey gave Joey the thumb up signal. Joey looked at his gauges and saw he still had plenty of air to deal with the situation. He pointed his index finger up and wagged it back and forth, telling her no. He was breaking a cardinal rule of cave diving by doing this.

The most important rule in cave diving was *Any diver can call the dive at any time for any reason with no questions asked.* So when a cave diver gave the thumb up signal to end a dive and exit, the only response all other cave divers were supposed to give was a thumb up and everyone was to exit the cave.

Except Jack couldn't exit the cave. And Joey couldn't leave Jack trapped in the cave. Even if it was Jack Johnson, and even if he had lied about rescuing both him and Lindsey. Joey still couldn't do that.

Joey looked at Lindsey and pointed back at Jack and again wagged his finger back and forth followed by a quick thumb up. Lindsey gave Joey the thumb up signal again, accentuating it with a pump of her fist. This time Joey emphatically shook his head back and forth and turned away from Lindsey to begin digging the sand out from beneath the boulder. Joey expected that Lindsey would probably leave him there to deal with Jack himself. That would be on her. He had to do what he felt was right.

Jack's hand flinched away as far as it could, which wasn't far, when Joey began digging from that side. At least he still had some sensation in his hand. His arm might not be crushed completely. Joey carefully dug another trench around the corner of the boulder from Jack but only got in about the length of his hand before he felt the hard limestone floor again. It looked like it was Jack's elbow that was pinched in between the fallen boulder and the hard surface of the floor.

The visibility was clearing even more, except in the area where Joey had been digging. Joey moved away from the boulder to try to get a wider picture of how Jack was trapped. That's when he noticed Lindsey hadn't left. He circled his light, asking if she was okay. She returned the okay signal. Joey looked back to the boulder. They had to get as much of the sand as they could cleared from underneath the fallen boulder. Then maybe they would be able to move it enough for Jack to pull his arm out.

Comfortable knowing that the fallen boulder was resting on a hard surface under the sandy bottom, Joey moved back to the side near Jack and began to quickly dig the sand away. He noticed Lindsey began digging from the other side.

About 10 minutes later they had relocated all the sand they could from under the boulder. Some sand from up the slope kept sliding down to replace what they had just removed but they were able to get quite a bit moved.

Joey turned to Jack and signaled for him to try to pull his arm out. He watched as Jack braced himself with his right hand and pushed back on the boulder pinning him down while trying to pull his left arm out. He didn't budge even an inch. Joey could see the pain on his face as he tried. Joey was at a loss on what to do next.

Checking his gauges, Joey noticed the pressure in both tanks had dropped to 800 psi in each. He had planned on beginning his exit when he reached 1200 psi, but they were less than 300 feet from the exit. He could push it to 400 psi, maybe even as low as 300 psi.

Turning toward Lindsey to see if she had any ideas, he saw her removing her stage tank. Joey wasn't ready to give up on Jack just yet. Sure, they could help him by leaving their stage tanks for him to breathe from, but calling for help and getting someone in the cave would take far too long. Leaving their stage tanks would only prolong Jack's suffering. Besides, Joey didn't know what kind of help was needed other than a crane to lift the boulder off Jack. And that wasn't possible.

Lindsey swam toward Joey with her stage tank held in front of her. He moved aside and let her pass. She swam to Jack's right side and stuck the bottom end of her stage tank under the boulder. That's when Joey noticed that side was angled up slightly. Apparently, Jack's

DPV, no longer a tube, was crushed beneath that side of the boulder providing enough clearance for Lindsey to get the bottom of her stage tank wedged into the gap.

Lindsey pulled up on the valve end, using it as leverage to try to move the boulder off Jack's arm. Joey thought he saw the boulder shift a little, but then the stage tank shifted underneath it and a plume of silt came flying out from under the boulder. Joey watched Jack's head drop as he slammed his right fist down on the floor when the boulder shifted its place and crushed his arm even more.

71

Lindsey

Lindsey watched in shock as Joey began digging the sand out from underneath the boulder. She couldn't believe Joey was helping Jack. After everything Jack had done to both of them, he didn't deserve any help. She tried to get Joey's attention by rapidly sweeping her light beam back and forth in front of him, but he either didn't notice or was ignoring her.

She watched Joey scoop out handful after handful of sand, pushing it down the slope beneath him. Jack used his free arm to scoop the sand pile that was growing beneath Joey farther down the slope. Lindsey began to worry that they would scoop too much and cause the boulder to shift and slide over them, trapping Joey as well.

Then she watched Joey stop and feel around for something underneath the boulder. Joey pulled his arm out and moved toward her. When he looked at her, she gave him the thumb up signal. Joey looked at his gauges and looked up at her and wagged his finger back and forth, telling her no. *What the hell!?!?!* He shouldn't be questioning her. Joey then pointed at Jack and wagged his finger again.

Lindsey made a fist with her thumb up and thrust it in front of Joey, insistent that they end the dive and exit the cave. This time Joey shook his head no and turned away from her. She almost lost her regulator when her jaw dropped in shock. She watched Joey as he resumed scooping the sand out from beneath the boulder.

As Lindsey watched Joey digging furiously to try to help Jack, she decided she couldn't leave him alone to deal with Jack. Just as she had made up her mind to not only stay, but to also help, Joey backed up from his work of scooping out sand. He noticed Lindsey and circled his light beam in front of her. She returned the signal.

Joey took a moment to look over the situation, then he moved back next to Jack to resume digging. Lindsey moved in from the other side and began digging around Jack's hand. Every now and then she scraped against his hand. She could tell by his response that he was in a lot of pain. She continued to dig out the sand closer to his hand, not really caring if she caused Jack more pain.

72

Joey

Joey pulled his stage tank off and shoved it underneath the boulder on the opposite side of Jack's arm. He had cleared enough sand to jam the bottom of his stage tank under it. He watched as Lindsey repositioned her stage tank on her side. Joey turned on his mask light so he could illuminate the area he was looking at and still use both hands. He looked toward Lindsey and held his right hand in the beam of the mask light and raised his index finger, middle finger, then ring finger, counting to three and gave her the okay signal. She returned the okay signal.

Turning to Jack, Joey pretended to push up on his stage tank and made a motion for Jack to pull his arm back. Jack held his right fist up and then pointed at the light on Joey's hand. Joey gave him the question mark signal. Jack pointed at Joey's light again and pointed around the corner toward his left hand. Joey suddenly realized Jack was telling him to remove the light from his hand.

Joey signaled to Lindsey to hold her position and moved to Jack's hand. He carefully pulled the light forward and away from Jack's hand. Joey watched as Jack wiggled his fingers slightly and then moved back behind his stage tank.

With Joey in position, he signaled Lindsey okay and they both dug their heels into the sandy bottom. Joey counted off to three with his fingers and they pushed up on their stage tanks at the same time as hard as they could.

Joey watched as the boulder shifted up slightly. It wasn't much, but apparently enough because Jack was able to pull his arm out a little. As Jack was pulling his arm back, the boulder shifted and crashed back down on top of it. Joey watched as Jack collapsed onto the sandy bottom and screamed through his regulator.

Joey looked around the corner of the boulder to see if Jack's hand was still visible on that side. The silt was too thick for him to see anything though. Joey set his stage tank down on the sand and moved to the other side while feeling along the bottom edge of the boulder. He didn't feel Jack's hand. It must be under the boulder now.

Joey moved back to the stage tank next to Jack. He tapped Jack on the shoulder and signaled him, asking if he was okay. Jack just grunted through his regulator. Joey couldn't be sure, but he thought Jack had just told him to fuck off. Joey considered doing just that and leaving the ungrateful bastard there to deal with the situation himself, which likely meant Jack dying.

Joey decided to be the better person and he ignored Jack. He repositioned his stage tank in the space between the bottom of the boulder and the floor and signaled Lindsey to try again. Joey tapped Jack on the shoulder and signaled him that they were going to try to raise the boulder a second time. This time Joey held his arm out in front of him and pulled it back quickly, indicating to Jack that he should move fast. Jack flipped him off with his right hand before turning back toward the boulder.

What an ass! Joey considered leaving him there again. Even in the position he was in, he was being such an egotistical prick. Then Joey decided maybe the best thing to do would be to rescue Jack. The rescuer gets rescued by one of his own victims. Joey wondered how that would play out on the social media sites.

Joey returned his attention back to the task at hand. He counted off again and signaled Lindsey to lift. They both pulled up on their tank valves. Joey felt the boulder rise slightly. This time Jack was quicker to yank his arm back away from the boulder. Just as Jack's hand cleared the boulder, it shifted off the stage tanks again and crashed down on the bottom. It also slid down the slope about a foot this time before coming to a stop.

Silt clouds appeared from where the boulder had come to a stop and obliterated the visibility for a moment. Fortunately, the floor in this area was composed of larger sand particles and the water current coming from behind them quickly began clearing away the smaller particles that hadn't yet settled back onto the floor.

Joey turned to Lindsey to see if she was okay. She was a few feet to his right and appeared to be unhurt. Joey circled his light beam in front of her and she immediately returned the signal. Joey then looked back at Jack. He was lying on the floor cradling his left arm. Joey swept his light beam back and forth on the floor in front of Jack's face. Jack looked up at Joey. Joey thought he could see tears in his eyes.

Lindsey had already started clipping her stage tank back in place. Joey turned to his stage tank, grabbed the valve, and pulled back on it. The stage tank didn't budge. It was wedged underneath the boulder. Joey tried to wiggle it back and forth to see if he could break it loose. As he did that, he saw the boulder start to shift and decided to leave the tank where it was. The stage tank might be the only thing keeping the boulder from sliding farther down the slope and on top of all three of them. Leaving a stage tank behind in the cave was beginning to be a habit.

Joey backed up and got on Jack's left side. He grabbed Jack's BC by the air bladder on that side and turned to Lindsey. He signaled Lindsey to do the same on her side. Jack tried to shake them off, but that movement must have caused more pain because he quickly gave in to them.

The three divers ascended up the chimney fissure, with Joey and Lindsey holding onto Jack in between them. Jack tried to fin but ended up just letting Lindsey and Joey pull him out. Any movement seemed to be too painful for him.

Joey glanced at his gauges. He had 500 psi in his left tank and 300 psi in his right tank. He made sure he was breathing from the regulator attached to his left tank as they reached the top of the fissure.

By the time they were back at 45 feet of depth, the visibility had cleared enough for them to see about 40 feet in front of them. Joey looked over to the boulder he had been searching before finding Jack. He couldn't believe the size of it. It was one thing to imagine the size based on counting 10-foot knots on his line. It was something else to actually see it. Jack was lucky he hadn't been underneath that boulder. There's no way he would have survived.

Lindsey and Joey swam toward the exit, pulling Jack along between them, stopping briefly at the beginning of the gold line to retrieve their oxygen tanks. Jack didn't have a decompression obligation but both Joey and Lindsey did. They had off gassed a little of the nitrogen buildup while getting Jack free, but they had also exerted themselves quite a bit. Fortunately, they only had 10 minutes of decompression at 10 feet of depth. Maybe Jim and Gary would be in the Deco Room and could take Jack from them and to the surface. Although there was nothing better that Joey would like to do than bring Jack, in the state he was in, to the surface to a crowd of other divers.

They swam and let the flow take them from the Rock Garden room to the Deco Room and quickly finned to the left to get out of the current. Joey looked around for Gary and Jim. No one else was there. Maybe Joey would get his wish after all.

Jack didn't have a decompression obligation since he had just begun his dive but considering the exertion and his injuries, and since he wasn't able to exit the cave without his and Lindsey's help, Joey grabbed his oxygen tank from where Jack had left it in the Deco Room and helped him switch regulators. Jack tried to do it on his own but was in too much pain. The three settled in to do their decompression stop.

73

Lindsey

Ten minutes later, after Lindsey and Joey cleared their decompression obligations, Lindsey turned to Joey and signaled she was clear by sweeping her palm flat over her dive computer display. Joey returned the signal. They each grabbed Jack's harness and began swimming out to the middle of the room to allow the current to push them out of the cave.

Lindsey had very mixed feelings. She had wanted to leave Jack in the cave to suffer the consequences. It would have served him right. But this was almost a sweeter revenge. With a crushed arm, there was no way Jack could claim this as his rescue. The rescuer had become the rescued. And by divers that he had claimed to rescue only weeks earlier. Lindsey hoped there would be a large crowd waiting for them at the surface. The bigger the better.

Joey and Lindsey turned the corner as soon as they cleared the overhead and had the surface above them. They kicked to get out of the current and position themselves over the sandy slope to the side of the opening. It wasn't as easy to do while also pulling Jack between them. The three of them side by side created a large sail against the water flowing out of the cave opening. They kicked hard until they were in the calm water just outside the reach of the current.

As they ascended up the gentle sandy slope to the shallows at the edge of the spring basin, Jack began to wiggle around to try to get them to release their grips on him. At first Lindsey thought he might be having a seizure and tried to pull him up to the surface to prevent him from drowning. But Jack was also finning as hard as he could to try to get away from them. He didn't put a lot of effort into it though, probably because he was in excruciating pain.

Jack's wiggling turned into thrashing and Lindsey finally released her hold on him. If he wanted to stand up on his own, she would let him. She looked over toward Joey and noticed he was still holding onto Jack. Lindsey decided she would let Joey deal with Jack and swam to the cinderblock wall lining the edge of the basin and stood up.

When her head cleared the surface, she saw several people standing on the grass in front of her. Jim and Gary were in front standing next to their tanks. There were at least four other divers in drysuits standing around, all with anxious looks on their faces. She saw an ambulance and a couple of police cars in the parking area. And between all the divers and the parking area was a bearded man with a long-lensed camera pointing toward her, snapping away.

Lindsey heard a splash behind her and turned around. Joey was standing up a few feet away. She looked down into the water and saw Jack still in a prone position. It looked like he was trying to get his tanks unclipped. She watched as his right tank fell away from his side and he teetered to the left due to the weight of the tank on that side. She continued to watch as he struggled to unclip that tank without success. He couldn't reach the bottom clip with his right hand and his left arm was not going to be doing anything useful for quite some time, if ever.

Lindsey finally stepped back and reached down to unclip the tank. She watched it fall away as Jack floated to the surface face down. He unclipped the other end of the tank and it fell the four feet to the sandy bottom. He tried to stand up but couldn't quite get the leverage to do so with the buoyancy of his drysuit and the incapacitation of his left arm fighting against him. Joey pushed down on his legs as he grabbed the top of Jack's harness and pulled him to a standing position.

Jack looked around the park with a bewildered look on his face. When he saw all the people standing on shore, he looked defeated. Although it was difficult to be sure with his mask still on his face. Then he reached up and tore his mask off. He tried to pull his neoprene hood off his head but couldn't do it one-handed. Joey helped with that as well.

With his head exposed Jack turned and looked at Joey and Lindsey and the look on his face transformed from a shocked look to a look of concern.

"Are y'all okay?" he asked them. "That was wild! I can't believe we just witnessed a collapse in there."

Lindsey couldn't believe what she was hearing. No thank you. No appreciation. Just a comment on the collapse.

"It's a good thing I was there to push y'all out of the way otherwise that boulder would've fallen right on top of both of y'all. As it was, I think it crushed my arm."

On hearing that Lindsey started laughing. She laughed hard. She laughed so hard tears began flowing down her cheeks and she couldn't catch her breath. The small crowd on shore just watched in disbelief as Lindsey continued to laugh at Jack. And then Joey joined in on the laughter.

Jack stood there between the two trying to continue with his story and claim another two rescues. But Lindsey and Joey were laughing so hard no one heard or cared. Not even the long-bearded reporter.

Epilogue

The other divers that Joey and Lindsey had seen going into the cave as they were exiting eventually made it back to the surface. On their way back, the silt had cleared significantly so they were able to see the gold line trapped beneath the large boulders. They exited uneventfully and surfaced about 20 minutes after Lindsey, Joey, and Jack had surfaced. They didn't know how close they had come to being under the collapse when it happened.

* * *

A month passed since the collapse in Jackson Blue. Lindsey and Joey had been back every weekend since to explore the area. Joey brought his GoPro to get video footage to upload to YouTube to share with non-diving friends and coworkers.

They brought a cloth tape measure with them on one dive to measure the sizes of the various boulders that had fallen. There were five boulders of various sizes, the largest one sitting on the shelf at the top of the chimney fissure. The other four were scattered on the sandy slope along the fissure.

Joey ran some rough calculations and estimated the largest boulder to weigh about 300 tons. The smallest of the boulders, the one that had pinned Jack down by his arm, weighed about 3 tons. It was a miracle he and Lindsey had been able to lift it enough for Jack to pull his arm out.

Jack got whisked off in an ambulance to get his arm attended to. The damage was so severe he had to be transferred to University of

Alabama at Birmingham Medical Center to have several reconstructive surgeries. Last Joey had heard, it was still unknown whether Jack would ever get full use of his left arm back.

Jack tried several more times to claim that he rescued Lindsey and Joey from the collapse. Even while the medics were attending to him, he was going on and on to the reporter/photographer about it. Fortunately, no one believed him this time. Not even the reporter.

Jim and Gary had exited the cave about 45 minutes before Lindsey, Joey, and Jack had surfaced. During that time, they had told the other divers what they had seen and how Lindsey and Joey had led them out of the cave to safety before heading back into the silted-out cave. By the time they surfaced everyone on shore already knew the true story.

This revelation discredited all of Jack's other claims. Jim and Gary told their version of what happened to them during their cave class. Joey told his version of what happened to him during his dive, including his own recklessness of scootering in passage he wasn't completely familiar with.

Lindsey decided not to say anything about what happened at Eddy Spring. The damage to Jack's reputation was already done and she didn't want to pull Emily and Alex into it. They had already been through enough and didn't need to be dragged through the mud, or silt, for Lindsey's sake.

AUTHOR'S NOTE

The first incident in the book, where Joey got stuck in a small parallel tunnel and got out by using a safety tank that had been staged nearby really occurred to a cave diver. A former student of mine and I had been doing exploration dives over 5000 feet inside the cave. Because of the long penetration distance involved, we placed a couple of safety tanks in the cave in case we were to have any issues and need additional air to breathe. One of those tanks was left directly in front of the traffic light that denotes the beginning of the Trash Room in Jackson Blue. Yes, it's a real place.

The diver that really did experience that incident knew about the safety tanks and was able to retrieve the safety tank at the traffic light and use it to safely exit the cave. Had that safety tank not been there, the diver would have breathed through all of his remaining air long before getting near the exit and perished in the cave. That's the only resemblance to reality from that part of the story.

* * *

The story about Parker Turner and Bill Gavin's dive is true. Turner and Gavin are real cave divers. Turner did die in Indian Spring after a sand avalanche trapped the two of them inside. The story in chapter 6 relates information about the dive as I heard it from various sources over the years. The details used may not be completely accurate, but most of the information is true.

Turner and Gavin were exploring the Wakulla Room that day. The Wakulla Room is 300 feet deep. A sand avalanche did occur while they were in the cave. And it is believed that Turner's efforts saved Gavin's life that day, at the cost of his own.

Continue reading below to see a possible explanation for the avalanche as studied by a late friend of mine, Doron Nof.

* * *

The story about the two students that were separated from their instructor was inspired by true events. There were a couple of cave diving students that did get separated from their instructor. The instructor did exit the cave and call for help. The students were found at the first breakdown and led out of the cave by another diver. The rest of the details in the story are fictional.

* * *

The cave collapse at the end of the book did occur. It happened sometime between the afternoon of Sunday, July 6, 2014, and the morning of Monday, July 7, 2014. On the morning of July 6, I was teaching a cave diving class and had my students do lost line drills in the cave at the exact spot where the 300-ton rock came down.

The next morning, a friend of mine, the same one that had been doing the exploration dives with the safety tanks placed in the cave, went back to dive Jackson Blue, and found the gold line buried under a couple of the smaller boulders as well as the large boulder at the top of the chimney fissure. Fortunately, this happened after all divers had already exited the cave and no one was harmed.

Doron Nof, Ph.D., a long-time faculty colleague in the Depts of Oceanography and Earth, Ocean and Atmospheric Science at the Florida State University, a cave diver, and good friend of mine, made it his life mission to study water movement. One study he is particularly well-known for involved the biblical phenomenon of the parting of the Red Sea.

One cave diving incident Dr. Nof studied was the death of Parker

Turner. Doron believed the cause of the sand avalanche that resulted in the death of Turner was the exhaust bubbles from the divers' exhalations displacing the sand and creating instability. The instability led to the sand avalanche that occurred in Indian Spring.

Doron believed the collapse in Jackson Blue was caused by the same phenomenon. The breathing exhaust bubbles from thousands of divers over the years rose to the ceiling and penetrated into the natural cracks in the limestone. Eventually, the bubbles expanded enough and caused the ceiling to become unstable.

It was very fortunate that the collapse happened overnight and not when cave divers were in the cave.

ABOUT THE AUTHOR

Rob Neto is an avid cave diver who lives in the Florida panhandle just minutes away from some of his favorite caves, Jackson Blue among them. He is an active cave explorer and retired cave and technical diving instructor. He spent more than 10 years teaching scuba diving in Arizona and Florida. He is also the author of the book Sidemount Diving The *Almost* Comprehensive Guide, the first comprehensive book about sidemount diving. With almost 300 pages of information and photos, Sidemount Diving is on its 2nd edition and has been translated into Dutch, German and Spanish, and is currently being translated into more languages. Rob published his first novel, *Beyond the Grate,* in July 2023. *Beyond the Grate* was awarded a Silver Award in Suspense Thrillers by the Global Book Awards in September 2023 and has received numerous reviews on Amazon, GoodReads, and Facebook. Rob is already working on completing the third book in the Beyond series, *Beyond Hope,* a story that completely takes place underwater on one long cave dive.

Rob is married to his wonderful, supportive wife of 21 years and has a household of furry family members. At the time of this publication his family consisted of four dogs, one inside cat, and several outside cats.

Coming Soon!

Beyond Hope

Another Joey Simmons and Lindsey Carter novel!

What do you do when you become separated from your dive buddy during a cave dive? How long do you look for your dive buddy? How far do you push your breathing air reserves before deciding you need to save yourself and exit the cave?

Beyond Hope goes in a completely different direction from the previous two books. The entire story takes place underwater during a cave dive.

Joey and Lindsey take their first trip to Mexico to see what the underwater caves there have to offer. One of the cave dives they do proves to be challenging, very challenging. It also pushes Joey and Lindsey to their limits while testing their faith and having them question some of their life choices.

Read on to see what happens to Joey and Lindsey on their next adventure.

1

Joey

Well, this lead didn't pan out. It was 200 feet long, maybe a bit longer. Not the 1000 plus feet I was hoping for. I still had to survey the line on the way out to know the exact length. But first I had to get out.

The tunnel was a decent size…at first. I was swimming along quickly, listening to the whirring sound coming from my large explorer reel as the spool rotated rapidly letting line out. I bought the explorer reel just for this trip. It held more than 1000 feet of cave line on its spool. I had high hopes that I would get to dump all the line from it into virgin cave passage at least once during our weeklong vacation.

This was the third day of the trip. We had two more days of cave diving. We had been doing two dives a day. The first two days, four dives, were duds. I never even had the opportunity to use the explorer reel.

Then today happened.

This was my first virgin cave passage. A passage that no other cave diver had ever found and been in. I was in a place on this earth - actually in this earth - that no other person had ever been. The first person there, and maybe the only person that will ever have entered this tunnel. The excitement of finding and venturing into it was almost too much to bear.

Lindsey and Gary stayed behind in the tunnel leading to this one. I'm not sure why they didn't follow. A little disappointed that they didn't follow. But at the same time, happy they hadn't.

While it would have been nice to share the excitement of this find and seeing the virgin cave passage, I was happy to be able to lay claim to it by myself. Happy to be able to tell others I had boldly gone where no man has gone before. *Yeah, I'm a little bit of a Trekkie.* I wouldn't have been able to claim that if they had followed. The going where no man has gone before part, not the Trekkie part.

After about 100 feet, the tunnel started to get smaller. Before the trip, I tied knots every ten feet on the cave line that was wrapped around the explorer reel. What a mess that was! First, unspooling the 800 feet of line that came on it. Then tying the knots as I spooled it back on. And of course, it got all tangled up…several times! Zoe, the family cat loved it, but she only made things worse by getting tangled up in the line. The additional 200 feet of line I put on it was so much easier to knot and spool on. If I ever buy another explorer reel, I'll try to order it without the line.

Anyway, as I got farther into this new tunnel, I was pretty sure I had counted ten knots. Kind of sure. In the excitement of the moment, I may have lost count.

Ten knots! One tenth of the line on my explorer reel!

The tunnel continued to get smaller. The walls got closer to each other. The ceiling dropped. But it wasn't too small for me to continue. So I pushed forward hoping it would open up and get bigger again around the next corner.

It didn't. It kept getting smaller and smaller until I couldn't go any farther. I was sandwiched between the floor and ceiling of the cave, snuggled in between the walls. Some might get claustrophobic from being in such a place. Not me. It felt comfortable. Cozy.

I aimed my light beam straight ahead. I swear it looked like it opened up 20 feet farther in. If only I could get through the restriction between me and where it gets bigger.

I tried pulling myself in. I anchored my heels on the ceiling and tried pushing myself in. I exhaled the air from my lungs trying to diminish my size. I pushed myself in and felt myself move, then I had second thoughts. What if I got stuck and couldn't expand my lungs enough to take in a breath?

I stopped and quickly pushed back before I did get stuck in a tighter spot. I laid there in my cozy cocoon, slowly breathing from my regulator, contemplating my situation.

It was no use. The tunnel was too small.

Resigned to the fact that this cave passage wasn't going anywhere, I secured the cave line I had just deployed around a small protrusion sticking out of the floor about a foot in front of my head. I wrapped the line around a few times before pulling my cutting tool off the sheath on my forearm and slicing the line about a foot and a half out from the wrap. I tied off the line then formed a loop on the end of it, hopeful that I would be able to use it sometime soon, preferably the next day or two.

It was a trick I learned from an old-time cave diver and explorer. Leave a loop at the end so it's easier to connect the line from the reel to the loop and continue pushing farther into unexplored territory. Yeah, I knew I had no luck getting through the restriction, but maybe the next day would be different. I could always eat one less taco at dinner. Always the optimist…

I placed a line arrow on the line pointing back to the way I had come. The arrow had my initials on it – JS. If anyone ever ventured into this small tunnel, they would see it and know I was the one to have found it. I hoped to leave many more arrows in this cave.

I formed a loop large enough for my fist to pass through on the end of the line still on the reel and tied a knot. I then reeled the loop in until there were just a few inches sticking out of the line guide on the reel. Placing the loop over the stop screw I snugged the line and rotated the stop screw clockwise until the reel was locked in place.

I tried to swing my arm around toward my back to secure the reel to a D ring. The problem was the reel was too big to fit back there in this particularly small tunnel. I clipped the reel to my left chest D ring instead, at least until I could back up enough to relocate it out of the way.

I started to back up. Only I didn't move. I couldn't move. I was stuck.

Flashbacks to my dive in Jackson Blue a year and a half earlier flew through my mind. It wasn't exactly the same. At least in this cave I could still see. There was no silt in this tunnel so nothing to obscure the visibility. And in Jackson Blue I was squeezed in by the wall on the right and the ceiling dropping down to the floor on the left. There had still been a bit of vertical space.

Here, in this cave in Mexico, I was squeezed in between the floor and the ceiling as well.

But instead of the smooth limestone of the Florida caves, the floors and ceiling of this passage were anything but smooth. It was like the cave had fingers that were reaching out and grabbing me and holding me in place.

That calm, relaxed feeling started to slip away as I felt my breathing rate increase. My heart started to race. I closed my eyes momentarily to try to calm down before the anxiety got the best of me and I panicked. Panic wouldn't do me any good. Especially in this tight coffin I had gotten myself stuck in.

Okay, maybe not the best analogy to help calm my nerves…

Think cozy thoughts again…

Wait! Lindsey might still be able to see me. I shielded the beam of the light mounted on the back of my left hand with my right palm and looked for the illumination of her light. I could see some light behind me, but it seemed far away. Hopefully she was looking toward me.

I crossed my fins, the cave diving signal for *I'M STUCK!!!!* I waited to feel Lindsey tug them to let me know she was there and ready to help. But nothing happened.

I shielded my light again. I still saw light coming from behind me. Lindsey must have been looking somewhere else and hadn't noticed my crossed fins. I pulled my left hand back and aimed the beam of light behind me. I then wiggled my hand back and forth in a slow rhythmic pattern trying to get her attention.

I waited again.

Still nothing. Why wasn't she responding to my light signal??

I wiggled my left hand frantically back and forth this time. A slow back and forth was meant to get the attention of the other diver on your team. A frantic movement was the signal for out of air. And there was only one way to respond to that.

But still there was no response. Lindsey must not have been able to see me.

I pulled my left hand back in front of me and tried once again to free myself. I wiggled my body side to side and back and forth. I couldn't move forward because the tunnel was too tight to go any farther. And something was holding onto me around the front of my waist preventing me from moving backwards. Something was digging into my belly.

I brought my right hand down and tried squeezing it between the floor and my abdomen. It was too tight, though. I couldn't get it quite far enough to feel for what was grabbing. Something was grabbing at my arm. I had sandwiched myself in pretty good.

Pulling my hand back in front of me, I noticed the dive computer on my wrist. Maybe that was the thing preventing my hand from reaching my waist. I slipped the dive computer up my forearm toward my elbow and brought my right hand back down along my body.

I reached in between my abdomen and the floor again. My fingertips brushed against the hard straight edge of something metallic. My harness buckle! Whatever was sticking up out of the floor had grabbed the edge of the buckle and was angling it up. I had to get the buckle over the protrusion. Then I should be able to back up.

Pushing off the ceiling with my feet again, I tried moving myself forward enough to get the buckle to lie flat against my belly. I should have been able to suck my gut in as I tried moving backwards and cleared whatever it was that was catching onto the buckle. Damn all the tasty Mexican food!

The buckle fell flat against me. I exhaled, letting out as much air from my lungs as I could and sucked in my gut. As I pushed myself backwards, I felt the buckle slide over something below me as it pushed deeper into my belly. I continued to push backwards until I felt the buckle ease off the pressure it had been exerting. Relaxing for a moment, I took a deep breath and continued to push myself backwards. Then something stopped me again.

I had only moved a few inches.

2

Lindsey

Where the hell was he going now? That boy! Always running off, or rather swimming off, to check out dark holes. Let him do this one on his own. I'm hanging back here with Gary.

Speaking of…

Dammit! Where was Gary going now?? Diving with these two was like trying to corral wild horses. They're always swimming off in different directions to check what might be some tunnel they think the previous explorers somehow missed.

The past two days diving with them had not been all that much fun. I just wanted to see the cave. Take in the beauty of the passages and the formations in them.

The caves in Mexico were very different compared to the caves in Florida. The formations that formed while the caves were still exposed to air held their own beauty that couldn't be found many other places.

And the haloclines! Where freshwater and saltwater met each other. Swimming below the halocline in the saltwater layer made it feel like we were swimming just below the surface. Swimming above it in the freshwater layer made it feel like we were soaring through the air just above the surface. The layers were so distinct. Until they were disturbed. The different layers mixed with each other and blurred out the visibility.

But all these idiots thought about was finding some tunnel that didn't have cave line in it yet. I didn't get it. Did they really think there was any virgin passage in this cave? Were they not seeing the beauty of these caves. Beauty unlike what any of us has experienced in the Florida caves? Don't get me wrong, the Florida caves hold their own beauty. But we live there and see them every day. We only see these caves once a year, if we're lucky.

Sure, this wasn't a cave that saw a lot of traffic. But it was thoroughly explored 30 years earlier. And others had been diving it looking for more passage since. What made Joey and Gary think the two of them, who had only been cave diving for three years, and had only been in this cave four times before this dive, were going to find something that cave divers with decades of experience and hundreds of dives in here didn't?

I just wanted to swim through the cave and enjoy the magic.

Well, I'll be damned! It looks like Joey may have found something after all.

It probably wasn't much. I doubted it would go very far, but if it made him happy to lay some line in it, so be it.

I better check on Gary.

Where did Gary go? I just saw his ridiculous yellow fins 30 feet in front of me a minute ago. This wasn't good. The three of us shouldn't be completely separated from each other like this. That wasn't the plan.

I glanced back into the tunnel Joey had just reeled line into and didn't see him anymore either. I looked back toward where I had last seen Gary before deciding to check on Joey first.

On the line of the tunnel we had come in on, I placed a line marker next to Joey's on the exit side of the line from Joey's ridiculously big explorer reel. This way Gary would know Joey and I both went down this new offshoot if he got back here before we did.

I started into the tunnel following Joey's line. A couple minutes later I saw Joey's light ahead. The ceiling was getting really low. Too low for my comfort, especially for two divers to be in it at the same time. I wasn't even sure two divers could fit in there. I doubted Joey would be able to go much farther so I turned around before getting into the really tight area and headed back to the line T where our markers were.

Back on the permanent line I looked around for Gary. No sign of him anywhere. I left my line marker in place and began swimming farther into the cave toward where I had last seen Gary. It was only a few minutes since I saw him. He couldn't have gone very far.

I swam slowly along the cave passage sweeping my light back and forth along both walls looking for a hole that might have enticed Gary to go explore it.

Gary should have left a line marker and should be deploying line from his explorer reel before leaving the permanent line in the tunnel we were in. Problem was I've already caught both Gary and Joey swimming off the line a few dozen feet to look at what they thought might be a lead. I've lectured them both about not doing this, but they always got so excited and forgot the rules when they saw something. They really thought they were going to find a lead to some huge new section that no one had found before.

"Come on, guys! This has to stop! Y'all need to run a line from the main line whenever you get more than 10 feet away from it. What y'all are doing is dangerous!" I told the boys as we sat waiting for our food in the taqueria where we were for dinner.

"Oh, com'on, Linds, it's not dangerous!" Joey replied. "Every time I swim off the line to check something out, I make sure I can see yours or Gary's light. I always stop before you get out of view."

"And what if something happens and the visibility gets silted out? Then what will you do?"

"There's hardly any silt in this cave. At least not where we've been looking."

"Yet... Joey, you know better. Would you do this back home in Florida?"

"Well, I guess not. But those caves are different."

"How so? It's still an underwater cave. And we've only done four dives in it

so far. You don't even know this cave. Every dive we do is in a new passage so how do you know you won't encounter any silt?"

"Com'on, Gary! Help me out here," Joey pleaded.

Gary put his hands up in surrender. "I'm staying out of this. This is between you two lovebirds. My partner isn't here so I'm free to do as I please," he said with a big grin on his face.

"Oh, yeah, mister! Let's just see what Jim thinks about that!"

I grabbed my phone and started to dial Jim's number.

"Okay, okay, okay!" Gary yelled as he grabbed my phone out of my hand. "I'll be better. I won't stray off the line unless I tie a jump spool onto it first."

"Joseph…"

Joey dropped his head and muttered, "Yes ma'am."

"What does that mean?"

"I'll be better too. No more wandering off without a line."

Apparently, that part had stuck with them. At least with Joey. This time he was using his explorer reel. Now, if I could only find Gary and make sure he was keeping his word.

After swimming for about five minutes, I still hadn't seen any sign of Gary. No lights. No bubbles. No silt. Nothing. And I hadn't seen any leads off this tunnel either. Would he have continued swimming farther into the cave?

We discussed this the night before over dinner. We needed to stay together. It was okay for them to swim a dozen feet or so off the permanent line to get a closer look, but any farther and they had to run a line. They had agreed to that. I didn't think of the possibility of one of them continuing to swim along the permanent line without the other two, though.

We had plenty of air. Probably enough to swim around in the cave another half hour before turning to begin our long swim back to the cenote where we had started. I didn't want to spend that half hour swimming around trying to keep these boys corralled. It was bad enough I had to do it at all.

I decided to swim another five minutes to look for Gary. Even if Joey turned around right after I turned back and started looking for Gary, it would take Joey a while to be back at the T. He already went far enough that he would want to get survey data of the line he placed.

Joey took a cave survey class right before this dive trip, but he hadn't had time to practice his new skills before we left on the trip. He did survey that one line in the area we visited the day before and that took him a while. This would be only his second time doing this outside of class.

It would take him several minutes.

Sweeping the light back and forth, I still didn't see anything. This was a dark cave. The walls were almost black. If not for the light gray color of the dive tanks we were using, we would probably blend right into the background. Well, except for Gary's yellow fins.

I occasionally covered the front of my dive light to shield the light beam looking for any illumination from Gary's dive light, but other than the soft glow of the numbers and letters on my dive computer displays, it was completely dark every time I shielded it.

Where the hell did he go?

Glancing at my dive computer, I saw I'd been swimming nine minutes since leaving the T. Close enough. I shielded my light one last time and looked into the darkness for any signs of Gary's dive light. I uncovered my light and swept the beam around the passage looking for visual signs, such as bubbles rushing along the ceiling or percolated silt hanging in the water column. Still nothing. Either Gary hadn't come this way, or it had been long enough since he had that there was nothing to indicate he was here.

I turned around and began swimming back to meet with Joey. Joey had been diving with Gary a lot more than I had. Maybe he would have an idea where Gary might have gone.

I looked at my dive computer. Twelve minutes since I left the T. Suddenly a feeling of anxiety came over me and I felt a slight tightness in my chest. I had already been separated from Joey for 12 minutes and had another eight minutes before getting back to him. Twenty minutes. That was a long time when it came to being underwater on a limited air supply. Plenty of time for him to survey any line he placed in that tunnel and take off looking for another lead. Plenty of time for him to remain separated from me and Gary.

I hastened my pace to try to get there before he took off to lord knows where.

If you liked this book and want to see more by Rob Neto, please visit www.RobNeto.com for a list of his other books. Rob has drafts of several more books, including three other books beyond the next one, Beyond Hope, for this series. This number will likely grow even more.

Once you're on the website, make sure to subscribe to the monthly newsletter. Email addresses are not sold or distributed, and you will only receive one email a month to update you on Rob's books and alert you to any price specials he may have going on.

Also, please take a moment to leave a review on Amazon. Reviews really do help to provide more exposure to the book. A simple statement is all that's needed to help boost exposure. But if you're so inclined, a more thorough review is always appreciated. Rob does read the reviews and use suggestions to help improve his writing.

See you in the next book!